Praise for
Her Dangerous Journey Home

"I adore queer fiction and interesting twists on patriarchal historical structures, and Lee Swanson delivers on these themes again and again during this exciting and dramatic novel. I picked up the storyline easily despite entering the work mid-series and was immediately enraptured by Christina's spirit, her bravery, her complexity, and her utter courage to stand up for what she wants in a world that would have her head for it."
– K.C. Finn, Readers' Favorite Reviews

"A superb storyteller and an expert on Hansa trade networks and medieval maritime culture, Lee Swanson has surpassed expectations yet again in this action-packed lesbian romance set in early-fourteenth-century England and pirate-infested Baltic waters. In this third volume of his compelling series **No Man Is Her Master**, he seamlessly weaves the myriad elements of exquisite historical fiction: authentic period detail, vivid description, engaging dialogue, and complex characters, along with adventure, intrigue, suspense, romance, passion, love, lust, revenge, adventure, and swashbuckling. . ."
- Dr. Theophilus C. Prousis, Professor of History Emeritus, University of North Florida

"Swanson has created passionate characters in a detailed medieval setting. You won't find any historical anachronisms in this well-researched historical fiction series."
- Jane Ann McLachlan, author of The Kingdom of Naples series

"Swanson's book is worth reading for the boldness of the subject and the crafting of the story."
– The Historical Fiction Company

D1257417

Novels by Lee Swanson

The Calling of Alex Tate

No Man's Chattel (**No Man is Her Master** Book 1)

Her Perilous Game (**No Man is Her Master** Book 2)

Her Dangerous Journey Home (**No Man is Her Master** Book 3)

Coming Soon

She Serves the Realm (**No Man is Her Master** Book 4)

Her Dangerous Journey Home

LEE SWANSON

Her Dangerous Journey Home
Book 3 in the No Man is Her Master Series
Merchant's Largesse Books

Copyright 2023 by Lee Swanson

Cover design by Tamian Wood,
www.BeyondDesignBooks.com

First Edition
ISBN-13: 978-1-736-2436-2-6 (paperback)
ISBN-10: 1-736-2436-2-6

Books>Historical Fiction>Medieval

For Karine, with love and thanks

Canonical Hours

Throughout *Her Dangerous Journey Home*, the canonical hours established by the Christian Church are used to tell time. Time variations are affected by seasonal differences in the rising and setting of the sun.

Matins:	Between 2:00 and 3:00 in the morning
Lauds:	Between 5:00 and 6:00 in the morning
Prime:	Around 7:00 AM or just prior to daybreak
Terce:	Around 9:00 in the morning
Sext:	Noon or when the sun is at its zenith
Nones:	Between 2:00 and 3:00 in the afternoon
Vespers:	Between 4:00 and 6:00 in the afternoon
Compline:	Between 7:00 and 9:00 in the evening

Chapter 1

An Unexpected Departure
London, October, 1310

Christina stood at her chamber window, staring down into the moonlit courtyard. Instinctively, her eyes moved across and registered each detail below, even as her mind was consumed by thoughts tumbling in her brain like flotsam on an angry sea. The frigid temperature outside created whorls of icy tracery on the inside of the thick, translucent glass; she ran her fingertips over the scars on her left forearm that the frostwork somewhat resembled. The room had steadily chilled since the fire in the hearth had burnt itself out hours before, causing gooseflesh on her naked skin. Yet, she remained so deeply engrossed in her thoughts, Christina hardly noticed the cold.

Could it really have been only a year ago that I was a simple girl, playing games with my friends and trying my best to avoid doing chores around the house? she marveled. *How much my life has changed since then. But it's not really my own life I lead now, is it?*

Not since the pirates attacked us at sea and Frederick was lost; that was when Christina ceased to be. Now, I exist as Frederick, and this house, my fortune, even a knighthood, all really belong to him. So very little can I claim for myself.

Christina's melancholy was interrupted by the sudden sensation of soft warmth pressed firmly against her back and buttocks. A pair of arms slowly extended around her middle, ending in two delicate hands that clasped gently together. A light kiss upon her shoulder-blade next, followed by the slight pressure of the other woman's cheek.

Christina slowly turned in the embrace until she stood looking downward into the upturned eyes of Lady Cecily Baldewyne. Christina extended her arms around Cecily's back and gripped her closer, forcing Cecily's full breasts to press firmly against her own. Christina lowered her head until their lips nearly touched, hesitating long enough to inhale her lover's sweet breath before giving in to their shared desire for a passionate kiss.

When their mouths parted, Christina asked, "Did I wake you, my love? It is still several hours before the dawn."

"No, my rising was my own doing. I must return to my own bedchamber now."

"No. Stay with me. Please," Christina pleaded, her mind a maelstrom of conflicting thoughts.

Cecily's full red lips parted into a wide grin, revealing her even, white teeth. She playfully pushed Christina from her, breaking their embrace. In an instant, she skipped away, gracefully scooping her white linen chemise from the floor.

Before exiting through the bedroom door, she looked back at Christina with fluttering doe-eyes.

"You can't be having the household staff believing their master makes a habit of bedding every saucy wench who comes to visit him. What kind of an example would you be setting?"

Although she spoke in a jocular manner, Christina perceived the other woman's words were only said half-jokingly. She watched as Cecily sniggered and nimbly held the chemise above her head, letting it fall over her sanguine curls before it dropped down over her voluptuous body. She laughed merrily then, raising her fingers to her lips and blowing a kiss toward Christina before dancing through the doorway and disappearing into the antechamber. A second or two later, Christina heard the outer door quietly open and close, leaving her alone with her thoughts.

Her feelings of self-loss had dissipated, however.

Although Frederick may claim credit for most of what I possess, Cecily's affection is a thing that is truly mine and mine alone, she declared fiercely to herself, with a welling certainty so strong she felt as if her heart were about to explode.

There was another realization that niggled at her though, this one so painful she tried to refuse its entrance into her foremost thoughts. Instead, she strode purposefully to bed and luxuriated between the sheets of Rennes linen still warm from the heat of Cecily's body. She buried her nose into the bottom sheet and inhaled deeply, virtually intoxicated by the mixed scent of musk and rosewater she would forthwith associate with thoughts of her lover. Delaying no further, Christina pulled the fur-lined coverlet up beneath her chin and tried to will herself to sleep.

After an interminable period of tossing and turning, she admitted defeat.

It is not just from my bedchamber Cecily must depart, but from my life as well. Today, I am dutybound to escort her to the Palace of Westminster as I had agreed. Once she is in service to the queen, she will have no time or opportunity for the likes of me!

Christina felt a palpable ache course through her core.

For weeks we voyaged southward from Berwick, inseparable within the close confines of the ship. Yet, nary a word passed between us beyond the limits of polite friendship. How was I to know she had come to love me? Am I so thick-headed I could not perceive her feelings? Even more, that I could not recognize my own love for her? Now, what good is this knowledge when she is expected at Westminster this very day?

These thoughts raced over and over in her mind, like a swift stream turning a heavy mill wheel. Yet, even after hours of consideration, she was no closer to a viable course of action to stay Cecily's departure.

Sitting up, she was surprised to notice the first vestiges of a dreary dawn creeping through her window. Christina moved to her antechamber and quickly dressed, beginning as always with the tiresome task of wrapping a length of linen repeatedly about her chest to bind the swell of her small breasts. She had nearly pulled on her boots when the door to the passageway began to open. Hoping it to be a returning Cecily, Christina was disappointed to see the slight form of Mary, one of the chambermaids, instead making her way purposefully into the room with an earthenware jug of fresh water, which she set on the dressing table before kneeling beside the fireplace to spark tinder for the morning fire.

"I won't be needing a fire this morning, Mary. I have plans to leave presently and to be out for the rest of the day," Christina directed as she moved forward from the deep shadows near the wall into the feeble light.

The maid turned about, startled by the sudden appearance of her master. She instantly recovered her wits, rising, then dropping swiftly into a graceful, full curtsy, her eyes demurely downcast.

"God be with you this morning, Master Frederick," she intoned, the lilting tones of her youthful voice betraying what

Christina believed to be her happiness at having one less duty to perform in her daily routine.

Or am I merely believing she is of a like mind as mine would be in such a situation? Christina considered as she felt her lips form a grin.

Rather than moving on to her next task, the chambermaid lingered, shifting her weight nervously from foot to foot. It was evident she had something she wished to say.

"Speak, Mary, please," Christina directed.

After a second's more delay, the girl blurted out, "Master Frederick, is it really true you were knighted by the king himself? And the Lady Cecily, are you . . .?"

"Escorting her to the Palace of Westminster this very day." Christina completed the girl's sentence somewhat brusquely. "That is, of course, by your leave?" A bit more sarcasm weighed down her voice than she had intended.

Mary's high cheekbones flushed crimson. It was clear to Christina the girl realized she had overstepped her place in the hierarchy of the household. Mary bowed her head slightly before resuming her work with a renewed intensity, moving from the antechamber to the bedroom to hide her obvious embarrassment from her master's eyes.

How correct was Cecily to depart my chamber before the morning, Christina thought thankfully? *Had this little gossipmonger discovered us abed together, the news would have spread over half of London by midday.*

Christina finished pulling the supple calves' leather of her right boot over her heel and up her own calf. Duplicating the action with the left, she rose and walked toward the door. She remained for a moment before exiting, considering whether to speak an encouraging word to the chambermaid.

I find myself having increasing affection for this girl, but she is too clever by half. Better she learns from me to wag her tongue more cautiously than from others who might teach her with the backs of their hands instead of with a sharp word.

She exited her apartments, intending first to check on Ziesolf, whose recovery from the wounds he incurred in the Scottish Marches had been worryingly slow, though encouragingly steady. Since first departing Lübeck over a year prior, he had been her trainer and advisor. He had also been the only man who knew her to be a woman. She could not imagine how she could manage her life without his sage guidance and wonderous sword arm.

At this point in his convalescence, the best treatment is rest, she reminded herself, deciding against entering his chamber. *He may very well still be asleep at this hour, especially since it is our first night back in our own beds.*

On the other hand, she knew the kitchen would already be abuzz with activity, as early morning was the time to begin baking and setting stews to simmer. She descended the broad stone stairway, intent on foraging a crust of bread and cup of weak ale to tide her over before partaking of a full breakfast with Cecily later in the solar. Just as she was turning the corner into the kitchen passageway, however, she heard voices in the great hall. Curious, she denied her stomach's demands and went to investigate the commotion.

Stepping through the thick archway into the massive room, Christina was surprised to find it deserted, the only sound the reverberating scuff of her boots on the limestone flagstones.

Could it have been my imagination, or perhaps some unsettled spirit from the house's past? She crossed herself despite the absurdity of her latter thought.

The answer to the mystery became evident as she again heard the sound of men talking, only this time from beyond the iron-reinforced oaken door leading into the yard outside. Christina strode through the portal and stood on the raised entrance portico, surprised by the sight before her. There were eight large, high-sided carts, each pulled by a team of plodding oxen, arranged in a loose procession about the perimeter of the open space. A small man stood beside a horse-drawn wagon in the lead craning his neck upward, engaged in earnest conversation with the man in the seat holding the reins. Noticing the lower man's massive forearms, she recognized him immediately, Black Peter, the manor's smith. She was just about to approach him when a figure waved at her from the group of men loitering in the middle of the yard. It was Jost, her apprentice. He moved toward her hurriedly.

"God's peace to you this day, Sir Frederick," he greeted.

"And to you, Jost. Though just Frederick or Cousin will do fine when we are in private conversation, Master Frederick if we are not," Christina wearily reminded him for the umpteenth time.

Fredrick to some, Christina to others. Master or Sir. How many names must I be ready to answer to? It surely makes my head ache,

"What's all this?" she asked her apprentice, changing the subject abruptly.

"Do you not remember, Master Frederick?" he responded with a look of alarm as though he may have misunderstood her and committed a grave error. "You told me last night of the cargo of wool that filled *Seelöwe's* hold; and that I should arrange to transport it here. Is that not correct?"

"Yes, of course," she replied hastily, loathe to admit she had indeed forgotten. "I am just surprised you have actioned my words so swiftly."

The young man's relief was palpable.

"Each of the last three late afternoons, heavy dark clouds have gathered in the east. Yet, no rain has fallen from them. I thought it prudent to convey the wool safely into our storerooms this morning rather than chance the storm holding off once again," Jost explained.

She considered his words carefully before agreeing with the wisdom of his decision.

I apologize to you, Mother. I was peeved when you sent this boy to me, thinking you had only compounded my burdens. Now, it seems he is well on the way to becoming indispensable.

"Well done, Cousin," she remarked before gazing about the yard once more. "In which of the warehouses do you plan to store the wool?"

She fixed her gaze upon the young man's face.

"I had planned on using the large one, there on the right. It seems quite dry inside and of a volume that would hold the entire cargo in one place," Jost replied.

Christina looked in the direction he indicated, focusing on the area in front of the sturdy wooden door of the storeroom where a slight depression in the ground's surface extended for approximately ten feet.

"Is there something wrong with my choice?"

He must have noticed her concerned expression.

"Should a heavy rain fall, water will certainly gather there." It was now Christina's finger that pointed. "It will then flow downhill, under the door, and into the storeroom."

Jost's mouth began to open but, before he could speak, Christina continued, already anticipating his arguments, "Yes, I know the wool would be placed upon the raised flooring, well above any water that might pool inside. The fleeces don't need to be immersed in the water to be damaged, however. They will also readily absorb dampness from overly moist air. At best, this will leave us hours of backbreaking work to dry them or, at worst, a sodden mess of worthless black mold fit only to be hauled away and discarded."

Jost's face turned ashen. His apology was cut off by Christina's raised hand, however.

"It was an honest mistake. You still have much to learn, Jost, but that is why you are an apprentice. If you knew everything already, you would be the master and I would be taking orders from you."

She clapped him on the back to emphasize she held no ill will.

"Now, what say we store the wool in those two, the second from the left and the smaller one in the middle?" she asked rhetorically, having previously conducted a careful inspection of those rooms herself.

"Yes, of course," he agreed without hesitation. "I will ensure everything is completed to your satisfaction, Master Frederick."

He looked at her as if still unsure whether he should apologize.

"Well then, get on with it," Christina said with a smirk, "Or are we to instead stay to make wager on the afternoon's weather?"

Relieved to be given leave to proceed, Jost ran to the lead cart and spoke for a few seconds with Peter. The smith yelled to the other men milling about the yard, who then either mounted the carts or fell into a rough formation behind.

I wish I was able to go with them, she thought wistfully as she watched the unwieldy procession wend its way out of the gates of the manor, turn down the uneven cobbles of Bucklersbury Street, and disappear on its way to the wharf where *Seelöwe* was moored.

9

Christina was alone in the yard. She moved her arms above her head and stretched the sinews of her body upward. She then turned her torso from side to side, causing her too-long unexercised muscles to protest. The idleness of the long voyage back to London had, in her mind at least, caused a worrying accumulation of body fat about her middle. She recalled the most obvious shared trait of the master merchants of Lübeck was a sprawling paunch of a belly and shuddered at the thought of degenerating into such a state. Several hours lifting and toting heavy sacks of wool would have proven to be an excellent first step in returning her body to its fighting trim.

Well, no chance of that now. Perhaps there will still be some work to do when I return.

The sudden reality of her impending journey to Westminster prompted Christina's mind to spring back to the dilemma she had failed to resolve the night before.

What are we to do? she asked herself for the hundredth time since the other woman had appeared unbidden into her bedchamber. *I know not who was the more surprised; her at the discovery of my true sex or I at her disclosure of the love she holds for me regardless of it.*

Should we delay the journey to Westminster? Certainly, Cecily can claim a sudden malady or undue fatigue resulting from the hardships of the voyage. But those would only substantiate a temporary delay, doing nothing to resolve our situation permanently. The fact remains she is a married woman, the wife of a nobleman at that. His claim to her is just, both in the eyes of the law and the Church. For her to desert her husband for another man is ungodly, for a woman, doubly-so. What are we to do?

It is not something I can decide alone. We must speak, Cecily and I, Christina concluded, striding back through the doorway and into the hall.

After trekking back up the stairs and entering the solar, she was surprised to find Trudi seated, slouched back on her favorite cushion. She smiled shyly at Christina, who remained standing, mystified at her boisterous friend's unusually reticent behavior.

"Come here," Trudi whispered, motioning for Christina to move beside her.

She did as she was bidden. Christina knelt upon the floor and Trudi reached out and took her hand, placing it to rest upon the lower middle of her coarsely-spun kirtle. With bated breath, Christina let Trudi press her hand more firmly upon the blue, woad-dyed wool. She felt the slight movement of her friend's quickening child and inhaled a sharp breath before springing forward, engulfing her life-long friend in a light embrace, all her other worries forgotten in this moment of pure joy.

Trudi pulled Christina tighter, remarking, "I'm not going to break you know," before pushing her back and rising to her feet. "I'll have Juliana prepare some breakfast for us, shall I?"

"How can I even think of food at a time like this?" Christina asked, still wide-eyed. "Besides, you should be conserving your strength. Let me find Juliana."

"Don't be a silly ass, Christina." Trudi chided. "It's still many months before I can even consider a laying-in time. What, should I spend nearly two seasons on my back, watching the race between my ass and my stomach to see which will grow bigger? No, I will do as every woman does, go about my work as usual until the time comes when I cannot."

Trudi exited the chamber, only to return a few minutes later.

"I've ordered us a hearty breakfast, which I am sure you sorely missed during your time in the North. A wastel loaf fresh from the oven, with cheese and butter, and some nice jellied pike. Even a few sweetmeats and fruits I know to be your favorites," she added with a wink.

Christina's mouth began to salivate. It could never be said her friend set a miserly table.

Unexpectantly, there was at slight knock at the door.

I know the kitchen staff is efficient, but I cannot believe them to be this swift to prepare and serve the feast Trudi described, Christina thought, a bit puzzled.

"Come," Trudi said.

The door opened and Cecily entered. Though she was dressed simply, her beauty was breathtaking. Her crimson curls blossomed out in a corona around the cream-colored skin of her face and her eyes gleamed like fine-cut emeralds well-set above the rubies of her lips.

"God's good day to you both," the noblewoman said merrily. "Please forgive me for my late rise this morn; I am not normally such a laggard."

"It is I who must apologize, my lady," Trudi responded deferentially. "Had I known you were awake, I would have offered to assist you dress."

Christina watched silently, relishing the company of these two women, each of whom she loved in her own way.

Made all the more delightful by my having no need to guard my every word and action, lest I disclose myself. Even though I sit here in man's dress, they and Ziesolf are the only ones who acknowledge me as the woman I truly am.

The food arrived and they seated themselves at the table, sharing words and laughter as liberally as the bountiful fare set before them.

The conversation lulled and Christina observed a change in Trudi's features, an uncertainty she seldom saw. Cecily looked up from her food and, noticing Christina's gaze, shifted her attention to Trudi as well.

"Um, Lady Cecily," Trudi began hesitantly, "I do not mean to overstep my place."

Cecily nodded, encouraging the other woman to continue.

". . . I am only a maid, though Master Frederick has been kind enough to raise me to the charge of his house and household. You, on the other hand, are a lady, whose kinship I understand extends even to the throne of this land. Thus, I have no right to ask this of you, but would you honor me and my new husband by attending our wedding feast this Martinsmas?

Cecily's radiant face seemed to brighten the room as she replied, "Oh, Trudi, you silly goose, it is I who would be honored to share in your special day. You think me above you, you who manage the household of this beautiful manor in London itself? I was lady of a single tower of only four rooms set in the wilderness of the Scottish Marches. I cooked, cleaned, washed clothes, and scrubbed piss from the wall where my husband's men chose to relieve themselves. I am a lady in name only and certainly no better than you. Rather, I would ask that you, who is truly the sister to Frederick, may regard me to be yours as well."

For once, Trudi could manage nothing to say; though the tears descending from her merry eyes clearly conveyed the joy Cecily's words had brought to her.

How can someone not love this woman who brings such happiness to others so naturally? Christina asked herself.

She gazed toward the window and was shocked to see the sun had already risen above the height of the second pane. Reality snapped her from her pleasant reverie as surely as a sudden plunge into icy water.

The hour when we must depart for Westminster fast approaches. If we are ever to discuss the mad possibility of a future together it must be now.

Christina locked eyes with Cecily and, after a second or two of silent communication, both slowly arose from their seats. Taking their leave of Trudi, they exited the solar.

There is so much I wish, nay, need to say, but how do I even begin? Christina's thoughts were a maelstrom as they stood together alone in the passageway.

Christina avoided Cecily's gaze, afraid of the rash words that might come tumbling from her mouth, a declaration crudely-formed and ill-advised, prompted not by coherent thought but the passion in her bosom.

Cecily was first to break the uncomfortable silence, stating, "I'll retrieve my cloak from my room. I shan't be more than a few minutes," before walking swiftly away.

Christina strode toward her own chambers, simultaneously attempting to formulate in her mind a plan that would keep them together; hoping against hope that, sometime on the hours-long journey to Westminster, she would unveil it, and Cecily would agree to it without hesitation.

Even that forlorn hope was denied her, however. Just as she grabbed her cloak, Christina heard hooves clattering into the yard.

What? Why are the wagons returning already? It's not possible they have been to the wharf and back filled with woolsacks in this short time.

Eager for any distraction from her fretting, Christina walked swiftly from her chamber and through the house. Once outside, she found Osbert, one of the yardmen, fastening the heavy wooden gates open. Already, one mounted man in royal livery was in the yard, while several others were turning the corner from the street to join him inside. In the group, she saw a pair of riders

14

markedly differed from the others: two richly-garbed young women astride splendid palfreys.

Completely baffled, Christina approached and proffered a formal greeting as the more splendidly-attired of the two women must be of high station indeed to warrant such a cortege.

"May the Lord bless you on this day, Your Grace."

Christina's words were accompanied with a courtly bow.

"And to you, sir, as well. Would it be you are Sir Frederick Kohl?" she asked in a temperate tone.

"Yes, Your Grace, I am."

Should I know this lady? It would be insulting to ask her name if she is of the greater nobility, especially since she seems to know mine.

She was saved from humiliation by the arrival of Cecily, who moved alongside Christina and said, "Dear lady aunt! I am so happy to see you!"

"Cecily? Is that really you?" cried the Lady of Glamorgan, Eleanor de Clare. "The last time I saw you we were no more than mere babes!"

Lady Eleanor impatiently gestured down to the guardsman nearest her. He and one of his fellows sprang from their horses and assisted her dismount. Her feet had barely touched the ground before she ran forward and up the stone steps, catching her niece in a warm embrace.

Christina had imagined Cecily's aunt would be middle-aged at the very least, with graying hair and a figure grown stout from multiple childbirths. Instead, she looked no older than Cecily, girlish in both appearance and action. Her hair was a light brown with reddish highlights, her face slightly more angular than Cecily's, but no less comely. Christina's assessment was cut short as she realized Eleanor had turned to face her.

"I have heard so much about you, Sir Frederick, that I feel I have long been in your acquaintance," Eleanor said.

Oh, shit! thought Christina apprehensively. *The source of her intelligence could only have been Queen Isabella, and she certainly holds no love for me.*

Before Christina could utter a word in her own defense, Eleanor continued, "Yes, my younger sister believes you to be a hero akin to those in the time of Arthur Pendragon, dashing around the countryside on mad quests and saving maidens from unspeakable dangers!" She laughed merrily.

"Sister?" was all Christina could manage in response.

Right now, I must seem more a dullard to Lady Eleanor than a hero.

Christina fumed at her suddenly-thick tongue.

"My younger sister Margaret, the wife of whom I believe to be a friend of yours, Piers Gaveston. It is he who entertains her with the tales of your exploits."

Now comprehending the source of Eleanor's information, Christina sought to determine the rationale for her visit.

"I am sure the earl greatly exaggerates my deeds, to make for a better tale, but may I ask why you honor us with the pleasure of your visit today?"

She waited, hoping her phrasing would be deemed adequate and without any trace of offense.

"Why, when I was told yesterday evening of the arrival of my niece's traveling chest, I was so overjoyed at the prospect of her arrival I scarcely slept at all. This morning, I could contain my impatience no longer, so I have come to collect her and return forthwith to Westminster."

Christina felt as if a blade of cold steel had just run through her, cleaving her heart in two.

No, you cannot have her! I have yet to speak to her, to declare my love plainly. Grant that small kindness, for God's sake!

But she did not speak the words, could not speak them. Instead, she looked helplessly at Cecily.

It was clear Eleanor's intent had caught Cecily unawares as well. Unlike Christina, however, she was able to find her tongue.

"How very thoughtful of you, Lady Eleanor," Cecily's lips formed a smile. "Would you perhaps tarry a while for some refreshment first? I am certain you would find the quality of Sir Frederick's hospitality to be quite pleasing"

"Unfortunately, no. I beg your indulgence, Sir Frederick, but my desire is to depart presently," Eleanor responded. "I have many tasks before me. Their majesties have plans to winter at the castle in Berwick. Consequently, I hope to attend Queen Isabella there no later than mid-November."

My God, does Lady Eleanor expect Cecily to accompany her to the North as well?

The thought sickened Christina. Has Cecily have escaped her terrible situation there, only to be expected to immediately return?

Cecily stepped forward to face Christina. Their eyes locked and Christina realized there was no recourse for either of them.

"Thank you, Sir Frederick, for all you have done for me. I owe you my life, and my eternal affection." Cecily spoke the words quietly before dipping into a deep curtsey.

Christina struggled against a sudden and insane impulse to take Cecily in her arms, proclaim her love for her to the world, and damn the consequences. Instead, she took a knee before her.

"May God and his angels protect you, Lady Cecily. Know you well I am your devoted servant."

They both arose.

Christina saw the solemn expression fixed on Cecily's face, knowing it must match the one on her own, masking the sorrow that lay inside her bosom like a cold stone.

"Do remember, Sir Frederick, I will be returning for Mistress Trudi's wedding feast," Cecily spoke reassuringly, her words a meager promise of future reunion.

"Of course," Christina replied with a wan smile, although any semblance of joy upon her visage was a lie.

Lady Eleanor's eyes narrowed, shifting from Christina to Cecily and then back again. Christina thought she saw shrewd comprehension flicker momentarily across the lady's face, but it disappeared before she could decide whether it had been real or just her imagination at play.

"I add my thanks to those of my niece for the attentiveness you have shown her," Eleanor said. "Now, adieu, Sir Frederick, I shan't think this will be the last time our paths will cross."

Eleanor grasped Cecily's hand and led her down the steps and into the yard. One of the riders brought a horse forward and the two dismounted men assisted first Eleanor and then Cecily into their saddles. Soon, the procession had disappeared, but Christina's eyes trailed long after them, as if she could see through the intervening structures and find her Cecily again, retaining the image of her beloved firmly in her mind.

She might have stood there all day, had she not heard a gruff voice declare from somewhere nearby, "Beautiful bit of horseflesh, they wuz, hey, sur?"

Christina glanced down at a small, older man with a wizened face staring up at her from the yard.

"Ya must be the master, I reckons. Mi name's Penny. I heered ya mite be needin' a groom," he said hopefully.

She had no heart for it and told the man to return later that afternoon to speak with Black Peter. Once more alone, Christina toyed with the idea of remaining frozen in place on the steps until Martinmas brought Cecily's return. After a few minutes, she sighed and thought better of it.

No matter how much I ache inside, there are still tasks that need attention. Why not approach those most disagreeable now, putting a crown on this most hellish of days? she thought bitterly.

Christina reentered the house, intent on leaving word she was departing. At first, she had thought to find Trudi, but knew her friend would take one look at her face and soon wheedle out the entire heartbreaking tale.

I have neither time, nor inclination, to spend the rest of the afternoon weeping and blubbering. Yes, Cecily is lost to me, and that is a fact I must now accept.

She sought out Ziesolf instead. The old knight had taken to habitually relaxing in the morning sun while sitting on one of the stone benches arranged around the perimeter of the kitchen garden. Opening the door, Christina was pleased to find that, although the sun's direct rays had deserted the space for the winter, Ziesolf had not.

His gaunt face brightened at her approach. Obviously happy for the company, he moved now without the aid of a walking stick, his ancient body slowly mending from the terrible wounds he had suffered in the North. He inched to the right side of the bench and motioned for her to sit beside him. Without preamble, she related her revised plan for the afternoon, now that there was no need to travel to Westminster. The bitterness in her voice was undisguisable. Ziesolf nodded in assent, saying nothing, but peering at her with a compassion she had rarely before perceived from the man. Strangely, his sympathy angered her. Before she could utter anything imprudent that she would surely later regret, she silently turned and trod swiftly from the house, wending her way Thameside in an ill-humor to answer the summons of the head alderman.

Chapter 2

A Matter of Honor, and of Vengeance
London, October, 1310

Christina's feet carried her southward along the route to the alderman's manor; however, she remained so distracted she could have been traveling toward any point of the compass rose and not known the difference. She grew increasingly sure with each passing step that she had made a calamitous mistake in not somehow postponing Cecily's departure. The certainty that they would never again discuss forging a life together gnawed at her stomach like a ravenous wolf.

She felt a tugging at her sleeve and, shaken from her painful contemplations, whirled about. There, a child of about six years stood before her with tearful eyes. Christina reached toward the pouch at her belt, seeking a half penny to give the waif she recognized as one of thousands of youthful beggars who encumbered London's streets.

"No," said the boy or girl.

Christina felt the child could be either.

The child snatched Christina's hand away from her purse and attempted to pull her toward a pestilent alleyway beside St. Stephen's church.

"Please!" The little one wailed. "Mi' mam's been hurt and she can't get up! There's blood all over!"

Christina found herself tugged into the alley. They turned a slight bend, after which she saw a ragged figure writhing on the mucky cobbles ahead. With her attention focused on the injured woman to her fore, she barely noticed a hint of movement out of the corner of her eye.

There was no time for thought. Reacting instinctively to the attack, she fell to the ground, forming her body into a tight ball and rolled forward, before springing upright once again. She moved into a fighting crouch and turned back to face her unknown assailant. A large bulk of a man stood with a dumbfounded expression on his heavily whiskered face. He now stared stupidly at the heavy wooden cudgel gripped in his meaty fist as if it had somehow magically passed through Christina's body before she had annoyingly moved out of the way.

The frustrations of her morning culminated into one big eruption in Christina's mind and she leaped forward, delivering a hard kick squarely into the man's face. He toppled like a felled tree and Christina threw herself upon him, pummeling him with her bare fists until her rage had abated, though there remained enough to fuel her desire to grab the stunned man 's forelock and rhythmically beat his head into the dirt.

Without warning, Christina felt a weight alight on her back. Thin arms encircled her head and taloned fingers sought to claw at her eyes and mouth. Unintelligible shrieks filled her ears as if she were bedeviled by hell's very demons. She shifted her weight

22

to the right and brought her arm over her head, catching the woman about the neck and dislodging her from her perch. Tucking her shoulder down, Christina lurched forward and tossed her assailant the ground. She then bent forward and drove her elbow into the nose of the child's mother, silencing her as she, like her large companion bleeding in the dirt, lost consciousness.

As Christina sprang to her feet, she heard rustling behind her. She spun and balanced her weight, ready for the new challenger.

The small boy who had lured her into the alley rushed past her, falling to his knees then splaying his diminutive body over that of his mother to shield her from further assault. Christina looked on, suddenly sickened by the pathetic scene.

I would have beaten the man's head into a pulp had the woman not stopped me. But why not? It was I who was attacked. Would the pair of them have shed a tear for me had that club bashed the brains from my head? I think not. They would have robbed and stripped me, leaving me to die naked and alone in this godforsaken gutter.

Still, she could not shake the strange feelings of guilt that crept along her spine like a spider.

Were the pair simply lawless, choosing this felonious trade over honest work? Or were they merely victims themselves, forced by desperate circumstances to risk execution in preference to their family's starvation?

The mother groaned slightly as she twisted about, gently dislodging her son beside her. She gazed up with fearful eyes, raising an arm in a pitiful attempt to ward off the further blows she believed were forthcoming.

"Is that your child?" Christina muttered through gritted teeth.

"Aye, John's me lad, Your Lordship."

The woman's voice trembled.

"And he, your husband?" Christina jabbing her thumb to indicate the man who was now attempting to sit up, one large paw rubbing at his wounded skull.

"Aye," the woman confirmed. Then, in a timid voice, she added, "Mercy. Please."

Christina straightened, uncertain what to do next.

She thought for a moment, then commanded, "Come here to me, John."

The boy hesitated, looking first to his mother, who nodded assent. He scrambled to his feet and cautiously approached Christina. The child's eyes widened as she dipped her fingers into her pouch and withdrew several pennies. She placed them gently in his hand and he backed away.

"Thank you, Lord," the mother said, sounding incredulous at this odd turn of events.

"Always think of him first, Mistress, and the man you wish him to become," Christina replied.

She circled around them and strode back to the street, resuming her journey toward the alderman's manor house. For the first time, she focused on the squalor and misery of the city's destitute, a stark contrast to the wealth and grandeur enjoyed by their more fortunate counterparts.

Can this really be God's will?

She rubbed her sore elbow as she turned onto Roperestrete to make the final approach to her destination.

Customarily, she would have paused for a few minutes to gaze upon the magnificent architectural detail of the alderman's home; however, today she felt no such compulsion to idle away her time admiring such a conspicuous display of prosperity and excess.

Instead, she strode to the gate and pulled heartily on the length of rope tied to the yard bell.

It was not long before a tall, comely young man in red livery and a burnished copper breast plate emerged from the house and walked toward the gate in graceful, measured steps.

Oh, my sweet Jesus, Christina groaned to herself, *not another one.*

A similarly attired sentry had greeted her on her last visit to the house, addressing her in a most rude manner until she had put him in his place. This man's manner, if anything, was even more supercilious than the first.

"Who are you and what is your business here?" he demanded, standing on the other side of the wrought iron gate and making no effort to permit her access.

"God's grace be with you, this day," Christina replied, struggling mightily to sound courteous. "I am Herr Frederick Kohl, master merchant of the Hansa, and I have come at the summons of Herr Volker."

The guard scowled, silently assessing her from head to foot before finally muttering, "Wait here," without so much as a "by-your-leave."

Turning on his heel, he vanished back into the manor. Christina waited, casually examining the raw knuckles of her right hand and forcing herself to patience. It was not long until he was back at the gate, but this time he parted it just sufficiently to permit her entrance. He then led her through the massive iron-strapped oaken doors and into the great hall that dwarfed even the massive chamber of her own abode. Beckoning her forward, he bid her to be seated on a solitary wooden chair. She sat facing the raised dais upon which the massive, intricately-carved seats of the aldermen were arranged; their plush, down-filled cushions hinting at a much more accommodating level of comfort than the hard, unyielding surface upon which she now rested. The guard then exited through a door to the rear of the chamber.

They clearly don't want anyone to mistake who is more important here.

Christina smiled ruefully, hoping she wouldn't be forced to wait too long. She wracked her memories of her prior visits, but could discern no pattern as to Volker's predilection for promptness . . . or lack thereof.

For the first time that day, it seemed her wishes would be fulfilled. A small procession soon entered the hall from a side door. Four young men came first, similarly attired to the one who had granted her access. Two more followed, dressed in clerical garments and far more elderly than the liverymen. Finally, the figure of Volker himself emerged, wearing an ill-fitting robe of darkest gray velvet trimmed lavishly in fox fur about the collar and sleeves. A matching chapeau encircled his near-bald pate. Christina's brain registered these features subconsciously, her mind preoccupied by the diminutive figure upon which Volker leaned for support: a woman who must be over forty years his junior, his wife, Katharine.

Although Katharine Volker was approximately the same age as Christina, a casual observer might believe her much younger, even pre-pubescent. She wore a fitted kirtle of alternating sky and dark blue brocade. Over this was an open-sleeved cyclas of finely-woven green linen lined with what appeared to be white silk. A bejeweled belt was fastened low about the slight swell of her hips while her hair fell scandalously loose over her spare shoulders. Slight of stature and of build, her face was as perfectly featured as that of an angel. The woman's appearance was deceiving; however, as her slight bosom held a heart as black as the bottom of the deepest hell-pit and in her fair head a conniving brain brimming with foul corruption.

Despite fully expecting Katharine to be present at the audience, the actual sight of her caused Christina to unconsciously knead the aching knuckles of her right hand. She always felt uncomfortable in the woman's presence, surely exacerbated by her shockingly forthright sexuality and conniving nature. Despite having no official standing in the hierarchy of the Hansa, Christina had no doubt of the complete sway Katharine held over her besotted husband and, through him, control of all the German merchants in London.

As was customary, Christina rose while the alderman set about finding his seat. On her part, Katharine remained standing by his side, seemingly daring Christina to broach protocol by sitting before her. Cognizant of the other woman's penchant for subtle games, Christina waited patiently until, finally, Katharine took her place beside her husband. Christina then regained her chair, resigned to the fact that, whatever unpleasantries should occur, the audience was finally about to begin.

"The good Lord has truly blessed us this day," Herr Volker began, making no attempt to conceal the sarcasm in his voice. "Frederick Kohl has finally seen fit to grace us with his esteemed presence."

"It was only yesterday that I returned to London," Christina protested, "I responded to your summons at the earliest practicable hour."

"Ah, yes, returned," Katharine mused, bringing her hands together to form a triangle that she rested on the table before her before lowering her rouge-stained lips lightly down to rest on their tips, apparently deeply in thought.

As if she has not planned every word, every gesture, she uses today far in advance, Christina thought, grudgingly admiring the woman's foxlike cunning.

Katharine's head rose and she boldly met Christina's gaze.

"Returned? From where exactly?"

Despite her best convictions, Christina already felt forced on the defensive.

"I was in the North, with one of my ships, carrying supplies to the king's forces there. Then I returned with a cargo of coarse wool. Is there a problem with this?" she asked, her ire mounting.

Why don't they just speak plainly? What this need for verbal sparring?

"None at all, Master Frederick, none at all. Calm yourself."

Volker shakily extended his liver-spotted hands forward in a placating gesture.

"Why, what else is a Hanseatic merchant expected to do, except trade?" he asked, though his rheumy eyes narrowed and his thin lips turned ever so slightly upward as if to belie the innocence of his question.

"Yes, what else, Master Frederick?" Katharine's voice echoed that of her husband, although her smile was much toothier, like that of a fox circling a wounded rabbit.

"I was also charged with carrying a confidential message northward, to the Earl of Cornwall," Christina stated evenly, figuring it best to tell the truth as she was certain the Volkers had already been apprised of the details of her journey by their spies.

"This is more problematic, I am afraid."

Volker pursed his lips thoughtfully.

"This is not a normal task for one of our merchants, engaging in espionage that could bring the wrath of the English government down upon all of our heads. Besides, which was incidental to the first, the opportunity to trade or the transmittal of the message? The chicken or the egg?"

"I was only warning a friend of a plot against him!" Christina's voice began to raise, "It was a matter of duty!"

"Yet, you ignored your duty to us to attend our meeting, as you were obliged to do as a master merchant of our assembly. Tell us, Master Frederick, are your sympathies now first to the Hansa or to the English?" Volker spoke deliberately, his rheumy eyes drilling directly into Christina's own.

"My loyalties are to the Hansa," Christina replied flatly, not knowing what else to say.

"Excellent!" Katharine exclaimed, clapping her small hands gleefully. "You see, dear husband, I told you we had nothing to fear! We should have no doubts he may be trusted."

Christina felt helpless before the cunning onslaught of Katharine and her manipulated husband, as if she had been thrown naked into a pit populated by two poisonous vipers.

"You are correct, of course, my lady wife, as always" Volker stated in a voice punctuated now by pronounced wheezing. "Herr Kohl, it is because of the confidence we have in your loyalty to the Hansa that I now share what I have to tell you."

Volker gave a great cough and convulsively spewed a large glob of phlegm onto the floor halfway to Christina's chair. She found it difficult to focus her attention on the alderman rather than what glistened on the flagstones before her like a large, wet slug. One of the clerics produced a cup of some sort of liquid, which Volker gulped down, the prominent Adam's apple of his gaunt throat moving up and down in time with his loud slurping sounds. He swiped the rich fabric of his sleeve across his mouth, then continued speaking.

"Two weeks ago, a merchant ship arrived from the Baltic. It carried, among other things, a petition from the councils of aldermen of the Wendish towns of Wismar, Rostock, and, most importantly, Lübeck. The document stated that, the dangers to merchant shipping posed by Danish and Swedish pirates, although always a threat, are becoming increasingly rampant. Consequently, they are requesting the assistance of German merchants everywhere within the Hansa in amassing a great fleet to bring war against the brigands and end their menace once and for all."

Katherine's broad smile betrayed the direction in which this tale was about to turn.

"When my husband related this request to me, I told him I could think of no one better to send to the assistance of our sister cities than you, Master Kohl!" The woman could withhold her glee no longer, her expression now clearly triumphant.

Nonetheless, Christina was dumbfounded by the implications of what she had been told.

"Why, I . . . I cannot possibly do such a thing," Christina stammered, her mind racing to formulate arguments sufficient to change the alderman's mind.

"I have responsibilities here. I have already laid plans for purchases and sales. How can I leave now?"

"The fleet will not form until spring, April at the earliest. This provides you ample time to bring your affairs into order." Katharine's voice was silky, filled with obvious pleasure at Christina's discomfort.

Finally, the little whore gains her revenge for my refusal to have sex with her. What's more, to marry her, as if anyone other than a senile dotard would sully himself with such a base creature!

"But I have no experience in such things," Christina protested.

"But is this not the Frederick Kohl who, hardly more than a year past, fought valiantly against these same pirates, successfully repelling their attempts to capture your own ship?" Katharine's tone grew harsher, almost accusatory. "Perhaps the news of your exploits was exaggerated, meant to curry unwarranted admiration and favor."

Christina bit her tongue, forcing herself to smolder silently rather than rise to the other woman's bait.

"You have even been made a knight. Sir Frederick now, isn't it?" Katharine continued. "Was this really for some valorous deed, or for a service of a, may I say, more personal nature?"

"Enough!" Christina snapped, springing to her feet and suddenly eager to lunge forward and smash the triumphant look from the young woman's face.

The guards gripped hard upon her shoulders, forcing her back down into the wooden chair.

"Are you really such a pitiful coward you would not leap at the opportunity to wreak vengeance on perhaps those very men responsible for the deaths of your father and sister?" Katharine's voice rang cold.

Images of Frederick and her father burst into her mind, but not as they had appeared in life. Her father's face was leathery gray and ruined by the ravages of the charnel worms. Frederick's visage was barely recognizable, gelatinous and bloated from its immersion in the waters at the bottom of the sea. She had encountered these figures countless times in her nightmares, always beseeching her to avenge them. Would the deaths of their murderers allow their souls to finally find God's grace, leaving Christina at last in peace?

For the moment, all other desires were thrust aside, even those for Cecily.

Christina arose again, this time slowly and deliberately. The guards must have once more moved to restrain her from behind, as she saw Volker's hand raise to stop them.

"I will do as you ask," Christina said in a quiet, measured voice, realizing she had been bested.

"See, that wasn't so difficult now, was it?" Katharine turned toward her husband and spoke in a reassuring voice. "Our dear Frederick had only to be reminded of his responsibilities."

Christina stood stiffly, her only thought being how much longer she would need to endure this excruciating charade.

Volker arose and tottered unsteadily toward the door leading further into the house.

Katharine ignored her husband, instead saying to Christina in a cheery voice, "Would you be so kind as to take some air with me, Sir Frederick?"

Without recourse, Christina could do no more than mutter, "As you wish, Frau Volker."

Katharine stood and capered lightly around the table, the felt slippers on her tiny feet making small, shuffling *shh-shhs* all the way. She drew alongside Christina and, with a girlish giggle, placed her delicate, white-fleshed hand upon Christina's stiffly held arm. It took great self-control for Christina not to recoil in revulsion.

In small, restrained steps they passed through the doorway into a day as leaden and cheerless as the dismal thoughts burrowing through Christina's mind like engorged grubs.

Katharine suddenly halted.

Christina looked down at her in surprise.

Katharine declared matter-of-factly, "It was I who dispatched the man who had been Gaveston's servant to you with the message to carry North." She gazed into Christina's face, clearly hoping to gauge the effect of her disclosure.

Christina met her stare, expressionless despite the strong desire to throttle the life from her nemesis.

I will not give her the satisfaction of knowing she has grievously wounded me yet again.

"I had already figured as much," Christina replied smoothly. "Gaveston was already aware of the threat posed to him by the Lords Ordainers."

"Too bad."

Katharine clucked her tongue with a hint of disappointment.

"I had hoped to surprise you with my news; instead, you had already reckoned as much. Hurrah, Frederick, hurrah! I believed I could disrupt your damnable string of trade successes, perhaps even be the cause of your death. Who knew? Instead, you return a hero, knighted by Edward himself. A hold full of cargo and a comely strumpet on your arm, for the love of sweet Jesus! Is there no end to your good fortune?"

Christina made no reply, instead merely meeting her gaze, expecting the woman to continue her self-centered rant.

"And what of me, you may ask?" Katharine's voice, though not rising in volume, certainly increased in its fervor. "I am left to wander the dusky hallways of this abode, friendless and alone with the knowledge I might have been yours. Wife of the great Frederick Kohl, had you not spurned me so cruelly. It is you I imagine as I straddle that toothless old fool you saw in there in bed at night, laboring feverishly to harden his prick sufficiently to gain at least a stroke or two before it falls shriveling from my slit. How you have condemned me, Frederick, to a vile purgatory of your own cruel device!"

33

"It was you who chose Volker, Katharine. You told me so yourself," Christina answered in defense.

"Only because I could not have you, Frederick!" she cried. "Would not my lips fit as sweetly about your cock as those of the woman from the North?"

Again, Christina refused to demean herself with a response.

Katharine's eyes narrowed; her cheeks flushed with splotches of heat.

"My mind is consumed by thoughts of you, Frederick. But, if I cannot have you, know you well that I will destroy you. My love prompts me to warn you of the hatred that I hold for your regard. Go, but do so ever so carefully. You will know not when I choose to strike."

Satisfied – at least for the moment - Katharine moved a few steps away. To a casual observer, the pair could have been discussing trifles no more alarming than lunch or the weather. An amiable smile once more upon her face, she nodded her head slightly in Christina's direction, turned and disappeared back into the manor.

Christina stood shaken, appalled at the depths of the other woman's depraved obsession. She walked quickly to the gate, resisting a near overwhelming urge to run. Once through it and into the street, she desired nothing further than the relatively safe confines of her own home. As she proceeded, however, her mind turned to the implications of the meetings that had transpired.

She had suspected Katharine's hand in the scheme to provoke her northward, but had thought it no more than a plot to rid her from the assembly of merchants, just as the council of aldermen was seeking to restrict their right to trade freely. That had made political sense. But now it seemed more likely Katharine's scheme spawned from vindictive hatred. Fear gripped Christina as she imagined the ability of Katharine, augmented by the power and influence of her compliant husband, to create deadly mischief. How could she protect those she loved most from Katharine's madness, especially from hundreds of miles away?

Returning home, she found the yard teeming with activity. The men were hard at work toting substantial sarplars of wool into the storeroom. Half the carts already stood empty, their oxen hobbled and the drivers afoot.

Coming out from the dark interior of the warehouse, Jost walked rapidly toward Christina, a gregarious grin appearing on his perspiring face.

"Hot work this is, even on a cold day such as this," he observed, wiping his sleeve across his sweaty brow.

"How far have you gotten?" Christina asked, though with little enthusiasm as her thoughts remained preoccupied with Katharine's threats.

"This is the second trip this afternoon, but I believe we will be at it for at least another day, maybe even one more after that."

He looked at Christina and his eyes narrowed.

"Is everything well, Cousin?"

Christina turned the question over in her mind.

Nothing is well at the present, but there is nothing he can do to make things better.

"Yes, of course," she lied. "I had trouble sleeping. That's all."

Apparently satisfied with his cousin's response, Jost changed the subject to one Christina found of far more interest.

"Have you ever seen such fleeces?"

Amazement tinged her cousin's voice.

"Why some must exceed twenty-five pounds in weight! Did you have a chance to see the shaggy buggers on the hoof?

"Aye," she replied, "You could have confused them for cattle at a casual glance. The rams must have exceeded three-hundred pounds, with the ewes nearly as large. Did you have the chance to examine the staple? Must be a foot and a half long, if it's an inch!"

Jost bobbed his head excitedly. Christina was happy to see the boy taking such an interest in the merchant's trade.

Soon, it will rest on his shoulders to see a profit is made for us.

A sudden recollection of her meeting at the alderman's manor clouded her mood once more.

"Will you be voyaging to Bruges soon?" Jost's question disrupted her darkening thoughts.

"Why?" she asked. Then, realizing the intent of his query, she continued, "Oh, do you mean to sell these fleeces? No, I'm afraid they are far too coarse to do for the finely woven Flemish fabrics. My thought is to inquire at the Weaver's Guild here. I was told this wool is well suited for worsted fabrics. Perhaps you would like to accompany me?"

"Yes, of course!" Jost replied, his rapid-paced head-bobs accentuating his excitement.

"Well, that is, of course, if we are ever able to finish our task here," she said dryly, gesturing toward the laboring men.

Jost looked in that direction, observing as she had that the workers' progress with the unloading had slowed noticeably. He trotted over to the storeroom with Christina following apace. He spoke a few sharp words of encouragement and their efforts doubled, though it was impossible to discern whether this was because of his cajoling or Christina's presence. Regardless, within a half-hour's time, the carts were once more wending their way to the wharf.

For the rest of the afternoon and into the dim light of evening, Christina threw herself into the physical pleasure to be had from hard manual labor. By the time they had finished for the night, well over half of the woolsacks were safely secured in the storerooms. She was pleased her exertions had largely blanked her mind of her worries and woes throughout the day. She realized she could not delay making plans for her upcoming departure forever, though just as she knew she could not long banish her thoughts of Cecily and what schemes would be required to reunite with her.

There will be time for reflection later, she decided with a rueful smile on her face. *For now, a hearty meal and a few cups of ale will do just fine.*

Later that night, she awoke with a start, her hand reaching frantically behind her, searching in vain for the telltale warmth of Cecily's body.

Although we have only shared the one night together as lovers, and not even all of that, it will forever seem amiss to not awaken with her beside me.

Christina sat up and gazed about the room forlornly.

She considered what to do with her day. She toyed with the idea once more of assisting with the unloading of *Seelöwe's* cargo, but thought better of it.

I don't want to make Jost think I am not confident he can supervise such a task.

She had no choice but to apprise both Trudi and Ziesolf of her meeting with Katharine and her husband.

At least the salient parts of it, she corrected herself.

This was not a task she relished, as she was certain both would be critical of the pathway she had chosen. Looking back, she was not sure she agreed with the decision she had made herself.

Christina decided to delay speaking with her two confidants until later.

She arose, now with a definite purpose in mind.

While sailing toward Bruges last summer, unaware of the perils to come, a random thought had popped into her consciousness.

I could arrange for Trudi to have her marriage take place in the manor's own chapel. Would that not be a wonderful surprise? Best of all, I can clean the place myself instead of employing the household staff. That way, Trudi will suspect nothing.

Intervening events had caused her to abandon the idea at the time, especially since she believed Trudi would already be Black Peter's wife upon her return from Berwick.

Now, it will be my gift to her to have her and Peter exchange their vows here. Besides, preparing the chapel for use will be a welcome diversion,

Christina grew increasingly enthusiastic about the plan.

Yesterday's labors proved beneficial to both my body and my soul. To have a project on which to work, instead of whiling away my time fretting about what is to come, will be doubly so.

Quickly dressing, she sped to the kitchen, exchanging greetings with Bess, the cook, and her helpers. Declining their offer to prepare a proper breakfast for her, Christina selected the remainder of a cocket loaf and a hard cheese and thrust them into a large pouch she carried at her side. She added an apple and a jug of weak ale to her collection and padded silently down the corridor and back up the stairs.

At the top, she turned and made her way into a disused wing of the mansion. A thick coating of dust on the window panes diffused the feeble sunlight even further. She resisted the childish urge to trace her fingers over the begrimed surface of the glass, not wishing to leave any clues that someone had been there recently. Suddenly, she halted and her head bobbed forcefully; the sound of her sneeze reverberating down the length of the hallway. She pressed a hand against the plastered limestone wall for support as she coughed up a bit of phlegm which, recalling Volker's disgusting display from the previous day, she decided to swallow instead of spit. Wiping her nose on the right sleeve of her tunic, she pressed on.

At the end of the passageway, she opened the elaborately-carved wooden door and stepped inside the forgotten chapel room. For a few seconds she tarried upon the large landing, gazing out upon the room before her.

Christina descended the broad stone steps to the floor below and lowered herself onto one of the pew benches. She opened the bag containing her breakfast. As she ate, she reappraised the condition of the chapel, pleased to confirm it as structurally sound and only in need of a thorough cleaning and some refurnishing. Finishing her evaluation and meal, she decided to collect what cleaning supplies she needed and make an immediate start.

Some four or five hours later, she leaned the chestnut wood handle of the besom against the side of the bench and dropped into the seat beside it, weary but in good spirits. The birch twigs of the brush, nearly new when she began, now showed a distinct curvature from heavy use. Christina leaned back and peered up, satisfied no evidence remained of the immense dust-encrusted cobwebs that had dangled from diverse areas of the ceiling. The long pole resting in the corner of the room had made short work of those, now so thickly wound around the upper extent of the pole that it appeared to be the end of an unlit torch.

Christina trailed her hand through the dust layer on the oaken seat of the bench.

Next time, I must remember to bring some beeswax to restore the sheen of the wood.

She added it to her mental checklist.

It was tempting to leave her cleaning implements in the chapel, though she feared Trudi's surprise may be spoiled should they be missed. In the end, she decided it less of a risk than chancing one of the household staff discovering her with the tools in hand. She wiped the sleeve of her tunic absentmindedly across her forehead but was aghast at the dark grime encrusting the fabric that had touched her face. As much dirt had probably fallen on her head as had accumulated on the floor. Leaving further cleaning of the room for another day, she departed the chapel, knowing she must visit her chamber for a thorough wash and a change of clothes before seeking out Trudi to put into motion the next part of her plan, presenting her with her wedding gift.

Besides, it is best to have her in a good mood before I tell her of yesterday's worrying events.

An hour later, a refreshed Christina found Trudi supervising the weekly changing of the rushes within the small hall of the manor. Christina breathed deeply, inhaling the scent of dried lavender and pennyroyal, Trudi's favorite mixture to dust over the rushes both to disguise unpleasant odors and to kill fleas.

"Come with me forthwith, Mistress," Christina directed, striving to keep her countenance impassive.

"Of course, Master Frederick," Trudi responded, albeit with a quizzical look. "Mary, will you ensure the work continues unabated in my absence?"

The young girl bobbed her head vigorously and the other maids quickened their efforts, knowing the lash of Mary's tongue to be sharper than that of their mistress.

Christina silently led Trudi to the manor's kitchens, then down the corridor leading to the winter garden. Just before exiting, she stopped and, facing to the right, opened the door before her. Christina made it to the middle of the room before pivoting and facing her mystified friend.

"These apartments are now yours. My wedding gift to you," Christina declared.

"Oh, my good Lord, Christina," Trudi exclaimed softly, overcome with astonishment. "Do you really intend for all of this to be mine?"

"Yes," Christina replied, now grinning broadly. "I can't abide the wailing of your newborn babe keeping me awake at all hours of the night."

Trudi ignored her friend's jest, saying instead, "There's so much of it. What maid lives in such splendor?"

"You're not 'just a maid,' you're my dearest friend. Besides, there are over forty rooms in the manor proper. What else am I to do with them?"

"Why, we could open a brothel!" Trudi said, eagerness tinging her voice.

"You're incorrigible, you lusty little tart!" Christina cried, laughing. "You're a respectable woman now, soon to be married. I think it only fitting for you and your husband to share an apartment of your own, rather than one small chamber. You can't very well sleep with him and the rest of the yardmen in the small hall, can you?"

Trudi giggled and hugged Christina tightly, clearly very happy. The apartment was on the ground floor of the house, down the passageway from the kitchens and across from the garden parlor. There were four rooms in all, with the central one housing a window that overlooked the kitchen garden. Despite the suite's relative privacy, it provided easy access to the kitchen and public rooms of the manor.

Christina had avoided worrying about the ramifications of her meeting with Katharine and her husband for most of the day, but felt she could delay no longer. Although Trudi would have certainly lingered longer in what would soon become her new home, she agreed to accompany Christina to the solar, stopping to retrieve a jug of ale along the way. After they had settled into their customary seats, Christina related what had occurred the previous day, beginning with her departure for the alderman's manor. She left out her private discussion with Katharine, however, as well as what had happened earlier betwixt her and Cecily. Though Trudi was her most intimate confidante, she still held a reluctance in sharing those feelings with anyone.

Unexpectedly, Trudi took the news well, displaying none of the histrionics that had occurred when Christina had informed her of her decision to go northward a few months prior. Her concern clearly showed in her worried expression, however. They spoke on, avoiding further discussion of the impending voyage for the time being. Trudi expressed concern for the family that had assailed Christina, wondering whether they should search them out to offer them work and sustenance at the manor.

"You have a good heart, Trudi, filled with Christian charity, but the world is overfilled with the destitute. On my journey to Volker's, I saw hundreds of starving souls begging for stale crusts of bread. We cannot save everyone in need, you and I, as if they were stray dogs dreaming of laying before a warm hearth and gnawing a meaty knuckle bone."

Trudi looked guilty.

"There are but five, Christina. Besides, they help keep the house rid of vermin."

"I doubt whether any of the hounds would put a foot forward to pursue a rat, given their stomachs are already full to bursting," Christina chuckled, then grew somber. "Yes, the family's plight has troubled me as well, Trudi. I will think on the matter further."

At that moment, Ziesolf entered the solar and took a seat. In a matter of minutes, Christina had once more related the salient point of her meeting with the alderman. Like Trudi, Ziesolf was deeply concerned for Christina's welfare. Although the voyage was still many months in the future, as a man of action he felt compelled to discuss plans for the provisioning of the voyage and beyond. As much as she would have preferred speaking of more pleasant matters, Christina acquiesced, knowing no number of distractions could delay the inevitability of what lay before her.

Chapter 3

Renewed Acquaintances
London, November, 1310

The first day of November dawned gloriously in London, a clear sky and a warmth in the air more reminiscent of a summer day than one in late autumn. Christina lounged casually upon a chair she had moved into the kitchen garden, contemplating the tasks she had accomplished over the past few weeks. She raised her face upward, enjoying the sun's soothing warmth on her skin.

She had completed her renovation of the chapel and, to the best of her knowledge, her activities had remained undiscovered. Christina was more than happy she was finished, having never much enjoyed household chores. More than once, she had considered tasking one of the maids to take over scrubbing of the parquet floor tiles, but she had persevered. The dripped candlewax had been scraped from the small side table, which had then been covered with a rich length of cloth before replacing the tapers, this time upon three matching silver candleholders she had purchased. All the wood had been polished to a high sheen and the silver cross upon the altar gleamed in the sunlight that passed through the cleaned windows. Christina had also coordinated with the priest at nearby St. Olave's Church, who had agreed to perform the ceremony at midday on Martinmas.

All that is left is to spring the surprise on Trudi.

At the thought of her longtime friend, Christina grinned.

Trudi had put the household maids to work cleaning her new abode thoroughly prior to beginning her move. While this was happening, she set about earmarking several pieces of furniture sitting unused in vacant rooms of the house. These were carried to the apartment by her fiancé, assisted by others of the yardmen. Finally, the maids brought soft furnishings to dress the rooms. What had been cold, empty space within the house was made homey and inviting, a suitable place to begin a happy and contented family. Although the apartment was completely ready for occupancy, Trudi had decided to wait until her wedding night to take up her new quarters within the house.

Imagine, after all her lusty talk, she assumes the role of the chaste wife! Christina sniggered. *Well, there's little chance of passing that off, what with her stomach growing larger each day! I'm relieved she will be well settled in to her new home before the time of her laying-in comes.*

Christina swiveled as the door from the house suddenly opened. A girl new to the household, Beatrix, if Christina remembered her name correctly, stepped purposefully forward. She stopped in front of Christina and performed a rather awkward looking curtesy.

"Sir Frederick," she began, eliciting a wince from Christina at the sound of the honorific. "A group of men on horseback have just arrived in the yard. One asks to speak with you."

Oh, sweet Jesus, Christina groaned, wondering what new devilment might be in store for her.

As she thanked the girl and walked into the manor, she wracked her brain, but could not imagine any horsemen who might have business with her. Exiting the great hall into the yard, the mystery dissolved in a most pleasant manner.

"Sir Giles!" she cried rushing forward to embrace the man who had just dismounted. "Peace be with you and those who ride by your side!"

"And to you, Sir Frederick," he replied good-naturedly, matching her hearty hug with one of his own.

"I did not expect to see you until next summer, if even that soon," Christina remarked. "But where are my manners? Please have your men come inside to enjoy my hospitality. My stableman will attend to your horses."

Despite the invitation Giles remained motionless, a slightly enigmatic smile fixed upon his lips.

"Are you so fickle, my friend, to have forgotten a lady to whom you once professed profound affection?" he asked, his eyes agleam.

Christina looked about frantically, assuming he could only be referring to Cecily. But there was no sign of her love. Her mood brightened, however, when she heard a familiar whinny from the horse being led before her.

"Pearl!" Christina shouted, moving forward to take the mare's bridle and stroking the damp coppery-colored hair of her neck.

"The same. I made you a promise at Berwick I would fetch her to you, a promise I have now kept. She is yours."

After one more affectionate pat of the horse, Christina said, "You have no idea how much joy you have brought to me, Giles. Now, by your leave, let us go inside."

"Penny, see to their mounts, if you please."

The groom, who had indeed been hired by Black Peter, called for two of the yardmen. The three men took the reins of the five horses and led them away to be stabled.

Christina was pleasantly surprised to find one of the trestle tables in the hall nearly bowed beneath the weight of a delectable assortment of foodstuffs and drink. While the others eagerly took a seat on the heavy oaken benches that flanked the table, Giles excused himself, remarking he had forgotten something outside. He returned to find everyone waiting impatiently for his return, to polite to commence their feast before their leader. He bade them to begin, a request they happily obeyed. He remained standing, however, holding in his hands a long bundle of hessian cloth. Christina's curiosity was piqued, but she was not quick enough to pose a question before Giles spoke.

"Before departing the North, I had occasion to once more travel to Roxburgh on the king's business. While there, Earl Piers instructed me to tell you he was extremely sorry to have not been at Berwick to witness your knighting, an auspicious event at any time made more so by the fact it was for one he considers a dear friend. He hoped this gift would be pleasing to you. A token of the esteem in which he holds you."

Giles handed the package to Christina, who was surprised by its considerable weight. She laid the object on the table and began to unwrap it. Beneath the burlap, she found a layer of cerecloth, a linen fabric infused with wax to render it waterproof. Removing this, she fell back in wonderment at what lay atop the table.

A broadsword, forged in a manner she had never before seen, one that created a distinctive wavy pattern within the steel. She guessed the tapering blade to be a bit over two feet long, with a broad fuller over half the length of the double-edged blade.

Plainly, the weapon held clear advantage over a falchion, as it could not only thrust and cut, but also slash on the backswing. Christina was enthralled by its elegance. She studied its quillon, slightly upturned at the ends and encrusted with four green stones regularly spaced on each side. A larger, matching stone was inset on either side of the round pommel. This was not just a weapon but a work of art crafted by a master smith.

Christina reached forward and clasped the soft leather wrapping of the hilt. As she closed her grip, she was amazed at how comfortable the weapon felt, almost as if it had been forged for her hand alone. She held the sword for examination, peering down its blade and finding it straight and true. She moved the sword slowly through the air above her, testing its weight and perfect balance. Gently, she brought the weapon down to rest on the cerecloth as if it were made of fragile eggshell, rather than hardened steel.

"I . . . I don't know what to say," Christina stammered, overcome by the generosity of Gaveston's gift.

"It is the most finely-wrought weapon I have ever seen," Giles commented in a low voice.

His companions made similar noises of affirmation before returned to their meal and jovial conversation. Eventually, none at the table could consume another bite. Drinking, on the other hand, was another matter. Christina and Giles prepared to retire to the solar, leaving the others to enjoy their ale more freely.

The door from the kitchen opened and Ziesolf entered the hall, thin lips upturning into a ghost of a smile as he recognized Giles. As he approached, the men-at-arms eyed the disfigured man with mild interest, though their drinking and good-natured banter continued unabated.

Sir Giles turned to them with a scowl.

"Mind your manners, you lot! This man is Sir Kurt Ziesolf, a brother of the Teutonic Knights, and one to whom I owe my life. He who slew a dozen Scots single-handedly at the Battle of the Tower two months ago and assisted Sir Frederick here in uncovering the treachery of the castellan at Roxburgh."

The young men scrambled to their feet, mouthing various words of apology to the man who had become the subject of a popular minstrel's song at King Edward's court.

"Return to your cups, lads," Ziesolf said with the ghost of a grimace, "Giles, you can't expect them to bow and scrape before every old codger they meet now, can you? Now, what fancy pig-sticker have we here?"

Ziesolf lifted Christina's new sword and examined it critically. The other men watched as he retreated a few feet from the table and then swung the weapon deftly. His rapid cuts and slashes lit the blade, caught by the sunlight streaming through the tall windows as if it were aflame. Satisfied, he returned the sword to its bed of cerecloth.

"Wonderfully crafted, it is," Ziesolf observed. "A true credit to the smith who forged it. One in the Holy Land, I would think."

The others at the table looked at him quizzically.

Ziesolf noticed their lack of understanding and pointed.

"See this pattern on the blade there? It was not etched on later; instead, it was part of the forging process. Damascus, it is named, after the Muslim city associated with its production. The steel is both flexible and strong, more important qualities than its beauty, I think."

Leaving Ziesolf to answer the young men's many questions, Christina and Giles adjourned to the solar.

Once seated inside, Christina faced her companion and said in a halting voice, "Do not think I am less than honored by the Earl's gift, it's just that I . . . I . . ."

She paused, searching for the right words.

Puzzled, Giles waited.

"Yes?"

"I . . . I don't know how to fight with such a sword! Throughout my life, I have only trained with a falchion which, as you know, is single-edged and weighted heavily forward. I am intelligent enough to realize this is a far different weapon, requiring a completely different fighting style, one with which I am totally unfamiliar. I could not trust carrying this sword into battle, not because of any deficiencies it possesses, but my own."

"Can you not be instructed by Herr Ziesolf?" he asked. "He wields a similar weapon. There are few his equal in its use."

"Yes, but . . ." Again, she hesitated. "He is still not recovered from his wounds, although he would not admit as such. I learn best through doing, not being told what to do. I cannot ask him to exert himself when, to do so, may sorely impact his health."

Giles nodded slowly before stating, "Although I cannot match Herr Ziesolf's prowess, I would be honored to train you in the sword's use, for the remaining weeks I will be in London at least."

Christina was relieved by Giles' offer, though his words aroused her curiosity.

"Only weeks? Where will you go after that?"

"Back to Berwick, I'm afraid."

His smile more of a grimace now.

"I am to escort the queen's lady, Eleanor de Clare, northward. After that, to spend the winter in snowbound revelries until Edward's campaign against the Bruce continues in the spring."

Christina's thoughts raced.

Would it not follow that, if Lady Eleanor were traveling north to serve Isabella, Cecily would be expected to accompany her aunt? If so, there would be no chance of her return before my own voyage to Lübeck in April. Are we cursed to travel the world as two ships forever bound on divergent courses?

A thought suddenly sprung into her mind.

"Giles . . ."

To make her question appear casual, she picked up her cup and examined its rim before continuing.

"Do you remember the varlet knight, Sir Edgar, who ran away into the night when the raiding party attacked the tower? Have you any knowledge of what became of him?"

She awaited his reply with bated breath.

"No," he said, studying Christina's face in mild interest. "His best outcome would have been to be killed by the Scots. Baron de Percy is a man who does not stomach cowardice, especially from one of his liegemen. For a man such as Sir Edgar, it would be preferable to be thought dead than brought to account."

Christina breathed a sigh of relief. It did not seem likely Cecily's husband would unexpectedly appear in London to reclaim his missing wife. Still, the outside chance the man still lived remained a possibility.

Giles and Christina spent the next hour in idle conversation.

Eventually, he remarked, "I once again thank you for your hospitality, Frederick, but I must now resume my journey to Westminster. I already fear my companions have imposed heavily on Herr Ziesolf to recount his chivalrous exploits, of which I am sure there are many."

Christina nodded in assent, though she enjoyed the man's company immensely.

"Come you on Sunday to the quintain field adjacent to the palace at sext, if that is agreeable, and we shall have a go at it," Giles suggested, clapping Christina's shoulder as he rose.

"Absolutely," she replied, overjoyed Giles had agreed to train with her.

They descended to the great hall where Ziesolf was regaling Giles' youthful companions with tales of marvelous deeds from his earlier life as a Teutonic knight. Seeing Giles, the men-at-arms rose to their feet, thanking the old knight for the benefit of his wisdom and voicing appreciation to Sir Frederick for the bounty of his kitchen. They then departed the hall as one, leaving a comfortable silence in their wake.

He seems like his old self, Christina thought happily, noticing the renewed energy in Ziesolf's step. *Perhaps I do as well. Not only will I have the pleasure of training with Giles, but I may also be so fortunate as to catch sight of Lady Cecily. Who knows upon whom God will smile next?*

She realized she could not spend the remainder of the day in idle anticipation. She had another task, one concerning her role as a merchant, not as a warrior or lover. She left the house and walked briskly to the hall of the Worshipful Company of Weavers. A clerk directed her to Master John Levestan, a guildmember in good standing. She began about the wool that lay in her storeroom, but he soon raised his hand, cutting her short.

"I do not mean to be rude, Master Frederick, but I desire to waste neither your time nor mine. I have no interest in long-staple wool, and I am fairly well assured the other members of our guild will take the same position."

Christina was stunned.

"If their wool is so useless, why do farmers raise such sheep?" she asked, speaking more sharply than she had intended.

"I did not say the wool is without value, merely that we London weavers prefer shorter, curlier, finer fibers that can be spun into woolen yarn," Levestan replied patiently. "The best market for your fleeces is in Norfolk, a county some one hundred miles to the north. The weavers there specialize in the manufacture of lighter, worsted fabrics best made from the longer, coarser staple. My best advice would be for you to offer your fleeces there."

Christina began to frame a sarcastic retort, but thought better of it.

He was only being honest. She sensed no guile in his words, not that there would have been a reason for it. The fleeces were in London, not the market in Norfolk. His information was valuable. Now she only had to determine how to make use of it.

"I thank you, Master Levestan. Your advice is most helpful to me," Christina remarked diplomatically.

She left feeling dismayed.

How am I to transport a shipload of this damnable wool a hundred miles to the north? The easiest way is merely to pack it back aboard Seelöwe, sail up the coast for a couple of days, and drop anchor in the port of Norwich. I should be able to make the roundtrip journey in a week, no more.

The thought of venturing out into winter seas again caused a shiver to pass down her spine.

Have I not tempted fate once this year already? she thought, recalling the fear she had felt as *der Greif* had fought against the savage storm that had nearly sent her to the bottom. *Would it be better to hire carts and transport the wool overland? Certainly safer, but also much more expensive. The ship and its crew are mine; the carts and their drovers are not. The journey could also take weeks. Am I willing to commit that much time to such an endeavor? And if not me, who? Surely not Jost but who else could perform the deed?*

"Damn it!" she exclaimed loudly, her frustration such she cared not who heard it. It seemed each task before her spawned two more, both more vexing than the last.

She had one more thing to do before returning home; one that, fortunately, was sure to restore her to her previously good humor. Christina walked to Cordwainer's Street, where sat the small shop of Averey Robinson, a young cordwainer who had fashioned a pair of poulaines for her the year prior. The man recalled her purchase and inquired as to the shoes' continued wear and comfort, both of which she assured were more than satisfactory. She then drew Gaveston's gift from the sheath she had borrowed from Ziesolf, which she wore on her belt. Even an artisan not accustomed to weaponry could appreciate the workmanship of such a weapon.

"I was wondering if you had skill in fashioning scabbards or, if not, had the name of someone you might recommend?" Christina entreated.

"I've made five for swords and several more for knives while I was an apprentice, so I do have some experience, although I would not profess to be an expert by any means."

The second tradesman today who has spoken honestly. Can this really be London town? she sniggered to herself.

He looked again at the blade, then said, "I would love to undertake this work for you, Master Frederick. If you agree, I will craft a sheath for your sword to the very best of my abilities. Should you find, upon your critical examination, it is unworthy, I will not oblige you to complete the purchase."

Christina gazed into the cordwainer's eyes for a few seconds, then slowly nodded. He placed the sword onto his workbench and deftly used a notched wooden stick similar to her ell-wand to take numerous measurements. Averey then asked her several questions concerning her preferences as to materials, design, and ornamentation. Afterwards, he asked her to return in a week to appraise the quality of his work.

Christina left the cordwainer's workshop with a feeling of satisfaction. She only hoped her confidence in the ability of the young man was not misplaced.

Although the next few days were busy, Christina felt they could not pass quickly enough. She awoke on Sunday morning excited at both the prospect of training with Giles and at the remote possibility of encountering Cecily.

After a thorough wash, she carefully set about selecting her clothes for the day, favoring choices that allowed comfort and good freedom of movement, yet not so worn and faded as to be embarrassing to wear in the shadow of the king's palace. She began with linen braies, a bit looser fitting than what was currently fashionable to permit an easier range of motion. She next pulled matching green chausses of soft wool over her feet and laced each in turn to the ties at the bottom of the braies. After binding her breasts snuggly, she selected one of her best linen shirts, pulling it over her head and allowing it to cascade down her body slightly past the extent of her braies. A light green wool tunic followed.

Until now, her ensemble was much the same as she wore any day; however, the next garment was definitely not. Christina picked a mulberry-colored garment that, although not unfashionable to wear on the street, was more suited for the practice of arms. The pourpoint was marvelously constructed, with felt padding sewn between the woolen outer layer and the linen inner toward the skin. The thickness of the felt varied, heavier on the chest and elbows and lighter elsewhere. The upper part of the gambeson was sewn in rhomboid shapes, while the lower was stitched horizontally. She slipped easily into the garment that extended to mid-thigh and buttoned it most of the way down the front. Moving her body through a range of motions, Christina was pleased the pourpoint in no way inhibited her movement.

She pulled on her boots and gave her toes a wiggle to ensure the concealed seam in her chausses would not cause any blisters. Satisfied, she selected a jaunty yellow cap accentuated with a single peacock feather and placed it on her head. Fastening her sword belt rakishly low upon her hips, she angled her Venetian looking glass to appraise her appearance. She felt a lump form in her throat as she remembered doing virtually the same thing the day of her sister's wedding feast.

How different I looked then; I was no more than a girl, and naked at that. Now, here I am garbed as a man. A knight at arms of all things. If only Frederick could see me now, she thought wistfully as she remembered how he had laughed at her as she appeared dressed in their father's old clothes. *He could joke all he wanted, if only he were here now and alive.*

She grabbed her cloak and made her way to the solar, where she found Ziesolf resting comfortably in his favored chair. He rose and looked her critically over from head to foot. Despite herself, she felt a bit nervous at his scrutiny. He came forward and adjusted her sword belt, positioning it to rest higher around her middle and cinching it tighter so it would remain so.

"It would not be a good thing if it fell around your ankles with a hostile blade thrusting toward you," Ziesolf mildly chastised her. "Better to look less fashionable than to be dead, I think. Eh?"

Christina said nothing, only grinned back at the man who, until now, had been her only teacher.

Other than those who have challenged me in combat, that is, she corrected herself.

Soon, Sarah brought forth from the kitchen a goodly selection of foodstuffs for Christina and Ziesolf with which to break the night's fast. With regret, Christina chose sparingly, resisting the urge to wolf down a large breakfast as was her custom. Ziesolf nodded approvingly at her restraint.

"Good. A fat belly will make you sluggish on the training field. It is also better to be a little hungry than to feel the need to make water or void your bowels. Giles may be puzzled by your peculiar need for privacy to attend to such matters," Ziesolf said.

Christina grimaced.

Why must everything that is so easy for everyone else, be so complicated for me? she lamented.

She knew the answer well, but still found the inequality between male and female anatomy to be one of God's most annoying jests.

When she had completed her meager meal, Christina bid adieu to Ziesolf. Somewhat alarmed by his words, she prudently decided to visit the privy chamber prior to leaving the grounds. Exiting, she was surprised to see the stableman standing in front of her.

"Will ya be on yur way ta Westminster now?" Penny asked matter-of-factly.

Are all my comings and goings such common knowledge among the staff? she thought to herself, already surmising the answer.

"Aye," she replied, "and what of it?"

"I figured as much. Took the liberty of saddlin' yur wee horse, that's all," he replied.

Horse? Why did I not think of that?

A feeling of unexpected pleasure surged through her. She had been so preoccupied with her worries she had forgotten about the spirited mare that now graced her stable. Traveling on horseback would certainly make the journey doubly enjoyable. Then, a sudden thought dampened her enthusiasm somewhat.

"Saddled, you said?" she asked the groom. "I do not recall a saddle being among the bits of tack in the stable."

What Christina did remember were the accoutrements for the cart horses which, until recently, had been the stable's sole inhabitants. She grimaced at the image of the well-worn, utilitarian harnesses she had noticed hanging from the overhead beams. Certainly, she couldn't be expected to ride through the streets of London looking like a farmer on his way to market, could she?

"I found one wedged way up into the rafters. A well-crafted bridle too. Lord knows how long they's been there," Penny answered. "I've been workin' 'em for a while now, cleanin' and workin' the leather with dubbin."

Still unconvinced, she waited impatiently while the groom disappeared into the stable. A few seconds later, he reappeared, leading Pearl by the reins. At the sight of her owner, the rouncey whinnied and tossed her head in delight. To Christina's amazement, the finely-tooled leather of an ornate riding saddle fairly gleamed from the horse's back.

Christina thanked the groom profusely for his good work. The elderly man brought his knuckle to his brow in acknowledgement and turned away to return to his other duties, but not before she noticed a toothy grin on his face. Eager to be on her way, she lithely vaulted onto the rouncey's back and settled comfortably into the saddle, reaching forward to gently stroke the horse's neck and whisper words of encouragement in her ear. Straightening up, Christina clicked her tongue and Pearl responded immediately, wheeling about smartly, exiting the yard, and beginning their journey to Westminster.

She set her steed at a steady, unhurried pace. She had allowed three hours to complete the journey, almost double the time she believed now necessary Astride a fine horse, for the first time she imagined she appeared a knight. She was more than a little pleased with herself as she noticed that, crowded though the streets were, people readily gave way before her.

Suddenly, something hit her high on her left cheekbone. More startled than hurt, she turned quickly to determine the source of the attack, reaching for her sword. A second projectile hit her forehead, similar in size to the first. About twenty feet ahead, she finally identified her assailants.: two boys, scruffily dressed, aged ten or twelve. They were poking each other and laughing uproariously until, seeing Christina had spotted them, they scrambled into the crowd, disappearing from view.

Christina allowed her sword to drop back into its scabbard, and straightened until she was once more sitting erectly in the saddle. She felt a trickle across her upper lip and tentatively moved her tongue forward, expecting the coppery taste of blood. Instead, she sampled the earthy taste of horse shit. She raised her hand to clean it off. but significant residue still adhered to her skin and was imbedded in her hair. She cleaned the bits of dung off her face as best she could while scanning the crowd for the faces of the two imps. The thought of the assault on her going unpunished left her increasingly irate until, unexpectedly, her anger dissipated as suddenly as it arose.

It was just two young scamps having a bit of fun. Trudi and I would have been happy to do the same when we were their age, if everyone in Lübeck hadn't known us by sight. Besides, it may have been God punishing me for my blasphemous thoughts, or more probably for my vanity. Although I cannot imagine those two ragamuffins as the Lord's angels come to Earth.

She regained her dignity as best she could and resumed her journey, albeit with a much less arrogant swagger about her.

Christina arrived at the quintain field well before the abbey bell sounded for sext. Not immediately seeing Giles, she felt a bit nervous. Not knowing what else to do, she looked about, seeing knots of men gathered together, laughing and joking in easy camaraderie. On the side of the plot furthest from the river was a long strip of churned ground, obviously a pathway made by running horses. At the end, she spotted the quintain, a wooden figure carved into the likeness of a Saracen, with a shield upon its left arm and a club in its right. As the breeze shifted, she was surprised to see the figure rotate slightly, evidence it was set upon a pivot. She envisioned a rider galloping down the pathway toward the quintain, striking it a blow with lance or sword and avoiding a counterstrike from the rotating club.

I hope there will be some who will compete at this today.

She smirked at the thought of trying it herself.

Her eyes moved to the other side of the field where townsmen were attaching cloth targets to a series of wooden casks extending the full length of the plot.

That must be over a thousand feet! Will swordsmen rush them in turn? If so, they will be well winded by the time they reach the last. But surely no weapon exists with such a range as this on its own.

After the last cloth was placed against the butts, a group of men congregated approximately two hundred feet before the first target, on which was placed not a bit of fabric, but an upright willow stave. Then they each took another stave in hand. In a minute, their intention became obvious.

"Sweet Virgin Mother!" she whispered. "Those are bows, but such as I have never seen!"

"Yes, English bowmen, Longshanks' secret weapon."

Startled, Christina turned to see Giles and another man she recognized as one of his companions from his visit to her home.

"God be with you this morning, Sir Frederick," Giles remarked amiably. "You do remember my squire, Thomas, do you not?"

She nodded, then turned to gaze once more at the bowmen.

While she watched in fascination, Giles said, "Each bow is approximately six feet in length and made of yew, with strings of hemp, flax, or silk. But it is not the bow that is the secret, it is the bowman. The king's father decreed that each male child would begin training at no more than ten years of age and that all able-bodied non-noble men would regularly practice until they became adept at ranges over two hundred paces. Many can exceed even that distance. It is customary here, as in many towns throughout the realm, to hold competitions on Sunday to ensure a ready force of competent archers is maintained."

"Unbelievable!" she exclaimed, as one of the bowmen fired an arrow that split the willow wand upon the first butt lengthwise.

"Should we get on to our own business, or would you rather watch the bowmen?" Giles asked mildly.

Hastily, Christina replied, "I would like very much to begin our training now, Sir Giles. I apologize for my distraction, but I have never seen this weapon, let alone observed it in practice. Why, it could completely change a battlefield. Imagine if we would have had a few of these bowmen with us at the tower. The Scots would have been dead long before they ever felt the bite of our swords!"

Giles' facial muscles tightened and his eyes narrowed. Christina's demeanor also sobered as they both momentarily recalled the comrades they had lost in the skirmish. Giles walked back toward the palace walls, accompanied by Thomas and

Christina. Soon they arrived beside a pile of assorted martial paraphernalia, obviously prepositioned by the pair. The squire extended his hand toward Christina and motioned his head in the direction of a nearby hitching rail. She passed him Pearl's reins before focusing her attention on Giles, who selected a pair of wooden swords and presented the hilt of one to Christina.

"Is this a jest?" she asked incredulously. "Do you believe me no more than a sprat?"

Giles met her gaze and said in a serious tone, "I believe it best to start with these. How can I show you how to make use of both sides of the blade if I cannot draw it against your body for fear of slicing your flesh? Even more importantly, you doing such a wound to me."

The corners of his mouth arose into a self-deprecating smile.

Obviously, he is right. When Frederick and I first found the falchions, we did little more than clang the blades together. When he later demonstrated what he had learned in his sessions with Ziesolf, the blades were so dull they could not cut through the fabric of our clothing.

Although she did recall the horrendous bruises the impact the blows of her brother's blade had raised on her skin, as hers had on his body.

We were lucky we did not permanently maim each other.

"Yes, I agree completely, Giles," she answered, matching the man's previously stern countenance before adding with a slight smirk, "The part about me doing injury to you, at least."

"Well, let us see if your cockiness is justified," he said, before drawing away a few yards and raising his wooden blade into a guard position.

With reluctance, Christina unbuckled her scabbard and placed it and the beautiful sword within it on the ground behind her. She then grasped the hilt of the wooden practice sword and gave a few tentative cuts through the air, pleased to find its weight and balance similar to that of her own blade. She nodded to Giles, indicating she was satisfied with the blade and ready to begin.

Christina advanced in a slight crouch; her weight well distributed onto the balls of her feet. Giles rushed forward into the attack, his weapon whistling through the air. Christina shifted her weight backward, avoiding the tip of the blade by a few inches. As Giles' blade passed beyond Christina's body, she thrust the tip of her own weapon forward, aiming for his heart. However, Giles stepped to the side, simultaneously pulling his weapon back along the outer edge of her thigh in what would have been a debilitating draw cut.

Christina swore viciously as she stepped backward to disengage from Giles' weapon. How could she have been so stupid? She'd been so eager to score a hit that she had disregarded his blade. If he'd been a true foe, she'd be dead. If Ziesolf wielded the wooden sword, she would have been bruised for a month, just so she wouldn't forget her mistake. Perhaps Giles was too courteous for that, but she vowed not to present him another opportunity so she could find out!

She advanced once more - this time more wary of her opponent's possible ploys. Giles snaked his blade forward diagonally from a high guard. She parried, deflecting his weapon to fall harmlessly where she had once stood while pulling her blade up and under his armpit. It was now his turn to concede space as he lifted his weapon in a slight salute to her own strike.

Their efforts continued for several minutes unabated. Their skill proved roughly equal at the beginning with Christina's superior speed and agility counter-balanced by Giles' familiarity with the double-edged blade. In strength, they were closely matched. As Christina became increasingly adept with her weapon's capabilities, however, she began to best her friend's efforts. After a particularly withering attack which ended with the flat of Christina's blade brought forward to fall gently against Giles' cheek, he stumbled backwards, raising his hand to abate any further attack.

"Peace!" he panted. "For God's sake, Frederick, you're like trying to fight an apparition. I think my sword has found you and then you're gone! Where did you learn to fight in this manner?"

Christina stood with eyes still fixed on her opponent, her sword arm trembling slightly with nervous energy. Steam blew from her nose into the chilled air as if she were a winded horse. She had no conscious thoughts, her movements automatic and reactive. Slowly, her muscles, taunt as bowstrings, began to relax. As she regained control of her body, she suddenly felt as if she would collapse to the ground.

"Herr Ziesolf was my teacher. What little I know I have learned from him."

Giles nodded, then gestured to his squire to bring forth a container of weak ale. Both he and Christina sucked liquid from the flask through their parched lips and down their dry throats. Although Giles took a seat on the ground, Christina remained standing. This had nothing to do with proving her fortitude, rather she was nursing a serious cramp in her left thigh she knew that, if not stretched, would contract, causing excruciating pain. She wiped her hand across her face, surprised to find it not encrusted with sweat as she expected. Only a white, salty residue clung to her cheeks and forehead. Her back, on the other hand, was awash in perspiration; her sodden linen shirt sticking to her skin. Although she could detect no smell, she expected she would absolutely be reeking from her exertions by the ride home.

Giles stood and stretched his sinews, an action almost immediately mirrored by Christina. Soon, they both felt ready to resume. This time, however, Giles indicated to his squire to assist Christina in donning a chainmail hauberk over her gambeson. She held her hands above her head and bent forward as Thomas deftly slipped the mail shirt over and down her body to the mid-point of her thighs.

Sweet Mary!

Christina groaned to herself as the weight of the mail settled primarily on her shoulders.

The arms of the garment, extending to her wrists, provided an additional burden as she sought to raise her practice sword to high guard. Thomas was not finished, however. He removed her hat and placed a quilted woolen arming cap upon her head, securing the ties firmly beneath her chin. Over this was placed a steel cap with a nasal guard, which was secured in a similar fashion by leather ties. Thomas then repeated the process with Giles while Christina sought to adjust her eyesight around the nasal piece.

And this damnable sweaty band across my tits is beginning to chaff! Fucking hell!

Whereas Christina had been the superior fighter previously, Giles was clearly the master of the two now. Christina's speed was negated by the weight of the mail, while Giles' experience in fighting in armor provided him a clear advantage. Additionally, the helm's nasal guard seemed to impede her vision at the most inopportune times, making her body an easy target for her friend's quick blade.

Shit, shit, shit!

Christina's frustration mounted as her opponent scored yet again. This time, it was Christina who backed away. With a restraint she did not feel, she signaled for a pause. What she really wanted to do was rush Giles, tackle him to the ground, and pummel him with her fists for embarrassing her so.

"Enough," she managed to gasp, determined to remain standing despite her body's demands she collapse.

Without being asked, Thomas approached and removed the helmet and cap. She then leaned forward as she had previously and he slipped the hauberk from her body, which suddenly felt light as a feather. She stretched her aching muscles while Thomas assisted Giles. This time they both sat, side-by-side, as they silently drank the tepid ale.

Giles spoke first.

"You are an extremely skilled swordsman, Frederick, superior to me, as I am superior to most of the king's men. That is good. You have little practice in armor though, and that is bad. As one of Edward's liegemen, you could rightfully be called upon to follow your lord into war as one of his knights. What would you do then?"

Christina stared at Giles, considering for the first time the full implications of her ascendance to knighthood.

"I understand, Giles," she began slowly, "This is all very new to me, but I do understand. I will make time every day to learn these skills."

In acknowledgement of their comradeship, he reached out and briefly put his arm around her shoulders.

"When might we meet again? You name the time, and I shall be here," she affirmed, noting to herself to consult with Ziesolf about obtaining armor of her own.

"Alas, my friend, I wish it were possible. However, it is not. I will be leaving the day after next and will require the morrow to prepare for my journey."

Christina gawked at him.

"But I thought you were not departing for some weeks yet?"

"The Lady of Glamorgan had a different opinion," replied Giles. "Remember, she hopes to join our lady, the queen, in Berwick in time for the yule. She does not travel as we do, Frederick. Each day will be a ride from one castle or stronghold to the next, where she may spend the night in a warm and comfortable bed. Some of these stops will only be for a night, while others will extend into days. As a result, we must leave immediately so as to comply with the queen's wishes."

It was neither Queen Isabella who occupied Christina's mind, nor even Giles. Her thoughts were only of her beloved Cecily, and the fact she had lost all hope of seeing her in mere hours.

Christina, realizing Giles was staring, awaiting a response, replied, "I am sorry to hear you must leave. Hopefully, we may schedule another session when their majesties return to London."

"I would be honored to do so, friend Frederick. I expect your skills in armored fighting will far exceed mine by that time, so I will fully expect a drubbing at your hands when next we meet," he replied cheerfully.

Giles and Thomas gathered the equipment from the ground and made their way toward a palace gate. For a brief second, Christina thought to hail them and ask if she might accompany them inside.

But what then? Do I demand to be taken to Eleanor de Clare's private apartments? Demand to see Cecily and plead with her not to accompany her lady northward as it is her duty to do? What right do I have to ask any of this? She is gone, Christina, and the sooner you accept this the sooner you can get on with your life.

With that, she untied her horse and struggled painfully into the saddle. She began the journey home, made even longer by the aches of her body and the pain in her heart.

Chapter 4

A Guest Most Welcome
London, November, 1310

The few remaining days before Trudi's nuptials filled the manor's residents with happy anticipation. This helped Christina to somewhat set aside the finality of the loss of Cecily. Although she still found her thoughts drifting sadly toward their too few precious days spent together, the sleeplessness she endured the night before the wedding stemmed from eager anticipation of the immediate future rather than mulling over past regrets.

Waking early, Christina hastily washed, dressed and made her way downstairs to find Mary, whose assistance she would need to prepare the chapel. She discovered the manor already swarming with frenetic activity. Over the past few days, the maids had thoroughly cleaned the public rooms. Now they had only to spread the fresh, fragrant rushes on the floor in anticipation of the evening's festivities. Most of the women not employed in this task were assisting Bess in preparing the myriad of delicious dishes that would be served at the wedding feast.

Christina discovered Mary supervising Margery and Heloise, two of the youngest maids, who were setting the tables in the great hall. Since Trudi was obviously otherwise occupied, the role of housekeeper had fallen to the young girl. Even though her promotion within the servant hierarchy was only temporary, it was plain to Christina she took her duties seriously. After the two girls had finished the first table. Mary went to the end and sighted down the row of pewter cups, instructing some to be moved forward and others back. The same was done for crockery and cutlery, until all were perfectly aligned. She then gave a curt bob of her head. As they moved on to the next table, Christina saw Margery roll her eyes skyward, a universal gesture of disrespect rendered by young girls everywhere. Heloise choked back a snorting laugh by placing her hand over her mouth, then quickly skipped to the next table and began to set the cups in their proper formation. The other girl was not so quick. Mary was beside her in an instant and she let out a yelp as the slender housekeeper gave her forearm a painful pinch.

"Sorry, miss!" Margery blurted, then ran to join her friend before she could receive a tongue-lashing in addition to the tweak.

Christina was happy to see Mary was not about to tolerate any foolishness from those in her charge. She did, however, feel sympathetic toward Margery as she had long ago mastered a more inconspicuous eye roll through constant practice when she thought her mother, Trudi's sister Anna, or her sister Marguerite wasn't looking.

"Oh, Mary," Christina said.

"Yes, Master?" she replied as she exercised her well-practiced little curtsey.

"I hate to take you away from your duties, but I have a special task for you. Can you break away for a few minutes?"

"Of course, Master Frederick. This lot know better than to muck about. I'll not be having Mistress Trudi's wedding be anything less than perfect!" Mary said fiercely.

"Good. Let's be off then."

Christina led Mary through the house to the chapel. She opened the door and they stepped inside,

"Sweet Mary!" the maid exclaimed; her mouth falling wide open. "I did not know this place existed. How is it so clean? None of we maids have worked here or I would have known about it."

"Aye," Christina replied as they descended the stone steps, pleased at Mary's unwitting compliment of her hard work. "What I want you to do is to see Osbert, the yardman, whom I have already tasked to obtain pine boughs and holly branches. Have him bring these hither. I would then like you to arrange them throughout the chapel as you best see fit. Have Bess provide you with rosemary sprigs from the kitchen garden and add these as well. Lastly, fetch a multitude of candles and ensure they are lit well prior to the ceremony, which will be soon after sext. I would do these things myself, but I have other matters to which I must attend. Can I trust you to do them in my stead?"

"Whatever pleases you, Master!" she answered exuberantly, then hastily added, "And Mistress Trudi as well, of course."

"And Mary?"

Christina fixed the girl with what she hoped was a stern look.

"Yes, Master?"

"Not a word to anyone. This is to be a surprise."

Mary's face beamed as she bobbed her head vigorously.

"By your leave?" she asked, nearly beside herself with eagerness to get on with her special task.

Christina nodded and Mary was off in an instant, taking the steps upward two at a time. As the girl disappeared through the doorway, Christina smiled and shook her head.

Was I ever so young?

She ascended the steps herself, albeit at a slower pace. Making her way up the hallway, she peered around the corner, pleased to find it deserted. She walked rapidly to the door to Trudi's chamber. Rapping quietly on the oaken portal, she looked once more in each direction to ensure she was not being observed. As the door opened Christina hastened inside, securing the latch behind her.

"It's a little bit early for the master of the house to claim the bride's first night, isn't it?" Trudi sniggered.

"Well, from the looks of your belly, wench, I'm actually more than a little late!" Christina snorted.

Both friends guffawed uproariously.

"Have you broken your fast this morning?" asked Christina, wiping merry tears from her eyes. "I can instruct one of the scullery girls to bring up a tray."

"No, thank you," Trudi replied shyly. "Believe it or not, I am without appetite. Besides, there will be more than ample food and drink at tonight's feast to compensate for anything I miss now."

The two women took seats in comfortable upholstered chairs arranged facing each other before the fire grate. For a few moments they sat in amiable silence, each alone with her own thoughts. Trudi spoke first.

"Are the preparations for the feast going well? Are you certain I am not needed?" she asked.

"No, absolutely not. As long as Bess rules the kitchen, there will never be a complaint about the quantity or quality of the food in this house."

"And Mary?" Trudi focused her question more pointedly.

"She is like a she-wolf and you her prized cub!" Christina remarked with a smile. "Nary an item will get out of place under her watch, believe you me. Although it was you who trained her, I might have thought she learned under Anna instead!"

They both giggled at the recollection of Trudi's stern sister, who had been Christina's mother's maid for years. Suddenly, tears came to Trudi's eyes, rolling in swiftly moving rivulets down her plump cheeks.

"I wish Anna were here. And my mother, and yours as well. It would only seem right," she said, her voice trailing off.

Christina rose and, taking Trudi's head in her hands, kissed her gently on the cheek.

"I miss them too. Well Anna not so much," Christina admitted. "But you have a new family now, a husband and a babe on the way. And you have me."

Trudi turned away, but not before Christina spied a look of worry on her face.

She frets that I am soon to leave her as well.

Uncomfortable with the melancholy turn of their conversation, Christina asked, "Should we not get you into the bath? It would be a shame to waste the girls' effort in lugging the hot water up here by allowing it to go cold."

Trudi nodded and moved adjacent to the wooden bathing vessel set before the fire, vapors of steam emanating into the air from its surface. She turned toward Christina and hesitated, a shy expression overtaking her face.

"Come now, little sister. It's not like I've never seen you naked!" Christina said, a bit bewildered at Trudi's reticence.

Trudi opened her smock and allowed it to slip off her shoulders, then fall to the floor. Christina gawked at her with amazement. This was not the Trudi she had known all her life standing before her. She was the first pregnant woman Christina had ever seen in the nude.

Trudi waited for Christina to speak, worrying her bottom lip between her teeth.

"You are the most beautiful woman I have ever seen. Peter is a fortunate man to call you wife," she whispered, hoping it to be the right thing to say.

Trudi smiled, clearly pleased by her friend's kind words.

Her expression turned mischievous and she remarked, "Well, are you going to help me into the tub, or should I just take a running leap?"

Christina steadied her friend's body as Trudi carefully moved first one leg and then another over the side of the bathing vessel and into the water. She then sat down, resting her back on the linen liner behind her. Christina rummaged about in the pouch she wore on her belt until she found a small parchment packet. Opening it, she removed an off-white, rectangular cake of soap approximately three inches in length. She held it first to her own nose, then to Trudi's.

"Smell this," she instructed. "I bought it from the pepperers' near the Eleanor Cross in Cheapside. The shopkeeper said the fragrance is sandalwood, and the soap is of the finest quality, from Castile in Spain."

Christina laid the soap to the side and pulled a small bottle from the pouch. She removed the stopper and poured a brownish, fragrant oil directly into the bath water. As soon as it fell upon the surface, a sensuous, musky odor began to permeate the room.

"This is an oil distilled from the glands of an animal called the civet. It is rumored to have a quickening effect on men," she added, somewhat embarrassed.

"I thank you, Christina, for your thoughtful gifts," Trudi remarked. "Though I'm somewhat unsure whether Peter will feel he is taking a wife, or a visit to the stews in Southwark."

Christina contorted her face into an evil scowl, scooped a handful of water, and splashed it onto Trudi's face, then joined her friend in laughter. After bathing, Trudi stood as Christina dried her thoroughly with multiple lengths of white linen toweling with blue embroidered borders. Laying the toweling aside, she took a wooden comb and worked it gently through Trudi's blond hair until it hung in straight sheets nearly down to her buttocks.

Christina helped the bride-to-be don a fine white linen smock, embroidered with small white birds upon the bodice. This was followed by a woolen kirtle of Lincoln green, the color associated with young love, and Trudi's favorite garment. The delay of the wedding had necessitated some last-minute alterations to accommodate her expanding girth, but adding a few inconspicuous gussets had assured a goodly fit. Christina extended a thin woolen girdle just above Trudi's hips. Madder-dyed red, it had a two-inch length of fine embroidery extending above the belt-chape. Lastly, a sideless linen surcoat of a verdulet blue-green color was added.

Trudi sat and Christina knelt before her, pulling tanne-colored woolen hose over her small feet and up to her mid-thigh, securing them with blue silk garters just under the knee. A pair of well-made brown leather turn-shoes completed Trudi's ensemble.

Christina then focused on her friend's hair, now dry enough to arrange. She separated the strands and braided them into plaits, interwoven with blue silken tape. These were pinned to the side and covered with a linen fillet, which was then enclosed by a linen kerchief pinned to the headband. Now finished dressing, Trudi arose, stepped a few feet away, and turned back toward Christina for her approval.

"Wait one moment," Christina said, exiting the door before Trudi could ask why. In her chamber, she retrieved her Venetian looking glass. She tarried only a moment, the thought of how much she missed her brother springing unbidden to her mind before returning to the bride-to-be. She angled the mirror so Trudi could contemplate her reflection. Judging from the bloom of her broad smile, she was well satisfied with Christina's efforts.

"You look lovely, Trudi," Christina commented, a lump rising in her throat.

Do I regret that I will never have an opportunity to marry?

An image of Cecily dressed thusly appeared in her mind.

She turned away, busying herself with picking up sundry items from the floor while she composed herself.

Trudi asked, "Should we not be off to the church soon? The time must be approaching and the walk will be several minutes at the speed I now move."

Some of Christina's good humor returned as she realized Trudi had not uncovered the secret of the chapel's rehabilitation.

"Yes, before too long. Wait here while I check to ensure Peter's family has arrived."

Although Peter and Trudi had a large circle of friends and acquaintances, they had decided to invite only those closest to them to the actual ceremony. For Trudi, this was Christina and Ziesolf. Peter's parents, his brother, and his sister-in-law represented the groom's family. Only Ziesolf had been aware the wedding would occur in the manor's chapel, rather than at the church of St. Olave.

Christina left Trudi's chamber and descended the stairs. Just before she stepped into the great hall, Mary called to her from the kitchen passage.

"Master!" she whispered loudly.

Christina turned, watching the young girl running toward her, her skirts held above her ankles to better her speed.

"Aye, Mary?" she answered, a knot forming in the pit of her stomach at the thought that some calamity had occurred.

"Master Frederick, a priest arrived at the door an hour ago asking for you. I told him I didn't know where you were, because I didn't know where you were. Where were you? Well, no matter. He said he was to perform a marriage ceremony here today. Well, I couldn't very well tell him to go away, could I? So, I brought him to the chapel and left him there while I returned to the kitchen to fetch him some food and drink, which I did. I brought it to him and he thanked and blessed me, so I think I did right. That is, if you think I did right. Did I?"

She gasped for air.

Christina silently cursed herself for forgetting about the priest's arrival.

"Well done, Mistress Mary!"

She was grateful for the girl's quick wit.

Mary's face flushed with pleasure at having again earned her master's praise. For an instant she beamed a smile up at Christina then, remembering her place, lowered her eyes modestly and dropped into her well-practiced curtsey.

"Has Peter's family arrived yet?"

"Yes, Master. He and Herr Ziesolf are sharing wine with them at a table as we speak here."

"Good. Now, run and let the priest know the bride and groom will be at the chapel presently."

After the merest hint of a dip, Mary ran up the stairs, taking the steps in twos and threes.

Christina entered the great hall. She saw Peter and Ziesolf seated at a table to the right of the one on the raised dais. After welcoming the visitors, she was happy to learn Ziesolf had already disclosed the ceremony was to be held in the manor chapel.

Christina could barely contain her mounting excitement as it seemed her clandestine plans for the wedding were successfully coming to fruition.

"Herr Ziesolf, would you be so kind as to escort our guests to the bottom of the stairway? For my part, I will gather Trudi from her room and out into the passageway. At that time, will all of you join us and we will walk together to the chapel, where the priest now awaits us?"

"But what if she is not yet ready, Sir Frederick?" Peter's mother asked cautiously. "Would it not be better to have one of us women check instead?"

"I have just minutes ago spoken with a trusted maid who assured me Mistress Trudi was only awaiting word to proceed," Christina glibly lied.

Anyway, who could be a more trusted maid than myself?

Not waiting to invite further suggestions, Christina took the stairs two at a time and rapped on the door to Trudi's chamber. Within seconds, the door opened and Trudi stepped out into the passageway. Christina offered her arm, at the same time flashing a wink at the other woman. The bride smiled serenely and placed her hand lightly on the sleeve of Christina's tunic. Suddenly, Trudi emitted a small gasp, startled at the sound of multiple footsteps echoing on the stairway below.

Realizing it must be the other members of the wedding party, she turned to Christina.

"Should we not be away to the church now? It makes small sense they should be walking up, only to be walking back down."

"Come," Christina instructed.

Baffled, Trudi accompanied her friend without further question, with the others following slightly to their rear. As they neared the chapel door, their destination became obvious. To Trudi, however, their purpose just grew more puzzling.

"Why are we coming here?" she asked in a near-hysterical whisper. "The chapel is a complete mess; I tasked none of the maids with cleaning it. Are you trying to embarrass me in front of Peter's people?"

"But you forget, there is one maid here who does not answer to your beck and call," Christina replied jauntily.

Even more mystified now, Trudi stepped through the doorway and onto the high landing of the chapel. She drew in a ragged breath, shocked at the beauty of the room before her. Boughs of aromatic pine circled the walls, their intoxicating fragrance melding with that of abundant rosemary sprigs. Branches of holly were placed above these, their merry red berries juxtaposed against the two shades of green. What must have been forty or more beeswax candles were strategically placed about the periphery of the room, their flames illuminating the small altar, causing the silver cross upon it to glow as if lighted from within. Trudi faced Christina with joyful, tear-filled eyes. She silently mouthed, "Thank you" and reached across unobtrusively to squeeze her friend's hand. Christina returned the pressure for an instant, then led Trudi carefully down the steps. Once they had descended, the others followed. Everyone now stood in somewhat of a line, facing the priest and about eight feet back from the altar.

Father Brand welcomed the group to the Lord's house, then asked, "Does the bride's father permit this marriage?"

Christina responded, "The bride's father is dead, while all of her other kin are far away in Lübeck town. I am the master of this house and possess lordship over this woman. As such, I agree to this marriage, as is my wont and right."

The priest then enquired, "Are the bride and groom related to each other?" to which Peter's father and Christina responded in the negative.

"And have the necessary banns been published?" Brand asked.

Christina replied, "Aye, they have."

Finally, he asked Peter and Trudi whether they consented freely to enter into marriage.

The couple briefly glanced toward each other, then simultaneously uttered, "Yes."

Ziesolf then read the dowry agreement. Although Peter had claimed none was necessary as Trudi was without any true family and they were both in Christina's service, she flatly refused his offer, believing it would be an affront to Trudi to be wed dowerless. The sum finally agreed upon was five English pounds, a small silver ingot, and the furnishings of their new apartment. Though an astronomical sum for a mere servant girl, Christina had never viewed Trudi so and would have gladly given more had Trudi consented. Consequently, Christina was more than satisfied with the arrangement. At this point, Peter presented Trudi with a small leather bag of thirteen coins, signifying he was content to allow her to manage the finances of their household. She accepted this from his hand. Christina knew it was customary to distribute this money to the needy later.

Peter now walked forward and stood before the priest. Trudi followed, taking her position at his distaff side, a custom representing that Eve was created from Adam's left rib.

In a clear voice, Peter plighted his troth, promising to, "have and to hold you, my sweet Mistress Trudi, at the bed and at the table, as my wife and I pledge to you the faith of my body, that I will be faithful to you and loyal with my body and my goods and that I will keep you in sickness and in health and in whatever condition it will please the Lord to place you, and that I shall not exchange you for better or worse until the end."

As was proper practice, Trudi remained silent. Father Brand delivered a homily on the sacredness of the marriage act. Afterward, he asked for the ring, which Peter's brother placed in his hand. The priest blessed the ring and handed it to Peter, who slid it on and off the first finger of her right, then the second, and finally allowed it to remain on the third. With each movement, he repeated, "In the name of the Father, and of the Son, and of the Holy Ghost, with this ring I thee wed."

Christina's thoughts strayed to herself speaking the same words to Cecily.

As Peter and Trudi knelt before the altar upon two cushions, the other attendees moved forward and held a length of linen as a canopy over the heads of the new couple while the priest said mass. When Father Brand finished, the canopy was removed and Peter and Trudi stood. The priest stepped forward and bestowed upon Peter the kiss of peace, which Peter than gave to Trudi. Following another short blessing, the ceremony was at an end.

They all departed the chapel and proceeded to the newlyweds' apartment, where Father Brand blessed the bedchamber. The formalities finally finished; the party moved to the great hall to begin the festivities of the wedding feast.

As she accompanied the others down the passageway, Christina's heart was swollen with joy for Trudi. She grinned, overhearing the growing sounds of happy talk and loud laughter from down the stairway. Within a couple of minutes, they stood before the door into the hall. Opening it, Christina was pummeled by a wave of warmth emanating from well over a hundred bodies. She stepped inside, recognizing most of those in attendance. The few she did not, she attributed to be guests of the groom and his family. She noticed Father Brand standing by himself along the right wall. Leaving Trudi, she met the priest and thanked him for performing the wedding service. He smiled and was about to reply when his attention was drawn to somewhere over Christina's right shoulder. The priest hurriedly excused himself and moved deeper into the room.

"By God's great cock! Ah hopes yur cellars run deep, or this lot will soon drain em dry, Yur Worship!" Reiniken shouted.

Christina was already bracing herself as she turned, for the blow she knew would certainly follow. As expected, she felt a huge, meaty paw clap her on the back with the force of a small felled tree. Although her shoulder felt numb, it mattered not, such was her joy.

"Wig!" she exclaimed, beating him with her hand on his upper arm for emphasis. "Where have you been? I haven't seen you since the day we returned from the North!"

She suddenly remembered his injury.

"I'm sorry, did I hurt you, your broken arm I mean?"

A puzzled look crossed Reiniken's broad face, then his mouth split open and he hooted uproariously, "You, Yur Worship, hurt me? Why, Ah've swatted flies harder off mi' ass when ah wuz shittin' then yur little taps! Besides, Ah've been gettin' a lot of exercise, bringin' ale to mouth, don't ya know. Good as new, Ah is, good as new!"

Same old Wig, Christina thought, overjoyed to see the man. *He's profane, ill-mannered, and a consummate sinner, but there is no more stalwart companion I would rather have beside me in a fight.*

"So, where's the new missus, eh?" Reiniken asked, grabbing two tankards of ale from the scullery maid Sarah, one of which he emptied in a gulp before thumping the empty vessel down on a nearby table. The other he nursed more judiciously.

"Over yonder," Christina pointed to where Trudi was standing, surrounded by a bevy of excited young women.

Ah can't figgur why a man would marry. Havin' someone tell - im what he kin do and who he kin fuck ain't livin', if ya ask me," Reiniken flashed Christina an uncommonly serious expression. "But if'n he were, he couldn't do better than Mistress Trudi, thet's fur damn sure. Lucky bastard, that smith!"

"That's one thing on which we can certainly agree, Wig. Sit for a minute, will you?"

As the massive man settled on the bench, Christina sat beside him. She had known he would not miss Trudi's wedding, so she had felt no hurry in asking him to accompany her to the Baltic. Now that he was here, there was no reason to delay any longer.

She motioned for one of the maids, who brought a hefty jug of ale and topped off Reiniken's tankard.

"Now, what's the big fuckin' secret, Yur Worship? Do ya wants mi ta kill some bastard?" He spoke in a conspiratorial voice, making the words sound like they were being dragged over sharp gravel. "Cause I will, ya know. Cut his heart out, strangle -im, whatever youse like!"

"Well," Christina said with an innocent smile, "That's exactly what I'd like you to do, Wig."

Shock appeared in Reiniken's eyes.

"Ah wuz just havin' a laugh!" he protested, "They hangs ya for shit lak thet here in London town! I means, Ah will if thet's whats ya need, but ya butter be damn shure!"

"It won't be in London, so you have no need to worry about that," she remarked.

"Well, where then? Is ya goin' up North agin? Good, if'n ya is. I still gots a score ta settle with them Scot bastards!"

"In a matter of speaking," Christina replied, enjoying the man's bafflement immensely.

"No more beatin' about the bush, fur fuck's sake! Make yurself plain or Ah'll spenk yur bare ass in front of everbody, ya damn pup!" Reiniken's voice became louder as his ire rose. A few people nearby turned their way with concern.

"All right, all right," Christina said hastily to placate him. "I am taking *Der Greif* to Lübeck, to join a fleet there that plans to seek pirates in the Skagerrak and the western Baltic, bring them to battle, and remove their threat forever."

"Mighty talk, but not so easy, I fugurs. Them's sneaky bastard, they are. You'll never find -em ashore, they's too well hidden for thet. So, youse'll have to get -em to come to youse on the sea. Too many ships, and they won't attack. Not enough, and its yur ass in the fire. Won't be easy, but Ah'm in," he said matter-of-factly. "When do we leave?"

"Glad to hear that, Wig," Christina said, happy he had agreed so readily. "I couldn't imagine doing it without your sword arm by my side."

"Ya don't think I'd let yur skinny ass have all the fun, do ya?"

He shaped his mouth into a gap-toothed grin.

Just as Christina began to formulate a retort, a sudden commotion at the back of the hall, near the door to the yard caught her ear.

"Ah've got a score to settle with those sons of bitches too. Split mi mate, Siegfried from gizzard to gullet on the trip here. So, it's personal, ya see," Reiniken added, eyes now scanning the same direction as Christina's, evaluating whether the situation required mayhem or some less violent attention.

"Oh, shit!" he exclaimed shaking his head, realizing Christina's interest in a conversation with him had been supplanted.

It was Cecily.

Christina rose slowly, as if in a trance. Her feet carried her forward, her pace quickening until she halted before the party of six individuals engaged in removing their heavy woolen traveling cloaks in the warmth of the room. The matching livery of the four male figures left little doubt they were royal retainers. The taller of the two women was older and well dressed, clearly a woman of high standing. Christina noticed these figures only in passing, her attention dominated by the remaining woman.

"Greetings to you all," Christina managed to say without tripping over her words too badly.

"And to you, Sir Frederick, Lady Agnes," Cecily said, rotating her head toward the matronly woman beside her while sweeping her hand toward Christina.

"This is the brave knight to whom I owe my life, as it was he and his stalwart companions who saved me from the ravages of the Scottish brigands."

Cecily's voice brought a sweet pain in Christina's bosom that threatened to tear her chest asunder. It took all of her resolve to not spring forward, take her into her arms, and kiss her enticing lips. Instead, Christina stood transfixed, gazing softly at Cecily.

The growing possibility of severe embarrassment was saved by the timely arrival of Mary, whose hand upon Christina's elbow broke the smitten woman from the spell.

"May I assist you in welcoming your guests, Master Frederick?"

"Thank you, Mistress Mary," Christina answered with relief. "Please have someone attend to our guests' cloaks and ensure these men are provided with food and drink."

Mary did as she had been instructed and soon Christina stood alone with Cecily and Lady Agnes.

Christina posed the question that had come to completely dominate her thoughts.

"I am pleased beyond words with your arrival, Lady Cecily, especially as I had been led to believe you were to accompany the Lady of Glamorgan to Berwick."

Cecily was strangely hesitant, leaving Christina concerned.

It was Lady Agnes who broke the silence.

"Lady Cecily has been unwell of late. Lady Eleanor believed it best her niece remains at Westminster until such time as she has, um, recovered."

Terror threatened to overwhelm Christina at the remembrance of another wedding feast, the one at which her sister was abruptly stricken with illness. An image of Margarete's feverish face filled her with horror.

"Sweet Jesus," she exclaimed, "I pray it is nothing serious."

"No, not really," Cecily managed, her bottom lip quivering.

Before Christina could interrogate Cecily further, Matthias, the master of *der Greif*, announced in a booming voice accustomed to sounding over wind and sea that everyone should take their seats as the feast was now to be served.

Christina led the two ladies to the front of the room, relieved to find space had been made at the dais table for them to sit adjacent to the master's chair. To the distaff side sat the beaming newlywed couple.

Trudi rose upon seeing Cecily and hurried around the table with a cry of delight. Cecily walked forward to intercept her path. Stopping a few paces before Cecily, Trudi, remembering decorum, paused and executed a careful curtsey. Cecily rushed forward and caught the new bride in a firm embrace, kissing her cheek, then smiling broadly as Trudi returned the favor.

Separating from the new bride, Cecily said, "I pray for God's lasting favor on you and your household, mistress. I hope this gift will be useful to you and add to the comfort of your new home."

Cecily motioned one of the liverymen forward. In his right hand was a copper pipkin, or small cooking pot. well-formed and forged with a width greater than its height to allow more food to be cooked in closer proximity to the flames of the hearth. If the pot had been intended for use in the manor's central kitchen, its limited capacity would have relegated its use primarily for the preparation of sauces. Conversely, it was the perfect size for cooking meals in Trudi's tiny household.

"Thank you, Lady Cecily! It is most perfect! Peter adds his appreciation as well, favoring as he does my mutton stews."

Trudi placed the pot on the side table on which the other wedding gifts were displayed. There were no vessels or jewelry of gold or silver here; instead, the table groaned under the weight of mostly practical items chosen to help the newlyweds prepare for their lives together. The yardman Osbert had fashioned a pair of wooden spoons with leaping fish carved into the handles, surprisingly intricate work for one with such large fingers as he. Along the same lines, Peter's friend Ranulf, a master smith in his own right, had forged a matched pair of eating knives, each set with a polished blue stone in the handle. There were several cloths of linen gifted from female members of the household staff, most notable being that which had been beautifully embroidered by Mary's nimble fingers. Each object, great or small, was a silent testament to the love and esteem each person present had for the mistress of Bokerel House.

Trudi turned and impulsively hugged Cecily once more. Not wanting to forestall the festivities any further, the two women moved to the head table, Cecily holding Trudi's hand before of her eyes as she admired her finely crafted wedding ring. Christina tried to recall whether Cecily had worn one of her own when first they met, but vexingly could not remember.

Soon they were all seated and joyous feasting began in earnest.

Bess' culinary skill was evidenced at its best by course after delectable course that appeared from the kitchens. After the trenchers, colored and spiced yellow with saffron, were distributed, the guests were soon treated to dishes of fat capon and a great beef in pepper sauce.

Oh, Sweet Mary, this is what I was waiting for! Christina thought gleefully as the baked lampreys, her personal favorite, were brought to the table.

This was followed by stuffed pig, stewed mutton, and roasted coneys. A third course of great tarts, glazed meat apples, and white milk leche came soon after. The availability of sweetmeats, tarts, jellied damsons and pears, custards, and burrebrede tempted diners on whose stomachs were already full to bursting.

As the first course was presented, a shawm could be heard above the revelers' heads. Many craned their necks to find a few musicians crowding the minstrel gallery set off the second-floor landing. A gittern, a citole, a rebec, and a sackbut soon joined in, creating a merry tune that set many of those seated below to tapping their feet or rapping their fingers upon the tables.

The consumption of food ebbing, Reiniken organized a few of the sailors present into moving the center tables back to form a clear space in the center of the room. Soon, a circle of men and women had formed. They looked about at each other, with no one offering to step into the middle. Out of the corner of her eye, Christina saw Mary, fairly bursting with exuberance, looking her way frantically. Christina nodded and the young maid was off like a flushed hare, ducking between two of the yardmen into the center of the Carole circle. Hardly stopping to catch her breath, she began singing a spritely tune about a young woman's revenge on her straying husband in a lovely soprano voice. The revelers joined fingers with those to their sides and danced a series of skipping steps to their left as the musicians accompanied Mary's sweet song.

Christina suddenly felt a hand fall upon her own. She looked toward Cecily, who smiled and gestured with a move of her head toward the dancers. As Mary's song came to an end, they joined the circle. In a few seconds, the maid began another song, a familiar tune about the woodchopper's daughter. Those not dancing pounded their tables, ostensibly to simulate the fall of the woodsman's ax, or to represent the young traveler's enjoyment of the maid's body, for those of a bawdier mind.

As they stepped to the rhythm of the music, Christina looked across the circle to see Jost's flushed face smiling broadly, as he held hands with the maid Sarah on one side and the cook, Bess, on the other. To her right was Reiniken, surprisingly light on his feet for one so huge, his sausage-sized fingers held tightly to each side by the slender hands of the two diminutive maids Mary had corrected the day prior. Although they came no higher than the pit of his heavily-muscled arms, the three executed the quickening steps of the dance in perfect precision.

As she danced, Christina offered a fervent prayer for the wellbeing of those around her, each of whom so close to her heart.

The dangers looming before her in the pirate-infested waters of the Skagerrak suddenly broke the surface of her mind like the leap of a great whale.

Pray God I survive to see such merriment in my house for years to come.

When the song ended, Christina felt Cecily's fingers leave hers. To her surprise, Cecily then stepped forward and exchanged places with Mary, whose slender right hand soon found Christina's. Cecily's voice was markedly different from that of Mary, a contralto tone as rich as butter. Although her body managed to keep in step to the music, Christina's eyes and thoughts had only one focus, the gorgeous woman before her.

After Cecily's song, the circle broke up as someone called for a farandole. Christina and Cecily returned to the head table to find Peter and Trudi readying themselves to depart.

"Leaving so soon, Mistress Trudi?" Christina asked, surprised her friend had not partaken of the dancing.

"Aye," she replied, moving her hand to her stomach, "The wee one is doing enough springing about for both of us right now. I thank ye for all you have done for me this day. You are not only the finest of masters, but the best friend a woman could have."

Trudi came forward and kissed Christina softly on the cheek.

The couple then unobtrusively departed without fanfare.

Trudi had put her foot down days before, refusing to countenance any idea of a bedding ceremony.

"Damn foolishness, that is, and an embarrassment as well. I don't think we need anyone to show us how to put the foot in the slipper. One look at my belly should be proof enough of that, for sure!" she had remarked firmly. "Let 'em drink themselves silly, that's all right. But when it's time for me to go to bed, I'll be going without the lot of them!"

Cecily laughed as Christina related the story, agreeing with Trudi's reasoning wholeheartedly.

Their knowledge that the evening was growing late spawned a momentary uncomfortable silence between the two.

"It will not be long until I will need to depart, Frederick. Lady Agnes does not well enjoy nighttime travel," Cecily said.

"I would not dream of sending you out into the cold darkness. I have more than enough rooms to accommodate all of you here," Christina protested, frantic Cecily might once more step from her life before they had got the chance to discuss whether they had any hope of a future together.

"Yes, that would be wonderful, Frederick," Cecily said, although she once more seemed somewhat preoccupied. "I must ask Lady Agnes. If she agrees, I will accept your hospitality once more, though our requirements will be small. The men may sleep in the hall. I am certain Agnes will insist she and I bed together."

"Of course, as is only right, Mi' lady," Christina replied, realizing Lady Agnes would not entertain a circumstance where Cecily's virtue might be compromised, particularly not in the abode of a strange young man with whom she already shared an obvious affection.

While Cecily moved to speak with Lady Agnes, Christina beckoned to Ziesolf, who was seated at a table with Osbert, Warin, Penny, and others of the yardmen. He arose with a sprightliness Christina had not noticed in the man even before he had incurred his latest wounds. As he approached, Christina looked to Cecily who nodded.

"Aye, Frederick?" he asked.

"Would you please arrange sleeping arrangements for the men who accompanied the ladies here tonight? As the hours grow late, Lady Cecily has decided it better to spend the night here than return to Westminster."

Ziesolf smirked.

"Oh, she has, has she? I suppose you had nothing to do with influencing that decision, did you?"

Christina cheeks warmed.

"Well, there was really no need to break me away from my cup. You see, I figured the two of you would come to that conclusion, so I've already found them a place in the small hall."

Christina thanked Ziesolf and scanned the room for Mary. As expected, she was still with the dancers, who were now engaged in a bucolic line dance. As Christina approached, Mary met her eye, in an instant, she was disengaged from the other dancers and skipping her way.

"Yes, Master?" she asked, her face now pleasantly flushed although she was not a bit out of breath from her exertions.

"Mary, I will need you to arrange a sleeping chamber for the ladies Agnes and Cecily for the night. I might suggest it be the one Lady Cecily occupied on her last visit here."

"Of course, Master Frederick. Will there be anything else?"

"No, thank you," Christina replied.

Mary dipped into her now familiar curtsy, then dashed off to perform her assigned task.

"Oh, Mary," Christina called her back.

The girl spun around to face her.

"I want to thank you for what you have done these last few days in Mistress Trudi's stead. You have been the very key to this day's success."

Her angular face beaming, Mary said in a throaty voice, "You're most welcome, Master. Words of praise have been few in my life, far outnumbered by slaps and kicks. I thank God every day that I serve in this house, and for you and Mistress Trudi."

Before Christina could say anything else, Mary dipped once more then sped away.

Turning, Christina was startled to find Cecily now stood directly in front of her.

"I too know the unpleasantness of serving a harsh master," Cecily whispered, sadness clouding her voice. "At least she is experiencing the joy that having one who is good brings."

Christina knew not what to say in response. Within seconds, Cecily's melancholy disappeared and she went to persuade Lady Agnes to join in the dancing. The merriment lasted for several more hours until the combined effect of excellent food, potent drink, and the warmth of the room began their slowing effect. Singly or in small groups, people began to wander off to their bedchambers, or to depart the manor if they were being accommodated elsewhere.

Mary appeared and tarried inconspicuously in the background while Christina bade Agnes and Cecily good night. The maid then led them away to their chamber leaving Christina staring after them, feeling as if she had missed another opportunity. Although there remained a few serious drinkers in the hall, she had no stomach for further reveling. Consequently, she strode purposefully to her own bed.

Stopping only to strip off her clothes, she was asleep nearly as soon as her head touched pillow. Her uncommonly dreamless slumber came to an abrupt end as she felt a warm hand extend across her naked middle. The full moon's light in the near-cloudless sky streamed through the window, making it simple to identify the figure lying next to her as she rolled over.

"I did not believe you could steal away, my love," Christina cooed as she reached her head forward and softly kissed Cecily's full, rosy lips.

"But is it really me?" Cecily asked, pulling away teasingly, "Or could it be a succubus, come to tempt you into carnal sin?"

"Perhaps both," Christina agreed.

She kissed Cecily once more. This time, Cecily's mouth opened, accepting the tip of the other woman's tongue across her bottom teeth, then meeting it with her own. Christina's lips moved forward, plunging her tongue deeper. Suddenly, she pulled away.

"But what of Lady Agnes? Are you not concerned she will notice your absence? I would not want your reputation besmirched throughout Isabella's court, despite my terrible desire for you."

"Once asleep, Lady Agnes slumbers like the dead, oblivious to any sound as her own snoring is as loud as a battle clarion. Besides, she knows I sometimes have need to be about at night or in the early morn."

Before she could inquire as to the reason why, Cecily interrupted her, sitting upright.

"Look at me, Christina."

Christina did as she was told, raising up as well and gazing the length of the beautiful nude body before her, from Cecily's delicate white feet to her crown of vibrant red locks, before settling back to look directly into the deep pools of green that were her eyes.

"I must tell you something," Cecily began hesitantly. "I did not travel north for the same reason Lady Eleanor did not accompany Isabella on campaign."

Christina wracked her brain, trying in vain to settle on a malady that might affect two apparently healthy young women so severely and in succession.

"I am with child, my love," Cecily stated simply, her eyes beginning to cloud.

"What?" Christina replied, dumbfounded. "But how?"

"Well, it certainly isn't yours, you silly goose!"

She laughed.

"As to 'how,' I don't really believe an explanation is needed. Suffice it to say my husband exercised his right to my body whenever he so desired, which was quite frequently. As with most women, I had little to say about the matter. At some time, his seed had the desired effect and I conceived. Early in the autumn, I figure most likely."

Sweet Mary!

Christina's mind could manage nothing more coherent.

"So, learning my sickness was the result of a baby quickening in my womb, my aunt decided it best to not subject me to the arduous journey northward, but rather to stay and deliver my child here. By that time, she was certain the king and queen would have returned to London, putting me in the right place after all."

A child. Should she be happy for Cecily, or commiserating her misfortune? Was she jealous? Did she have a right to be? Clearly, a child was one thing she could never give to Cecily, regardless of her love and desire for her.

"What are your thoughts, my dearest?" Cecily asked in a concerned voice.

"I . . . I don't know, actually," Christina responded truthfully. "Your husband was an overbearing pig and a vile coward, but I believe a child should be blameless for his father's deeds, regardless of the teachings of the Church. As for you, how could I feel any differently? My love is constant as the rise of the sun each morn."

She took Cecily's hand in hers and brought it to her lips, kissing it gently before laying it on her breast.

"But this only makes our lives together more impossible," Cecily stated in a flat voice. "I will birth my husband's child at the palace. All in attendance will soon be aware of that fact. I will remain his wife in their eyes as well, so there will be scant opportunity to steal time away with you, and never alone. Above all, looming like a dark cloud, is the possibility Sir Edgar may one day appear, demanding the return of his wife and child, a request supported by both civil and ecclesiastical law. I will either need to go with him or flee to a nunnery, neither of which looms well for a future together, Christina."

Christina had been mulling a mad idea over while Cecily spoke.

"There is another possibility," she stated, the other woman now gazing at her with rapt attention. "We could leave England entirely, go far beyond the laws of its borders. I have money and ships and loyal men to sail them. All we would need do is board and sail away; then we would be free to live our lives any way we see fit."

"But where would we go? To Lübeck?"

"No, probably not," Christina admitted, "We would live in constant fear someone would see through my disguise and recognize me. No, we would need to venture further afield. Not even Bruges would be totally safe. Perhaps to the Mediterranean, even to Venice itself."

Cecily's expression was blank. It was apparent to Christina she knew nothing of these destinations, perhaps only of the names. Then her expression changed, to one of avid eagerness.

"Yes, oh yes! Let us leave today! Wherever you go, it is my wish to be at your side!"

Christina reached out and combed her fingers through Cecily's thick, cherry-red hair, pushing it away from her face. She then moved her hand to her cheek, tracing it along her unblemished alabaster skin.

"I wish it were that simple, my beloved Cecily, but it is not," Christina responded wistfully. "The sea is awash with tumultuous storms this time of year, as I myself have experienced. I would not risk your safety, even if you were not burdened by pregnancy. No, we must be patient, and pray fortune favors us until after you have recovered from your birthing. Then, we will be off, never again to part from each other."

"But what will we do until that time?" Cecily's pleading gouged at Christina's heart. "I cannot bear the thought of being without your touch for a moment, let alone a day, a week, or a month! Let us go now, I pray you, my love!"

She drew Cecily into a tight embrace, the entirety of the universe existing only within their intertwined bodies. After a full minute, they drew apart.

"We must be content with what time the Lord allows us. I will be training at Westminster each week. Will you do me the favor of walking with me along the river, if the weather is pleasant? I have heard a mother's light exercise is beneficial for her quickening babe," Christina said.

"Of course," Cecily replied, an inch of her impish smile revealed by the pale moonlight filtering through the thick window glass. "But for now, I have other exertions in mind, certainly of a more strenuous nature!"

Cecily grabbed Christina's hair and pulled her roughly toward her. Their passionate lips met, tongues entwining, exploring the depths of each other's mouths. Their lovemaking lasted for the better part of an hour, then they embraced each other for a few precious minutes more as the slickness of their perspiring bodies began to grow cold.

Cecily rose and went into the antechamber. Christina followed, taking the linen cloth from her lover's hand. She poured cold water from the pitcher into the bowl and set about washing the musky smell of their lovemaking from Cecily's body. Cecily slipped her chemise over her head, letting it slide down before arching her head and kissing the taller woman tenderly. Turning and padding to the door on silent, bare feet, in an instant more she was gone with a finality that was almost as if she had never been there at all.

Christina closed the door and skipped and twirled like a giddy young girl back into her bedchamber. She flopped into her bed, astounded by what had transpired that night.

There is a chance for us after all!

She felt nearly intoxicated with joy. She vowed nothing short of God's divine will would keep her from returning from Lübeck and into the arms of the woman she loved.

Chapter 5

Preparations
London, March, 1311

The amiable weather of early November 1310 departed from London and a savage winter took its place, the cold gnawing at the city as if a ravenous beast. The Thames froze over, making its glassy, solid surface the easiest means of transporting commerce across the river. Although the wealthy enjoyed the novelty of taking sport upon the ice, the frigid temperatures brought no joy to the poor of the city, who shivered and starved without respite. When they died, they were stacked outside the city walls like cordwood, the ground too hard to dig graves.

Christina saw to it her household experienced no ill effects from the cold, having had the foresight to stockpile ample cured foodstuffs and great mounds of firewood over the summer. That said, she suffered in ways unrelated to the plights of others. Never one to grow accustomed to a sedentary lifestyle, she chafed under the forced inactivity brought on by the severe winter. She paced the passageways of the manor house, her mind formulating plans for her voyage to Lübeck in the spring, only to find fault in each and discard them as doubts crept in. Most of all, her heart was rent by long days of separation from Cecily, interspaced by their all too infrequent opportunities to be together.

Christina had been invited to the Twelfth Night festivities at Westminster, but her time there with Cecily had been shared by the company of a virtual throng of courtiers and other noble visitors. Consequently, the words they were able to exchange were mere pleasantries, alluding nothing to the intense passion they shared in their souls. The same could be said for the instances when Cecily was able to escape the palace to walk Thameside with Christina. Heavily bundled against the cold and closely accompanied by other ladies of the court, Christina scarcely believed it was actually Cecily who walked beside her, had it not been for the stray lock of crimson hair that sometimes escaped her hood to confirm the fact.

As with all things, the winter eventually passed. The days became warmer and smiles returned to the faces of people on the street. Well, to some at least. The city regained its vibrancy as the routines of life returned once more to normal.

In Parliament, the Lords Ordainers continued to argue over how best to restraint their worrisome monarch and rid the kingdom once and for all of his despised favorite, Piers Gaveston. The February death of the Earl of Lincoln, one of the group's most moderate members, eased the way for more severe measures to be proposed, making a decisive clash with King Edward all but inevitable. The king and his court remained at Berwick, while Christina's friend Gaveston waited at Bamburgh Castle, longing for the thaw that would permit their forces to foray afield. With luck, they hoped to bring the wily Bruce to battle, secure an undeniable victory, and return to London as conquering heroes.

Only this outcome could swerve public opinion in their favor and away from that of the Ordainers.

It was nearing April when the waters of the great river thawed and it became once more navigable. Christina knew it would still be some weeks more before the same could be said for the Trave and the short twelve-mile journey up its length to Lübeck would become possible. Those weeks, however, would barely be enough to accomplish all that was necessary to do before her departure.

Christina arose from her bed early. Filled with a nervous energy she had not felt for some time, she washed and dressed swiftly. She then descended the stairs and made her way down the kitchen passageway to Trudi's apartments. Trudi's voice granted her entrance at the door and she stepped inside the warm and homey antechamber. Although there were only a couple of tapers lit, Christina readily discerned Trudi sitting in the comfortable chair she had favored so in the upstairs solar, but which had now become part of her own furnishings.

"How fare thee, sister?" Christina asked, trying to keep worry from her voice.

"Much the same, I'm afraid," she replied. "I thought I was clever marrying Peter. Certainly, one so slight would only sire manageable babes. But look at me, will you? Could he have snuck in one of the carthorses to do his business for him?"

Christina guffawed at Trudi's sarcastic jibe. The pregnant woman must be well into her ninth month with child and her girth seemed enormous.

It has been well over a month since I have seen Cecily. I wonder if her body is already undergoing a similar change?

Although Trudi largely maintained her customary good humor, Christina could tell she was becoming frazzled from her growing burden. She seemed already exhausted, despite the day just beginning.

"Did you manage some sleep last night?" Christina queried.

"Aye, a bit at least. I finally ordered poor Peter out of the bed so I wouldn't keep him awake the whole night through."

"So, the perpetrator of the deed suffers as well, eh?"

Trudi gazed at her with an exasperated expression.

"Really? Well, let him strap his damned anvil about his middle for the day, then we can talk about a shared experience!" she snorted derisively.

Christina was unsure whether her friend spoke in jest, or in ill-humor, so she made no further comment.

Arising to leave, she said," I will have Mary send one of the maids to sit with you. I do not believe you should chance being alone. The babe must certainly come this day or one of the next."

"Aye," Trudi said wearily, then, "How I wish you could be here, Christina, although there is no way you can, of course. There is no one I would rather have with me when the time comes."

Christina moved forward and kissed Trudi on her forehead.

"Before I leave on today's errand, there is something that I have for you."

She reached into her pouch and rummaged around with her fingers. Finding what she sought, she pulled out a large pink-colored stone attached to a long leather cord. She reached forward and placed the cord about Trudi's neck.

"This is a coral stone. It is said to provide relief from pain during childbirth."

Trudi picked up and examined the stone. She impulsively moved forward and kissed her friend's lips; that and her brimming eyes conveyed her pleasure with the gift and the love she felt for her dear friend more than mere words.

Departing the apartment, Christina found Mary in the great hall. Only a few words were needed to spark her into action. She immediately called Margery from where she and Heloise were hard at work scrubbing the flagstones of the floor.

"Gather a few of the honied wheat cakes Bess has just taken from the oven and a flagon of wine from the cellar and go sit with Mistress Trudi. You may take two for yourself, but no more, mind you. Now, at the quick girl, before they grow cold!"

As Margery fled from the room, Christina observed her slowing to stick out her tongue at her friend who was still at the thankless task of scrubbing the floors. Heloise returned the rude gesture, but too late to have any effect as Margery was already around the screen and well into the kitchen passageway.

"Would you prefer to break your fast here, or in the solar, Master Frederick?" Mary asked.

"Here, Mary, thank you. I believe Herr Ziesolf will soon be joining me."

"As you wish," she replied, before curtseying and leaving the room for the kitchen.

Should I tell her she needn't curtsey every bloody time she comes and goes?

Christina decided it was a habit so ingrained in the girl it had become part of her persona.

What does it hurt, anyway? Maybe I should ask Trudi to do it as well?

She laughed inwardly at the thought of the insolent response she would likely receive.

Hearing nearby footsteps, Christina looked up to see Ziesolf approaching. She was well-satisfied to note the man walked with scarcely a limp, nor did he seem to favor any other part of his body.

For all rights and purposes, he seemed fully recovered from his terrible injury. Now, it was only the advancement of age that he had left to combat.

Good, he seems well enough to accompany me for the fitting of my personal armor today.

"Good day, Sir Knight," Ziesolf hailed in his raspy voice.

"And to you, Herr Ziesolf, God's favor be with you this day," Christina responded.

As Ziesolf took his seat, the serving maid Sarah appeared with a tray of food for the two diners. Christina and Ziesolf exchanged snippets of local gossip, interspersed with periods of silence while they focused their attention on the hearty fare before them. Before they had finished, the maid reappeared with a plate of the honied wheat cakes, which cheered Christina mightily as she had become fearful that none remained.

Working a large bite of the cake around in her mouth so she could speak, Christina asked, "You will accompany me to the armorer, will you not?"

"If you wish, of course."

They soon finished their repast and departed together for the Coleman Street workshop of Manekin le Hauberger, one of London's most skilled artificers of metal.

Christina and Ziesolf were greeted by the smith, who showed them inside the large wooden building that held his forge.

Manekin's excellence as an armorer was recognized throughout the city and, as such, he had many more seeking his wares than he could possibly serve. Certainly, he was under no compulsion to forge armor for a newly knighted foreigner ahead of accepting undertakings from London's higher nobility. But the coincidence that he was a boon friend of Christina's smith, Black Peter, and a guest at his wedding to Trudi, was cause enough for him to accept her request.

As they made their way through the building, several of Manekin's subordinates were hard at work, shaping glowing metal that would one day protect English fighting men from those who sought to do them harm. Christina felt ready to swoon from the combined effects of oppressive heat and infernal noise. Manekin led them across the workshop floor and through an internal door. Closing the door behind them greatly reduced both the din and temperature from outside, and they were finally able to converse, albeit using loud voices.

How fortunate I am to be here, Christina marveled, as Manekin instructed her to stand to the side of the room.

"First, the chausses," Manekin instructed, fetching two mail leggings from a box and dumping them on the floor before her feet. "Now, lean back and hike up your gambeson to your middle."

Surprised by the armorer's request, Christina looked behind her and saw a length of planking attached to the wall at an angle. She did as she was told and found it fit her back quite comfortably. Manekin took her left foot and lifted it, the image of a farrier doing so with a horse's hoof flashing through her mind as she took her weight off that leg. He then slipped off her boot. In its place he pulled one of the mail leggings up to the middle of her thigh before securing its points to the ties dangling from her belt. After that, he adjusted the leather sole of the garment until it fit comfortably on her foot, knotting a cord about her ankle to hold it into place. He repeated the process with her right leg before standing back and asking Christina to walk about as he assessed the fit more closely.

Christina stood and lowered the hem of her gambeson back down over her thighs.

As she moved about the room she observed in amazement, "They weigh so little! I can hardly believe I am wearing them!"

"Well," Manekin said, a satisfied smile on his thin lips, "it's all about getting the weight properly distributed, you know. Additionally, I have used a more open weave to reduce the weight, as you requested. Shall we proceed further?"

Christina nodded. She had struggled with the concept of personal armor for weeks, conversing with Ziesolf long into the night as to the relative merits of different materials and designs. Although she was wealthy enough to afford full plate, she dismissed that choice immediately. She knew the weight and awkwardness of such armor would take away her greatest advantages, speed and flexibility, while accentuating her relative inferiority to most men in strength.

Conversely, she had also considered a full suit of leather armor, or *cuir bouilli* as called by the French. The boiled leather was very light, a definite advantage. The rigidity of the material and its relatively poor protection for the wearer were serious drawbacks, however. Dismissing this, Christina and Ziesolf had settled on a suit primarily constituted of mail.

Manekin went once more to the wooden box that held the chausses, reached over, and pulled out a hauberk. Christina raised her hands above her head and leaned over as she had done for Giles' squire, Thomas. The armorer pulled the garment over her upper body. He brought the full sleeves over her arms and she wiggled her hands into the mail-backed leather mittens at their ends. Finally, he pulled the hauberk down until it rested its full length along her body.

"See how the palms are slashed to allow you to free your hands, if need be, without having to remove the entire shirt?" Ziesolf pointed out, as Manekin secured the hauberk with additional points at the wrist and elbow.

"Aye," Christina agreed, pleased by the armorer's forethought.

"I have reduced the weight considerably, as I said, but this also somewhat reduces the protection to the wearer," Manekin remarked. "We may compensate for this weakness with this."

The armorer went to the side of the room and picked up a cured leather breastplate with overlapping iron plates riveted to the front. He asked Christina to hold this tightly upon her chest while he moved behind her to secure it snugly to her body with two large buckles.

Christina stepped away and executed a range of motions to assess to what degree she was restricted. She was quite pleased to find the fit to be perfect, the weight of the garments so well distributed that it felt natural, rather like an increase in her own body weight rather than a burden that she bore. The rigidity of the breastplate was annoying, but she hoped it would become less so through wear.

If not, I can always set it to the side and wear the rest.

Manekin secured a linen arming cap upon her head, followed by a mail coif complete with an aventail that extended down over her neck and shoulders. Finally, he set an open bascinet helm upon the coif, affixing it with ties under her chin. The nasal guard was uncommonly narrow, as Christina had specified.

"I can't very well effectively fight if the damn nasal makes me cross-eyed," she had told Manekin when she had first visited the workshop for him to take measurements.

Now, fully attired in armor masterfully constructed for full protection without inhibiting her fighting style, Christina was well satisfied she would be an even match for Sir Giles, or a knight of a similar skill level. As to whether she would ever have the occasion to use the armor for actual combat was something she seriously doubted.

After all, I'm just a merchant. Violence usually finds me suddenly, without advance notice. But will that be true for the future? she mused, recalling Giles' gentle chiding concerning her obligation to the one who made her a knight. Besides, I am presently voyaging to the Baltic to fight, not to trade. It is reassuring though, to have such protection at hand should the need arise.

Ziesolf helped Christina from her armor, placing each item on the floor beside her. When he finished, Manekin produced two substantial leather bags, demonstrating with the deftness of a skilled artisan how best to pack the pieces so the load would be evenly distributed and not rattle against each other. After paying Manekin the agreed upon sixteen silver marks for his good work, Christina and Ziesolf picked up the bags and departed the artificer's shop.

"This is excellent workmanship, Frederick," Ziesolf commented as they made their way back home. "It probably weighs half of that to which I am accustomed. The rings of the mail are well made, the rivets in each ring solidly set. The protection should be very good, but not so exceptional that you should become complacent. The lightness of the armor's construction comes at a cost, you know."

"Of course," Christina agreed, too pleased by her new purchase to risk any disagreement. "But I believe its use will be wholly relegated to the training field, where the worst damage I could suffer is a wounded ego."

"But what if it is not? What if one day your armor is all that stays an enemy's blade from feasting on your entrails? Be prepared, that's all I am saying."

They traveled the remainder of the way in silence, as Christina mulled over the implications of Ziesolf's advice.

As they entered the yard of the manor, Christina was surprised to see four strangers standing silently just inside the gate. She followed their eyes, all locked on another man conversing with Peter, the smith. Their clothes were clearly homespun, multiple patches on them evidencing long and hard wear. The men's footwear was similarly in poor repair, with two of the four having lengths of cloth wrapped repeatedly about their shoes to keep them from falling apart. It was clear each was a commoner, and probably from the lower end of that social class at that.

She added her bag to Ziesolf's burden, approaching Peter as Ziesolf went inside.

"God be with you both."

"And to you, Master Frederick," Peter replied as the other man took a step back and lowered his head in silent obeisance.

"Is there a problem here?" Christina asked, gazing at the stranger with a neutral expression.

"No . . . no, none at all, Mi 'lord!" he exclaimed, his pale face blanching even further.

"These men seek employment," Peter stated. "There has been little work available over the winter and they have had a rough go of it keeping home and hearth together for their families. Alan here vows they are good men, who are willing to provide honest work for a bit of coin or food in kind."

Christina considered Peter's words. There had been little enough to do over the winter for the men already receiving regular pay from her. Now, with her imminent departure, it seemed highly unlikely additional hands would be needed, especially those who seemed no more than day laborers, at best.

I wish I could do more, she thought, imagining their discouragement of returning home to the hungry and sad faces of their families.

She started to reach for her purse, hoping the gift of a silver penny each would somewhat allay their wretchedness for at least a day or two.

She paused, then asked without much hope, "Do you have any skills I might find useful?"

"Aye!" Alan's eyes showed a faint glimmer of hope. "Gilbert was a stonemason's apprentice for a time and Nicholas is good with beasts, nary a one he meets can resist his ways. I've done a bit of thatching in my day, as well. We all have strong backs and won't give you any trouble, sir. Please."

The man's tone was desperate.

As I had feared, Christina thought with a sick feeling forming in her stomach. *They have nothing I need, beyond the ability of moving things from here to there.*

Out of the corner of her eye, Christina saw one of the other men detach himself from the group and walk toward her. He stopped a few paces before her, bowed clumsily, then straightened as she motioned with her hand for him to rise.

"Pardon me, Mi 'lord, but have you been training with your sword on Sundays at Westminster green?" he asked.

"Yes, I have frequently visited there over the winter. Why is it that you asked?"

"Why, me and my mates have just been saying that we thought it was you," he replied.

Christina grew impatient.

Am I now to answer to these ragamuffins as to my daily whereabouts? she thought, determined to bring this diversion to an end.

Before she could speak, however, he said, "We thought it was you watching us."

Suddenly her mind clicked, her irritation dissipating.

"Watching you? Are you bowmen?" she asked with amazement, the image of a mass of English arrows speeding from the deck of *der Greif* to transfix a number of terrified Danish pirates suddenly blossoming in her mind.

"Aye, we are, all of us," Alan resumed speaking for the group. "Godfrey here is the best shot of us all. I think we all would have starved this winter if he hadn't taken most of the king's prizes."

Godfrey blushed and said nothing.

Christina looked from man to man. Each was well-formed, but with a curious overdevelopment of the right side of his upper torso. She could not believe her possible good fortune.

"Alan, meet me on the green at sunrise tomorrow. If your skill with your bows is as you promise, your families need worry no more, as you will be made men."

Alan struggled to speak past the lump forming in his throat.

"Thank you, Mi 'lord, thank you! We'll be there, don't you worry, sir! With our bows, to be sure!

"Go then," Christina replied, dismissing the men. "I will see you on the morrow."

Alan and Godfrey both bowed deeply and backed away from where Christina and Peter stood. They spoke a few excited words to their fellows and then all began backing out of the yard, grinning and jostling each other as they departed.

Before they could leave, however, Christina called out.

"Alan?"

A stricken look appeared on the man's face as if he feared his good fortune was about to be snatched away.

"Aye, Mi' lord?"

"Might it be possible to round out your group with a few more men? A total of ten or twelve would do nicely."

His expression changed to one of relief.

"Aye!" he shouted and, in a few seconds, they turned up the street and were gone.

"Thank you, Master Frederick. As I said, I believe them to be honest men. You have done a generous thing here."

"God favors those who do charitable acts, Peter," Christina replied, flashing the smith a merry little wink. "If their ability as archers is as skilled as those I observed on the green, he is about to reward me several times over."

The butts were already emplaced when Christina arrived at Westminster the next day, securing Pearl's bridle to the rail as she had done so many times before. She saw a dozen men huddling closely together against the chilled wind, the five she had met the day prior as well as seven she did not know. Each carried a longbow in his hand, several lengthier even than the men who held them. They busied themselves stringing their bows as she neared. By the time she was within hailing distance, they were already prepared to nock their first arrow.

"Good day to you fellows," she remarked loudly to ensure she was heard over the gusting wind.

"God be with you, Mi 'lord," Alan replied, the other men murmuring their agreement. "Shall we shoot now?"

Good. Better to be right at it than to waste time talking.

Alan stepped a few paces away from the other men and stuck five arrows into the mushy soil beside his right foot, holding a sixth at the ready in his right hand. He looked at Christina for a second before pointing his bow in his extended left hand straight toward the nearest target, turning his head in the same direction. With a smooth, powerful movement, he drew his bowstring back with his first two fingers until the tail of the arrow was just touching the corner of his mouth, directly under his aiming eye. He adjusted his weight slightly on his rear foot and let fly at the first target, his arrow splitting the willow stave neatly before penetrating solidly into the butt.

Christina's jaw dropped.

Alan neither hesitated to survey his initial shot, nor to revel in its excellence. Instead, he snatched his next arrow neatly and repeated his movements, only this time raising his left hand a few degrees to aim at the next target in line. He released his arrow, which hit the piece of cloth attached to the butt squarely only an instant prior to the next arrow speeding downrange. The final two arrows were already aloft before the two before them had found their mark.

Sweet Mary, Mother of Mercy! In less than a minute, five men would have died before Alan's bow, with no sound to mark their passing beyond the thwack of the bowstring and rushing sound of his speeding arrow! If the others prove a fraction of Alan's worth, der Greif will carry a surprise the likes of which these varlets of the North have never seen!

Christina was not disappointed. Each archer took his turn, sending his arrows toward the targets with a similar rate of fire. There were a couple of misses at the final target, but any foe unlucky enough to be at a hundred and fifty yards or less would have been skewered without exception. Now, there was only Godfrey remaining to take his turn.

Unlike the others, he stuck eleven arrows into the soil beside him. Christina noticed his arrows appeared somewhat different than those who had taken a turn before him.

"We were using flight arrows for the further targets. These were long, light, and winged with narrower feathers to travel longer distances more easily. His are sheaf arrows, with broad, barbed points, designed to kill rather than to look pretty. Watch this now, Mi 'lord," Alan said.

The speed of Godfrey's bow was astounding. He worked up the range of target, before sighting back down again. Although Christina had not counted the seconds as she intended, so focused was she on observing the man's skill, the elapsed time could not have been more than a single minute. More importantly, each arrow had found its mark.

Godfrey returned to his fellows, who clapped him on the back and murmured words of congratulations. They then turned and looked toward Christina, expressions of eagerness, uncertainty, and trepidation spread equally among the lot.

She stood frozen, in sharp contrast to her mind that now worked feverishly.

I need these men. They will surely guarantee us victory against the pirates!

She finally managed to say, "Do you know who I am?"

The men looked at each other in apparent confusion.

After a few seconds, Alan answered, "Sir Frederick the German, Mi 'lord."

"Is that what the local people call me?" Christina exclaimed, digressing for a moment before continuing. "Well, Sir Frederick, at least, Sir Frederick Kohl, to be more exact. This day you have my word as a knight that I do have work for you. That is, if you agree to it."

"For all of us, Mi 'lord?" asked one man, a quaver in his voice.

He had been one of the men whose furthest arrow had strayed from hitting the cloth.

"Aye, all of you," Christina answered, perceiving the look of relief on the archer's face. "In two weeks, my ship will depart London, sailing to the Baltic Sea and the north German coast. We will join a fleet seeking to hunt out several pirate vessels that plague the waters there. I confess it will not be easy, as these brigands are wily, have fast ships, and know the coastline like no others. They are also merciless, and will not hesitate to kill you before you have the pleasure of ending their misbegotten lives. I believe we will be gone no more than six months but, it is the sea, so who knows?"

"Six months from our families, sir?" another of the archers asked hesitantly.

"If the king had required us, we would have been freezing our ballocks off chasing the Scots in the north for just as long or longer," Godfrey muttered. "At least it will be summer now. You can do without a belly-warmer, Will!"

"And the pay, Mi 'lord?" asked Alan, changing the subject.

"Will you consent to being your men's captain, Alan?" Christina asked.

Alan gazed back at the group of bowmen to gauge their consensus. They looked at each other for a second before voicing a unanimous chorus of "ayes."

"I guess so," Alan chuckled.

"Well, that will be six pence for you each day between now and when we sail. Three for everyone else, except four for Godfrey. I will pay half now, and half when you show up at dockside. At that time, I will also advance you two months' pay for while you are at sea. Ensure your wives are there, so your families will want for nothing while you are away. Alan, you will be responsible for ensuring every man comes with extra staves, bowstrings, and side weapons. Are we in agreement?"

Again, Alan looked to the men who had just acknowledged him as their leader. They nodded vigorously; grins spread across their mouths revealing a varying number of teeth.

"I guess we belong to you, Sir Frederick. And what about arrows?" he asked.

"Let me know when you have made arrangements for their purchase. I will send a cart to your fletcher to fetch them, as well as to render payment. Any other questions?"

The men voiced nothing further. Christina provided directions to *der Greif's* moorage and counted out the archers' advancements, handing them to Alan for further disbursement before bidding them farewell and beginning to cross the field back to where Pearl was tethered. After a few paces, she stopped and took a longing glance back at the Palace of Westminster.

If only Cecily would appear. Seeing her, even from a distance would make my happiness with this day complete.

There was no movement, however, other than that of the sentries posted at the gate. Certainly not a flash of crimson hair tousling in the wind. Christina chided herself to be content with what fortune had already provided her. She walked the rest of the way with a spring in her step.

The archers will provide an advantage no pirate would anticipate. If we can lure them within a hundred yards, they may all be dead before we fear them boarding us. Still, eight or ten good sword or axmen would be prudent to add to the ship's company. I will speak to Wig about this, I'm sure he knows a few scoundrels he might rely upon to stand beside him in a scrap. Combined with the hearty crew already manning the ship, we will be more than a match for anyone. Perhaps, we will return sooner rather than later.

So pleased was she with her arrangement with the bowmen she had to restrain herself from dancing about like one mad.

Impatient to share her good news with Ziesolf, she mounted her mare and urged her into an easy canter, a command to which the high-spirited palfrey eagerly complied. The pair kept up this pace until they entered the city, where the increasingly crowded streets forced them into a more prudent walk. Although their progress had slowed, Christina's thoughts still raced.

She had no more than passed through her own gates when she spotted Jost running toward her down the steps of the manor. Clearly, he had been sitting there, waiting for her return.

"Frederick!" he cried, even before he arrived in front of her. The young man wore a look of wild alarm.

"Yes, Jost, what is it?" she asked, a sick feeling beginning in her stomach as such behavior by her apprentice had heralded evil portents in the past.

He stopped before her and bent to catch his breath.

"It's Mistress Trudi, Master Frederick! Her babe is coming!"

"Well, what did you expect, Jost? That it would hold up inside her, only to crawl out undetected in the middle of the night?"

Christina considered bloodying his nose for alarming her so.

"No, not really," he said a bit ashamedly. "It's just that I've never been around a woman when she was birthing. I was the youngest child, so I don't really know what I'm supposed to do."

"Nothing. Nothing but praying to Saint Margaret for the health of her and her child," she said gently, now feeling pity for her cousin, rather than anger. "It's all in God's caring hands now. Who is with her?"

"Bess and the midwife, for sure. Mary or Sarah, or maybe both, I'm not sure. They pushed me right out the door, so I have no way of telling."

"As they would me, I'm sure," Christina replied, frustration evident in her voice.

It's almost worth revealing myself to the other women if it means being with Trudi, she thought ruefully.

"And Peter?" she asked.

"Can you not hear?" Jost replied, a quizzical expression fixed on his face.

It took only an instant for her to determine the father-to-be was in his workshop. The loud, rhythmic clanging of a large hammer on metal sounded clearly from the smithy. Christina dismounted and handed Pearl's reins to Penny, who had been observing her interchange with Jost from a respectful distance. He ran his hand over the clear sweat dampening the horse's neck and smiled, happy her master had seen fit to provide her with a hearty workout. He led the mare away for a good grooming and some sweet fodder.

Christina and Jost walked to the far corner of the yard and opened the door to the small building. A wave of heat rushed to greet their faces as they stepped inside the dimly lit space. The forge burned brightly at the other side of the floor, illuminating the face of the man firing a length of metal which he held by a pair of long tongs in the reddish white coals.

Sensing he had company; Peter withdrew the iron and placed it carefully upon a metal surfaced bench. His normally taciturn expression was replaced by deep furrows of worry etched across his forehead and around his mouth. He wiped sweat from his face on a soiled length of toweling and tossed it to the side before approaching his visitors.

"Can we talk outside, Peter?" Christina asked, "It's hotter than the hinges of hell in here!"

119

"As you wish," he replied with a slight upturn of his mouth, "Not something a smith really notices much."

Once more in the cool, spring air, Christina asked, "Is there any word yet?"

"No, nothing," he replied, his expression returning to one of concern. "I was just about ready to leave our apartments shortly after sunrise when I heard her cry out from the bed chamber. I rushed inside and saw her standing, a look of shock upon her face and a puddle below her on the floor. I helped her to the side of the bed, but she was in too much pain to sit. Vowing to leave her for only for an instant, I ran to fetch Mistress Bess."

Christina and Jost stood silently, waiting for him to continue.

"Well, Bess sent Sarah off for the midwife and we hurried to Trudi's side. As soon as she passed into the bedchamber, she closed the door behind her, forbidding me from my wife's side. I waited in the anteroom for a while before Sarah returned with the midwife, who shooed me out of our lodging entirely. She said it could be ages yet. That's when I decided to come here. Beating on metal takes your mind off other things, you see."

Christina clapped the apprehensive smith reassuringly upon his shoulder, murmuring a few words of encouragement that she did not feel herself. She knew childbirth was a painful, dangerous task, and even the healthiest of mothers could sometimes become sickened and die within a day or two of delivery.

The babe is even more at risk, she thought, determined to not voice such a concern aloud. *Somewhere in heaven Marguerite sits alongside two of our mother's other children who lived not a week.*

The outside door to the manor opened and all heads in the small group in the courtyard turned in unison. Mary's slim figure walked out and down the steps carrying three cups in one hand

and a flagon of dark wine in the other. She halted before Christina and dipped into a curtesy.

"God be with you this day, Master Frederick, and to you as well Master Peter," she said in her sweet, soprano voice. "I thought you might be liking a drink."

Jost, she pointedly ignored. There must be some trouble between them of which Christina was unaware. She vowed to observe the interactions between the pair most closely, perhaps even to alert Trudi to do the same in her absence. Both of the young people had become far too integral to the functioning of her household to ignore any rift between them.

Mary distributed the cups into ready hands, then poured each a measure from the flagon.

"Mistress, pray you any news of my wife?" asked Peter.

"Though I have not been in to see her myself, Sarah told me she is well, but not yet ready to be seated upon the birthing chair. The pains are not yet coming close together, but she is pale and unsettled, as one would imagine at such a time," she replied. "I pray mightily for her health and that of her unborn child."

"As do we all," Christina whispered.

Leaving the bottle, Mary departed to return to her duties inside. Within a few minutes, Christina led Peter and Jost into the hall, where they took a seat on a bench at one of the trestle tables. Although it was clear Peter was preoccupied, she figured it as good a time as any to lay plans for the functioning of the manor while she was away. Before she could begin, however, Ziesolf entered the room. She hailed him over and he joined the group.

Initially, she had been adamant that he not accompany her on the upcoming voyage. Between his advancing age and the severity of his still-healing wounds, the arduousness of an extended stay at sea, along with the possibility of heavy fighting, posed a real danger to his health. It seemed foolhardy for him to even consider taking such a risk.

But this is Ziesolf.

She gazed at the man sitting across from her and shook her head in admiration.

Who would have thought him capable of cutting through the Scots at the tower like a scythe through winter wheat? Or that any man, let alone one of his age, would recover so quickly from the injuries that nearly felled him only a few months past? Going in harm's way without his sword or, just as importantly, his counsel would be foolhardy. Besides, should I become injured, he is the only person beyond two pregnant women who could treat my wounds. I'm certainly not asking either of them, so Ziesolf it must be.

"How fared the archers?" Ziesolf asked.

"Amazingly!" Christina responded, slapping her hand on the table with unrestrained glee. She rose and leaned forward until her face was only inches from that of the old knight. "From seventy-eight arrows sent downrange up to 250 yards, only two missed their mark. Such men will be worth their weight in gold, I feel. They agreed to the terms we discussed and Alan assured me they will be ready by the time we set sail."

"Truly, this will be a most nasty surprise for our foes," Ziesolf's lips curled wolfishly.

"Aye," she agreed, regaining her seat before directing her next words toward Peter.

"With the harsh winter past and . . . um . . . other possible threats that have come to light," Christina began, referring indirectly to Katharine Volker's implicitly threatening words, "you must be very vigilant against those who wish to thieve or render other mischief onto us. I believe it would be wise to hire additional watchmen to guard against this. I leave the decision as to who and how many in your capable hands. But knowing you have posted a couple of burly fellows at the gates both day and night will greatly ease my worry."

"I will see to it immediately," Peter replied.

"Well, perhaps after you greet your child into the world would be soon enough," Christina retorted with a chuckle.

"Now, as for you, Jost," she said, turning to her young apprentice. "Again, I place the fortunes of my business in your capable hands. I have already contracted with Master Butiler for his second shearing."

"Why not the first, Master Frederick?" he replied with a puzzled expression. "You turned an excellent profit this past year by being among the first wool ships to Bruges in the spring. Would it not make sense to do the same again?"

"Normally, I would readily agree with you," Christina began patiently, happy to see Jost again proving capable of independent thinking. "Sadly, this year I run short of my supply of ships. *der Greif* will carry a crew of fighting men aboard, leaving no room for cargo other than provisions. *Seelöwe* will accompany us, carrying the Lincoln fleeces in her hold. Both ships will make land in Norwich, a market town that greatly favors this type of wool, or so I have been led to believe. If so, *Seelöwe* will substitute her old cargo for a new one, hopefully of worsted cloth. She will then accompany *der Greif* north, turning to Lübeck while we continue on to join the search for pirates. Thorsten will undoubtedly need to wait in Lübeck for the arrival of the *Winterfahrer* from Novgorod and their cargo of furs. He will return to London - hopefully, with a king's ransom in pelts. It is only then you will have a ship available to send to Bruges."

"So why pay a premium price for the first shearing, only to have it sit in the storeroom for months?" Jost concluded with a groan, "I'm such an idiot!"

"No, not really," Christina remarked reassuringly. "It is good you ask questions. That is how to best learn. Imagine, if you had not posed the question, instead just purchasing the first clip. Then you truly would have been an idiot, because I would have been a poorer man!"

Everyone at the table chuckled, save for Jost, who sat with a serious expression. After this, they discussed other matters; some significant, others not so much. Nearly six hours later, Christina went to fetch yet another bottle of wine, as several of its predecessors had already been drained dry. They were filling their cups for the second time from the flagon when the door to the kitchen passageway burst open and the maid Sarah ran toward them as fast as her short legs could carry her.

"Master Peter, come quickly!" she said breathlessly.

"What . . . what's wrong?"

His anxiety evident as his face noticeably blanched.

"Come . . . come meet your son!" Sarah replied, a toothy grin exploding across her broad face.

"A son?" Peter repeated. He turned to each of the others, who were now also standing, repeating the words as if they had not just now heard them. Then he shouted, "A son! I have a son!"

There was a joyous round of congratulations, as each felt relieved the smith's anxious waiting was finally ended.

"And Mistress Trudi?" Christina asked, hoping Sarah's good humor was indicative the mother fared well.

"Tired, but in good spirits, Master Frederick. Forgive me, sir, for not saying so more plainly."

"Quite alright, Sarah," Christina's relief was palpable. "Do you think it possible for us to see them?"

Sarah's expression turned to one of confusion, then she said, "Um . . . I will ask Bess. Come back with me to the apartment and wait outside. I'll ask and let you know."

They hurried through the corridors, finally arriving outside the door to the couple's chambers. Sarah went inside, returning in a few moments with her arms folded across her chest, clearly barring the men from what remained a solely female domain.

"Bess says come back in an hour. Everything is fine. We just need to get things tidied up."

Disappointed, Christina and the others returned to the hall where they raised their glasses in salute to Trudi, Peter, and the couple's new son. Through some mysterious means, word had spread throughout the household and maids and yardmen alike took a few minutes from their duties to come by and congratulate the new father. Before they knew it, the hour had elapsed and they returned to the apartment. This time, Sarah ushered them immediately inside the antechamber. She opened the door to the bedchamber and motioned for Peter to enter.

Christina felt somewhat perturbed at being excluded.

After all, it is my house and I have known her longer than everyone here put together. By rights, it should have been me mopping her brow during the birth, if only I didn't have to play out this damned masquerade.

Her feelings of being slighted passed quickly, however, as she begrudgingly admitted Peter's right to be the first to see his new son somewhat exceeded her own. After what seemed an eternity, he returned to the antechamber, only this time with a small bundle held carefully in his arms. When he was within a couple of paces of Christina, he held his treasure forward for her to see.

The infant was wrapped from shoulders to feet in linen swaddling bands dyed a light green, with only the face and toes exposed. The bands were tied snugly; to provide warmth, encourage the limbs to grow straight, and for support. As she looked into his face, the baby's eyes opened and he gazed back at her soundlessly.

"This is the most beautiful child I have ever seen!" Jost exclaimed, crowding closer. "Look how his eyes follow the sound of my voice. Already he begins to piece together the world!"

"How can I but agree?" Christina said. "No man could hope for a finer son than this, Peter."

She reached out and ever so gently touched the baby's cheek, reveling in the warmth of the new life before her.

"May I see, Trudi?" she whispered.

"Yes, please. She was asking for you. The midwife said it would be improper for a man to enter her birthing chamber, but my sweet wife implored her to go to hell, she'd see whomsoever she wanted. So, they came to an agreement you would be the exception."

Almost before Peter had finished speaking, Christina was through the door and beside Trudi's bed. She looked down upon the exhausted face of her dear friend, the paleness of whom gave her cause for alarm. Trudi looked up and gave a wan smile.

"Well, that wasn't so bad," she said in a tired voice. "Although I told Peter it would be a day or two before he can see about planting a brother for him inside me."

"Oh, Trudi!" Christina exclaimed, using all her self-control to keep from flinging her arms about the woman's neck and smothering her face with kisses. "Your baby is perfect, a true gift from God Almighty. I pray the pair of you enjoy long and prosperous lives."

"Amen," Trudi whispered, her eyes fluttering as she resisted in vain the urge to slumber.

Christina caught up her hand and held it tightly, willing her own strength to aid her friend's recovery. After a few seconds, Trudi could no longer deny her body's need for rest and fell into a tranquil sleep. Christina placed her friend's fingers gently on the coverlet and left the room.

She stopped briefly to congratulate Peter once more and look upon the infant who, like his mother, was now fast asleep. Reluctantly, she departed. She walked toward her own chamber, but hesitated at the top of the stairway. Turning right instead, she trod down the passageway to the chapel, where she knelt before the altar and prayed fervent for the health of the newborn child and his mother.

And watch over Cecily, she added, and her unborn babe as well. She is deserving of your love, sweet Jesus, much more so than I, your most unworthy servant. If you may favor only one of us, please let it be her.

Finally, she rose and returned to her own door.

For once, everything seems right with the world, or at least my little part of it. Trudi appears to have weathered the birth well, her babe is strong and alert, and my preparations to depart London are near completion. But how long before the tide of fortune begins to ebb? Will I ever return to see the women I love again, to share their joy in watching their children grow? How I wish I knew.

Chapter 6

The Voyage North
On to Norwich, April, 1311

Much of the way along the Queenhithe moorages stood quiet in the eerie wisps of the early morning fog, save for the irregular sound of the water's splashing against the revetments and the deeper tones of ships' hulls rhythmically booming against the fenders of the quay. The flurry of activity along the length of the wharf where *der Greif* and *Seelöwe* were docked stood in sharp contrast to the idyllic scene of silent ships sedately rocking to and fro to their left and right. Several men scurried about with the single-mindedness of a swarm of ants to load cargo, provisions, and stores for the extended voyage that lay ahead.

Christina and Ziesolf stood well out of the men's way, leaving the direct supervision of the work to the masters of the two ships, but ready to offer a sharp command should the need arise. Already, the massive cargo of Lincoln fleeces had been secured in the cavernous hold of *Seelöwe*. Christina had inspected the cloth bags herself, ensuring they were well-placed on the risers to protect them from absorbing any stray bilgewater. She found everything as it should be, with only the provisions for the crew remaining to be stowed. It was not this ship that now consumed Christina's attention, but rather *der Greif.*

Matthias, the ship's master, and Christina had planned extensively for what they hoped was every eventuality. Spare strake timber and strips of lath, yards of additional sailcloth, small barrels of tar, and bags of moss to use as caulking were brought on board, followed by two small crates of iron nails and sintels that had been forged by Peter in his smithy.

"Hopefully, we will not be needing to make any serious repairs," Christina said as they watched the crates hauled on deck, "Either because of sea or battle."

"Aye," replied Ziesolf, "But it's better to bring the materials back unused than to not have what you want when you need it."

A wagon loaded with six wooden kegs clattered noisily up the cobbles. When the driver brought his carthorse to a halt, all twelve of the bowmen Christina had hired moved forward to lift the barrels to the ground. They pried the lids off the casks and, taking the contents out from inside, counted and examined the arrows. After a considerable length of time, they seemed satisfied as they placed the arrows back inside the kegs. While the others worked at this task, Alan walked over to where Christina and Ziesolf stood observing.

"Six hundred in each, with only a few needing to be re-feathered. Five kegs of sheaf arrows and one of flight, that's 300 arrows per man as I figure it. Seems like we're in for some good sport," he said dryly.

"I hope it's enough," Christina said.

"Do you know what every English archer carries at his belt, Sir Frederick?" Alan asked with a twinkle in his eye.

"No, what?" Christina replied, mystified at the question.

Ziesolf, who had heard the familiar English boast before, chuckled softly.

"Twenty-four Scottish souls, one for each arrow," Alan stated emphatically. "We have enough."

Christina was well pleased with the man's self-assurance.

Ziesolf asked, "Well said, but will they seek out Danish hearts with the same enthusiasm?"

"You have given our families full bellies for the first time in months," Alan replied, "You point out who it is needs killing, then just sit back and count the bodies!"

He gave Christina a confident wink and returned to assist his fellows to finish with the arrows.

A loud voice sounded from behind them.

"As usual, yur poor men bustin' ther asses workin' and ya standin' on the side, scratchin' yur balls! Oh, to be Frederick fuckin' Kohl!"

Christina turned to see Reiniken swaggering his way at the head of a group of five men.

"Good day to you, Wig!" she shouted happily, having not seen the man since Trudi's wedding. "Some of us have to use our brains instead of our backs, that's all."

"Fuck!" he retorted. I've bashed in many a head, and the brains that splashed out a' the skulls of the thinkers looked like so much puddin', same as the doers!"

"So, who are these fine fellows you have behind you?" Christina asked, knowing Reiniken's profanity-laced repartee could continue on for hours.

"Dregs of the drinkin' holes, this lot is, Yur Worship!" he turned to indicate the men with a sweep of his beefy hand. "Each 'un carefully chosen from the mud and piss of London's dankest back alleys, they is. This 'un's Tiny Tom.''

Reiniken pointed at a short, dark-haired young man with a wide, expressionless face.

"Not much to look at, is he? But quicker than a baited fox, mayhaps even as quick as you? And this big bastard is Henry, like the old-time English kings, ya know, only throne he ever sat on is the shitter though."

"Yes, Henry and I have already met."

Christina was pleased his face bore no permanent damage from her furious pummeling in November. She waited for the man to recognize her as well.

A crestfallen expression appeared on Henry's face, which turned slowly to look first at Christina, then Reiniken, then back to Christina again.

Before Henry could speak, Christina said, "Good to have you aboard, Henry. How fares your family?"

"Good, very good, thank ye fur askin', Mi 'lord," Henry replied, shuffling his feet about nervously.

Christina reached into her money pouch, pulled out a shilling and gave it to Henry.

"It will be a few hours at least before we depart. Hurry now to your wife and give her this, to make things easier while you're away at sea."

Before Henry could depart, Christina added, "Oh, and Henry, tell her sorry about her nose."

Reiniken smirked.

"Ah can't wait to hear that story."

"Not from me, you won't Wig," she remarked. "Do any of you other men have a family?"

A redheaded man named Alf, raised his hand.

"Ya lyin' shit!" retorted Reiniken. "Ya gots no wife, unless ya married toothless Lizzy down in the stews last night after ya had yur way with her."

"Shut yur mouth, ya miserable whoreson!" Alf replied, "It's me mum needs lookin' after. She's got no one, since me da died. Do mothers count, sir?"

"Aye, Alf, they do," Christina replied, giving him a shilling as well. "Now, to your mother and straight back, do you hear?"

"And if I has to come lookin' for ya, mark me, ya'll be comin' back a gelding, shur as shit," Reiniken stared at the man through slitted eyelids.

Alf departed at a trot as Reiniken introduced the other two men as Fawkes and Ham.

"Likely lads," Ziesolf remarked sternly, "But can they fight?"

"Same old One-Eye, eh?" Reiniken remarked, "Straight to the point, just lak yur blade. Well, they shan't be ma first choice if I was settin' up a battle rank. Not enuf discipline fur that. But if'n the fight is anythin' lak what we fought before, it's more lak a bar brawl than one fit fur soldiers. 'N these fuckers kin more than hold their own in that kind of scrap."

Ziesolf muttered, "Aye," apparently satisfied with Reiniken's assessment of his men's mettle.

With all of the ships' companies present, save for the two men who would be returning shortly, there were few details left to attend to before they were fully prepared to set sail. Ziesolf and Christina boarded *der Greif* to confer with Matthias and Thorsten, who were already engaged in conversation.

Despite the fresh breeze, the fetid vapors of the effluent-filled river, joined with the fusty smell of the ship's wood, permeated the air on deck. It was a familiar scent to Christina, almost a malodorous welcome home. She resisted the impulse to hold her nose as she and Ziesolf joined the two sailing masters at the landward railing of the main deck

"Will we be able to depart today?" Christina asked.

"Aye, we should have a good ebb tide in an hour or so," Matthias replied, "Not much wind, but we'll make do."

Thorsten stroked the coarse curls of his thick, black beard and said nothing, seemingly agreeing with the older man's assessment.

"What remains to come on board?" Ziesolf asked.

"From what I believe, only the fresh provisions," Thorsten said. "We'll eat fresh beef and bread for the next few days, probably all the way to Norwich. There, we'll replenish our fresh stores before heading north again. With any luck, we'll be in Lübeck before we have to crack a barrel of salt cod."

"Speak for yourself," Matthias retorted. "We'll not have the good fortune to be going ashore, not for a while at least, as we're heading right back out into the Skagerrak. At least we've got enough beer to keep the men reasonably happy."

Their conversation ended abruptly end as Christina spied Jost unexpectedly hurrying toward where they stood.

What can be wrong?

She jumped onto the cobbled way and walked over to meet her apprentice.

Surely, he understood all of my instructions, or else he would have already sought further clarification.

"How go the preparations, cousin?" Jost asked, bending over slightly to catch his breath.

"Good enough, at least when I'm not needlessly interrupted."

"Oh, sorry for that," he replied glibly, reaching into his tunic to retrieve a folded and sealed sheet of parchment. "It's from Westminster Palace. I thought you would be wanting to have it before you left but, I wouldn't want to take you away from your tasks. I'm sure it can wait until you return."

Christina muttered, "Still your wicked tongue, you young rogue," before snatching the message from his hand."

She examined the seal which, although unbroken, she did not recognize. Jost waited beside her, should the missive cause his master to direct action on his part. With mounting trepidation, Christina opened the parchment and began to read.

To My Valiant Knight, Sir Frederick Kohl, from His Most Ardent Admirer, Lady Cecily Baldewyne,

God be praised this missive finds you happy and that you and your household enjoy good health in Hs almighty grace. They are good and honest people and well deserve the kindness and largesse bestowed on them by such a just and honest master as yourself.

As for me, I am in good spirits, although the babe growing within my womb saps my strength increasingly. I am within my laying-in now and can no longer leave my apartments here. This is very difficult for me, as I have roamed the fields and woodlands freely near my tower since I was a child. Increasingly, I long for our walks along the river, especially now that springtime comes to the land.

There is little news to report of the campaign in the North, only that the king dispatched Earl Gaveston to parlay with the Bruce before Christmas, but little became of it, if anything at all. His majesty also moved the King's Bench and the Lord Exchequer to

York, but whether this is because he envisions his stay in the North to grow longer or to protect these royal offices from being seized by the Lords Ordainers, I do not know.

Know ye well that I spent time each day before my confinement in chapel, praying for the success of your impending journey and your safe return to London town. Now, the Lord must hear my supplications for the same directly from my mouth to his ears. The message remains the same, save said with even greater fervency, "Take care of your most worthy servant, Frederick, and speed him back to the bosom of those whom love him best."

So, take care, my friend most beloved. Take no more risks than need be, although I fear this request will fall too often on deaf ears. Place trust in those beside you; Herr Ziesolf, Goodman Reiniken, Master Matthias. and the others. Know you well that, though I am a simple and weak woman, I would be there fighting beside you, if I did not face a different manner of challenge in the days ahead.

May the Holy Virgin and Her son, Lord Jesus Christ, send mighty angels to help you defeat your enemies and guide your path back home.

Until that blessed time, I will remain your most loyal servant and humble petitioner for as long as my body draws breath upon this Earth.

Lady Cecily

Christina slowly refolded the parchment and slipped it into the front of her tunic, placing it directly over her heart.

How I love her! How I miss her!

Christina's heart felt rent in two.

There has been some consolation in knowing she was somewhat near me these past months, but each day's sail will take me further from her side now, eliminating even that small solace!

She denied herself tears, knowing they would serve no useful purpose. Rather, she strengthened her resolve to speed her return to London. A sudden thought came to her.

How cagily she worded her missive! It alludes to nothing improper between us, had it been intercepted by unfriendly eyes.

The unbidden image of Katharine Volker's conniving face caused an involuntary shudder to course through her body.

Yet, I am left with no doubt as to the feelings that unite her heart to mine. What a woman she is!

She looked up to discover Jost still waiting and looking concerned. She smiled at the young man, causing his expression to relax. Then she moved forward and embraced him, the first time she had ever done so. His body stiffened briefly at her unexpected touch, then relaxed. She released her hold and stepped back to stare earnestly into his eyes.

"Thank you, Jost. For this and for your good service. I could not hope for a finer apprentice."

"Nor I a better master," he replied. "Godspeed, Frederick. Please come back to us unharmed."

He offered his hand, which Christina clasped firmly before he turned and departed. Four hours later, just as the tide ceased its movement, Christina, her ships, and those aboard them did the same, as the crewmen freed the hawsers that held them to their moorages. Other men hauled in unison to hoist their ship's huge rectangular sail and angled it a few degrees to better catch the now steady breeze blowing from the west. Just after they passed under the Great Bridge, the tide began to ebb, adding to their traveling speed. Within a short while the convoy was moving downstream at a brisk five knots.

Even at this speed, Christina realized it would take almost a full twenty-four-hours to reach the open sea outside the Thames' expansive estuary. Consequently, she, Matthias, and Thorsten decided it more prudent to anchor somewhere below Greenwich when the light began to fade rather than to chance the treacherous sandbars at the river's mouth at night. The following morning, they planned to sail on the tide down the remainder of the river's course. After a night at anchor in the relatively calm waters of the estuary, they would travel north; hopefully reaching their destination in a day or two. It was a leisurely schedule, one far too slow for Christina's liking. She was as eager to speed their way as a spirited mare fighting her bit. The experience and proven wisdom of her two sailing masters stilled any protests she might have lodged, however.

She moved to the portside of *der Greif* and gazed out at the slowly passing verdant countryside. In some places, the green expanse was interrupted by patches of white sheep gorging themselves on the thick grass. The harsh calls of waterfowl emanated from the increasingly marshy shoreline, at times augmented by the chirping of their more musical songbird cousins. The gentle rocking of the boat and the warmth of the afternoon sun blended into a hypnotic concert and Christina was well on her way to slumber when she was jarred awake by the sound of a heavy nearby splash.

"The damned idjit's fallen in the fuckin' water!" one of Reiniken's men exclaimed.

"Shit!" Christina said under her breath, fearing she would need to dive into the cold water to rescue the unfortunate man. Before she could kick off her boots; however, she heard a second, less noisy, splash. She peered over the freeboard. A man swam powerfully toward the first, who thrashed in a fit of extreme panic. Gotz, one of the more experienced mariners aboard, had the presence of mind to run to the stern with a length of rope and toss it expertly toward the struggling man. The rescuer, whom she was astonished to identify as the hulking Henry, arrived at the same time, reaching up to catch the last few feet of the line. Holding fast to the rope with his right hand, he used his left to scoop around the now exhausted victim.

"Drop the sail! Look lively, you lot!"

Several crewmen hastened to obey Matthias' command.

Slowly, the ship lost way until its forward motion mirrored that of the ebbing tidal waters beneath it. More men crowded to the stern and hauled up a limp figure with a shock of reddish hair: Alf, one of Reiniken's toughs. Removing the rope that had been secured under his armpits, they let him fall rather roughly to the deck, where he laid on his side, retching up a copious amount of brackish water. The men ignored him as they lowered the rope once more. Within seconds, the lumbering figure of Henry was hauled aboard.

The other men congratulated Henry, clapping him on the back and punching his arm playfully. As Alf struggled to his feet to join in the camaraderie, Christina made her way toward the men.

"What the hell happened here, Alf?" she demanded angrily.

"Well, me -n the lads, we wuz lookin' over th- side, and Ah guess, well Ah guess Ah slipped and fell in th- river," he answered.

"It's lucky ya decided to go fur a swim here, ya silly bastard. If'n we wuz still in London, ya'd have come up with a mouthful of somebody's shit!" Reiniken retorted.

The other men laughed uproariously, only to fall immediately silent as Christina yelled, "Shut your miserable fucking gobs, the whole misbegotten lot of you!"

The men looked at each other. Some who did not have the measure of the spare young figure before them looked as though they might answer back. Those who had sailed with her before held their tongues, having witnessed the consequences of challenging her authority.

"If you would have drowned, you stupid son of a bitch, I would have hunted your mother down when we returned to London and beat every penny of that shilling I gave you out of her worthless ass, so help me God!"

Even Reiniken raised his eyebrows slightly at the vehemence in her voice. He had seen her angry before, even to the point of violence, but never to the degree before him now.

"If this can happen now, how much easier it will be when we're on the open sea, rolling and pitching like the dregs at the bottom of a cup of ale you swirl before swilling it down. If you're in the water there, the sea will have the ship away with the next wave. No one can come to save you. You'll die alone watching us disappear into the distance. My best advice would be to take a big swallow of water, so it's a quick death," Christina's words were filled with acrimony as she fixed the man with a withering stare.

"Sorry, Mi 'lord," Alf replied in a meek voice.

"Damned right you are! Now, get out of my sight before I have you fitted with a leg iron. That way, if it happens again, you go straight to the bottom and none of us will be any the wiser, except when we're happy to find a bit more in our rations!"

Alf scuttled away, eager to distance himself from the fury of Christina's tongue.

"And you," she began again, now directing her comments toward Henry, "that was a damned foolish thing to do, Henry, do you know that?"

Henry said nothing, only dropping his eyes submissively like an abused beast accustomed to feeling the lash.

"But it was brave as well. Alf was fortunate you were there for him," she said, not mentioning she was only seconds away from diving to rescue the man herself. "In the North, there are tales of a creature known as a walrus."

"Ah don't know wha' thet is, Mi' lord," he replied.

"Well, it's a huge sea creature, bigger than a cow, but so slow and awkward on land a man can dance rings around it.

Henry looked at her, his slow wit trying to comprehend the point Christina was making.

"But, when the walrus slides into the water, it's quick and swims as powerfully as a seal. You, Henry, are our walrus"

The group around him began cheering once more, chanting "walrus" several times. Henry blinked confusedly, still not comprehending the meaning of Christina's little speech. But the other men's reactions, coupled with the unexpected bonus of not sharing in Alf's tongue-lashing from Christina, were sufficient to spark a broken-toothed grin.

Christina was thankful Alf's dunking was the only excitement for the day. The two ships continued to make good progress well into twilight, then anchored several feet from shore in a broad bend of the river's course. By the time the rising sun sent shimmers of light across the water so intense they hurt the eye, the men aboard were awake and chaffing to resume their journey. This was not to be, however, as the strong current would have moved them back up the river, rather than downstream. Combined with a slight breeze blowing from the southeast directly against their sail, they had no alternative but to patiently wait for the changing tide.

Spotting Reiniken standing alone on the sterncastle, Christina climbed the stairs to where the man stood.

"God's day to ya, Yur Worship," he said.

"And to you, Wig," she replied, "What mischief is it you are up to this fine morning?"

"Nothin' much, just standin' here thinkin' yur payin' me good coin to stand in the sun scratchin' my bollocks."

"While other times I'm paying you to freeze your ass off while you're trying to fend off a few dozen Danish berserkers trying to detach those same bollocks from your body, let's not forget," Christina remarked dryly.

"God's bloody eyes, Yur Worship, can't ya let a fella enjoy hisself fur even a minit?" he complained, then joined her in outright laughter.

Reiniken's attention abruptly shifted to somewhere past Christina's ear.

"Will ya look at that, will ya?"

She turned around to discover a couple of the archers had fetched their bows and brought them on deck. After bending the yew wood and attaching bowstrings, they scanned the immediate shoreline, then fixed their gazes upon a young horse chestnut, only the upper branches of which could be seen from where Christina stood. From their animated conversation, it was evident they had spotted something at the tree's base. One fellow lowered his bow and pointed, while the other reached into his belt to withdraw an arrow. A second later, his bowstring twanged and the arrow flew several hundred feet. Reiniken and Christina could not discern the target from their angle, or whether it had been hit. A silent glance passed between them before both ambled down to where the archers were standing.

Before they could close to within speaking distance, the other archer, whom Christina recognized as Godfrey, launched an arrow as well.

Sensing their approach, Godfrey turned and said, "God be with you, Mi' lord, and to you, Goodman Reiniken."

"And to you," she replied, "Are you and Gilbert here set on repelling some ferocious unseen attackers who threaten us this early morn?"

"Aye," Gilbert interjected with a serious expression. "Savage beasties they were, lurking in the brush, just waiting for a chance to leap aboard and savage our throats with their great fangs!"

Both Christina and Reiniken scoured the shoreline for several seconds before finally detecting the objects of the two archers' interest. Two fat, grayish conies lay motionless upon the grass, each transfixed by an arrow. Christina reckoned the range to be at least 150 feet from the deck where they stood.

"Excellent shooting!" she exclaimed.

"Is this sum trickery?" Reiniken asked suspiciously, clearly not believing such skill with a bow was possible. "Ah've been in the field with the fuckin' emperor's own crossbowmen an' nivir saw nothin' lak thet! Ah don't . . ."

Reiniken's words were cut short by the sizzle of another arrow let fly. His head swiveled toward Godfrey, the shooter. Christina's attention shifted to the land bordering the river, where she witnessed the final struggles of a third cony, this one secured to a larch sapling by the arrow shaft through its neck.

Reiniken turned, his eyes following Christina's pointing finger. His jaw dropped open, at a loss for words for perhaps the only time since Christina had met the man.

"Jesus sufferin' on the cross!" he exclaimed. "Do ya think Ah mite give it a go?"

The two archers glanced at each other noncommittally, then Godfrey replied, "Certainly, you can use my bow, if you wish."

Reiniken took the man's bow in his left hand, bringing it nearer his face to examine it more closely. He then held it out before him and sighted across his hand toward the riverbank. Satisfied he had the measure of the weapon; he turned his head toward Godfrey who handed him an arrow.

To Christina, it appeared as if the proportions of the bow had diminished in Reiniken's enormous hand. Whereas the length of it had exceeded Godfrey's height by a good three to four inches, it reached barely to the chin of her much larger companion. Although she was unsure of Wig's ability to match the accuracy of the English archers, she was certainly not expecting what transpired next.

Reiniken notched the arrow and pulled back on the bowstring. He managed only to reach half its possible extension before he was unable to move it any further. The massive muscles from his shoulder to his bicep strained until he finally gained another inch or two. After about five seconds of this effort, his left hand started to tremble and the head of the arrow moved in little circles. Recognizing defeat, he relaxed the tension on the bowstring and released it from his grasp. Still holding the arrow in his right hand, he rotated his arm in its socket, working out the kinks and spasms in the sinews of his upper body.

"Wha' fuckin' witchcraft is this?" Reiniken demanded. "Ah gots twice the muscle of both of youse together! But ya kin draw an arrow lak ya wuz pluckin' a lute, while Ah can't do shit whit it!"

"No witchery, just practice," Godfrey replied calmly. "I shot my first arrow at the age of six, from a three-foot hazelwood bow crafted by mi' da. I thought I was a real man, having a bow and all, but that's when I learned that to be an archer was work, not play. I was taught how to lay my body to the bow, to draw from the eye and hip as much as the arm. If I forgot, a quick smack helped me to remember the next time."

Reiniken said nothing, but still seemed unconvinced.

"You are certainly the larger man betwixt us, but I'm not so sure I agree you have more muscle, at least for those necessary to pull a bow. Feel here, in my arm and shoulder," Godfrey directed, turning his back toward Reiniken.

Reiniken did as asked, then his expression grew more and more surprised as he felt along the right shoulder of the other man's cowl and tunic to discover an unexpectedly large, firm mass of muscle beneath. A comparative examination of the left side disclosed no more than what would normally be expected.

Godfrey turned once more to face Reiniken and Christina.

"If you would have been trained as was I, friend Reiniken, the king could have stationed you on the English coast and let you bombard the French into submission across the channel," Godfrey said with a wolfish grin.

"Aye!" Reiniken replied loudly, matching Godfrey's smirk. "Fuck the lot of -em. Never met a Frenchie worth a shit anyway. Now, Ah gots one more question."

Godfrey raised his eyebrows slightly.

"Which one of youse are goin' fur a swim to fetch them conies? Nothin' lak a bit of fresh rabbit stew to ease the journey along, don't ya think, Yur Worship?" Reiniken said, hooting with laughter as he dug his elbow not so gently into Christina's ribs.

As they turned away to let the bowmen decide how best to retrieve their prizes, Reiniken said in an unexpectedly serious voice, "There's gonna be a lot of dyin' comin' at the hands uv them English bastards."

The next three days passed pleasantly enough as they were blessed with favorable winds and calm seas. On the morning of the fifth day since they departed London, they anchored outside the Wensum River, awaiting the flood tide to aid them upriver to Norwich. After a few hours, Matthias detected the faint landward pull of the tidal change, so he hoisted the anchor and set the sail to its best advantage. By late afternoon, they were moored quayside at what they discovered later to be St. Anne's dock.

Although Christina was eager to complete the sale of her fleeces in Norwich and then be on with the main objective of their journey, she had learned that successful trading required some degree of patience, though this was not among her most sterling virtues. Nor was it a quality possessed by the men aboard the ships, who chafed to enjoy the pleasures of an unfamiliar town. As she stepped onto the quay, she noticed the men eying her eagerly, awaiting the word they were free to go drinking and whoring. She chose to ignore them.

They'll see what I'm up to soon enough. Let me determine first if there is work needs to be done.

She boarded *Seelöwe* and descended forthwith into the ship's hold, which she happily found to be devoid of seawater. Christina undertook her customary careful inspection of the woolsacks, finding neither evidence of dampness nor of vermin damage. Satisfied her cargo was unblemished and saleable, she ascended the stairway back onto the deck where Thorsten stood with crossed arms, awaiting her arrival and further instructions.

"Everything seems to be in order," she stated. "It is too late in the day to determine if a weavers' guild exists or, if not, to make inquiries among the locals as to who might be in the market to make a purchase."

"Aye," he replied. "I've already set the night's watch. Will you be needing the others for anything?"

"No, I guess not," she responded slowly.

She was reluctant to chance the sailors and other men getting into mischief in town, but she could think of no plausible excuse to deny them their pleasure.

"Just make certain they're back here in the morning, ready for work, and not puking their guts out in some alleyway somewhere. If I'm lucky, we'll have the cargo away tomorrow, or the next day at the latest."

Leaving Thorsten, Christina returned to *der Greif* to repeat her decision to Matthias. Afterwards, now with idle time on her hands, she decided to wander into town herself to sample the local fare. Accompanied by Ziesolf, she set off at a leisurely pace toward the market square. They encountered few other people until they turned onto King Street, where a throng of pedestrian activity crowded the way. After traveling no more than a few hundred feet northward, Christina spied a large, well-kept three-story inn with a painted sign on its front proclaiming it to be "The Golden Fleece."

"A most auspicious name," agreed Ziesolf after she pointed out the signboard to him.

"Aye, and it would surely deny fortune should we not venture inside, don't you think?" she responded. "Besides, we might chance into a conversation with a bureller or weaver who might know someone of their ilk in the market for our load of fleeces."

"A bureller? I am not acquainted with that term," Ziesolf's forehead creased slightly.

"Master Butiler informed me a bureller is the term for one who spins the thread from the wool, especially used here in the Midlands," Christina replied, secretly pleased.

It was rare she had information unknown to her companion.

"Well then," he said briskly, "A tankard of ale and a knowledgeable bureller. It makes no difference in which order they come before us!"

They made their way across to the other side of the street, mounted a couple of shallow steps and then entered a spacious and surprisingly light-filled common room. Though just early evening, fifty or sixty men were already hard at their cups, filling the air with loud talk and laughter, the stench of sweating bodies and stale beer creating the curious aroma that uniquely permeated such establishments. As Ziesolf moved to lay claim to one of the few tables still unoccupied in the room, Christina approached the massive bar of well-polished oak that extended for what she believed to be forty feet or more.

"God's favor be with you this day," she declared amiably to the stout middle-aged man behind the bar. "Two tankards of ale, if it pleases you."

He looked at Christina quizzically.

"Did ya not see the ale pole was not up? No ale today, I'm sorry to say. But we do have fresh beer a-plenty, so there's no need to go thirsty."

"Aye, beer's definitely a winsome substitute. And food?" she added hopefully.

"I didn't think you were from around here, good sir," the barman replied, ignoring her last question for the time being. "Even the Easterlings living hereabouts know of the food at The Golden Fleece."

Christina waited for the man to explain further.

"On Fridays, my Margaret spends all day making lamb shank pies, with a gravy so thick it'll hardly slop from your trencher. It's lucky you got here early; they'll be long gone by dark."

Christina's mouth watered at the barman's description of his woman's specialty.

"Absolutely, two of the pies as well then." she declared, paying him the three pennies he requested.

She strolled over to their table where she found Ziesolf already in a dialog with two of the other patrons of the establishment.

"This is Hugh and Walter, two men in good standing of the town's weavers' guild," Ziesolf said by way of introduction. "And this is Master Frederick Kohl."

God's teeth! Can we really be so fortunate as to make such an acquaintance so soon?

"So, it's him that has the wool, eh?" the one Christina believed to be Hugh asked Ziesolf.

"Aye, the very one," she answered with measured pleasantness, not wanting to push the conversation.

"And how many sarplar has ya gots?" the other man added, breaking his silence.

"Sixty-two to be exact."

"Sweet Jesus," Walter remarked after sounding a low whistle. "That would keep our burellers busy until our first shearing."

148

Since this response sounded encouraging to Christina, she ventured to ask, "Do you have an interest? In making a purchase, that is."

"A few sacks to be sure," Walter replied.

By the holy tears of the Virgin! Christina groaned inwardly. *I have no time for this. Selling the cargo piecemeal could take weeks or even months. By that time, they will be shearing their own flocks and the value of my fleeces will certainly diminish measurably. Not only that, but I will be too late to join the fleet in Lübeck. Hell, no! This simply will not do!*

A portly woman arrived with the tankards of beer Christina had ordered. She savored a deep draught of the foamy brew, then continued to speak.

"Because I have pressing business elsewhere, I had not intended to market them so. Could not the guild undertake to purchase my cargo in bulk?" she asked hopefully.

Hugh stroked his closely clipped beard slowly and looked toward his fellow weaver as if to get his thoughts.

"It's possible," Walter said slowly. "We will have to gather our masters together to discuss the idea."

"And when do you believe such a meeting is possible?" Christina queried, realizing that, in her desperation, she was indeed pressing the man.

"I would think it would take two days, perhaps three, to gets you an answer."

Damn!

She cursed at the misfortune of her circumstances, but realized there was nothing she could do to speed their response.

"Would you care to examine the wool, to attest to its fine quality?" she asked in a sudden burst of inspiration.

Again, the two men looked at each other.

"Aye," Hugh said finally. "It wouldn't do no harm, especially if you do decide to sell it separately."

Walter nodded his assent.

"Fine. Would tomorrow at midday suit you? Our ship is moored at St. Anne's wharf," Christina replied.

"A bit later would be preferable. Perhaps when the bells toll nones?" responded Hugh.

Christina agreed.

"We'll be there. For now, we'd better get to our guild master to let him know what you have asked."

Within seconds of the two weavers' departure, the stout woman arrived with two coarse tourte trenchers, each containing a substantial shortcrust pie baked golden brown. When Christina cut into the crust with her eating knife, it exploded with a thick, rich gravy brimming with savory chunks of lamb shank, as well as carrot, turnip, parsnip, and leek. By the time she finished, Christina had not only consumed the pie's crust and contents, but also much of the sopping innards of her trencher. Leaning back on her bench to ease the pressure on her swollen stomach, she took a long swallow of her second tankard of beer.

"I will have to ask Bess if she knows how to make such a dish," Christina remarked to Ziesolf, who was still chasing pools of gravy with bits of bread, albeit at a more leisurely pace.

"A most flavorsome meal, I will agree," he replied before filling his mouth with a last bit of meat.

"So, what now?" she asked.

"Hopefully, these two will be able to arrange what they promised, and the guild will make an offer. If not, would it be such a bad thing to leave *Seelöwe* moored here, in Norwich, while *der Greif* continues north? The weavers and burellers could make their purchases in small lots over a period of time, and we would not be impeded from our principal task. Remember, Thorsten customarily traded on his own accord, without the ship's owner being aboard. Also, it could be several months before the *Winterfahrer* arrive in Lübeck from Novgorod. Do you think it any better for *Seelöwe* to be moored in Lübeck awaiting them than here in Norwich?"

Christina gritted her teeth. As usual, Ziesolf's suggestion seemed perfectly reasonable.

Why did I not consider this alternative? she thought, upset at her own thickheadedness.

"You are absolutely correct," she responded. "That is exactly what we will do. Now, to more pressing matters. I wonder if they have a room available?"

Given a choice, Christina almost always preferred a bed on land over her sea cabin.

With the prospect looming ahead of months at sea, an accommodation ashore for a few days would be a blessing, she thought, recalling fondly the rooms at The Tabard Inn in London.

Given the general tidiness of the Golden Fleece, and the fresh rushes intermingled with dry lavender spread across the floor, she anticipated the lodging would be more than acceptable.

Christina chatted with Ziesolf until they had drained the last dregs of their tankards. As they rose from the table, Christina instructed her friend to arrange for ten sarplars to be raised from *Seelöwe's* hold in the morning and placed on the dock for the weavers' inspection.

"Ten?" he asked, eyebrows raised in mild surprise.

"Aye. I realize four would be customary but, anything I can do to convince these louts I am bargaining in good faith; I will try.

Besides, it will give the men something to do while we're in port besides raising a tankard and chasing the local whores. I'm beginning to feel my charity extends too generously to the prosperity of the stews of this land."

Flashing a quick grin, Ziesolf departed for the ships. Christina returned to query the barman as to the availability of a chamber.

"A sleeping room? Sure," said the barman. "Come with me."

He led her up a flight of stairs to a narrow, dimly lit corridor that extended for what she inferred was the length of the building. What appeared to be pinewood doors were spaced periodically to the left and right. The barman opened the third door to the left and stood aside to let Christina enter. Courtesy of a small window, the light inside was slightly better than that in the passageway. What it revealed, however, left her aghast.

Inside were eight beds, each of a wooden frame strung with rope. What were clearly straw-stuffed mattresses encased in canvas were allocated two to a bed. It was not the beds themselves that caused her concern, but the fact that each was already occupied. Some had two or even three occupants, sleeping companionably while emitting loud snores and other night sounds. In one, an older man lay on his side facing away from the door, his thin left arm draped around the shoulder of the hefty woman beside him. The rhythmic writhing of their torsos beneath the thin blanket that covered them made it evident they were engaged in coupling. To Christina, the entire scene appeared as if captured from the depth of the inferno itself.

"One penny for the night be the going rate," the barman stated matter-of-factly.

"Do you not have something more . . . private?" Christina asked, closing the door behind her with a substantial thud.

"Private? No. Well, see it's the feast of St. George today and the town is full of revelers. This is the best I can do, I'm afraid," he replied, clearly impatient to return downstairs.

She thanked him, but declined his offer forthwith.

As she was leaving the inn, he called out to her, "If you still have need of a room tomorrow, I can give you my very best for two pence, if you're here early enough that is. You can have that one all to yourself."

Surprised at her turn of good fortune, Christina readily agreed.

Now, she had only to retrace her steps back to the moorage. The crowds that choked Kings Street earlier had largely dissipated now, leaving only drunken revelers to pass her by. A few lit rush torches were already smoldering outside the drinking establishments, scenting the cool night air with aromatic smoke. As she left the main thoroughfare, she was left with only the fading twilight to guide her.

Abruptly, she was gripped with the sensation of being followed. She turned and scanned the street behind her. Nothing seemed out of place. The few pedestrians appeared to be going innocently about their way, paying her no particular attention.

It's just walking at night through a strange, somewhat deserted part of town that has my nerves frayed.

She loosened her sword in its scabbard just in case, happy her status as a knight entitled her to travel thusly armed.

A stone clattered noisily behind her, accompanied by the swift patter of muffled footsteps.

This time she wheeled about with her weapon at the ready, hoping the mere sight of her blade would dissuade any cutpurse or more aggressive thief from tempting a nasty fate. Again, she detected no one.

153

Suddenly, she stopped, a dire thought finding her mind.

Could Katharine Volker's talons stretch even to here?

How could she have known Norwich was their destination, and then have gotten word to a compliant henchman so quickly? Could there be a traitor in their midst? Or was she just conjuring unsubstantiated fears from the air?

She walked more carefully now, halting intermittently while keeping her sword at the ready should an attack occur. Minutes later, she was thankful to make out the silhouettes of her two ships and a group of men clustered to their fore, drinking, and talking quietly. She placed her sword back into its sheath and moved to join Thorsten, Matthias, Ziesolf, and a few others.

"Kurt had said you were fixing to stay onshore," Matthias mentioned, "Changed your mind?"

"Nothing available," Christina replied noncommittally. "I'll see all of you in the morning. Rest well."

She boarded *der Greif* and went to her cabin. She sighed as she regarded her hard bunk, thinking that even the thick straw mattresses at the inn would have been much more comfortable. She had considered having one made of goose down sewn for the voyage, but decided against it, knowing it would be worse than useless should it become drenched in seawater.

Christina disrobed, taking off everything but her linen shirt. After a quick wash and her prayers, she went to her bed and climbed under the top sheet, blanket, and coverlet.

She fell into a troubled sleep, beset by nightmarish visitations from her dead brother and sister, both Marguerite and Frederick murmuring a name in her ear she could not quite make out. These ghosts faded into the shadows and were replaced by an indistinct figure who hovered just out of sight. Without warning, she felt a weight settle upon her chest, one that grew heavier and heavier. She cried out for help, but could only manage a throaty whisper.

She awoke and bolted upright, gasping for air. Her wild eyes scanned left and right, but could find no other presence in the moonlit cabin, corporeal or supernatural. Her racing heart began to slow.

Although quite weary from the day's events, she could not return to sleep. Each time she closed her eyes, the thought of an unknown person with an unwholesome interest in her whereabouts filled her mind.

The idea that it might be some rogue, seeking to prey on a solitary traveler on a dark, deserted street, seemed almost reassuring. That happenstance could play out on any night, in any town. But, somehow, the theory seemed not to fit.

I feel as though he was merely content to watch, to learn. I sense I must be on guard while we are here. I'll ask Ziesolf to warn the others.

Chapter 7

An Old Acquaintance
Norwich, April, 1311

Christina awoke the next morning feeling revitalized and a bit ashamed she had let a few random noises in the night alarm her.

I simply let my imagination run wild, she chided herself. *Next, I'll be seeing spirits floating along the walls and trolls below the bridges. Don't be such a child, Christina, for God's sake!*

She dressed quickly, grabbing a crust of bread to gnaw on while she stepped out on the deck to judge the day. Although the slight wind was chilling, the clear skies promised some warmth as the day progressed. The sun was already a couple of fingers above the horizon, though scant few upon the ships.

Clear evidence of the efforts put into their merrymaking, she thought, happy they had found pleasure in one of their final nights ashore for perhaps several weeks.

She returned to her cabin and fetched a tankard of ale, as the staleness of the loaf had parched her. Once more outside, she was glad to see more men appearing on deck; however, several appeared worse for wear, the debilitating effects of strong drink still upon them. Despite this hindrance, within the hour Thorsten and Matthias had organized those not totally incapacitated into a work party that began to move the required number of woolsacks from the hold in a more or less efficient manner.

As mid-afternoon approached, the men finished their work and the ten sarplar lay upon the wharf-side, ready for inspection. Finished with their labors for the time being, most went below deck to nurse aching heads or volatile stomachs, or simply to enjoy the sleep they had lost out night prior. The crews' absence did not depopulate the wharf; however, as their place was taken by a growing number of onlookers.

Christina had not foreseen that a crowd would form to observe the weavers' inspection of the wool but, as she thought more about it, it did make sense. Other weavers or burellers who might contribute to the purchase would want to see firsthand what they were being asked to help fund. Others, not directly involved, still might envision how such a transaction could benefit them. While some might simply be curious about a group of foreign merchants displaying their wares for all to see. Regardless of their motivations, the number of onlookers soon swelled to a hundred or more.

As the sun reached its summit, Walter and Hugh appeared, as promised. They made a swift, but thorough, inspection of the wool, their experienced hands and eyes appraising the quality of the longwool fleeces.

When they finished, Hugh said to Christina, "The wool's quality is as you told us. The staple lengths are over seven inches, indicating a single shearing. Almost all have a fine crimp and most have spiral tips. Good luster, no sign of discoloration or mold. It would be a pleasure to work with such upon my loom."

"We will inform our brother guildsmen of this when we meet on the morrow," Walter added. "If they are in agreement, we may be able to make you an offer soon after. Shall we find you here?"

"No," Christina replied, "I have taken a room at The Golden Fleece, where we first met."

"Good," said Hugh. "Until tomorrow then."

As Christina watched the two men depart, her gaze idly drifted over the ranks of onlookers. As she surveyed their faces, she froze on one that seemed somehow familiar. But, as she looked again, trying to find the man's visage once more, she could not. Whoever he was, he had already disappeared.

What the hell, Christina? First, last night, and now this. You're as skittish as a yearling fowl. How good it will be to complete my business here and depart. I hope my insecurity is associated with this place only and not some stymieing mental affliction that will plague me elsewhere as well.

She left the task of re-stowing the cargo in the capable hands of the two sailing masters and searched out Ziesolf, who had been observing the activity on the quay from the sterncastle of *der Greif.* Drawing up alongside the man, she informed him of what the weavers had told her.

"Good news then, eh?" he asked, then looked at her quizzically, "Or not?"

Sometimes, he's just too perceptive for his own good, she thought testily.

"No, it's good, very good in fact," she replied in better humor than she felt, "It's just that I believed I recognized someone in the crowd."

"Who?"

"Well, that's the frustrating part. Someone I knew, but who, I'm not certain," she remarked, realizing she probably made no sense at all.

She sought to recall his features. It had only been a swift glance; she could only remember dark hair and a flowing beard of similar hue. She considered him tall, at least compared to those who stood beside him. All she knew as fact was the figure filled her with a sense of foreboding far beyond what one would expect after such a random encounter.

The beard! Without it, his identity would be clear!

"Richard!"

"What? Are you certain?" Ziesolf asked, aghast.

"As sure as I am it is you who stands before me. The same misbegotten whoreson who plotted the deaths of my father and brother and blamed the murder of my uncle upon me. I nearly swung from the gallows because of him!"

"And?" Ziesolf stared steadily into her eyes.

"And what?" she asked, exasperated. "I only cleaved three fingers from him in London. Now, I aim to hunt him down and end his wretched life like I should have then, that's what!"

"You faced him in trial by combat and he submitted. You were forbidden to take his life then and you cannot take it now," he said in a calm voice. "He was banished only from London. He has a right to live here. To kill him without cause would be murder."

"But I have causes. Plenty of them!"

"None that could be lawfully proven here."

"Damn you, Ziesolf!" she shouted, overcome with rage. "What about the person who was following me last night?"

"And you have proof this was Richard and that he had deadly intentions toward you?"

Christina stood mutely in defeat, squinting fiercely to forestall tears. She dug her nails into their palms to keep from screaming.

Ziesolf waited patiently for her fury to dissipate, which it eventually did after several minutes.

"Oh, sod it, "she muttered, swiping at her eyes. "If you won't let me gut the bastard, can we at least go see what Goodwife Margaret has prepared for today's sup?"

Approaching the Golden Fleece, Christina's foul mood improved somewhat when she saw the establishment displaying its ale-pole protruding from a small window over the doorway. Although the homebrewed beer they had enjoyed the day before had slaked their thirst, she much preferred the flavor of ale, especially when freshly brewed. Her step quickened as she imagined a gulp of it running down her dry throat.

Inside, she was surprised to find the common room almost devoid of customers. Somewhat a creature of habit, Ziesolf chose to sit at the same table, despite there being others to choose from. Christina ordered two tankards of ale and then asked the barman whether the room he had previously offered was still available.

"Aye," he replied, wiping his hands on a towel, before addressing the woman who had served them their food the previous day. "Margery love, will you fetch these two gentlemen tankards of ale whilst I show this one the Bishop's Rest?"

"Already at it, Tuck, ya dalcop," she replied good-naturedly.

Curious name for a room in an inn, Christina mused as she followed the man she now knew as Tuck up the same stairway as before. *Sometime in the past a high-ranking church official may have had reason to spend the night away from prying eyes, for whatever illicit reason one can only guess,* she thought with a grin, aware that even churchmen had failings of the flesh at times.

Reaching the third floor this time, Tuck turned to the right and opened the door to a generous-sized room with a large bed dominating the floor space. Although the bottom mattress was stuffed with straw, there was little doubt the top was down-filled. A plain white coverlet was atop, which appeared newly laundered. A few other articles of sturdy wooden construction completed the furnishings of the room.

Although I doubt it would please a bishop's taste for extravagance, it will certainly satisfy mine, she thought.

"I'll take it," she announced, "For two nights, if you will."

"Two for you alone, three for the pair of you," Tuck replied.

His statement confounded Christina.

I had not considered whether Ziesolf would prefer lodging ashore as well. He has always preferred to stay aboard ship in the past, but that was before his most recent injury. Should I ask him? I have never shared a bed with a man, let alone someone I know as well as Ziesolf. It would be passingly strange as he knows me for the woman I am. Would he . . .? She let the thought drift off into nothingness, rather than completing it, which would have forced her to consider it seriously.

"Just me, thank you," she said, paying him the four pennies.

They returned to the common room where Ziesolf was already sampling the new ale.

"How is it?" Christina queried, once more contemplating whether she should ask Ziesolf whether he would prefer to spend the night ashore.

"Good to very good," he replied. "By the way, I took the liberty to order two spitted hens."

Christina's stomach growled in anticipation.

Although a few individuals intermittently entered the room as they dined, their presence perked no particular interest. Once finished, Ziesolf departed for the ships while Christina lingered over another tankard of ale. By the time she finished, it was nearly dark outside. Suddenly fatigued by the combination of an early rise and abundant food and drink in her belly, she returned to her room, removed her boots and sword belt, and laid upon the bed fully clothed. Though she only anticipated resting a few minutes, she was soon fast asleep.

Christina woke with a start at the sound of heavy, impatient knocking on the door. Although groggy, she quickly recalled the door's location and padded in that direction. After a moment's fumbling to find the latch, she opened the door to see Ziesolf's grim visage faintly illuminated in the small lanthorn's light.

"Come. There has been a problem aboard *Seelöwe*. Someone's been killed."

Christina's heart sank as she turned to pull on her boots. Buckling on her sword belt, she grabbed her cloak and the two of them departed the inn at speed. Ziesolf provided a succinct rendition of what had occurred as they quickly walked toward the moorage. Christina remained quiet for the most part, other than voicing a few pertinent questions.

Arriving at the ships, Christina and Ziesolf leaped aboard and moved toward the forecastle, where six of the men in her employ had gathered. Noticing their approach, the archers and sailors formed into a rough semicircle facing toward her. Looking down toward the men's feet, Christina saw someone else, a someone who was lying in a motionless heap.

She was distracted by a terrible stench arising from the starboard side of the ship. She vowed to investigate it later as there were more pressing matters at hand.

"Alright, where's Gilbert?" she demanded.

"Over there, on the steps," Thorsten said pointing toward the young archer.

Christina walked toward the archer and said gently, "Tell me what happened."

He stood up, still gripping his bow in his fist. He looked toward Christina helplessly, unable to speak.

"Take your time," she said encouragingly.

After a minute of struggling with himself, Gilbert finally said, "I killed him. He was just a boy and I killed him!"

"From the start, please, from the start," Christina instructed.

"My head was still a bit thick from last night, so I volunteered to stand Peter's watch so's he could go with everyone else. It was just after dark and I was standing on the sterncastle of *der Greif* over there. Well, I had my bow out and I was taking sight at the stars, as if I was going to shoot one of them from out of the sky, you know?"

Christina nodded patiently.

"I heard a scurrying sound coming from *Seelöwe*, like a rat, only bigger. I squinted into the darkness and saw somebody shimmying up the mooring pile before jumping onto the deck. He reached over the side and that's when I saw the other one, in a small boat floating alongside. So, he throws a line up to the one on the ship, who catches it as neatly as you please. He then starts hauling up a bucket, which I figured was filled with something since it was taking quite a bit of effort to lift it. That's when I smelled it, the stink of birch bark pitch., so I knew then he was up to no good.

So that's what I smelled! Christina realized.

Gilbert continued his recollection.

"While he was finishing raising the line, the one in the boat was striking a flint to light a torch. I don't have much learning, but even I could figure out what they were up to. If he poured the pitch on the wool in the hold, the ship would be ablaze in a minute or two.

So, I put an arrow into the eye of the one on the deck just as he was bringing the bucket over the side. By the time I reached for another arrow, the one in the boat had dived into the water. That's his boat down there," Gilbert pointed over the side of *Seelöwe*. "I don't know where he swam off to, but far away from here, I'll bet."

"You've done well, Gilbert," Christina remarked, clapping the man on his back.

"It's the first man I've ever shot," he replied, misery etched on his face. "He's just a boy, can't be more than thirteen or fourteen years old. A damned shame, it is, his life ending like this. Someone surely put him up to this. It can't just be a prank the two of them thought up on their own."

"What do we do now?" Thorsten asked.

What indeed? Christina's thoughts echoed.

Perhaps the easiest thing would be to remove the arrow and dump the body overboard, disavowing any knowledge of the boy's death to anyone who came asking questions. The problem was it would only be natural for the local bailiff to call it murder, without hearing a contradictory story. Who then to blame the killing on? Two ships full of strangers, many of whom were archers. Likely, the whole lot of them would be thrown in prison until a confession could be beaten from someone. No, far better to report the crime than to attempt to cover it up.

"We notify the bailiff of what happened, that's what," she remarked firmly.

"Should we send for him now?" Thorsten replied.

"No, I don't think so," Christina responded. "First, we have no idea where we might find him and the few people still about this time of night would probably have more cause to avoid the law than to fetch it. Second, he will be neither less dead now, nor more so in the morning. The circumstances and the evidence of the crime will not change between now and dawn. Third, the last thing we want to do is put the man in a foul mood by waking him in the middle of the night. Thorsten, Matthias, set double watches, in case we receive other unwelcome visitors this eve. The rest of you, go to sleep, I will sit by the body until the morning."

While the others drifted off, Ziesolf remained.

"Better that I stay with him," he said. Before Christina could argue, he continued, "You will need a clear head in the morning when you speak with the bailiff. Who knows what he may ask of you after? You may also need to negotiate with the weavers after their meeting. I, on the other hand, have nothing to do other than to sample Goodwife Margery's hearty fare once more."

Although it seemed to her as if she were shirking part of her responsibilities, Christina could not dispute Ziesolf's logic. She thanked him for his wise counsel and walked away, but to her cabin aboard *der Greif* rather than to the inn. This way, she would be readily available should some other mischief occur.

She had considered whether to discuss with Ziesolf the possibility of Richard's hand being behind the attack, but held her tongue. Without any proof of Richard's involvement, she knew Ziesolf would take the same position he had previously,

No point getting irate for nothing, she concluded, although remembrance of the warm, comfortable bed she had vacated at the inn was upsetting enough.

Arising early the next morning, Christina left her cabin and walked the short distance to *Seelöwe*. She found Ziesolf just as she had left him the night before, placidly sitting on the steps a short distance from the dead boy's body. She left and headed into town after confirming there had been no further incidents in the night.

At The Golden Fleece, she queried Tuck as to where she might find the bailiff. He informed her Norwich subscribed to a leet system, one in which the town was divided into four districts, each with its own bailiff. He directed her a short distance away, to the home of William Bateman, who served in the position for the section of town called Conesford.

In fewer than ten minutes, she was standing before a sturdy house built primarily of gray-colored field stone. She pulled on the bell rope placed adjacent to the door and was soon led inside by a servant. The bailiff was breaking his fast at a table in the kitchen. He was a rather rotund man with a florid complexion who looked up at Christina from his meal with moderate interest.

"Yes?" he inquired.

Christina explained who she was and the events of the previous evening that had prompted her visit. The bailiff's face grew increasingly severe as she continued, interrupting only with a few brief requests for clarification. When she had finished, he stared at her briefly and sighed. Taking one last bite of an aromatic cheese, the smell of which caused Christina's stomach to rumble, he stood up and took a long pull from his tankard. Without a word, he disappeared from the room, only to return a few minutes later with a light cloak in hand.

"Let's be off then, shall we?" he said, already half out the door.

The bailiff walked at a surprising pace for a man of such girth, his speed made more startling by the shortness of his legs. They passed several people along the way, most of whom it seemed were acquainted with Bateman. He had a greeting and a word to say to most, housewives out for their morning shop and tradesmen going about their business alike. Despite this, they soon arrived at St. Anne's wharf.

Instead of immediately boarding *Seelöwe* to examine the corpse, Bateman stopped a hundred feet before and requested that Christina repeat her rendition of what had occurred the night before. As she spoke, Bateman's gaze passed from ship to ship, clearly reenacting the event in his mind. When she finished, he asked to go aboard *Seelöwe*.

Bateman seemed intelligent, diligent, and popular, uncommon attributes for one in such a position. This man could go far in the governance of this land, should he have such a desire.

The body lay untouched. One of the sailors had suggested covering it with a tarp as an act of Christian mercy, but Ziesolf had refused, not wishing to disturb the circumstances of the boy's death in any way.

Bateman looked down for a few minutes, silently assessing the veracity of Christina's words versus the evidence on hand before shifting his gaze to the group of men standing about, watching.

"Which is he who claims this arrow?" the bailiff asked.

"It . . . it is mine, Mi 'lord," stammered Gilbert.

"Damned fine shot, I must say, and at night as well," Bateman stated. "Are you the most accurate archer of the company aboard these ships?"

"Oh no, Mi' lord! Godfrey and Alan are the best. After that I may be middlin', depending on the day," Gilbert replied modestly.

"Is it common practice for German merchants to fill their ships with the king's archers, as well as cargo?" the bailiff asked Christina in an innocent tone belied by his shrewd stare.

She groaned inwardly. She had not mentioned her primary mission to anyone in Norwich previously, but saw no way around it now. Consequently, she provided the bailiff with a truncated version of what had in fact prompted her to undertake the journey.

"Quite some story indeed, Master Frederick," Bateman commented. "And a worthy mission as well, I might add. The Baltic is not the only sea plagued by those who wish to become rich by stealing from the toil of others. The Channel waters north of here abound with such scoundrels. Many ships have arrived with happy tales of having outrun suspicious vessels, shortening sail only when reaching the safety of the flow of the Wensum. Sweet Jesus alone knows how many were not so fortunate."

He crossed himself piously before continuing to speak.

"But I have no control over what happens at sea, only events occurring within my jurisdiction. Now, Gilbert, give me your version of what happened last night. Everyone else, silence, if you please," he instructed.

Gilbert's version was identical to Christina's.

Bateman knelt next to the corpse and began a thorough examination. He rotated the head to ensure the man's neck had not been broken, then searched for signs of a struggle or other wounds that Christina and Gilbert had neglected to disclose. Finally, he checked the boy's clothing for any possible clues they might provide.

"Ah ha," Bateman proclaimed in a low voice.

The men crowded closer to get a better look.

"Get back, you lot, before I remember you've got work to do!" Matthias scolded, the wrinkles of his ancient, leathery face folding into a fearsome scowl.

Reluctantly, the men edged back.

By this time, Bateman had regained his feet. In his hands was a small, rough-spun linen bag, clearly with something inside. He fumbled with the drawstring before tipping it into his palm. He held it out toward Christina.

"Four shillings, shiny ones at that" the bailiff stated. "It's always more appealing when the coins are gleaming. Not a fortune, but clearly more than this poor lad has ever seen in his life. This amount of money would tempt many an honest man to commit dark deeds. Desperate times cause men to do desperate things."

Christina nodded, perceiving what had seemingly prompted the boy to attempt the foul deed.

"So, do you know of anyone who might have instigated this crime?" Bateman asked casually, although his eyes were sharp.

Who indeed would have such interest in doing her harm? Surely, even Katharine Volker's considerable influence could not extend this far. Or could it? And what of Richard? His previous foul deeds had been motivated by money, but there was no obvious material gain for him to benefit from here. Was he now motivated by hatred for her alone?

Why must everything in my life be so convoluted?

She returned her attention to the bailiff.

"Perhaps one person," she began, deciding her fears concerning Katharine Volker's involvement were too outlandish to voice. "A man named Richard. Much bad blood has passed between us."

Christina provided a description to Bateman; disappointingly, he claimed he had no recollection of such an individual. The bailiff did say he would make inquiries among the merchant community to find if any had knowledge of the man.

"All seems to be in order here, Master Frederick. I apologize for this act of lawlessness you have endured, but do not believe you have suffered a physical or financial loss because of it. I might suggest confession may be in order for your man Gilbert here, who seems greatly troubled by his act. Perhaps it would be good for the souls of all of you, if I may be so bold, to do so before you continue your odyssey. But that is a matter best between you and God."

Christina thanked the bailiff and he began to leave. Before going over the side of the ship, he turned back.

"I will send a couple of men to fetch the body. I might suggest you keep your men from going into town, for a couple of days at least. This boy was someone's son, someone's brother, someone's friend. I do not want to make it easy for those who knew him to seek revenge, regardless of the fact it was he who brought his fate upon himself."

Saying that, he departed as swiftly as he had come.

I can't wait to leave this damned place, Christina thought furiously. *Now, I'll have a disgruntled crew on my hands as well as trying to placate what seems to be reluctant buyers, all the while trying to avoid having my fucking ships sunk by who the hell knows who! Damn it!*

In less than an hour, the two men Bateman had promised arrived. Christina's stomach lurched nervously when she noted they were accompanied by the bailiff himself. As the men placed the body on a litter and covered it with a length of cloth, Bateman drew her to the side.

"It seems we are beset with a rash of dead boys this morning," he abruptly stated in a low voice.

"Huh?" Christina responded, dumbfounded.

"Another has been found, dumped into a pig yard near St. Stephens. No arrow and no coins this time. Instead, he had been stabbed in the chest and his throat cut for good measure. I have to ask, did your man Gilbert leave the ship after he shot the boy last night?"

"To the best of my knowledge, no," Christina replied carefully. "Why do you ask?"

"From what you say, he was the only one of your men who saw the one in the boat, only how he would have found him later, that far from here and in the dark, I don't know. So, either our second victim was bragging about his new wealth and someone killed him for it, or his benefactor was none too pleased he and his accomplice failed at their task and didn't want to leave any tongue-wagging loose ends about. It might even be the two deaths are unconnected, but that would be one hell of a coincidence,"

Bateman massaged his temples with his fingers, as if to ease an apparent aching in his head, or possibly to stimulate his thoughts.

"Clearly, this is my problem and not yours. Good day to you, Master Frederick, for the second, and I hope final, time today."

Again, the bailiff left the ship and hurried from sight. The two ships' masters set the men at a myriad of small tasks that always seemed to need to be done on a wooden sailing vessel. As for Christina, she busied herself with cleaning her own small cabin, scrubbing away at stubborn bits of filth that had probably lodged themselves on the journey to Berwick or Bruges, or even before. She then sat down with her ledger, catching the entries up-to-date and rechecking sums she already knew to be correct.

As she thumbed the page over, she discovered the letter she had received from Cecily the day of their departure. She slowly re-read each word, savoring their sweet taste like a cup of fine wine. Her thoughts turned to her beloved, wondering as to her health and that of her unborn child. Her mind churned in frustration as she realized she could know no more than what was already expressed on the sheet of parchment. Finally, she felt she could endure no more time-wasting.

Once more on deck, she located Ziesolf speaking with Matthias near the ship's mast.

"Pardon me Matthias, but may I borrow Herr Ziesolf?" she asked. "I had made arrangements to meet with the prospective purchasers of *Seelöwe's* cargo and the time now grows near."

Matthias excused himself and went to have a word with a crewman who was mending one of the heavy mooring hawsers that had begun to fray.

"Although I would not imagine we would be blatantly attacked in the common room of The Golden Fleece, it might be prudent to add to our numbers, just in case. Now, who do you think would serve us well should a bar fight occur?"

She flashed a knowing smile.

Ziesolf sighed, nodding his head in response.

They located Reiniken in the cargo hold, spearing rats and mice. Although Matthias kept an immaculate ship, free of the miscellaneous detritus and muck common on most others, the pesky creatures had a knack for finding their way aboard and stealing away into the slightest hidey-hole. As the rodents could reproduce at a prodigious rate, it was vital to eradicate them immediately in ones and twos, rather than wait until they amassed in the hundreds. This was especially true since the hold was dedicated to the quartering of the additional contingent of fighting men. The rats viewed human flesh as a delicacy and their bites became easily and seriously infected. Many men returned from voyages minus digits or even limbs thanks to attacks from members of *Rattus rattus*.

As Christina and Ziesolf approached, "Reiniken turned and extended his spear in their direction. Impaled on the point was a large black rat, still struggling in its death throes.

"Tough little bastards, they is, Yur Worship," he grinned, crashing the spear downward into one of the ship's ribs with a loud thud. "But not tough enuf, ya see. Would ya lak a haunch or belly meat to chew on now, or wait for it in tonight's stew?"

Christina inwardly shuddered at the thought. She knew better than to let on to Reiniken she was squeamish, however, as that would only make her the butt of the man's jests far into the foreseeable future.

With months of shared time ahead at sea, that's just too damned long.

"No, Wig, I've already lunched. Add them to your pile over there, as I see no worth to them at all except to feed the fishes. Now, the mice are something different. When you have enough, you can skin the lot and give them to your lady friends as presents. They shave their eyebrows, cut the pelts into slivers and paste them on in their place, you know."

Christina returned his smile.

Reiniken's face grew serious as he mulled over her revelation.

"Saints be praised!" he finally remarked with mock astonishment. "Ah'd niver imagined such. Of course, it's the udder end Ah'm more interested in. Sum of the women Ah knows would needs ta skin a hefty-sized ship's rat ta have enough ta replace their cunny fur!"

"Much as I hate to cut your fun short down here," Christina began, gladly changing the subject, "I have a proposition for you. You can either continue your sport, or come with us to an establishment with flavorsome food and new ale, all to be had on my coin. Choice is yours, of course."

"Well, I was jus' getting' started," he objected. He paused a second, seemingly mulling over a difficult decision, before replying. "Oh well, anythin' fur ya, Yur Worship!"

Reiniken added the stabbed rat's bloody carcass to the pile of four or five others he had amassed.

"Don't any of ya go away, mi lovelies! Ah'll be back to spear youse sum company!"

In a short time, the three were comfortably situated at Ziesolf's customary table at the Golden Fleece, wooden tankards of ale in their hands. As Reiniken entertained them with his irreverent wit, Christina and Ziesolf casually scanned the faces of the other customers. They were pleased to see none viewed them with anything beyond casual curiosity, certainly no belligerence. By the time they had finished their meals of baked pike and root vegetables, the two weavers had appeared, recognized them, and approached their table.

After the drama of the day's other activities, the negotiations seemed almost anticlimactic. The weaving community of Norwich was certainly interested in procuring Christina's wool, which established a most favorable starting point. The complication, however, was the guild's reluctance to part with their coin, preferring instead to trade for finished worsted material, which they referred to as *stuff*, rather than cloth. By the time they reached an agreement, the weavers had offered 230 silver marks, the remainder to be made up by several lengths of worsted weave. Although she was disinclined to accept the fabric in trade, Christina realized it was the best offer she was likely to receive at the time.

At least acceptance will conclude our business here and we can continue onward, praise heaven.

In the early afternoon of the following day, Christina and a few of her men proceeded to the building the weavers of Norwich used as their guildhall. As they had agreed at the Golden Fleece the day before, Hugh and Walter were present, along with several rolls of worsted stuff from which she was to make her choice to total a

174

value of 660 marks. Although she was unfamiliar with worsted fabrics, she was impressed by the tightness of the weave as well as its slick feel, which Hugh claimed to be very rain resistant. The dyes seemed to have set well, especially in those lengths that were multicolored. Somewhat worrying was the overall light weight of the fabric, which would be ill-suited for the cold winters of the Baltic coast.

But for those of wealth, who are not relegated to wear a single set of garments year-round, a light fabric for summer may prove desirable, she mused optimistically. *I might even have a tunic crafted for myself.*

With that in mind, she began by selecting those rolls she most preferred herself, measuring them with her ell-wand and recording their lengths in her ledger. One or other of the two men would then cite a price which, after a certain degree of haggling, would be agreed upon. By the end, she was satisfied to have accumulated eight lengths of the worsted material, which the two men directed a group of laborers to load onto two large carts. She walked alongside the lumbering oxen as the carts slowly wended their way toward the wharf. By the time they arrived, other carters were just finishing rolling away with the last of the woolsacks from *Seelöwe's* hold. Within a short time, the rolls of fabric were being carried inside the ship and Thorsten and Christina were supervising their safe placement on board.

The sun had not yet set over the town when all the tasks associated with loading the cargo were finally completed. The ships had already taken on fresh provisions the day before, so there was naught more to do in preparation of their departure on the morning's ebb tide. She briefly considered delaying their sailing for a day or two while she procured additional cargo to better fill *Seelöwe's* cavernous hold. As it was, the rolls of fabric took up little more than a quarter of the space. She decided against it, however, as the only commodity of high value was additional worsted stuff, the salability of which in Lübeck she was uncertain. Besides, she had another plan.

Speaking with Thorsten and Matthias, she instructed them to distribute half of the fighting men from onboard *der Greif* to *Seelöwe*. That way, if they should be attacked on the voyage to Lübeck, each ship's company would be reinforced. Christina shuddered as she recalled how her brother's vessel, *der Heiligen Maria*, had been separated from *der Greif* on her voyage from Lübeck and taken.

I will not allow such a thing to happen again, she declared, offering a brief prayer for the soul of her brother.

As the masters of the two ships departed to seek out Reiniken and Alan, Christina felt once more at a loss as to how to while away the evening.

I agreed with the bailiff it is probably unwise for our men to be turned loose on the town after the deaths of two of their own. Besides, it's never wise to let a crew celebrate the night before sailing, especially if one plans an early morning departure. But two of us should not be a problem, should it? she pondered innocently, then went to fetch Ziesolf.

Shortly thereafter, they were again seated in The Golden Fleece, enjoying roasted capon with small loaves of suety black bread with their ale. While they ate, Christina glanced ruefully upwards, imagining the comfortable room somewhere above their heads for which she had already paid. She reluctantly dismissed the thought of spending her final night at the inn, somewhat convincing herself such a splendid repast instead of ship's store was reward enough.

Their meal finished, the two set out to return to *der Greif*. By now, the streets were dark, save for a few puddles of light outside of a tavern or two where torches were lit. As they turned toward the river, even these disappeared, forcing them to navigate by the sliver of the moon in the night sky.

Suddenly, loud voices broke their companionable silence. A hundred yards or so to their fore a group of four men appeared, seemingly well down in their cups. They swayed toward Christina and Ziesolf, sharing laughter, shouts, and a couple of jugs from which they took frequent pulls. As they neared, Christina cast a sideways glance at Ziesolf.

"Something seems amiss here. Their laughter seems wooden, almost forced. They put the jug to their lips, but do not tip it up enough to drink," she whispered.

"Aye," Ziesolf, muttered from the side of his mouth, "They seem more intent on intersecting our path than being on their way. Beware here, I think."

Ziesolf angled slightly away from the men toward the other side of the street, followed closely by Christina. Their actions were mirrored by the seemingly gregarious group, who now called out to Ziesolf, offering to share their drink. They closed to within about ten feet suspiciously fast, especially for ones supposedly heavily inebriated.

They moved as if to pass between Ziesolf and Christina. The outward man of the group seemed to misjudge the distance and looked as though he would inadvertently bump into her. At the last second, she saw the glimmer of a long knife blade appear in his hand, its sharp tip moving toward the center of her stomach. She grabbed his hand in both of hers and twisted it violently, forcing his arm behind his back and thrusting the blade deep into his own kidney. The man groaned heavily and fell to his knees for a second or two before fully collapsing upon the cobbles.

Christina grabbed her cloak with her left hand and threw it in the face of the next assailant. He used his left arm to intercept the garment while he advanced another step, threatening her with a massive filthy meat cleaver that looked capable of easily chopping ox bones. Christina's sword leaped from its scabbard, then forward into a thrust that neatly skewered the man's neck. She retracted her blade, his neck gurgling blood even after his hand found the wound and tried in vain to staunch the spray. As he collapsed, she saw Ziesolf calmly cleaning his sword blade on the tunic of one of the two men dead at his feet.

"What took you so long?" he asked innocently. "I thought to take the second of yours, but then considered it more polite to share equally. So, should we just leave them here, hoping we can get away in the morning before they are discovered? I don't believe anyone saw what transpired."

"No, I don't think so," Christina responded, retrieving her cloak and wiping her blade on her second victim. "If they are found, the bailiff will certainly infer our men are involved. His investigation could well delay our departure. I am certainly loath to spend even one additional hour in this damnable town, let alone what might be days."

They returned with the bailiff within the hour and found the scene just as they had left it. Bateman immediately moved to examine the wounds on the bodies to ensure they correlated with the information Christina had provided on the way there. Afterwards, he asked to see their swords, examining each closely. He then smelled the weapons deeply before returning them to their owners.

"It appears to have likely happened as you related, Sir Frederick," the bailiff said. "The wounds are as you described them and match the blades of your weapons. Although you have already wiped your blades dry, the rusty iron smell of fresh blood is still upon them. Thus, it seems you have done the killing yourselves, in what appears to be self-defense."

"Thank you, Master Bailiff," Christina replied courteously.

Bateman's mouth pursed into a sour smile.

"Yes, self-defense, but there are factors involved here well beyond my ken. You say you have done nothing to offend anyone; yet, the bodies stack up around you like baker's loaves. The only lead you can provide concerns a mysterious man whom no one seems to know. It seems violence is prone to follow in your wake as hungry gulls do the herring fleet. Although I do not believe you are to blame here, you do seem to be the catalyst. Please leave our town in the morning, or I will need to take more drastic measures."

Christina nodded vigorously. Although departing had already been her intent, it did not hurt to let the bailiff believe his words had an immediate effect. Leaving Bateman to his work, Christina and Ziesolf walked the remaining way back to the wharf quickly. Once aboard, Christina spent most of the night awake, praying no other incident would occur to impede them from departing.

The tide began to ebb an hour past sunup and the lines were loosened from the mooring pilings. Slowly, the two ships began to pull out into the middle of the river where the current was strongest. The day was overcast and cold, leaving Christina shivering slightly. She was about to return to her cabin when she saw a figure appear on the wharf where her ships had been tied only a few minutes prior.

Richard.

His gaze upon her held such malevolence that it seemed almost palpable.

The man lifted his gloved right hand until it was at eye level, then reached his left over and slowly removed the glove from the other, revealing only a thumb and forefinger. The other three fingers had been neatly cut away.

"Richard!" she screamed with white-hot loathing. "You puking sard-dribble How could I not have been certain this had your foul stench on it all along? This time, nothing short of God's own mighty hand will stay me from my vengeance!"

She turned toward the man at the tiller.

"Turn the ship about, Matthias! Take us back to the fucking wharf, I say!"

Suddenly, she felt a hand on her arm. She spun about, pushing Ziesolf roughly away in an act so unexpected he nearly fell to the deck headfirst before catching himself on the ship's freeboard. She seemed not to see him as he again approached, this time holding both of her shoulders firmly.

"Belay that command, Matthias," he yelled at the helmsman who looked at the two figures in confusion. Then, to Christina, he said, "You do not want to do this. You have no proof against the man. He disposed of all who could connect him to his crimes. Bateman can do nothing without evidence."

Christina pushed Ziesolf away.

"Who was it that said anything about the damned bailiff? I will hunt the son of a bitch down myself, rip his heart from his chest, and shove it up his ass for good measure! Do you not recall what he has done to me?"

"I do remember," Ziesolf replied softly. "You have every right to take his life; but it is the cost for this that I cannot allow you to pay. For a stranger to kill a man, one who has now established himself within the town, would be viewed as an act of unmitigated murder, regardless of your claims to the otherwise. Although Bateman appears to be an honest and diligent official, he has made it plain his toleration for us grows thin. To return to Norwich simply to murder one of its citizens will not likely regain his favor."

"If Matthias will not turn the ship about, I will swim to shore myself," Christina declared, sitting down on the hatch cover and beginning to take off her boots."

"With a sword strapped to you?" Matthias asked mildly. "Already the distance grows wide to the shore. Are you certain this is a wise course of action?"

Frustrated beyond her ability to control herself, she muttered, "Go fuck yourself, old man, and everyone else can as well!" before stomping off to her cabin and slamming the door shut behind her.

It was early in the afternoon before she felt certain enough in her ability to control the fury that seethed within her to reappear back on deck. Although several of the ship's complement were performing various tasks in the area, they avoided going near her for fear of evoking her wrath. Even Reiniken, upon seeing her, disappeared into the hold, evidently preferring the company of the ship's rats to her foul mood. She moved to the deserted forecastle of the ship, hoping to cool her burning rage.

The cold spray of the sea on Christina's face was a welcome relief. She saw with satisfaction they were sailing almost due east, making for the waters near the Frisian coast. She knew Matthias would then navigate northward into the Skagerrak, then southward through the Kattegat and into the Baltic Sea. With favorable winds, they could near Lübeck in a couple of weeks.

If not, who knows? she thought pessimistically.

She turned and gazed sternward. The ship's huge rectangular sail was almost squarely set and was well filled, confirming her earlier appraisal of *der Greif's* course. She was not so pleased by what she saw off the starboard beam, however. In the far distance, some four or five leagues astern of *Seelöwe*, two other ships labored on what appeared to be an identical course.

"They've been on our asses for the past few hours or so," Ziesolf said, walking up the stairs to join Christina on the forecastle. "We've begun to pull away now, either through a shift in wind or Matthias' superior seamanship."

"They may be innocent enough," Christina remarked. "After all, there is no promise we are to have the entire sea to ourselves. But, with all the talk of pirates, do you think we should heave to and discover if their intentions are good or bad?"

"Well, I know putting sword to a few murderous rogues would likely brighten your temperament, but I don't believe you are set on clearing the world's oceans of every last knave who preys upon the weakness of others. Besides, every skirmish has the possibility of weakening us in some way, either through loss of men or damages to our ship. Better to conserve our resources for the battles we have sworn to fight, rather than waste them on those we have not."

Although she would have liked to pose an argument, Christina chose to bite her tongue

As always, his words make sense, Although, with the mood I'm in right now, I can think of nothing more satisfying than matching steel with some belligerent lout.

Seelöwe and *der Greif* did not slacken their speed, nor did the other ships continue their possible pursuit. Gradually, their mysterious followers changed their heading a few points southward until they were no more than two dark dots. Finally, they disappeared altogether. Christina was left alone with her ships, the sea and sky, and her black thoughts of those who schemed to do her ill.

Chapter 8

Changing Tactics
The Baltic Sea, May, 1311

Two weeks after their departure from Norwich, Christina's thirst for action became a reality.

"Sorry sons-of-whores, just like when they attacked my father's ships three years ago! Have they no imagination?" Christina muttered, keeping a close watch on the small, swift vessels closing on them through the calm waters to their starboard side.

"If it is a successful tactic, why would they have reason to change? There are very few who escape their clutches to disclose their strategies to others," Ziesolf replied, his good eye fixed in the same direction.

It was a motley flotilla bearing down on them, fixing to pin Christina's larger, slower cog between them and the marshy shallows along the Jutland coastal expanse. In a favorable wind, they might have been able to distance themselves from the two pursuing vessels, each half the size of *der Greif.* They had no chance of doing so, however, against the three fast and maneuverable schnigges that accompanied them, especially as they were capable of running down their prey through the use of oars, if need be.

And they have the wind, what little there is of it, Christina murmured to herself as *der Greif* crawled along at about two knots per hour, *and what they believe to be an easy quarry. But perhaps we are not so helpless after all, eh?*

The two ewer ships could carry fifty or more fighting men each, but likely no more than twenty to thirty. Added to the fifteen or twenty onboard each of the schnigges and their foes would conservatively number nearly a hundred. Luckily, only three or four of the enemy vessels could attack at one time, but that seemed more than enough. The men would be armed with their preferred weapons of choice; falchions, axes, maces, and only Satan himself knew what else. A few may have crossbows, a good weapon to demoralize a normal crew into surrendering without a fight.

Against this threat, the crew of *der Greif* numbered just fourteen souls - valiant men all who knew how to fight, but clearly unable to mount more than a futile resistance against such a number.

At least that's what those Danish bastards believe they will be facing, Christina thought with quiet satisfaction.

Der Greif's crew would be reinforced by Reiniken and his men, vicious brawlers who knew how to scrap in a free-for-all, whether in a tavern or on a deck at sea. Combined with the advantage provided by the high freeboard integral to the cog's design, she relished the image of the bloody mayhem these men would exact on any of the attackers who raised their stupid heads over the ship's sides.

If they even do.

Divided between the two castles at the bow and stern of the vessel were Alan, Godfrey, and the ten other archers. Before each was a wooden trough, filled with dirt. The heads of dozens of arrows were thrust into the soft earth. Although Christina believed their insistence upon readying their arrows in this manner to be no pure superstition, she had readily agreed, wanting nothing to interfere with their ability to swiftly mete out death upon their unsuspecting assailants.

For now, they crouched out of sight beneath the railings. When Christina gave the signal, they would spring up and search out their initial targets, followed by what she hoped would be a series of several more.

She and Ziesolf had decided the archers would loosen their first arrows when the attacking ships closed to within about 150 feet. This was still beyond the effective range of any crossbowmen, who probably would not be prepared to fire their weapons anyway at that distance, believing their victims to not possess ranged weapons of any kind. Consequently, her archers' first task would be to eliminate any enemy bowmen before their weapons could be brought to bear.

After that, God willing, it will turn into a fucking slaughter.

Despite the greater agility of the smaller vessels, it still would take several minutes for the pirates to turn their vessels and work their way out of her archers' range. During that time, the bowmen would maintain a withering rate of fire, sweeping their open and unprotected decks.

And then we will merrily sail away, she thought, although not without worry as she was well aware plans never seemed to work as successfully as one imagined.

The schnigges were closer now, their angle of approach narrowing, like a pack of bounding hounds cutting off the escape of a great stag. The only seeming alternatives for *der Greif's* master now would be to surrender outright or succumb to a vicious and deadly boarding.

"Do you believe the schnigges will attack on their own, or will they merely attempt to harry and slow us until the ewers catch up?" Christina asked.

"Why would they wait? I am sure they believe each are our equal in numbers, and their inferiors in fighting skill. Much preferable to capture us and split our cargo among three crews than delay to let the larger ships take the lion's share."

The lead ship was now less than a league away, Christina could pick out some details now from what had been only an hour or so before a tiny dark speck. The sail was now visible, and she believed she could discern two or three heads moving about in the bow, although this may only have been her imagination.

There was a gentle roll upon the water, not even enough to put the few gulls that bobbed noisily alongside *der Greif's* starboard side to flight.

We have been truly blessed by the weather on this voyage, praise *be to God. Even the men aboard who have never ventured into deep water have suffered few effects of seasickness. At the mouth of the Trave, when we took back aboard the fighting men who had been detailed to Seelöwe, all seemed to be hale and in good spirits. Since then, our luck has held and the sea is doing little to disrupt the aim of our bowmen today.*

She could clearly make out figures on the small, fast pursuing ships as they had closed to under half a league.

"The greedy bastards are prob'ly already countin' how many whores their share of their prize will buy 'em," Reiniken laughed as he joined them. "Little do they know the only tits they'll be squeezin' today are those of the Valkyries carryin' them off to fuckin' Valhalla!"

"Don't get overconfident, Reiniken," Ziesolf warned.

"Can ya believe old One-Eye?" the huge man said to Christina, shaking his shaggy head heavily from side to side. "Ah swear he'd worry his balls away if he held -em in his hand. What is it that could goes wrong?"

Christina was torn between Ziesolf's air of caution and Reiniken's confidence.

A good place to be, she decided thoughtfully.

"Ah, see how those two surge to pull ahead, while the third adjusts its course to intercept us. That way, they can attack us from the front and both sides. If the fighting lasts longer than expected, they still have the two ewers to take us from the rear," Ziesolf observed. "It will not be long now."

Christina grasped the starboard braces tightly to quell her mounting excitement.

The old knight's words were prophetic as no more than a half-hour later, the first two ships had crossed their bow a few thousand feet before them. As expected, they lowered their sails, now relying exclusively on the banks of oars that lined their sides to propel their ships. With the maneuverability this strategy provided, a confrontation between *der Greif* and the enemy craft could seemingly now only be averted through divine intervention.

"And it looks like God has no interest in interfering here today," Christina muttered, causing the bowmen squatting beside her in the forecastle to turn their heads in surprise.

She glanced to the right, happy to see the other schnigge no more than five hundred feet off their side. With luck, they would be able to engage all these ships more or less simultaneously.

As *der Greif* neared the two craft before it, Christina was able to make out three or four crossbowmen in the bow of each ship. She relayed this information to her bowmen, who acknowledged her words with a simple nod.

Good. Our archers should be able to take out their ranged weapons with their first volley. With any luck, that is.

Unexpectedly, one of the pirates in the lead craft waived a signal to the ship off their now starboard beam.

Of, course, thought Cristina, wolfishly exposing her teeth. *They believe their best advantage lays in their men attacking us simultaneously. The bastards don't realize they are playing exactly into our hands!*

At that, the approach of the boats, which had playing out over the past hours as if in a slow-motion dream, was followed by a burst of action.

"Now!" Christina yelled, turning to waive frantically to Ziesolf, who had moved to join the second contingent of bowmen hidden in the stern castle. He relayed her order and the six archers arose, almost immediately finding targets upon their starboard foe.

By the time she returned her attention to her surroundings, she was amazed to see most of the men were already reaching for their third or even fourth arrow. Christina's attention now shifted to assess the effects of their barrage. What she saw below her was utter devastation.

Every crossbowman was slouched this way or that, his lifeless body punctured deeply with at least two arrows in his head or upper torso. Behind them, several of their companions had suffered a similar fate, some still gripping their oars; a were few scattered about open decks that had offered little concealment from the fire that had rained down on them. Without sail or any rowers left to propel them, the small ships drifted slowly toward *der Greif*, where Alan and his companions snuffed out the screams and moans of the few of their crews still living with the same deftness as two moist fingers on a candle's flame. The archers in the bow then shifted their aim to the remaining men about the starboard ship, its sail still drawing it closer toward Christina's cog, despite assuredly there being none aboard who wished it to do so.

"Should we be ready to hop aboard, in case a few of the bastards want to surrender?" Reiniken asked.

She had not considered that possibility. Her thoughts went back a year and a half, to the first time she had sailed these waters.

I had been hardly more than a child then. But would they have granted mercy to me, especially when they found I was a girl? No, they each would have taken a turn on me, as well as Trudi, before they sold us to slavers in the east. Or, if they fancied us sufficiently, they would have kept us, to be raped again and again, until they tired of their sport. They offered no quarter to Father, or Frederick. They can expect none from me!

"No! We are too few to take prisoners. I want no man aboard risking himself unnecessarily. Let our arrows give answer to their cowardly pleading!"

Reiniken looked at her strangely, as if seeing her truly for the first time. Then he nodded, returning to the main deck to be ready in case she changed her mind. She did not.

Among the few of the schnigge's crew still numbering among the living, some begged for mercy, while the rest could only voice guttural groans. Blood was everywhere, mostly pooling below deep arrow wounds but, at times, spraying spectacularly into the air from nicked arteries. As her archers put a merciful end to the remaining pirates' suffering, Christina's resolve weakened. She felt a familiar lurch in her belly and considered making her way to her cabin, rather than further witnessing such slaughter.

You will stay, damn you! Christina ordered herself. *You cannot ask others to do what you cannot stomach.*

"Matthias!" she shouted to her ship's master. "Take in the sail! Then get some men aboard to get those schnigges under control!"

Matthias had been ready for her order. He ordered men to the rigging lines, who adjusted *der Greif's* course slightly to alleviate any damage that might result from the impact of the inevitable collision with the onrushing schnigge. Even so, there was a loud thump when the two ships ground together, causing several of those aboard *der Greif* to reach out to solid wood to steady themselves. On the other ship, there were none left alive to do so.

Seconds later, the great sheet of linen was dropped and *der Greif* immediately lost what little way it had. It now bobbed upon the placid sea, floating calmly amongst its three victims.

Leaving Matthias to secure their prizes, Christina and the archers from the bow hurried to join their fellows astern. Mounting the castle, she was relieved to see the ewers still closing, now only several thousand feet astern.

"They believe everything has gone to plan, not realizing it has gone to shit for them instead," Ziesolf said with a thin smile.

"Aye," She replied, "And I want them to keep thinking that, until it's too late for them too. Alan, have your archers lay their bows against the railing. I have need for you to be actors as well."

Alan appeared befuddled.

"Now, I want you to engage in what appears to be a desperate struggle with each other, only for the love of Christ be careful you don't trip and go over the side. This should draw their ships nearer, as they will believe the fight is still in doubt. Ziesolf, tell the rest of the men to make a mighty clanging with their weapons, with much shouting and profanity thrown in to season the sauce. By the time they realize they are being duped, they'll be within range of our arrows, and you know what that means."

Now realizing Christina's intent, Alan sped away to relay her instructions to his men.

Moments later, the archers were heartily engaged in their ploy, aiming massive blows at each other's heads that missed by inches but, from a distance, looked crushing. A hand directed toward a stomach simulated a knife thrust, causing the recipient to crumple into a dramatic death throe only to rise again a few seconds later like Lazarus. Christina wielded her sword mightily above her head, though her downward blows were directed nowhere near anyone else. Their mock battle may have drawn volleys of rotten vegetables from unimpressed onlookers of a pageant wagon or inn yard, but she hoped it sufficient to deceive the men on the ewers.

Stepping to the rail to catch her breath, Christina took a second to listen to the sounds of simulated fighting around her. Men on the main deck were beating metal against metal, raising a din so mighty she feared for an instant their attackers may find it suspicious. Gazing astern, she was relieved to see the ewers still rushing onward under full sail. She was not, however, so happy to discover one had pulled ahead of the other by a good measure.

"Shit!" she exclaimed to no one in particular.

If they remain like this there is no way we can engage them simultaneously. We cannot withhold our fire on the first, giving the second time to catch up. If we do, we'll undoubtedly be boarded, giving up the advantage of our archers. We'll just have to chance losing the other ewer; *I'll not be endangering any of our men today if I can help it!*

"Take that, you base varlet!" Christina shouted as she reentered the fray, bringing her sword down to within six inches of Gilbert's head in a simulated braining of the man.

Gilbert theatrically scrunched up his face and stuck out his tongue from the side of his mouth before toppling to the deck.

Although each ewer was approximately twice the size of the three small ships *der Greif* had already engaged, the cog's sterncastle still towered over their decks, providing an almost unimpeded view of the length of the ship. As she looked down upon the comparatively slender deck of the other vessel, Christina was amazed to count over thirty of the pirates arrayed before her, each seemingly eager to board what he believed to be what must now be a near-defenseless prize. She was delighted to see none of them holding a crossbow; if any did possess one, he had set it aside for fear of hitting one of his own comrades. Consequently, there was none aboard the pirate's ship to mount even a token ranged defense against her archers.

Because of this, Christina hesitated until the enemy ship had drawn no more than a hundred feet astern and slightly to starboard before giving the longbowmen the order to engage with the enemy. She watched with amazement as the deadly shafts of their arrows found homes in the chests and heads of their unwary quarry. The archers began with the targets furthest away, causing those closer to view with horror the appalling wounds inflicted on their comrades and hear their dying screams. This technique, well known to hunters, caused those in the bow of the ship to freeze in terror, unwilling to flee into what they considered a killing zone. Their inactivity provided them no defense whatsoever and soon they shared the fate of those who had fallen behind them. Within a couple of minutes, Christina could discern no obvious sign of life aboard the enemy vessel.

Having witnessed the end of their unfortunate comrades first-hand, the men of the other ewer were drastically adjusting their sail, seeking to distance between themselves from *der Greif*. A few of the archers found new targets even as the ship began to pull away, reducing its company by at least another five or six men before out of range, heading to the northeast like a whipped cur to lick its wounds.

"Another fuckin' mess ya've gotten us into, Yur Worship," Reiniken exclaimed, looking down at the corpses that littered the other vessels, "Fur a little fucker, ya shure seem to attract death like flies to a sweet pile a shit. The good thing is, it allus seems like the other poor bastards comin' out on the short end of the stick!"

Christina felt her stomach again grow unsettled as she gazed over the lifeless bodies, imagining the scene must resemble the stacked corpses of the men, women, and children outside the city walls of London who had succumbed to the winter cold. Out of the corner of her eye, she was startled to see sudden movement upon the ewer before realizing it was a few of *der Greif's* sailors already striking its mainsail.

"So, what do we do with this lot?" Matthias asked as he walked across the deck toward Christina.

She had not thought about the pirate vessels other than how to achieve their defeat, so it took a bit of time for Christina to realize the intent of his question.

"Do we have enough crewmen to sail them to Lübeck?" she inquired. "We certainly can't leave them just floating here for their brothers to recover and it seems a shame to burn them."

"Aye," Matthias answered, seemingly to everything. "Especially since we didn't lose a single man in the scrap. I'll probably need to use a few of your men to flesh out crews for them. It should be an easy sail of a couple of days, if the weather holds fair, that is. I don't think we need to worry about that other lot returning but, if they do, we should be able to spot them far enough away to bring everyone back aboard and regroup."

"That's what we'll do then. Thank you, Matthias. Let's get at it, shall we?"

As Matthias strode away to arrange the division of the men to provide a skeleton crew for each of the ships, Reiniken cleared his throat and expertly spat a wad of yellow phlegm over the side of *der Greif* to gain Christina's attention.

"'Scuse me, Yur Worship, but what about the spoils?"

Christina was baffled.

"What do you mean, Wig?"

"The spoils," he repeated, gesturing toward the masses of bodies in the ships.

Now understanding, she asked heatedly, "Are we no better than corpse robbers now?"

"It's not the same thing, Master Frederick," Ziesolf interjected. "Unless you have other plans, these men will not receive a burial, with weeping families to mourn them and receive their goods. Instead, they will unceremoniously be dumped into the sea, taking what they have to be shared out amongst the fishes, who care not for trinkets and coins. Better their belongings be distributed amongst the living who risked their lives to put them there."

"I don't know," Christina muttered, mulling the morality of emptying the newly dead's pockets. "It seems sacrilegious."

"It has been a custom on the battlefield since time immemorial. It also prompts the men to fight harder, knowing there is an opportunity for reward after," Ziesolf added.

Somewhat against her Christian sensibilities, she chose to reluctantly agreed.

"Now, how are you going to go about doing it?" Ziesolf asked with a smirk.

"For Christ's sake, what does it matter? Just let them do it!" she said testily, perplexed by yet another unforeseen complication she had no idea how to address.

"Well, if you simply allow the men who board the ships first to take everything, the others will be angry and you're likely to have scuffles on hand, if not outright fighting."

Shit!

Christina mulled over Ziesolf's words.

The last thing I need are divisions and jealously among the men I need to rely on and who must count on each other.

Taking a deep breath, she pondered a minute before replying.

"All right, then. Tell Matthias to have his men search each body before dumping it in the sea, taking anything of value. Instruct them they are to keep nothing for themselves. Everything is to be brought back to *der Greif* and placed upon the deck hatch."

Ziesolf and Reiniken gazed at Christina with intense interest, waiting for her to continue.

"The coin will be totaled and evenly divided. Afterwards, every man will draw lots to see who has first choice among the items that remain. When the final man selects, he will go again, and the process will proceed in reverse. This will continue until everything is gone."

Both men nodded, finding Christina's method of sharing the spoils fair and equitable.

"I will not choose," she continued. "Instead, I claim the ewer as my prize, to dispose of how I decide. The schnigges will be offered for sale in Lübeck, with two-thirds of the proceeds going to the men and the remaining third to me. That is my decision."

Within a couple of hours, the decks of the pirate ships were devoid of the bodies of their previous crews and a large mass of coins, jewelry, weapons, and assorted other goods was strewn across the deck hatch of *der Greif*. Simultaneously, the archers retrieved whatever arrows were salvageable for later use. In the meantime, Christina had numbered thirty-two small bits of parchment, placing them in a wooden bucket over which she placed a scrap of cloth. Each of the men now came forward, placing their hand beneath the cloth and grasping one of the pieces of parchment in his fingers. Some shouted with glee at the selection of a single-digit number, while others cursed heartily, finding theirs to be in the twenties or thirties. Others simply stared at the parchment dumbly, not possessing even the rudimentary skill of recognizing written numbers, delaying their reaction until one of their mates informed them of their selection.

It was a pleasant enough diversion for men whose lives had been at risk only a few hours prior.

The first to choose was Gilbert, the young archer, who selected a silver ring with a glistening purple amethyst inset. Gotz, the assistant helmsman, chose an enamel and gold bracelet. Each man took his turn after that, selecting mostly jewelry, except Tiny Tom, who was pleased with his selection of a beautifully tooled Byzantine sword. Their comrade Henry, however, had an eye for something else. Among the remaining articles was a pair of heavy leather boots so enormous Christina could have fitted both her feet inside one of them.

Henry grabbed them when it came his turn and, smiling blissfully, pulled them onto his large, filthy feet, exclaiming, "Ah've niver had the lak before!"

"Jesus! It must a taken a full-grown bull fur each boot, Henry!" Reiniken hooted as the rest of the company joined in the laughter.

Henry minded them not, pleased as he was with his new prize.

Christina's attention shifted from the men's levity to a small object revealed after Henry grabbed the boots from the hatch. It was a small, but distinctive, gold filigree and enamel cross upon a delicate gold chain. Her brother Frederick had worn an identical one nearly every day since their father gifted it to him for his twelfth birthday.

It must be his!

Her mouth fell open in disbelief.

She was barely able to restrain herself from rushing forward, remembering the rules she had set forth for divvying the spoils.

A few more men made their choices and then it was Reiniken's turn. He carefully looked over the remaining items, then stuck his meaty paw forward and grasped Frederick's cross and chain. Christina audibly gasped as she saw her family heirloom disappear from the hatch cover.

Soon, the remaining items were apportioned and the men dispersed to their assigned ships.

Christina went to her cabin filled with overwhelming melancholy. Unexpectedly, she heard a heavy thudding at her door. She opened it to find the massive bulk of Reiniken almost completely filling the space before her.

"God be with ya, Yur Worship," he began, seemingly somewhat embarrassed.

"And you, Wig. What can I do for you?"

"Well, ya see, Ah noticed ya lookin' at this little trinket, lak Ah never seen ya pine fur somethin' before. So, Ah thoughts it must mean somethin' to ya. And since ya'd already said ya wasn't taking a turn, I thoughts the only way ya could get it is if'n somebody got it fur ya. Well, that somebody was me, I guess."

Reiniken held the cross out and dropped it into her hand.

"Thank you, Wig. It does mean a great deal to me. It belonged to my . . . sister, the one who died on the journey to London. Let me pay you for it."

She fumbled for her purse.

"Naw!" Reiniken said sharply, "Yuv been very good to me, you and yur household. I niver had a family, but youse are about the closest thing to it. It's a gift, Master Frederick, and ya don't expect to be paid fur a gift, do ya?"

"No, Wig, I wouldn't," Christina said softly, "But thank you nonetheless. You have no idea how much this means to me."

"Well, I better be getting' back to my duties, before we start slobberin' all over each other. Besides, that whoreson Matthias will put his boot up my ass if I don't."

With that, he abruptly left, although Christina stood for several minutes in her doorway, examining the cross before finally admitting to herself it not what her father had given Frederick. Her smile remained, however, her heart warmed at Reiniken's unexpected generosity.

It was not a quick return to Lübeck. Matthias felt it best for the flotilla of undermanned vessels to remain bunched together. As a result, they were restricted to travel at the speed of the slowest amongst them, which changed often as the inexperienced crews of the smaller boats sometimes lost the wind entirely.

At least the weather remains fair and there has been no further harassment from pirate vessels, Christina thought, pleased with her continued good fortune.

Now, *der Greif* and the other members of her little flotilla stood once more outside the mouth of the Trave. Though she should have been happy they arrived without incident, her mind was troubled by another sort of problem instead.

Should I risk going to visit my mother? If I am seen by someone I know, my entire masquerade could be unraveled. Or am I using this reason merely as an excuse?

Christina had no doubts the news of the four pirate vessels' capture would spread through Lübeck like a raging fire.

It would be common knowledge that the captain who orchestrated such a victory was Frederick Kohl, son of Mechtild Kohl and her late alderman husband, Thomas. Surely, all the Kohl family's acquaintances would call by the house on Engelsgrube to convey their congratulations. There was no way Christina's mother would not know her daughter was nearby.

Mechtild would expect Christina to visit her, albeit in her guise as Frederick. But what if she tried to dissuade her from returning to her task of ferreting out pirates, believing it too dangerous for a young woman, just as Trudi did before Christina traveled to Berwick. Could she openly defy her mother? What if she inadvertently disclosed that Christina was her daughter, not her son, to her houseguests? And what about the family maid, Anna? Could she be trusted?

Oh, my damnable head hurts! Christina thought miserably.

As usual, Christina sought out Ziesolf for counsel, both for his wisdom and the fact he was the only one who knew both her eagerness to visit her mother and why she would be reluctant to do so.

"Hmm," he said, gazing intently into her face.

"What do you mean 'Hmm?'" she responded in frustration. "Can you not provide me better advice than that?"

"It is difficult for me to say, as you are not being honest with yourself, I think. In addition to the reasons you gave, I believe you also fear confronting the ghosts that haunt your memories. How many times have you called out in your sleep to Marguerite, or Frederick, or your father? I think you are not yet ready to walk the halls where you once laughed and loved with them."

Christina said nothing, but her thoughts churned furiously.

Could that truly be the reason for my hesitancy?

"When you saw the cross that somewhat resembled that worn by Frederick, I believed you would leap forth and snatch it. So eager were you to gain something you believed to be his you would break the rules you yourself set to gain it."

"Christ's Holy Cods! Does your singular old eye miss nothing?"

"The fact remains it is a great risk for you to enter Lübeck, whatever other factors trouble you to do so," he continued, ignoring her outburst. "Perhaps it would be better if it is me who goes in command of the captured vessels. I believe I am known sufficiently within the council of the aldermen to be accepted in your stead, if they so summon you. I will also call on your mother, conveying the news you are well and plan to visit her soon. To put her off is the best I can do, I am afraid. I have too much respect for the woman to tell her that her daughter may return to London without speaking with her, for I would then be the cause for rending her heart, I think. If that is what you wish, I will not be a part of it."

Ziesolf looked at her silently, waiting patiently for her decision.

Christina hesitated, mulling over her options.

Doesn't he realize to not see her would break my heart as well? she thought as she fought to control the growing lump in her throat.

In the end she decided she must accept Ziesolf's offer.

"Yes, I believe what you say seems the best course of action. Please also contact Thorsten and have him bring our men back to *der Greif* along with fresh provisions. I would like to speak to him concerning the state of trade in the town."

Ziesolf walked toward the door.

"And Kurt?" she asked in a quiet voice.

"Aye?" he asked, looking back.

"Thank you . . . for understanding."

Three days hence, Ziesolf and the others returned aboard *Seelöwe*. As the men went about transferring the supplies from ship to ship, Thorsten found Christina on the sterncastle observing their activity.

"God's days have been good to you, Master Frederick," he said with a happy expression. "It seems your plans could not have worked any better. Congratulations on your great victory."

"Thank you, Thorsten," she replied, slightly embarrassed by his praise. "And Our Lord's blessing on you as well. How is life among the merchants of Lübeck?"

"Not so well, it seems. The harsh winter past has put a great strain on the resources of the city and it's only the fact of its great wealth that has minimized the hardship of its citizenry."

Thank God their suffering has been comparatively light, she thought, remembering the grim toll the cold had taken among the people of London

But grain reserves had dipped lower than ever in recent memory and a favorable harvest in Prussia was fervently prayed for in all the city's churches. The winter has also driven the pirates to become even more voracious than in years past, which were bad enough in their own right. As yet, there was no word from the *Winterfahrer* to Novgorod the Great. This was expected since the ice of the far eastern Baltic had not yet melted, let alone that upon the Volkhov River. So, Lübeck's merchants waited, and what trade did transpire was of a low level.

"It's most troubling to hear there are hard times even here," she said.

The great circle of trade amongst the four major *kontore*, or major trade outposts of the Hansa, had been stilled by the winter. The furs, honey, and wax of Novgorod would soon flow southward, destined for London and its ancillary ports. English wool would be passed on to Bruges and other Flemish towns to be woven into rich fabrics highly prized in the Russian principalities. Flowing southward, from the other major entrepot, Bergen, were vast numbers of barrels of salted herring and slabs of dried codfish, essential commodities to every market, as they were required to feed the populace on the many meatless days specified by the Church. When this interchange of products was disrupted, whether by piracy or weather, everyone suffered, but especially the merchants.

After exchanging words of encouragement and hopes for continued good fortune with Christina, Thorsten departed, to be replaced by Ziesolf a few minutes later.

"Your mother sends you her love, Christina," he spoke in a low voice, to ensure no one overheard him address her by her true name. "She is disappointed she will have to wait to see you in person, but understands your need for caution. She says she is well and has no reason to ask God for anything, beyond your own continued health and safety. She sends you this."

He set the middling-sized wooden box he was carrying down on the deck and stepped back. Curious, Christina went to her knees and reached forward to pry the lid from the container. As she did, her nose was assailed by a range of aromas recalled with fondness. The slightly acrid smell of jellied lampreys made identifying the small container's contents quite simple. Her heart leaped as she opened a roll of parchment to find a dozen fresh almond tarts. Five more of her favorite foods were also present, a fortune of culinary delicacies.

"Your mother said, 'The best gift to give my Christina is one that ends up in her belly.' From the expression, she still knows you very well, eh?" Ziesolf beamed at her obvious pleasure.

"Yes, she does," Christina said softly, choking back the lump in her throat.

I should have visited her myself, she thought, realizing her mistake.

"Now, about the sale of the captured ships. There were no immediate offers, but Thorsten feels confident there will be growing interest over the coming weeks as the days grow warmer. The ewer, as you directed, is safely birthed and will be inspected and repaired as needed."

"Yes, well done," she replied automatically, still turning over in her mind what a terrible blunder she had made in deciding not to call on her mother.

"As to the news concerning the city's campaign against the pirates. The results have been very lukewarm at best, save for your own. Three ships have had encounters, with no vessels captured and one lost. The aldermen claim victory, of course, as several of the freebooters were killed. Although more men of Lübeck's fleet died, the town's manpower resources are much greater as well. Consequently, the aldermen portray it as a war of attrition, which has not been popular among the populace as it is they and their friends and families being sacrificed."

"As always, it is the leaders who are so brave with the lives of others, while they risk nothing" she commented bitterly.

"Which brings us to you, the darling now of Lübeck's masses. When I informed the council of aldermen of our victory, they expressed disbelief, coming near to calling me a liar, if you can believe that. It took them seeing the ships with their own eyes, to convince them your utter defeat of the pirates was real."

"I bet that left a sour taste in the bastards' mouths."

Ziesolf smiled.

"In public, they congratulated you, although it seems they took undue credit for masterminding your victories when, as we both know, their only part was in directing the letter that brought you here. Now, they fete you as der Löwe, a veritable reincarnation of Lübeck's founder, Henry the Lion."

Christina snorted.

"Maybe they will give me a statue on the market square, or some such ridiculous shit. If so, I hope they make it a naked one with massive cock and balls!"

They both laughed uproariously before Ziesolf continued.

"They have also directed you to appear before them at your earliest convenience - probably to constrain your campaign so you do not outshine the efforts of the others more directly under their control. Actual victory matters little in comparison to their own prestige, I am afraid."

"As it always seems to be," Christina agreed. "Well, there is scant possibility of my accepting their invitation, now or ever. Someone would quickly call me out as an imposter of the great Frederick Kohl!"

She hesitated a few seconds before adding, "Not to change the subject, but I have been thinking."

"An always dangerous thing," Ziesolf interjected.

Christina screwed her face into what she hoped was an offensive scowl then continued.

"Should we not allow the other half of our men to enjoy a couple of days in the town as well? It would seem only just. I would hate for them to believe themselves ill-treated in comparison to their fellows."

Ziesolf considered the idea for a minute before replying.

"No," he answered at last. "Under normal circumstances, it would make sense to eliminate any reason for jealousy amongst the men, especially when the company is as factionalized as it already is. But, if our departure is delayed, it would be difficult to deny the aldermen's command. You would be forced to appear before them and the entire city would turn out to behold the return of the prodigal son. It would only take one person with a loud mouth to recognize you for who you are - or are not - and to create a disaster for you that would far outweigh a few mildly disgruntled subordinates. No, I strongly advise we leave at once."

Christina was chagrined by the old knight's counsel, but knew he was right in his reasoning.

But if we allowed our voyage to be delayed, it would provide me the opportunity to visit my mother, righting my previous wrong. Am I to be denied all chance at redemption?

It seemed she already knew the answer to that.

With the transfer of the remaining provisions from *Seelöwe* now completed, Christina bid Thorsten farewell.

Her final words to her sailing master were, "Should the aldermen question you as to my whereabouts, tell them I have returned to the hunt. If they need to speak to me, direct them to the location where the pirates most frequent and I will be more than happy to hear them."

Thorsten agreed to do as she asked and offered his hand, which she grasped firmly.

"Good luck and Godspeed, Master Frederick. . . and good hunting," he added.

Christina watched the man return to his own vessel.

After a few minutes, a familiar sound drew her back to the deck of *der Greif*. Already, the slight wind was beginning to swell the sail of the ship, moving it steadily away from land. She gazed back toward *Seelöwe*, resting at anchor until the slack tide signaled when the ship could begin its return upriver to Lübeck. Eventually, the vessel became indistinguishable from the greenish black sea and greying skies that engulfed it.

Four days later, *der Greif* rocked gently to and fro, restrained by its anchor chain a quarter-mile off the lichen-covered rocks of the Eastern Coast of the island of Anholt. Christina stood on the sterncastle, gazing out with growing concern at the thickening fogbank rolling toward her from the Swedish mainland.

To remain at anchor was all they could do for the time being. There were far too many shoals, sandbanks, and shallows to sail about blindly. Plus, the island afforded some protection against approaching pirate vessels from one direction at least.

A sizeable group of men congregated on the main deck, just forward of the mast. Realizing large gatherings on sea voyages often indicated growing unrest, Christina grew somewhat alarmed. As she moved to investigate, her fears evaporated as she heard Reiniken speaking in an uncommonly low voice.

"Aye, it wur about twenty years ago, in this very spot, that mi pa sawr it. A low fogbank caught 'em unawares, and they soon found themselves in pitch black, tho' it were the middle of the day. Everythin' went quiet-like, then the seals on the island there started their damn barkin', like ten thousand hell hounds announcin' the comin' of old Scratch himself. Then, quiet again until a rushin' sound started, like a swift ship cuttin' through the water with a gale wind fillin' its sail."

Reiniken's audience of archers, toughs, and sailors stood captivated, hanging on his every word. Christina had to admit she wasn't too far from the same. She waited impatiently for him to take a swig of ale before continuing.

"Then, they sees it! It was the *stoor worm*! Dragon worm! Two hundred feet long with a head as big as a house!"

"Well, what was it? A dragon or a worm? It sure as fuck can't be both," grumbled Henry.

"Shut yur hole and let 'im finish, fur the love 'a Christ!" old Gotz replied.

Christina was certain he had most probably heard Reiniken's version of the story before.

"Like I wuz sayin'," Reiniken glared at Henry, "it was a big fucker, with eyes thet glowed and flamed like an All-Hollows bonfire, and it was comin' straight for mi pa's ship! It opened its jaws and out flicked a forked tongue, which it used like a pair of smith's tongs to pick up the ship and shake it in the air like a terrier does a big rat! Well, mi pa wuz thrown out, landin' by luck in the soft lichen on the island over there."

The men in the audience looked around nervously, both in the direction the tale teller had indicated as well as toward the fog bank that had now narrowed their world to only a few thousand feet in the other direction.

"The others were not so lucky. *The stoor worm* dived down into the water, still holdin' the ship tight. It never came back up, or so mi' pa said."

"What happened next?" asked Gilbert, the archer.

"Well, mi pa knew the Danish king owned a huntin' lodge on the island, so he figured he might be able to hold up there 'til another ship came. So's, he goes there, opens the door, and what do ya think he finds?"

The men looked at each other, but no one ventured a guess.

A great hall full of bullshit, just like this story, Christina thought wryly, but held her tongue. *Let them steady their nerves with a bit of amusement. The whole ship's company can't very well stand at their stations for hours on end with weapons in hand, imagining every fleck in the distance to be our enemy. Besides, a double watch has already been set. What more can I do?*

"A great hall," Reiniken seemed to have stolen Christina's thoughts. "A vast chamber, with tables and benches enough to feast a thousand men. But that weren't what really caught his eye. What did were seven gorgeous young women, three with hair of red, three of gold, and one of darkest black. They wore skirts of precious fabrics that would make His Worship's little cock hard; silks, brocades, and the likes. But mi pa weren't lookin' at their skirts neither."

Not one of the men said a word now, so captivated were they by Reiniken's skill as a storyteller.

"Above the jeweled belts of their skirts they wore not a damned thing! Their tits were right there for anyone to see! Mi pa can't take his eyes off em, having never seen such a variety of shapes and sizes of women's tits at one time. Then they start coming toward him, and he gets embarrassed like, thinking they're gonna yell at him for staring at their bare chests. But, no. Instead, they take him by the hand and lead him into a bed chamber where they spend the night fuckin' him every which way."

The fog has now completely enveloped the ship, cutting visibility down to no more than a few feet.

"He sleeps late," Reiniken continued, "worn out by his efforts of the night before. When he gets up, the women are nowhere in sight, but he hears em, you know. So, he goes to the window and looks out into the sea. Well, there they are swimmin' and frolickin' in the water. But when one dives down, he don't see legs. No, it's a fish tail instead! He'd been fuckin' a school of mermaids! They never came back on shore to share his bed after that, just swim around temptin' him from the water. That is until nine months later, when the one with black hair comes ashore one night with her belly all swollen. In no time at all, she squeezes out a whelp, and gives it to mi pa, then slips back into the ocean."

His enthralled audience leaned forward, hanging on Reiniken's every word.

He looks at it and it's the handsomest little bastard any father could hope for, 'cept for one thing. It's got a fuckin' tail, like its ma. Well, he thinks, there's just one thing to do. He takes out his guttin' knife and splits the tail down the middle, so's its now like a pair of legs instead. Shortly after, a ship comes ashore and takes em back to the mainland."

"What about the boy?" demanded Gilbert, "What happened to his son?"

"Well, ya sees, thet wee one grew up to be me," Reiniken responded calmly.

"What a load of horse shit!" declared Henry, the others nodding and muttering their agreement.

"I can prove it to you," Reiniken stated matter-of-factly.

This stilled the men completely. They held their tongues, waiting for the huge man to continue.

Reiniken pulled up his shirt and reached swiftly down the front of his braies. Within a second or two his hand reappeared, holding at least a foot's length of inert eel."

"See, I gots me a fish cock!" he shouted, brandishing it toward the other men, who hooted and guffawed uproariously.

Despite her best efforts to restrain herself, Christina's own laughter was amongst the loudest.

She was just about to order the men back to their duties when an enormous din was heard. The air was inundated with what seemed thousands of discordant roars, barks, honks, and growls. The men grew suddenly quiet, looking about wildly gripped by inherent superstitions now magnified by Reiniken's bardic tale. A sudden wave of unreasonable fear caused the hair on Christina's neck to rise before she calmed, realizing the origin of the noise.

"It's just the seals basking over on the island's shore," she shouted, stilling the men's terror somewhat.

Although she knew the sound was not derived from a supernatural source, her concern remained high.

Did something alarm the beasts? she wondered, considering whether a pirate vessel could be attempting to sneak near under the fog's cover.

A sudden premonition filled her with a certainty that it had.

Christina now felt *der Greif* to be at its most vulnerable. Gone was their supreme advantage - the ability to sight their enemy at a distance and engage them with the greater range of her archers before a threat could be posed. It had worked flawlessly previously, but that was then. This was now.

She leaned on the mast and looked toward the starboard side of the ship. Despite the fog, she could just discern the top of the oaken planking.

That's good. I can station archers here along the center beam of the ship and plug the bastards as they stick their heads up over the side. Kill -em all and journey back to England just as fast as our sail will carry us. Back to Cecily. Her mind involuntarily conjuring the image of the one person never far from her thoughts.

Reluctantly returning her attention to the task at hand, she shifted her gaze portside, only to find the planking in this direction to be completely obscured. She took two full steps closer before she could make out its top edge.

Probably, it's the position of the sun causing the difference, she postulated. Whatever the cause, it would make killing anyone emerging portside a much more difficult proposition. *Well, unless this wretched miasma clears, it is the best strategy I can devise.*

Christina sought out Alan and relayed her plan. There would be eight men placed along the centerline of the main deck, four focused to each side. She emphasized they must be able to see the top edge of the side strake; otherwise, they must inch closer until they could do so. Two archers would remain in each castle to defend against a surprise attack there.

Next, she called Ziesolf, Matthias and Reiniken together to plan for the placement of their men in the ship's defense. This called for their most accomplished fighters to be intermingled among the archers on the main deck, as this was where Christina expected an attack most likely to be concentrated.

Leaving her lieutenants to arrange their forces, Christina went to her cabin and made use of her slops bucket. Refreshed after a quick bite of bread and cheese and a swig of ale, she regarded the leather bags that held her armor and considered whether it would provide an advantage in the anticipated coming encounter with the next group of pirates.

Last time, I knew the bastards would never get close enough to take a swing at me, but this could be different. In this damnable fog, they might be in our faces before we know it. It would be reassuring to be protected by mail should a blade flash toward me. But, should I inadvertently fall into the sea, my strength as a swimmer will be to no avail as its weight will sink me directly to the bottom. A wound might not kill me, but two lungs full of sea water certainly will. I think I'll save the armor for when I am firmly on solid ground.

Christina took a deep breath, then slowly exhaled. She examined her mind for any hint of the nervousness and fear she had felt when confronting pirates on her first voyage, from Lübeck to London. She found none.

The circumstances are quite different now. We are the hunters, not the hunted, and I am no longer a vulnerable young girl dressed in her father's old clothes with an ancient falchion in her trembling hand. I have been trained in fighting by the best and tested more than once in battle. Behold, you bastards, I am death and I offer no mercy!

She returned to the deck and viewed the defenders' placement with satisfaction. She was less pleased by the degree of haphazard noise heard about the ship.

"Quiet!" she hissed. "We might actually be able to hear the sons-a-bitches coming if you stop your damned gabbing!"

"Hear 'em, Yur Worship?" Reiniken replied good-naturedly. "Why. Ah bet we kin smell the fuckers from a mile away. A steady diet of salt cod will make yur shit stink like somethin' crawled up inside yur plughole and died!"

"Shut your gob, Wig!" Christina spoke vehemently. "Not only might we hear them, but they can certainly hear us! They can navigate right toward the sound of your fucking big, loud voice, leading them right toward us. Don't you realize we're at a disadvantage here?"

Reiniken looked more than a little unsettled by Christina's outburst but silenced himself as did the rest of the men. It now became a test of nerves as minutes dragged into hours. The fog seemed to cling to the timbers of the ship, like a wooden spoon swirled by spirits in an accursed stewpot. Every small sound prompted those aboard *der Greif* to bring their weapons to the ready, only to relax after a few anxious moments of nonaction.

Suddenly, a substantial bump seemed to reverberate through the ship. This was followed by a smaller one accompanied by the distinctive scraping of two wooden surfaces rubbing against one another. Christina looked toward a gesturing Reiniken who stood a few figures to her right. He was lifting his head and exaggerating a sniffing motion. Then he looked back toward her and grinned.

I'll be damned!

She returned his smile.

I can smell a distinctively fishy smell, strong enough to make me want to gag. Wig was right!

That's when the first grapple came over the port side, followed in quick succession by several more; most of which Christina could not see, but registered them by the distinctive clunk as they hit the thick timbers of the deck. A hand appeared, clutching the upper strake for support, followed by the indistinct outline of a head. That's when she heard the twang of Alan's bowstring and felt the rush of air displaced by the arrow speeding only a few inches from her cheek toward its target. The man boarding the vessel emitted a heavy groan. From his eye, a bloody rose bloomed. There was no sign of the arrow's fletching; the impetus of its flight had pushed it completely through his skull. The attacker fell, landing in the area from whence he came with a thud, dead before he could utter a second moan.

Two other pirates attempted to board *der Greif*, one from each side, both meeting with the same fate as the first. There then came a lull in the action, during which Christina feared the attackers were concocting an alternative plan. She passed the word down the line of defenders to be vigilant, knowing it to be unnecessary; nevertheless, she felt compelled to say something.

Unexpectedly, she heard the sound of heavy axes chopping wood. It took her a few seconds to realize the pirates were attempting a breach through the oaken strakes of the side of the ship. She cursed herself for not considering that possibility.

"To the side!" she yelled. "Target the bastards with the axes!"

The bowmen dutifully rushed forward and peered over the side of the ship, seeking their intended targets. Suddenly, Alan fell back, clutching at his hip. Two or three more quarrels cut through the air; however, they failed to find a target of flesh and blood. Then, another of the archers disappeared off the side of the ship, mortally wounded by a crossbow bolt buried deeply within his throat. From below came the sound of jeering and laughter, although it did not last for long.

Without thought for her own safety, Christina moved forward.

She saw the remaining two bowmen calmly scan the deck of the ewer revealed below them. They located four of the crossbowmen frantically working to rearm their weapons. Two were straining mightily to draw and latch the bowstring, their right feet inserted into a cocking stirrup at the front of the bow to stabilize the weapon. Both of these were dispatched with the longbowmen's nocked arrows. The reloading process of the other two pirates was even more laborious as their crossbows were of a windlass type, requiring the bowstring to be drawn by cranking. Each of these men were killed before they could complete their task and take aim once more. The two longbowmen, each drawing another arrow from his belt, scanned the mass of scrambling humanity below them for their next victims.

Another crossbowman stepped from behind the ewer's mast where he had concealed himself while he was reloading his weapon. His bolt hit Gilbert squarely in his stomach with enough force to throw him onto his back, where he lay screaming in pain. The remaining longbowman let his arrow fly toward his cunning adversary, who had already returned to his safe haven behind the mast. A couple of thrown daggers from the other pirates, though failing to find their targets, were enough to force the lone archer and Christina to retreat to the relative safety offered nearer the ship's centerline.

While her attention had been drawn to what had transpired to port, the action to starboard had tilted even more in the pirate's favor. Although two of the longbowmen remained unharmed, the other two were certainly dead. Even more dire, the number and frequency of quarrels sizzling through the fog indicated at least two or three of the crossbowmen on that side were still alive and aggressively seeking the lives of Christina's men.

The harassing fire ceased and loud shouting replaced it.

They're attacking now, and why not?

Christina stepped forth and dragged the wounded Gilbert to a sitting position against the mainmast.

They must have double or triple our numbers and they believe they have negated our bowmen. Now, the fighting begins in earnest!

"Challenge the bastards before they can set foot on the deck!" Ziesolf shouted.

Christina looked toward where she had heard his voice, but her view was met by a wall of the ever-present fog.

"Clear, damn you!" she yelled as if she could convince the ill-timed weather dissipate by force of will alone.

She had no more time to divert her attention, as the grapples set deeper into the strakes as the weight of men climbing their ropes was added.

Christina stepped forward cautiously, aware the threat from the crossbowmen had not been completely eradicated. Without warning, a boarding pike thrust up, its sharp spike seeking to split her face. She parried it with her sword, the force of her swing pinning it against the top strake of the ship. She released it instantly, drawing her blade back in a backhand slice directed at the massive, bearded head that had suddenly appeared. The reverse edge of her blade cut deeply into the side of his neck, nearly severing his spine and causing his now lifeless head to loll. She had neither time to congratulate herself, nor thank Gaveston for his gift of this double-edged wonder or Giles for training her in its use. Already, another foe was stepping clumsily over the side of the ship.

She whirled her sword over her head and brought it down in a diagonal cut that caught the man on his lower thigh. The impetus of her swing sliced through the flesh, shattered the underlying bone, and passed through the other side, cleanly severing the leg and leaving the man to collapse in the growing puddle of blood and piss where he would end his days.

Control yourself, Christina, damn you!

She realized she could not continue to expend such massive amounts of energy on delivering a single, horrible wound.

A plucked artery will kill just as surely as a beheading. Although not half as satisfying to administer! She grinned through lips already parched by her efforts.

To her right, she saw a man shinny up a boarding hook as lithely as if he were a performing monkey. He leaped to the deck and landed on his feet, crouching down as he looked to select a target for the wicked *hiebmesser* he carried in his grip. He swiveled his head left and saw Reiniken, already engaged with two assailants simultaneously. The man rose to a crouch and attempted to sneak behind Reiniken, thinking to mount a craven attack on the giant of a man from his rear.

Christina bolted forward, her earlier admonition to herself now forgotten. Her sword sang through the air in a broad slash against her adversary's side, slicing into liver, kidney, and stomach as easily if she were butchering a beast for the entrails of a hearty pie. The dark blood oozing toward her hand down the blade's fuller guaranteed this man would trouble them no further.

"I sawr -im, Yur Worship!" Reiniken shouted, kicking his remaining adversary squarely in the groin. When his opponent doubled over, Reiniken brought his immense boot upward to meet his face with a sickening crunch. The man toppled toward Christina, who skewed his neck with her blade, just in case.

"I know, Wig!" she shouted madly, overpowered by the adrenaline flowing through her body. "Can't let you get ahead of me now, can I?" How many is that for you so far? Two?"

"Four, if you'd a left mi' the little fucker there!"

He pointed the tip of his huge sword toward the man Christina had gutted. "Or are ya gonna claim half a this -un?"

He used the toe of his boot to indicate the one he had kicked.

"No, no." she replied, "It seems there are more than enough to go around, Wig."

All signs of humor in Christina disappeared as quickly as they had arisen.

On the starboard side, Ziesolf's blade anchored a defense that was holding, but only just. Already, a few of her men had fallen, whether dead, wounded, or merely exhausted, she did not have time to assess. She offered a quick word to God for their souls and stepped once more into the fray.

"Fuck!" she screamed as a lucky crossbow bolt grazed the top of her shoulder.

Less than a second later, a large-bellied man loped toward her, with seemingly no more than a loincloth only intermittently concealing his swollen genitals. He raised a great maul over his head, the round, wooden handle at least three feet long in his sweaty palms.

Christina threw herself forward, rotating her body so she landed on her back. She felt a rush of wind as the maul passed through the air where she had stood only a breath before. With both hands on her sword's hilt, she pushed the blade up through the man's gut and into his vital organs above. He collapsed immediately, pinning her to the deck by his great bulk. She lay there, wriggling to free herself while the man's body fluids leaked into her mouth and stung her eyes. She felt herself retch, fearing she was fated to drown on her own vomit.

With sudden fear, she felt the man's weight diminish, then vanish completely. She looked up to see Wig looming over her, laughing uncontrollably.

"Christ's Holy Cods!" Reiniken exclaimed, extending his meaty paw to assist her to her feet. "Was ya lookin' to take yurself a fuckin' trophy?"

He used the tip of his sword to gesture toward the man's now fully exposed genitalia.

"I 'spose ya now want to count 'im as two, do ya?"

"Thanks, Wig, but save the jests for later," she answered, bending down to retrieve her sword from the man's body. "Other business to attend to now!"

Christina stepped past her rescuer and saw two more pirates had gained the deck.

Damn, how many of them are there? We can't keep this up forever!

She had no idea how many of her men still survived, let alone were capable of forming a defense. Soon, even she, Reiniken, and Ziesolf would be overcome, by sheer weight of numbers if not by skill. The two on the deck were approaching, brandishing wicked blades in their hands and obvious foul deeds in their hearts. Movement to her left side only added to the odds against her.

Without any warning, she heard a thwack, followed seconds later by another. The two men before her toppled, poplar shafts ending in goose feather fletching protruding from their backs.

Christina gazed about her with amazement.

The fog's clearing! Praise be to God, it's clearing!

She looked forward and saw the two archers who had shot the arrows as plain as day. Already, they had loosed two more, throwing the odds on the main deck more favorably toward *der Greif's* victory. Behind her, she heard more music to her ears – that of the bowmen's craft from the sterncastle, though whether they were targeting enemies on the deck or on the ships below, she had no idea.

Christina ran forward to join those who still struggled to defeat the pirates still upright on *der Greif's* deck. Without warning came a staggering blow to the back of her head. The sudden pain was white-hot, the intensity nothing like she had ever experienced. She staggered blindly, blade slashing wildly. But her sword felt too heavy and soon it slipped from her hand and onto the deck. For once, her body could not be subjugated by her strong spirit. She crumpled to the ground as all about her faded.

Then, there was nothing.

Chapter 9

An Unexpected Invitation
London, June, 1311

"Would you be having a bit more of that cheese?" the kitchen maid asked.

"Aye," Jost replied, navigating his answer past a mouth already crammed with wholesome foodstuffs.

He swallowed the large bolus of bread, cheese, and meat before answering more completely.

"I would indeed. Thank you, Sarah."

The comely young woman made her way back into the kitchen larder, leaving Jost alone in the great hall. The yard laborers had not yet arrived to break their fast and the maids and kitchen staff had eaten much earlier. Usually, only Frederick would have taken his morning repast around this time, though Ziesolf and Trudi would sometimes alter their schedules to keep him company. Although his cousin had now been gone over two months, Jost felt it would be somehow unlucky to change their routine, almost as if it would portent Frederick was not to return.

Well, that would be silly, wouldn't it? Jost reassured himself as Sarah sat another ample wedge of cheese in front of him before returning to her other tasks in the kitchen. *Frederick is a renowned fighter, knighted by King Edward himself, for the love of God. I cannot believe any so-called pirates could cause him worry, especially with the likes of Herr Ziesolf and Wig Reiniken by his side.*

Still, he offered a silent prayer for his cousin's success and well-being, just in case.

After finishing breakfast, Jost walked outside to the yard. The sun beamed down from a cloudless sky, warming his body and chasing the memory of the winter cold from his bones. The slight, swirling breeze in the air buoyed the myriad of birds aloft on its intermittent updrafts. Gulls, ravens, and songbirds of several types filled the air with their varied calls, creating a cacophonous background. As he approached the storeroom at the furthest right side of the yard, Peter strode forth from his smithy and set an intercepting course.

"God be with you on such a fine day, young Jost," Peter greeted him cordially.

"And may He smile on you and your family as He does on the Earth this morn," Jost replied. "Are the lads ready?"

"Aye, and eager to get on with it, s'truth," replied the smith. "This new drain is quite an undertaking, but the results will be well worth the effort, I believe."

This storeroom has long been the subject of my master's consternation, thought Jost. *It is by far the largest of the four stores on site, easily capable of holding two hundred sarplar of wool and a bit more besides. Yet, it is virtually unusable for our primary trade commodity, relegated instead to hold only the most nonperishable of goods. Any substantial amount of rain leaves ground water to run over the lip of the door jamb curb to pool inside on the packed earth of the floor. The resultant dampness in the air would permeate wool, furs, or fabric, causing them to grow moldy and worthless.*

Jost recalled the embarrassment he had felt as Frederick patiently explained this to him. If he had not, Jost would have packed the entire stock of Lincoln fleeces into the storeroom, resulting in its complete ruin. Now, he looked to make amends for his stupidity.

He had originally thought to merely raise the curb, but this would not halt seepage from an even greater pool passing through the earth beneath the door and into the room. To re-level the entire yard to reverse the flow of rainwater away from the storerooms would be a monumental task, requiring much more labor than he had available. Jost had decided instead to create a large stone-lined sump before the entrance to the storeroom, covering it with an iron grate Simon was creating in his forge. The sump would then be drained through a wooden conduit buried beneath the yard's surface, connecting to the privy hole above the city's sewers.

The angle of drop needed to be calculated closely. Too little, and the sump would soon fill, leaving the problem much as before. Too much, and the conduit could back up with sewage, clogging the conduit and stopping the flow of water as well. Mistress Trudi would not be pleased if the conduit backed up, filling the floor of her husband's smithy with rancid shit.

Peter had detailed four of the yardmen to Jost, who directed them to begin at once. Soon, they were hard at work, using their pickaxes and wooden shovels to begin shaping the sump. While they were doing this, he used a line of linen thread to create a straight line between the privy and where the edge of the sump would lie. Jost took a piece of chalk and marked the line across the dirt and cobbles of the yard. This task complete, he went to see how Stephen, the carpenter, was progressing with the fabrication of the sections of wooden conduit.

Jost found the carpenter and his apprentice hard at work, using an auger to bore through the center of several lengths of elm trunk wood. Although he had figured a four-inch diameter hole would be sufficient to keep the sump drained, Jost had instructed Stephen to auger a six-inch hole, just in case.

Far easier to make the hole bigger and not need it, than to make it too small and have to dig it back up and start anew, he thought prudently.

Work on the drainage system progressed unabated until a few minutes after the bell of St. Olave's church signaled the hour of sext. Another, sharper-toned bell sounded, this one attached to the outside gate of the yard. Why was the watchman not moving to answer its call? Jost looked about to see Warin was nearly up to his belly shoveling out dirt from the sump hole.

I'll do it myself; better so than to let it disrupt work on the drains.

In a few seconds, he was at the wrought iron door of the gateway. Jost opened it to discover a haughty young man elaborately garbed in a uniform of some kind sewn from an assortment of rich fabrics primarily of blue, black, and red.

"Well, boy, is your purpose in this household to stand gawking at those who call here?" the man inquired sarcastically.

"No . . . no, of course not," Jost replied haltingly.

"Good. Now that we have that settled, perhaps you are adroit enough to move aside and let me enter."

"May I ask your business here first, Mi 'lord?" Jost asked, trying to regain some control over the conversation.

"Why, of course, good sir. Of course!" the man replied with a sudden good-natured air. "My purpose is to stand out in a shit-covered street, answering the silly fucking questions of some half-witted country bumpkin! It's what I live for, you see."

All mock humor gone, his face reddened and twisted with impatient anger.

"Now, stand aside or be damned!" he bellowed.

Jost was about to do as the man demanded, then hesitated.

There is no way my cousin would permit himself to be cowed by such arrogance. His garments may be expensive, but it is still only livery, the clothing specified by the master he serves. While Frederick is away, I am master of his holdings and certainly need not be subservient to this swaggering fop that stands before me!

"If you carry a message from your master, deliver it now, for I am the head of this household in the absence of Sir Frederick," Jost said evenly. "If not, depart and trouble us no more."

Jost felt his stomach churn. He had never spoken to anyone so dismissively. He tried to keep his face expressionless, though he struggled to keep from spewing the remnants of his breakfast all over the boorish stranger. Somehow, that pleasant image settled his nerves somewhat.

The courier looked at him with exasperation, then reached into the large tooled-leather pouch attached to his belt, withdrew a folded sheet of parchment, and thrust it at Jost.

"Fine. I would not want to tarry a minute longer in such a crude barnyard as this! The message is for the apprentice to Master Frederick Kohl, Jost be his name."

Surprised the message was for him, Jost reached forward to receive the parchment. At the last second, the rude messenger drew it back.

"How can I be sure you will deliver it to him?" he asked suspiciously. "Sometimes disgruntled servants intercept private message, seeking to parlay them into profit from the enemies of their masters. I think it likely you might be one such varlet."

"I am Jost," he replied, weary of the man's endless games. "My master is Sir Frederick."

The courier's face became somewhat less imperious, eyebrows lowering and sneer softening. He moved his hand forward, this time allowing Jost to take the missive. He then resumed his haughty expression.

"I hope you can read. If not, I'm certainly not going to speak it to you!"

He offered a contemptuous smirk before turning up the street and swiftly walking away.

Saints above! Jost thought as he closed and latched the gate. *What master could tolerate such an unpleasant knave as his servant?*

Overwhelmed with curiosity as to what message he could possibly be the recipient, he examined the red wax seal over the parchment fold. Shock widened his eyes; it was one of only a few he could recognize by sight, a seated merchant holding a tablet inscribed with a column of three fleeces in bas-relief. With growing dread, he broke the seal and opened the missive from the chief alderman.

Fear gripped his guts and gave them an evil twist, nearly incapacitated him then and there.

A summons to appear before the aldermen, he realized with despair, *addressed to me personally. What have I done? Certainly nothing that would incur the interest of the leaders of London's Hanseatics!*

Another monstrous idea leapt into his suddenly feverish mind.

What if it is about Frederick? I know he and the aldermen have sometimes been at odds. What if they seek information about him from me, or even plan to ask that I betray him?

Jost crumpled the parchment and threw it away from him as if it were a thing accursed.

I would never do such a thing, even if they tortured me!

Although he often felt uncomfortable around his cousin, it was not from fear but from awe. Frederick was no more than a year or two his elder; yet, he had lived nearly another lifetime full of adventure. He had fought pirates, uncovered murderous plots, and fought the English king's enemies and been knighted for it.

"And what have I done with my life?" Jost mused in a low voice. "Well, I've measured fabrics and counted fleeces. Now, I'm trying to figure out how to move a puddle of water from one end of the yard to the other. Hardly a comparison, I'd think. One thing of which I am certain, I'm sure as hell not adding betrayal to my paltry list of accomplishments."

"Did ya say somethin' to me, Master Jost?" Warin asked, the hefty watchman having suddenly appeared beside him. "Ah didn't hears ya, if ya did."

"No," Jost answered with a forced smile, "I was just talking with myself."

"Best ways to keeps a secret," Warin's huge mouth broke into a grin at his own attempt at a jest, revealing teeth that resembled the broken and canted stones in a derelict church graveyard.

Jost laughed, more to make Warin feel good about his effort at humor than anything else. What Warin lacked in intelligence, he more than made up for in loyalty and an affable nature. He was much favored by every member of the household.

Realizing Jost had not been addressing him, Warin returned to his labors. Jost was left alone with his uncertainties as to how to proceed. After a few minutes, he decided his best course of action was to discuss the matter with Trudi.

If Jost were to describe the hierarchy of the estate, he would obviously place Frederick at its head, though both Ziesolf and Trudi spoke to him as equals. If Ziesolf were there, he would probably speak with him concerning what to expect from the alderman; but he was not. That left Trudi.

Passing through the door and into the great hall, Jost walked on toward Trudi and Peter's apartments.

It seemed odd to be consulting a woman concerning business affairs, but the connection between Frederick and Trudi was certainly beyond that of mere master and maid. Jost knew they had known each other all their lives, but it went much further beyond that. She was his confidant in all matters. Likewise, Jost believed there was nothing Trudi would not do for Frederick.

Strangely, her love for him had not extended to his bed, at least Jost so believed. Trudi was one of the most flirtatious women he had ever encountered, a quality that had caused him great embarrassment upon his arrival at Bokerel House. He had misinterpreted her friendly smile and easy banter as an invitation for something more.

As had others, he thought in his defense.

Both he and Malcolm, the now dead stableboy, had been completely infatuated with her. Their quarrels had led to blows, each intended to win a prize that was not being offered. In the end, they had both been rebuffed, as Trudi had settled her eye on Black Peter. In retrospect, he held the young woman no grudge, nor believed she had unduly led him on. He realized now Trudi was one of those rare people who reveled in making others feel good about themselves.

Perhaps that is what draws Frederick so close to her? he mused as he knocked upon the door of her apartments.

"Aye!" Trudi's voice sounded from inside, "Give me a minute to separate this greedy little bugger from my tit!"

True to her word, she soon opened the door A look of surprised pleasure appeared on her face as she invited him inside. Although she had gained weight during her pregnancy, her roundish face surrounded by her golden locks remained as comely as ever. She unceremoniously plopped down in an upholstered chair, wiped her hair from her eyes, and emitted a loud sigh from her full, pinkish lips.

"A bit of advice to you, Jost," she said in a worn voice. "A wet nurse is worth her weight in vair. Don't be so stubborn as to think your babe will only thrive upon your woman's own milk alone."

"I'll definitely remember that, Mistress Trudi," he replied with a laugh. "How fares your young master?"

"Him?"

She nodded toward the cradle in the opposite corner.

"Growing by leaps and bounds, he is. He'll be bigger than his father by the time he's ten, this one," Trudi's musical laughter joined his own before abruptly being cut off as a serious tone overtook her voice.

"Now, I don't suppose you broke away from your project in the yard just to bring a ray of sunshine to my day, did you? What is it that troubles you, lad?"

Jost recounted his encounter with the chief alderman's servant as well as the contents of the parchment he had received.

"I know there is a long history of strife between Frederick and the chief aldermen, both old and new, but have not been made privy to the details. Now I am required to attend upon Herr Volker, and I am both uncertain as to what he might ask - as well as how I should respond. Obviously, I cannot question my cousin how to proceed. Therefore, I am here to ask the advice of his closest counselor."

When he finished, he waited to gauge Trudi's reaction with troubled eyes.

"The chief alderman is like most men, self-centered and avaricious. Weigh each of his words closely with this in mind: 'What gain does this provide him?' Recognizing this, you should be able to avoid any major pratfalls. Agree to nothing forthwith, take time to seek counsel among those you trust first."

Jost nodded, agreeing with the sense of Trudi's words.

"Now, that is the easy part. Herr Volker is elderly and, from what Master Frederick intimates, no longer quick of wit. You should have no difficulty in outmaneuvering him," Trudi continued hesitantly.

Is she holding something back? Jost wondered.

"No, Volker is not the problem," she began again, "It is his wife, Katharine, the daughter of the previous chief alderman. Let it suffice to say Frederick finds her to be young, beautiful, and extremely intelligent. She is the schemer whose great influence engenders all her husband's actions. A great animosity exists between her and Frederick. She waits like a poisonous adder for the opportunity to strike, to deal him a deadly blow. Do not trust her, Jost. Ever."

"I understand, Mistress Trudi, and thank thee Your sage advice is most appreciated."

"Sage? Me?" Trudi giggled and threw a cushion toward her guest, striking him squarely. "Why, do I now have gray whiskers sprouting from my chin? You certainly have a way with words for the ladies, you young scamp! Now, be off with you before you start complimenting me on the fair broadening of my fat arse!"

Jost stood swiftly, a flush of embarrassment budding on his cheeks and spreading outward. Trudi too sprang to her feet and, laughing cheerfully, skipped across the floor to the young man, catching him in a tight embrace and kissing him loudly on both cheeks before releasing him.

The frantic beating of his heart slowed as he realized Trudi had been speaking in jest and that he had not inadvertently offended her. He took his leave and departed, his legs carrying him back in the direction of the yard and the work on his drain project. As he walked, he mulled over Trudi's words.

Why does Katharine Volker hold such hatred in her bosom for Frederick? Certainly, my cousin's activities as a merchant would hold no interest for a mere woman, regardless of whether her husband is the chief alderman or not. It must be something personal then. But what?

He was descending the steps into the yard, when he abruptly stopped, a new thought leaping into his mind.

Could he have attempted to take advantage of her? Perhaps Frederick is strangely attracted to women who are already claimed by other men, he deduced, somewhat aghast at his conclusion. *It is clear to everyone in the household he loves the lady Cecily with all his heart, despite her already being married. It is evident her feelings for him run just as deeply. Could it be he professed similar feelings to Katharine Volker, but she chose to rebuff his advances? What happened next to evoke such hatred in her heart?*

Jost shuddered at the possibilities.

He knew only too well the consequences of committing undesired advances. Just before Frederick's departure, Jost had found himself alone in the fabric stores with Mary, who had assumed the duties of housekeeper during the latter stages of Trudi's pregnancy. She had come seeking appropriate lengths of suitable fabric to dress the tables in one of the unused rooms on the second floor she was converting to a guest chamber. She had greeted him in a friendly enough manner and he had ceased the work he was doing to show her a very fine remnant of tansy and woad dyed damask in the rear of the room.

Reaching the cloth, he turned to show it to her. Instead of looking at the cloth, however, she directed the gaze of her voluminous doe eyes toward his own. He looked at her angular, comely face, surrounded by thick and lustrous brown hair. She smiled encouragingly. Without any more thought, he leaned forward, placing his lips gently on hers. She placed her small hand delicately upon the back of his neck, drawing him closer.

Jost had felt his manhood stirring, growing hard and erect. He slipped his right hand behind the maid's back, moving it downward to cup her slender, almost boyish, buttocks. He then moved forward, pressing her petite body between the mound of fabric and his own. His hands fell upon her skirts, clumsily attempting to lift them upwards.

"Ouch!" he yelled, nearly overwhelmed by the agony erupting in his groin, as her knee found its intended mark.

He quickly backed away, forgetting about baring Mary's sex as he instinctively sought to relieve the intense agony in his own. She moved faster, however, shocking him with a swinging blow from the back of her hand across his face. He stumbled backwards, tears forming in his eyes from both his pain and embarrassment. Mary took a step forward and smoothed her skirts back in place. She took one more and thrust her slender index finger into the center of his chest.

"What kind of a girl do you take me for?" she had demanded. "A bit of cuddle and peck, aye, but if you think I'd let you have my maidenhead just like that, you've figured wrong! I thought you were different, a gentleman like your cousin. But, you're just a lecherous wee bastard, like the rest of 'em. You think us servant women welcome your randy sport, but we don't, especially when you force it upon us!"

Jost stood dumbly before her, unable to move. She shook her finger angrily beneath his nose for emphasis.

"If you ever try to force yourself upon me again, young master," Mary spoke slowly, deliberately, with unconcealed venom, "I will cut off your cock and feed it to the dogs. The same holds true if I hear tales of you doing it to any of the other women in this house. Do you understand me?"

Not knowing what else to do, Jost had mutely nodded. Mary had given him one last, lingering glare before grabbing the fabric and storming from the room.

He had lived the next few days in fear, dreading the thought she would divulge his misbehavior to Frederick, or worse, to Trudi. Although it would have greatly embarrassed him to displease his cousin, it would have been far worse in his mind to incur the wrath of the housekeeper. He had heard the fury in her voice as she berated Frederick before he left for Berwick. He had not caught all her angry words and those he had understood made little sense. Regardless, her voice had left little doubt in his mind he would do anything to save himself such a bollocking. Luckily for him, Mary had held her tongue, but the incident had caused him to avoid her presence whenever possible, and to squirm uncomfortably if he could not.

I'll never understand women, especially those who are English. If my cousin had such an experience with Katharine Volker, I pity him more than I condemn him. I only know I must be careful to avoid misconstruing any such friendly encouragement on her part, should such an occasion arise.

234

Jost returned to a problem he much better understood, how to move rainwater across the courtyard. He vigorously threw himself into his work, leaving the impending meeting with the chief alderman far from his immediate thoughts and his difficulties with women even further.

Chapter 10

A Proposition, of Sorts
London, June, 1311

"There, now don't you look a sight?"

Trudi stepped back to view him more fully.

Jost's lips formed a ghost of a smile, though he felt self-conscious as the center of attention.

"I thought it would fit you perfectly, and I was right now, wasn't I?"

Jost agreed. Trudi had suggested he borrow some of his cousin's clothes for his visit to the house of the alderman, a subtle hint at the non-suitability of his own. He had never really thought about it, satisfied to wear the same frayed shirt and threadbare tunic until they were so soiled his cousin would remind him that he did, in fact, possess other garments. Now, wearing Frederick's snugly tailored cotehardie, particolored of green and brown, he felt a pride in himself that belied his habitual insecurities.

Trudi next drew forth a burgundy-colored chaperon. Unexpectedly, she placed the hole intended for the face over the top of the straw-colored hair upon his head. This left the *cornette* tail and the cape portion of the hood hanging loose from the top his head. She wound the tail one turn about the top and then tucked it under, leaving a length to dangle to the side of his face.

"Is this really necessary?" he asked, somewhat skeptical.

"Yes, it is!" she replied good-naturedly. "Do you want to be taken for a bumpkin, freshly fallen off a farm wagon, or as the chief apprentice of a successful merchant master?"

"I'm Frederick's only apprentice," he grumbled in response.

"And it's no wonder he has but one, if this is how much trouble they are!" she retorted with a sour look.

"I'm sorry," he quickly apologized, not wishing to evoke ire from the woman. "I'm just not used to someone making such a fuss over me."

Trudi's face softened.

"In Master Frederick's absence, you represent his business interests and place in society. No one else here can do that, not Peter and certainly not me. I will not allow you to cause him shame. Do you understand me?"

He gulped.

"Yes, Mistress."

"Good," Trudi said briskly. "Now off with you!"

Jost thanked her before departing Bokerel House and beginning his journey to the alderman's manor. Although he knew the route, he paid close attention to where he was going, halting several times to gather his bearings.

"The last thing I need is to lose my way and arrive late," he muttered to himself. "I'll probably make a buffoon of myself anyway, but let it be after I begin speaking, not before."

He soon arrived, much earlier than the stipulated hour of nones. He considered whiling away some time gazing out upon the

Thames that flowed within a couple of hundred feet from where he stood.

What if I get distracted? he fretted. *The next thing I know, I'll hear the church bells tolling nones and I'll be tardy after all. No, certainly better early than late.*

He approached the beautifully worked wrought-iron gate. Another time, he might stop to admire its craftsmanship, but not today. His sole focus was to complete his task and depart - hopefully, without reflecting embarrassment upon his master and his household. He pulled the bell rope, took one step backward, and waited.

Unexpectedly, the man who opened the gate was the same one who had delivered the summons to him two days prior. Jost's heart sank, fully expecting to be the target for the servant's disdain once more, most assuredly magnified by the knowledge the man was now on his own ground.

"Aye, come forth, young master. The chief alderman is expecting you," the man spoke pleasantly, nearly groveling in the pleasantness of his invitation.

What the hell? Jost thought, the hairs on the back of his neck rising with unease. *Is there something afoot here I am missing?*

Vowing even greater caution, Jost stepped through the gate and into the massive manor yard. He was ushered quickly into the cavernous great hall, much grander even than the one at Bokerel House. There he waited, nervously picking at the previously unnoticed grime beneath his fingernails for several minutes. Eventually, a door set into the front wall of the chamber opened. Through it hobbled an elderly, wispy-haired man in a midnight blue houppelande, elaborately trimmed in what Jost believed to be sable fur of an exquisite quality, dark brown and ending in silver tips. He was followed through the portal by four young men outfitted in the same livery pattern as the one at the front gate. They assisted him to the center of six elaborately carved chairs sitting behind an immense wooden table on the raised dais at the front of the room. Had it been positioned by itself, Jost could have easily taken it for a throne.

"God be with you," the man who was most certainly the chief alderman began.

"And to you, Mi' lord," Jost responded, executing a clumsy, short bow.

"I have called you here today to inquire as to the health and success of your master. Have you received any word as to how he fares?" the old man asked in a surprisingly friendly tone.

Jost replied to the negative, as no message had been received from Frederick in the months since he had sailed. The alderman asked a few more questions that were rather inane in nature, all of which Jost was able to answer with short, direct responses. This was fortunate, as his attention was increasingly drawn to a small figure who had appeared at the elaborately carved railing of the minstrel's gallery high above the floor of the chamber.

Peering down from above, it would be easy to confuse her with something unearthly, like an angel flown from heaven. Her rich, dark-brown hair loosely framed a youthful face perfect in symmetry and feature. Suddenly, her lips parted in a friendly smile that could only be directed at him. Embarrassed she had noticed his bold stare; he dropped his eyes swiftly back to focus on the old man who was posing yet another meaningless question.

Jost's response was straightforward, stating, "Yes, Mi' lord," while resisting mightily the impulse to again regard the lovely creature hovering above.

Thankfully, the chief alderman seemed to have at last wearied of his endless questioning and rose abruptly, signaling the end to their somewhat bewildering meeting. The old man and his retainers departed through the same door through which they had entered, leaving Jost to stand alone in the hall, confounded as to what he was expected to do next. Somewhat guiltily, he raised his gaze back to the minstrel's gallery, but now found it uninhabited. He felt acutely disappointed to not behold her face once more. Realizing there was nothing more for him there, he turned and strode out. Jost stepped into the harsh afternoon light that baked the courtyard and then, placing his hand above his brow to help deflect the sun's glare, he was astounded to see the young woman from the gallery strolling in his direction.

Or is she even that? Jost wondered. *Might she be just a child?*

It was difficult to determine, as he judged her to be only about five feet in stature. The faint swelling of womanly breasts concealed beneath the fabric of her kirtle only partially convinced him of her adulthood.

"God's blessing upon you this day, good sir," she said in a pleasant breathy voice when the distance between them had closed to only a few feet.

"Ur. . . um . . . thank you," Jost managed, his faculties overcome by the woman's sheer beauty.

Her skin was the color of fresh milk, without blemish or imperfection. It made for the perfect contrast to her almond-shaped, deep green eyes, which she had enhanced further by kohling the surrounding lash lines. She gazed upon Jost with a keen interest he had never perceived before from a woman.

"You are most welcome!" she replied laughingly, but gaily rather than with scorn. "I am Katharine."

Katharine? His mind recoiled in shock. *Volker's wife? No, it is impossible! This small, young girl cannot be wed to such a man as he. Surely, she must be his daughter. Nay, a granddaughter!*

As he collected his wits, he noticed her staring at him expectantly, the smile on her pleasant red lips now becoming slightly brittle.

"I am Jost, apprentice to Master Frederick Kohl," he managed without stumbling once again over his words.

"Yes, I know. I saw you in the great hall,"

Her smile once again grew warm and inviting.

"I saw you there as well," he replied, before the remembrance of his impertinent gawking caused him to redden with embarrassment. "It is a magnificent manor," he quickly observed, hoping to change the subject.

"Oh, yes, it is, isn't it?" Katharine said, then giggled slightly for some reason Jost could not discern. "Would you like to see it? I could act as your guide."

"Would Herr Volker not take offense at an uninvited guest traipsing through his home? Or Frau Volker?" Jost added, remembering Trudi's warning. Despite his trepidation, he could imagine nothing more pleasant than prolonging his time with this delightful young woman.

"Oh, no, I do not believe so!"

Again, she tittered musically at a jest to which he was not privy.

"Besides, we can hide if we see either of them coming. I know oh so many hidden places!"

He gazed into her mischievously twinkling eyes and surrendered; he would chance almost anything to please her.

"Well then, let us be off!" she cried, grabbing his hand to pull him after her.

He almost pulled back from her touch, shocked at her boldness. Instead, his hand tightened slightly around the small palm and slender fingers. In a few seconds, they had passed through a side door leading into a long passageway with stairs at the end. They ascended to the floor above and entered the first of several imposing chambers. In each room, Katharine kept up a running commentary on its architectural details, furnishings, and decorative arts. The only person he had ever met with a similar familiarity of such matters was his cousin Frederick, who certainly would not have been privy to the secrets of this structure. Jost asked a few questions at first, but then was content to remain silent, devoting his energies to stealing admiring glances at his delightful companion rather than expanding his knowledge.

As they walked through the many corridors, Katharine posed several questions to Jost concerning himself, his duties, and his feelings toward his cousin. Although they seemed to him to be rather pointed at times, he replied to each as best he could, pleased that she took such an interest in him.

He grew somewhat wary when the young woman began to inquire about Frederick's trade in the commodity of wool.

"It seems to be a rather peculiar interest for a woman," he remarked, gazing at her with a wry smile. "No offense intended," he added quickly.

"And none taken, Master Jost," she replied, although the sudden flush that rushed to her ivory cheeks seemed to belie the friendliness of her response. "You see, having been the recipient of possibly questionable guidance, I have invested heavily in a large quantity of fleeces, committing almost the entirety of my inherited largesse to their purchase. I believe I am in need of the assistance of one whom I can trust."

"Although my experience is limited, I would be more than happy to help you in any way," Jost said, in a manner he hoped she would perceive as gallant.

He could think of few things more agreeable at the moment than earning this young woman's appreciation and gratitude.

Katharine's small mouth formed into a most fetching, toothy smile before she stated, "That would be so kind of you, Jost, but let us talk again of this matter later. For now, I'm happy enough just to enjoy the pleasure of your company."

After what seemed like hours of exploration, they arrived at one last set of apartments, their entrance barred by a massive oaken door upon which an elaborately detailed garden scene had been carved. An apple tree in full bloom stood in the middle, surrounded by intricately twined grapevines and flowers. It was the most beautiful thing Jost had ever seen.

"The Garden of Eden," Katharine remarked, tittering to herself once more at a jest beyond his ken.

Once inside, his wonderment grew. Although the anteroom in which they stood was quite large, it was made cozy and intimate by the richly woven tapestries that adorned every available wall, save that of the outer which allowed the afternoon's remaining light to stream into the chamber through multi-colored panes of stained glass. The fireplace was uncommonly large for such a room, with a marble surround and a carved frieze above.

My sweet Lord! thought Jost, suddenly fearful, *this must be the very chambers of the chief alderman himself. No one else could be allotted such opulence. What would become of me if he discovered us here?*

His young companion seemed completely familiar with the chamber, opening a hidden door in the side wall to reveal a garderobe. She then threw herself down upon a low divan, upholstered with eggshell blue silk, her skirts daringly riding up to reveal her dainty, white, bare calves. Jost gulped and looked away, once again embarrassed, this time at what he recognized as his stirring arousal. Unconcerned, Katharine laughed and sat upright, patting the seat next to her in clear invitation. He gazed about the room nervously, believing Volker would burst in at any moment.

"Join me, Jost," Katharine said in a low husky voice, a demand rather than a request.

As he did as he was told, seating himself only a few inches from her, she reached to the adjacent table and took a flagon of wine into her hands. She put the bottle to her lips and took a long draught. When she pulled it away, remnants of the rose-colored liquid escaped from her mouth, wetting her delicate chin. She passed the bottle to Jost, who drank from it as well. She retrieved the flagon from him and returned it to the table. She looked at him with a cheery glint in her eye and suddenly stood upright. She reached once more for Jost's hand, which he gave to her without any hesitation.

She led him to another beautifully carved door in the side wall. They passed through into what was obviously the bed chamber, a sight that once more brought amazement to Jost's eyes.

The room resembled nothing more than a Muslim sultan's harem, or at least what Jost imagined one to be from the stories he had overheard from two old men who claimed to have fought in the seventh crusade under the command of King Louis IX of France. The chamber was awash with hangings of every hue of silk, cushions of strange shapes and diverse sizes, and what must have been twenty or thirty beeswax candles. A pleasant, musky scent hung heavily in the air. Dominating the floor area was an enormous, raised bed, with towering posts draped with gauzy material that fell in sweeping curves to the floor. The entire room evoked fantasies of wealth, splendor, and decadence.

"Who would have known Herr Volker enjoyed such pleasures?" Jost marveled aloud.

"Herr Volker, here?" Katharine giggled before turning to stare boldly into his eyes. "Why this is not my husband's chamber. It is mine own."

Your husband?" Jost replied in incoherent confusion. "Why, you said we would hide if we saw Frau Volker."

"Yes, I mislead you, dear Jost," she tittered, her eyes twinkling mischievously. "But would you have so willingly come with me had you known I was Volker's wife?"

"But you cannot be Katharine Volker!"

"Why? Because I am young and beautiful and he is old and, well, not?" she remarked, turning away from him. "Or do you not find me so, Jost?"

"No, yes, um...," he struggled, unsure as to which question he should reply to first, before finding his tongue to state boldly, "You are the loveliest creature I have ever beheld."

"Really?"

She turned to face him.

"Yes."

She raised up to her toes and turned her face upward, kissing him very gently on his lips. He replied in kind, being careful to apply no more pressure than what he received. He realized what he was doing was wrong, that to engage in pleasures of the flesh with a married woman was a sin that could damn him to hell eternally. That she was the chief alderman's wife and a woman he had been warned against endangered his mortal flesh as well. Yet, he did not break away, too smitten now to resist her.

Her lips parted slightly and he felt the tip of her tongue seeking to probe his mouth. He opened his own and tasted the intoxicating flavor of some exotic spice in his mouth. He broke their kiss with a start, astonished by the feel of her fingers on the outside of his braies, gently touching his now firmly erect manhood. He brought his lips down on hers once more, her touch emboldening him to respond with one of his own.

Jost reached for Katharine's skirts, intent on pulling them upward. Without warning, Katharine stepped away from him.

"I . . . I'm sorry. I didn't . . .," he stammered, memories of Mary's reaction to similar advances echoing in his mid.

"Silence, you stupid boy!" Katharine snapped with unexpected ire. "Unlace me! Now!"

Katharine raised her right arm above her head. With fingers suddenly lacking dexterity, he untied the lacings down the side of her kirtle. The woman shrugged off the garment, then raised the underlying chemise over her head and threw it violently to the side. Jost gawked at the now nude woman before him, a sight such as he had never beheld in his short life.

"Oh, for the love of Sweet Jesus!" she exclaimed exasperated, reaching forward to hastily remove his clothing as well.

After she had finished her irksome task, she reached forward to grasp him with unexpected strength to throw him bodily upon the bed. She leaped forward atop him, sliding him easily within her moist cleft. She rode him like a wild animal; the violent rhythm of her thrusting thighs forced him to spew his seed deeply within her after only a few seconds. She screamed aloud with frustration, then leaned forward to slap his face savagely to and fro with her dainty hand. Having no idea what to do next, he lay there docilely beneath her, waiting patiently like a dumb beast soon to be slaughtered.

246

She then dismounted him, throwing herself testily to the other side of the soft, goose feather mattress facing away from him.

Jost had no idea what he was expected to do next. After a few minutes of considering his options, he eventually rolled onto his side, moving closer to the woman he had seemingly disappointed so badly. He reached out and placed his hand hesitantly upon her shoulder. She, in turn, grabbed it roughly and laid it upon her firm left breast.

"Have you never had a woman before?" Katharine asked in an icy voice without turning her head.

"No," he replied, ashamed by his admission.

"Tis a pity," she remarked briskly before rolling over to face him. "For what were you waiting?"

"Ah . . . um . . .," he mumbled, having no possible response that would make him appear less stupid than he currently felt.

"Never mind," she said with a sigh, clearly irritated by him. "Now, did you mean what you said about helping me with my fleeces, or were you only lying to convince me to let you have your way with me?"

"No, never!" he replied with alarm, hoping to somehow win his way back into the lady's good graces. "I will assist you in any way I can!"

"That's my good, good, boy," Katharine cooed, her previous coldness toward him seemingly now forgotten.

Jost felt a rush of relief at her renewed friendliness.

"My husband will probably come to seek me out soon," she said in a matter-of-fact manner.

A jolt of sudden terror coursed through Jost's veins. He swiftly began to rise from the bed, only to be stayed by Katharine's hand on his shoulder.

"Soon," she repeated, "but not now."

She pulled him atop her, sliding her hands down between their bodies to knead and stroke his pillicock. Within a few seconds, he had regained his hardness and entered her once more. He began to rock his hips gently, afraid of hurting the tiny woman beneath him. Unexpectedly, Katharine reached behind his buttocks and dug her fingernails deep into his soft flesh.

"Deeper, you damnable lout!" she raged wildly, "Put your back into it!"

Jost obeyed as best he could, although his ardor was somewhat hampered by the fear they would be discovered by the woman's husband. Katharine began to match his strokes with her own pelvic movements, twining her legs around him tightly and pulling his body down to place all of his weight upon hers. Without warning, her back arched and he felt his cock gripped by a spasming within her sex. For the second time, he felt his own release occur.

She turned her body, causing his to fall beside her.

"Better," she said, her face flushed with heat "Much better."

Jost smiled, glad he had pleased her this time.

"Now, get yourself dressed and I will tell you what I require," she said, beginning to pull on her clothing.

A half hour later, he was walking down the streets that led back to Bokerel House. Murky thoughts wriggled through his mind like a nest of eels disturbed from a muddy river bottom. He wondered whether he had only dreamed his encounter with Katharine Volker, that she had not shared her bed and body with him. Yet, he knew their shared passion had been real, just as real as her plans to intertwine her business with that of his cousin, Frederick.

"To the benefit of all," she had claimed assuredly.

Jost wasn't so sure. Her explanation had been somewhat vague, necessitated by their haste to avoid discovery by her husband, she had claimed. He had sought to ask questions, only to see a hurt expression appear on her face.

"Do you not trust me, my darling Jost?" she had asked, eyes wide and mournful.

"Yes, of course I do," he had replied without hesitation.

She had finished describing what she planned and he readily agreed, knowing he had received no such authority from Frederick to do so.

It mattered not. Jost realized he would sell his immortal soul to Satan himself, should that be Katharine's desire.

Chapter 11

Home
Lübeck, June, 1311

It was very, very dark.

Go back to sleep, Christina commanded herself.

She wasn't sure whether she obeyed, as she experienced none of that in-between period between consciousness and slumber - that time when you think about what you have done yesterday, or need to do tomorrow. Instead, she was there, wherever there was, and then she was not.

When she awoke, dust particles danced across the field of her vision, illuminated by a soft glow that filled the room; yet, emanated from no discernable source. For some odd reason, her other senses seemed to have not yet engaged; she could neither hear nor taste, smell nor feel. She seemed to be a disembodied spirit, floating . . . somewhere.

Then her brain made the connection.

I'm in my own chamber!

The two carved wooden ponies, red and blue, waited patiently on the table beside her bed, always ready for a hard-fought race across its surface. In the chair in the corner of the room sat Bette, one of the few dolls she had been gifted that she could tolerate.

That's because she teaches me bad words, Christina thought with a girlish giggle.

Her mood darkened as another consideration occurred to her.

Is it time for breakfast? If it is, why hasn't Anna come to dress me yet? Is she eating all of the cakes herself?

Grumpy now, Christina determined she would pull her clothes on and race to the kitchen to claim her share of her mother's fresh baked oatcakes. She struggled mightily but found she could not move. After minutes of single-minded effort, she managed to raise her hand off the bed and up toward her chest. What she found both shocked and terrified her.

"What's happened to me?" she shouted.

Though her lips made no sound, her shout was deafening in her mind.

What's happened to me? She posed the question to herself once more, this time realizing she had not spoken it aloud.

This was not the body of a girl; rather, it displayed the features of a grown woman. In amazement, Christina moved her fingers unsteadily over the swell of a full breast, where she had expected to feel a flat chest. She moved her hand down, encountering outlying tufts of coarse curly hair somewhat below her navel. Her exploration halted there; the conclusion now incontrovertible.

What's happened to me? she asked herself a third time, not just questioning whatever sorcery had aged her body so, but also why she could not focus her swirling thoughts. Her head began to ache as her frustration mounted. *Why am I so confused?*

She plunged back into the dark place without willing it; the place where thought was forbidden and time was meaningless.

Christina's eyes slowly opened again. She was relieved to discover that the world that greeted her now looked quite natural and familiar.

How long have I been asleep this time? she wondered futilely, having no means to fix either a starting or ending point to her slumber.

A quick examination of her body revealed everything as it should be.

That's good, she thought humorously, *I'd hate to have discovered that I'm now a grandmother.*

She suddenly noticed a figure in the room, one she knew well.

"Anna! Come to me. Help me!" she cried, but the sounds again failed to materialize from her throat.

As the maid walked about the room, Christina noticed another, less discernable, figure moving behind her.

"Marguerite! What are you doing in my room? You'd better get out or I'm going to tell Mother!"

But Marguerite just hid behind Anna's skirts, poking her head out every now and then to smile at Christina before disappearing once more.

Why is she playing such childish games? Is this not the night of her marriage feast? If she isn't careful, she'll be late and that will embarrass Mother and Father in front of everyone who matters in Lübeck!

"Marguerite, you'd better stop!"

But she was no longer there.

In her place was . . . Frederick. He did not crouch in the shadows; instead, he stood boldly beside where she lay in her bed, almost close enough to reach had she the strength to do so.

Christina smiled up at her brother, whom she loved beyond all others. He grinned back, but his face had changed subtlety. It was slightly more angular, with a more pronounced jawline. As she stared at him, Frederick's hair, although remaining the same color, grew fuller. In shock, she realized it was not her brother standing before her, but herself.

A sudden rush of faces passed before her eyes. Some she had loved, others hated, and still others whom she had lost.

She managed a small whimper. With shock, she realized she had actually heard it.

Now, the faces were juxtaposed against various settings as if part of some confounding memory game.

No, Anna did not go to London! she recalled firmly. *It was my other, younger sister!*

She fumbled for her name, but it eluded her. She moved on.

Yes, Piers . . . Piers Gaveston, in the castle! she thought, enormously please with herself for remembering. *But which castle?*

She felt unable to answer until, finally, the pieces connected.

Both of them! He was at the Tower in London as well as Roxburgh, in the Scottish Marches. I like the man. He's helped me and I've helped him! And Anna's sister is Trudi, and I like her too . . . a lot!

Suddenly, the people and places she had correctly associated became scrambled once more. Her vision clouded with what she knew to be tears of frustration, but she was unable to raise her hand to her face to wipe them away.

I've never felt so abandoned, so alone. Why won't someone help me?

As her vision cleared slightly, she saw her mother: sitting on her bed beside her and gazing down at her, deep concern upon the woman's lined face. Christina tried to lift her arms, to reach out to touch her somehow, but was unable.

Why can't I speak? Christina wondered with mounting horror. *Where was I before I was here? What was I doing? Am I dead? If I'm with my mother, is she dead as well?*

Ignoring the sharpening pain in her head, Christina focused all her will on recalling what she could remember of the recent past. A perplexing series of images moved through her mind: of ships, of blood, of death. Then they were gone, only to be replaced by the all-too-familiar darkness.

Am I dead? she once more posed the simple question to herself, matter-of-factly, without fear or concern.

Christina received no confirmation from the darkness; instead, what little grip she had on her world began to recede once more.

Just before losing consciousness, she heard her mother say, "I love you, my Christina."

Chapter 12

***

A Plan Comes Together
Lübeck, July, 1311

Christina awoke with a start, slowly allowing the world around her to come into focus. It was warm. No, hot. She felt the thin, perspiration-soaked sheet move with her as she squirmed slightly to make her position more comfortable.

What time of day is this? she wondered, attempting to judge the angle of the sun streaming through the windows. *Windows? Where the hell am I? Certainly not aboard der Greif, that's for damn sure.*

Her mind felt as foggy as the sea had been, when she could last recall any details at all.

How long have I been here? she wondered, realizing she couldn't even venture a guess.

Clearly, the only means to finding answers lay with first rising from her bed. Thus, Christina struggled to get one elbow beneath her, lifting her head a few inches. A sudden pain exploded inside her skull and she dropped it back onto the pillow. Gritting her teeth, she repeated her first effort only, this time, rather than falling back when the pain came, she swung her legs over the side of the bed and sat upright.

Blackness fought to grip her brain, eliciting a sudden lurch in her stomach that caused a small amount of thick, rancid, yellow bile to eject from her lips and out upon the sheet that still covered half of her nakedness. She felt herself grow unsteady once more as her eyes fought to focus.

"Christina!" a female voice cried.

Christina felt herself suddenly supported by a pair of strong arms that held her tightly to a clothed bosom. Realizing she was no longer in danger of collapsing to the floor; she directed her pitifully limited reserve of strength to the task of clearing her vision. Suddenly, her eyes focused and sensory recognition threatened to overwhelm her.

"Mother?" she asked with incredulity, recognizing not only the individual who held her, but also the chamber in which they sat as her own.

"Oh, yes, Christina! My dear, dear Christina!" Mechtild Kohl replied, sobbing. "I thought I had lost you, that you would never awaken. But now you have, thank our merciful God!"

The pain and blackness grudgingly receded from Christina's mind; yet, she knew they had not been completely overcome. They only awaited an opportunity to defeat her once more.

"How am I here? I was standing on the deck of *der Greif*, in the fog. There was fighting, then no more . . ." she muttered haltingly, her memories still somewhat enmeshed with her hallucinations while unconscious.

"You were injured. A terrible blow fell upon the back of your head. Herr Ziesolf and that large fellow took you aboard a schnigge and sped you here while you lay unconscious for three days. For five more you have lain in your own bed, neither opening your eyes, nor emitting a sound other than low moans. I almost despaired for you, my daughter, but knew I must remain strong. I will not let death claim the last of my children," Christina's mother spoke resolutely.

"*Der Greif?*" Christina asked fearfully. "How fared the battle?"

"You will need to gain the particulars from Herr Ziesolf, I'm afraid. Let it suffice to say you were victorious and your ship sits safely within our harbor."

"Thank the sweet Virgin for her mercy," Christina said softly, finding herself yearning for sleep once more.

Mechtild Kohl gently guided her daughter's body back down onto her bed.

"You rest now," she said, "The only important thing is for you to regain your strength. We will talk more later."

Christina's mother walked quietly to the voluminous cabinet at the side of the room and withdrew a clean bleached linen sheet. She stripped the damp one from her daughter's naked body, looking with concern at the large number of scars, bruises, and abrasions evident upon her pale flesh. Placing the clean sheet gently over the drowsy young woman, she walked to the door, stopping to take one last loving look at her.

"Thank you for coming back to me," she said in a low voice before exiting the room, leaving Christina alone once more.

It might have been that evening or the next when Christina again gained consciousness. This time, she had no doubt as to her whereabouts or what had transpired. She sat up with only a modicum of head-throbbing, took a deep breath, then stood upright for the first time in over a week. Feeling as helpless as a newborn colt, she began to sway, finally placing her hand upon the wall to steady herself. After a few moments, she felt strong enough to continue her journey to the trunk where her clothes had been stored ever since she had been a small child.

Christina worked her way carefully to her knees, then opened the lid. As expected, an assortment of clothing was neatly folded and stacked within; however, she had not considered they would all be female garments.

"Christ's nails," she exclaimed in a low whisper, "How long has it been since I have worn such clothing?"

She thought about donning the garb before her, both because there seemed no alternative and because she was a bit curious to see herself as a woman for the first time in almost two years. In the end, she decided against it, resolving to await her mother's return before getting dressed.

Walking back to the bed, she noticed a small bell had been placed upon the table alongside. Reasoning her mother had left it there for her, Christina gave it a try.

She waited patiently for a few minutes. Having elicited no apparent response, Christina was contemplating ringing the bell once more when the door opened. To her surprise, it was not her mother who entered the room, but her maid, Anna. Embarrassed, Christina scrambled to pull the sheet over her unclothed body.

"I don't know why you're bothering with that," Anna said briskly, "It's not like I haven't seen every square inch of you before, and scrubbed it clean as well, I might add."

"Oh . . . good day to you, Anna," Christina replied, "It's just that I was expecting my mother, that's all."

"She's sleeping," the maid replied." And about time too. I don't think she closed her eyes for more than ten minutes at a time since they brought you back; insensible, and seemingly at death's door."

Anna had always been fiercely protective of Mechtild Kohl. It was certainly one of her better qualities, along with being efficient and hardworking. To Christina, however, she had always been stern, unemotional, and a little frightening. She thanked God she had been able to trick her mother into letting Trudi come with her to London instead of Anna. How things might have turned out differently if she had not!

"Anna," Christina said in what she hoped was a declarative voice, "I need to get dressed. Fetch me my clothes, if you please."

The maid looked at her strangely for a second, clearly unaccustomed to being spoken to in such a manner by a person over whom she had always felt control. She moved toward the trunk that Christina had explored only a few minutes prior.

"No, not those. I need the clothing I was wearing when I was brought here, or others that are . . . similar."

Anna's thin lips pinched together, as if she wanted to say something but then decided against it. She nodded curtly, then departed the chamber. A few minutes later, she returned, carrying a stack of clean, folded clothing, as well as Christina's boots. She placed the footwear on the floor and the clothing on the bed.

"Here, let me help you dress," Anna said, then added in a slightly softer tone, "If you would like."

"Yes, please," Christina replied, sensing their previous relationship had somehow changed by the now deferential tone of the maid's response.

As Anna wrapped the length of linen fabric snugly about Christina's chest, she asked, "And what of my sister, Trudi? Does she serve you well?"

Though her words were spoken casually, Christina detected deep concern in them.

"Yes," answered Christina, "She has been a true godsend to me. Soon after my arrival in London, my aunt bequeathed her home to me, a manor house of some forty-six rooms, more or less. Trudi has assumed the role of housekeeper there, with a staff of over twenty servants to manage, most hardly younger than herself. The household is contented, runs efficiently, and is maintained to my liking. I could not ask for more."

Anna sat down on a nearby bench, seeming overcome with amazement at Christina's description of the new-found competence of a younger sister whom she had always criticized as a vain, empty-headed girl. She had made it readily apparent to Trudi that she felt her too concerned with creating mischief and flirting with boys to be trusted with anything more than menial tasks. Distraught at her sister's harsh condemnations, Christina had had to repeatedly still her friend's ragged sobs and reassure her of her self-worth.

With an expression of guilty remorse, Anna rose from her seat and began dressing Christina once more.

"Anna?"

"Yes?"

"There's more," Christina said, grinning as she turned to face the maid. "Trudi is married now, to the master of my yard, a smith. They have a young son, newly born only days before I departed."

Anna stared at Christina, her jaw hanging. It was several seconds before she was able to speak.

"Married? A son?" she exclaimed. "What have you two girls been up to while you've been away? Can these be the same brats that got into some sort of devilment nearly every day when they were little? By the blessed Virgin, Christina, how the two of you have changed!"

"Many things do, Anna."

Without thinking, Christina moved forward and hugged the older woman, an action she had never before done willingly. A lifetime of petty animosity between the two seemed to melt away as Anna returned the embrace, stiffly at first, then more naturally.

Once Christina was clothed, the two women went to the solar of the house. Christina was happy to be seated, as even the short walk between the rooms of the house had nearly exhausted her. Her mother joined her in a matter of minutes, accompanied by Anna carrying a large tray of delicious foodstuffs. Sitting it down upon the circular table, Anna departed, although with a lilt to her step and a pleasant expression that Christina hadn't once noticed throughout her childhood.

"Hold your head downward," Mechtild Kohl brusquely instructed her daughter.

Christina complied. Her mother poked lightly about the thick bandaging on the back of Christina's skull, eliciting a few winces and a slight cry of pain from her daughter when her finger probed too near the still-tender area of her swollen scalp. Eventually, she stepped away. Christina gazed now into her mother's eyes; her question evident despite being left unspoken.

"There seems to be no permanent damage as far as I can tell, although it seems miraculous to say so. The skull seems to be uncracked and the swelling has gone down considerably. You were fortunate, my daughter. Clearly, our God had you under his blessed protection."

She smiled slightly, then crossed herself.

It had been days since Christina had ingested anything more substantial than a few drops of wine. She attempted to gulp down the food with her usual enthusiasm, but could manage only a few bites before her stomach felt queasy. She pushed her plate away and hurriedly clamped her hand over her mouth as her stomach began to convulse.

"It will take time, my daughter."

Her mother chuckled.

"Your appetite will certainly return, as will then Anna's concerns with an empty larder. Rest now, then try some more later. Do you feel well enough to chat?"

Christina did. They spoke for what seemed hours, the shadows growing long until they disappeared altogether. Anna entered and lit a few candles about the chamber. The room enveloped them in the remnants of the day's heat and the soft glow from the flickering flames. Eventually, Christina nodded off to sleep, feeling a contentment she had seldom experienced in her life. Sometime later that night she awoke and returned to her own chamber.

In the faint light of the half moon, Christina gazed about the room in which she had slept nearly every night of her life, up to her departure to London nearly two years prior. There was really no reason to look, she knew the placement of the bed, the small table beside it, and every other article in the room by heart.

Her mother had left everything exactly as it had always been; yet, Christina felt strangely out of place in her childhood home. She recalled when she had turned fourteen years old and had wanted to wear her favorite woad-blue kirtle to Katrey Wendler's wedding feast. She remembered her tears of frustration as, despite her best efforts, she had been unable to pull the sturdy fabric down over the broadened hips of a woman who was no longer a child. Like the kirtle, her home had remained the same, it was she who no longer fit.

She did not go back to her slumbers easily, her thoughts turning away from the pleasure of reuniting with her mother to other, more troublesome ones outside the family home on Engelsgrube.

Awakening the next morning, Christina's return to the real world became complete.

Soon after breaking her fast, she was sitting with her mother in the solar when Anna entered, accompanied by Ziesolf. Knowing there was much he and her daughter had to discuss, Mechtild departed with the maid, softly closing the door behind them.

Ziesolf moved forward and, displaying uncommon emotion, patted Christina gently on the shoulder, murmuring, "My good, good girl. How happy I am to see you have returned to us."

"You always told me I was too hard-headed," Christina teased, "Maybe that is a good thing after all."

Ziesolf ignored the jibe.

"How do you feel?" he asked, staring at her intently. no doubt to judge the tenor of her response.

"Like shit, truthfully. My head aches much of the time and I feel as weak as a newly born babe. I can only take a few nibbles at one sitting, despite the fact Mother sets vast quantities of my favorite foods before me."

"You are young and healthy and will soon return to your normal self," Ziesolf reassured.

A few moments of silence ensued, each reluctant to broach the subject that was foremost in their minds. Finally, Christina could wait no longer.

"Kurt?" she began, "The battle. What happened?"

Ziesolf sunk into the chair her mother had vacated and pulled it closer.

"It was a near thing," he said in a low voice. "More and more of our attackers were boarding, threatening to overwhelm our diminished numbers."

Christina sighed and asked the question that had plagued since she had awakened the day before.

"Who was it we lost?"

"As you know, the lead archer Alan received a bolt through his hip. Luckily, it missed anything vital and he is well on the mend. His man Gilbert was not so fortunate. His wound is serious and his life is still in some doubt. He rests at the Hospital of the Holy Spirit, under the care of Brother Udo. Do you remember him?"

She nodded. Of course, she remembered the friar unable to save Marguerite when she fell ill. Hopefully, he would have more success treating the wounds of the young bowman.

"The man Reiniken refers to as Tiny Tom took a bad slice to the side, but his ribs kept it from reaching his vitals. Reiniken sewed him up, all the while the injured man kept up such a steady stream of foul curses that Wig started laughing so hard, he pulled the thread right out and had to start over again. Tom kept silent after that, fixing Reiniken with a murderous stare the whole time. He'll be fine."

Christina knew there was worse news to come. She didn't have long to wait.

"One of the archers, Edward by name, was the first to fall. Two sailors, Aldstan and Luit, were killed during the clash on the deck. Another of Reiniken's men, the large one called Henry, also died. Besides that, there were only bruises and bumps, other than yourself, of course."

She felt an aching sorrow grow inside her as she recalled the faces of the men who had given their lives in her service. She had known them all, not a difficult accomplishment considering the long days at sea in the tight quarters aboard ship. For some reason, the death of Henry troubled her the most, although she probably knew him the least.

Probably from having seen his wife and child.

The image of their forlorn faces would surely plague many of her future dreams.

Ziesolf waited patiently for Christina to speak. He knew the losses bothered her more than she would ever admit aloud.

"What now?" she asked after a few pregnant seconds.

"The aldermen have inquired several times concerning your condition, requesting you to appear before them as soon as you have recovered your wits. Although you have, thank God, done so, I have not informed them of this fact. Better you do not appear in public, yes?"

"Absolutely."

"So, in your absence and as your lieutenant, they have made me privy to their plans. Do you recall Ulbert Geldersen?"

"Yes," she replied, without fondness.

He was one of the senior aldermen of the council. His father had been a member of Cologne's *Richerzeche*, or "Rich Man's Club," who had left that city as the result of some mysterious controversy. Settling in Lübeck, his wealth had continued to grow as well as his influence in the city's government. After the elder's death, his holdings were inherited by his son. Ulbert Geldersen had often argued with Christina's father, who had found him to be a disagreeable and arrogant man. Christina believed Geldersen had pursued her sister Marguerite as a bride for his own son, but her father had flatly refused any negotiations to that end. Christina groaned, afraid to hear what was coming next.

"He has been placed in charge of the fleet of ships hunting the pirates. In this capacity, he is nominally your superior, in Lübeck's eyes at least."

"Bull shit! As if I would subordinate myself to that varlet!"

Ignoring her outburst, Ziesolf continued.

"He is very frustrated, as there has been scant success in the campaign. Townspeople are beginning to whisper it is because of his poor leadership. You, on the other hand, are feted as a hero, capturing six enemy vessels and killing more than a hundred of the foes. Knowing this man, he must be raging with jealousy. He knows he must own a victory, and soon."

Why do men have to be so fucking stupid? she thought wearily. *Why does it matter who gets credit, as long as the task gets done?*

"Now, he believes the opportunity is before him," Ziesolf continued, "Under extreme torture, one of the pirates disclosed the location of their base, a village on the Jutland peninsula across the Kattegat west of Anholt. Geldersen now musters what ships and men he can to lead on an attack."

"And what of us?" Christina replied, "What part is *der Greif* to play in this plan?"

"The last thing Geldersen wants is to share the glory of ridding the threat to shipping in the Kattegat once and for all with anyone, let alone you. He has directed that our men will come ashore some distance from the village and take up positions nearby. That will leave his forces to conduct the actual attack, while we will only be able to engage those who flee."

Christina kneaded her temples as her head began to pound once more.

It seemed straightforward. The number of able-bodied men among the pirates must have been greatly reduced, placing the odds clearly in Geldersen's favor. If they stand and fight, that is. But, if they realize they are greatly outnumbered, what then? It seems sensible they would retreat, rather than stand and be killed. Could the entire pirate force be driven toward Christina's meager forces? Although the pirates were less in numbers than they once were, certainly there are many more of them remaining than there were of her men.

"What if they run toward us?" she asked.

"Then we get very busy," Ziesolf replied, a grim smile fixed on his face. "Should they get past us, you are to blame. Should they kill us, you are to blame. Should we stop them, he receives the credit. Can you see how such a strategy would appeal to him?"

Christina understood the attractiveness of such a plan to the man's ego.

"When does he intend to depart?"

"Four days hence. Will you be well enough to sail?" he asked with a look of concern. "Your injury was severe and you have not had sufficient time to fully recover."

"Try and stop me," Christina responded fiercely, her lips forming wolfish grin. "There will be bloody hell to pay for those we have lost."

Over the ensuing days, Christina began to regain her strength, although she chafed at the forced inactivity of remaining sequestered inside the house. She had hoped to sneak out to the wharf where *der Greif* was anchored, but her mother had scolded her, as she had done throughout her daughter's life. She had reminded Christina of the risk involved in not only being recognized for who she was - but also for who she was not - prompting a more forceful summons from the alderman she could not ignore. Although she wanted to argue, Christina could not dispute her mother's words. Consequently, she was forced to leave the preparations for the forthcoming voyage in the capable hands of Matthias and Ziesolf.

With time on her hands, Christina spent hours regaling her mother with the events that had occurred in her life since sailing from Lübeck as an impetuous, immature girl. She omitted any reference to her shared love with Cecily, believing it would be beyond her mother's ken, who would consider it to be a cardinal sin that would damn her daughter's soul forever. Afterwards, she felt guilty about her intentional deception.

Was she ashamed? One would believe she must be if she was afraid to share her feelings for Cecily with her mother. But there was more to it. Not only were Cecily and Christina two women, but Cecily was also the wife of another. Regardless of the churlishness of Cecily's husband, their marriage was blessed by God and subsequently consummated, evidenced by the child that grew within her womb. Would a son proclaim his love proudly to his mother for a woman under the same circumstances?

In the end, she decided to remain silent for the time being. Christina realized their reunion was nearing its end and had no desire to depart with a new wedge of misunderstanding thrust between them.

Perhaps if the opportunity presents itself . . .

Despite the growing anticipation in the city surrounding the rumors of Ulbert Geldersen's imminent foray against the pirates, an event even more important in the eyes of the citizens soon occurred, overshadowing all else. The ships of the *Winterfahrer* had finally returned from the city of Novgorod. Considerable anxiety had grown throughout the city over the past weeks as never before had the hardy merchants who had wintered in the harsh environment of 'Rus returned so late in the year. Soon, tales of the Volkhov River being frozen nearly down to its bottom emerged, with the normal mid-April thaw being delayed well into May. Even then, the waters were not navigable as massive floes of ice locked and jammed the river nearly its entire length. This was only part of the journey, however, as a portage was necessary to enter Lake Lagoda, the next step of the arduous journey. From there, they sailed down the Neva River until they emerged at the island of Kronstadt near its mouth. Here, the merchants transferred their cargo to their larger ocean-going ships and navigated the full length of the Baltic back to their home port.

The dark, foreboding winter did have a bright spot, however. The plummeting temperatures prompted fur-bearing animals in the region to grow thicker, more luxurious coats. Consequently, the German ships were nearly groaning under the load of cask after cask of northern gray squirrel furs. Particularly desirable squirrel pelt types were separately bundled as they were graded as gray and white vair, grey gris, and white miniver. Beaver, ermine, sable, and other exotic pelts constituted the remainder of their cargoes, along with substantial amounts of wax and honey. Reunions with long-separated families were joyous but hasty, as preparations began for immediate distribution of these riches to markets across Europe.

Christina knew her mother's investment in shares of the cargoes of four ships would soon be making their way directly onto *Seelöwe*, which would depart for London as soon as loading was complete. What was left over would be stored on the fourth floor of the house on Engelsgrube, awaiting the return of *der Greif.*

Perhaps I will even try to purchase more, Christina speculated. *I have the two ewer vessels at my disposal, should I decide to crew them rather than arrange for their sale.*

At last, the day approached for the departure of Geldersen's small fleet. Although he had only been successful in procuring five cogs for his mission, their decks would be crowded with nearly 160 men. Although others of the council urged Geldersen to wait until more ships arrived, he was undeterred.

Ziesolf, trying to mimic Geldersen's grating voice, quoted his response as, "Our prisoner told us his band had been reduced to no more than fifty men of fighting age. What need have we to wait? We outnumber them by three to one already, and each of ours is worth three of them!"

Christina gave a derisive snort.

She imagined a large number of Lübeck's citizenry would turn out in the early morning chill to watch the ships slowly depart from their moorages into a stately line to progress the approximate ten miles to the sea. Some would wave and shout to the men on board the cogs, while others would choose to watch silently, offering prayers for the safe return of their fathers, husbands, and sons. Geldersen would pose stiffly erect atop the sterncastle of his ship, his hand resting firmly on the railing, gazing toward the horizon, almost as if he were already posing for his victory portrait.

Christina had decided to forego this spectacle, choosing instead to depart her family's home, board *der Greif*, and leave with the previous evening's tide. Now, her cog rocked gently at anchor, patiently awaiting the arrival of the other ships. Alone on the sterncastle of her vessel, Christina stared toward the mouth of the Trave; however, her thoughts were back in Lübeck, recalling her mother's farewell words.

"You know I do not think you should do this," Mechtild Kohl had said firmly, "You have neither fully recovered from your injury, nor regained your strength."

As Christina opened her mouth to argue, her mother held up her hand, the same gesture she had always used to still her daughter's protests. She then reached down and clasped both of Christina's hands firmly in her own.

"But you are no longer the obstinate child who needed to be controlled for her own good. Now, you are an adult who makes her own decisions, profiting or suffering from their consequences as the Lord's will dictates. Your life is further complicated by the double life you have chosen to lead. But, since I cannot stop you, I may only fervently pray for your safety and success, in this as in all your ventures."

"Thank you, Mother. I will be careful. I promise."

"Do not make promises you will not keep," her mother replied with a merry gleam in her eye. "I have known you too long to believe you will approach any challenge cautiously."

She knows me well, Christina mused with a smile.

"Will I see you again?" Mechtild Kohl asked, suddenly changing the subject.

"Yes. No. I'm not sure," Christina replied, confused as to what response to make to future plans she had not yet considered. "Certainly, at some time, but I am not sure when."

Her mother gazed at her with a sad smile, her grip on her daughter's hands growing tighter.

"This answer gives me hope. Go now, with my blessing. You have done well for yourself, Christina, remarkably so. You've gained fortune and accomplishment far beyond what might be expected of any man of your few years, and absolutely impossible for one of our sex. But do remember, my child, wealth and renown do not always guarantee happiness."

Christina's heart nearly burst from the affection she felt for her mother then, and suddenly, she felt compelled to rid their relationship of the last secret between them.

"Mother," Christina suddenly blurted out, "I have found someone who does make me happy."

Her mother's eyebrows raised in surprise.

"Her name is Cecily and she is a lady of the English nobility."

Her mother's eyes narrowed and she looked down, randomly picking at a loose thread on the cuff of her chemise for a few long seconds. Her gaze arose and her expression softened.

"I am not familiar with such . . . um . . . an arrangement," she said, choosing her words carefully. "I only know this constitutes another dangerous path, one in which you must tread very, very lightly. Again, I will not criticize the choices you have made. Instead, I will pray doubly the Lord not hold you in his disfavor for them."

She leaned forward and kissed Christina lightly on the cheek, then turned and walked away.

Christina felt as if a burden had been removed from her life. She thought to call after her mother, to reaffirm her love for her. She declined, deciding the terms of their parting to have satisfied both of their needs.

As Christina was gathering her things from her chamber, a light knock sounded at her door. She opened it, surprised to find Anna standing outside.

"Oh, Anna, I was not expecting you."

"I am sorry to intrude upon you," Anna replied somewhat stiffly before holding something in her hands out toward Christina. "Would you be so kind as to give this to my sister? It is something I have made with my own hands for her babe."

Christina looked down to see a small linen coverlet, covered with intricately embroidered birds and flowers.

"I am certain she will love it," she said, smiling encouragingly. "As will her son."

"Please tell her I wish her well and hope that someday we will meet again."

"I will, Anna," Christina replied, touched by the woman's unexpected tenderness.

The sudden appearance of a cog emerging from the mouth of the Trave broke her sentimental reverie. From her elevated position on the aft castle, she was soon able to see the other four members of the flotilla following closely behind. Already, Matthias was ordering *der Greif's* anchor to be raised from the bay's bottom. The sails of Geldersen's vessels began to catch the land breeze more fully, billowing majestically to push the vessels northward at a stately five knots. Matthias expertly brought *der Greif* behind their formation, approximately three hundred yards in their wake.

With God's mercy, this will be the end of it, she thought. *One final confrontation, then home to England.*

Two days later, Geldersen's ships halted their progress off the small Jutland village of Grenaa, less than a half day's sail from the mouth of the inlet leading to the pirates' lair. *Der Greif,* however, did not join the other cogs at their anchorage. Instead, Christina's ship sailed resolutely forward, alone once more.

"This is the riskiest part of the plan," Ziesolf admitted, standing at his customary post at the forecastle of the ship.

"What? That we travel on by ourselves to make a landfall on an unknown coast, or that we must then trek overland and take up positions above our adversary's village undetected? What could be risky about that?" Christina laughed mirthlessly.

273

It is dangerous, with many aspects that can easily go very wrong.

"The potential peril is real, but undetected is the key word here. Should the pirates discover us before Geldersen makes his attack, they could turn their full might upon us. The archers provide us a tremendous advantage, but what if the land is forested, or we are caught among the reed beds that stretch for miles in the low-lying areas of the shore? Alternatively, they could just ignore us, waiting until night to attack us in the dark. Any of these eventualities would make us the distraction, allowing Geldersen's ships to possibly approach unobserved. Is this what he intended?"

"Maybe not," Christina replied dryly, "But I'm certain he would not shed many tears for our demise if it somehow enabled his own glorious victory."

They passed the entrance to the fjord that, a few miles further along its course, would eventually lead to the Danish town of Randers. Christina had wondered how the pirates had managed to conceal their activities from the ships that would most certainly carry commerce along the waterway to the sea. Ziesolf had told her the aldermen's prisoner had revealed his village was located along a small tributary, some two or three miles from the coast, whose entrance was well obscured by reed beds. Should any ship's master become too curious and choose to investigate this secondary waterway more closely, his curiosity would likely cost him his ship.

A little over an hour later, Christina believed they had passed far enough beyond the inlet to make their landing. She communicated this to Matthias, who would choose the exact position of their disembarkation, as well as the time. The ship's master took several minutes to make a careful examination of the waters leading to the beach before finally deciding.

"There," he said, pointing to a point of sand which, to Christina, differed in no way from those to its left and right. "We will wait until high tide, then you and your men can wade ashore with hardly getting your feet wet."

Christina was about to ask Mattias why he chose that spot, but thought better of it. She trusted the man completely in such matters; besides, she could now see the slightly darker finger of water stretching toward Mattias' selected landing site. Clearly, the greater depth would allow the ship to be navigated closer to shore, within a few yards of dry land.

Three hours of impatient waiting finally resulted in a favorable switching of tidal flows. Two more and Christina's small band of warriors were safely ashore. Although she was wet almost to her knee she was not complaining. She had greatly feared that, should they be required to disembark in deeper waters, her men's lives would be in danger as she knew several of them could not swim.

Christina drew a deep breath. Everything had progressed well to this point, but would it continue to do so?

If Geldersen's informer was truthful. If we have navigated correctly. If the pirates are in their village and not somewhere at sea. Too many "ifs" for my liking, she muttered under her breath as she took her first steps inland toward their designated position above the pirate hamlet. *But what choice do we have? We're just going to have to trust in the Lord and hope for the best.*

In a short time, they had progressed across the white sands of the beach, only to encounter an extensive marshland populated with an overgrowth of reeds. Christina fixed her position with the sun and led her small party in what she hoped was a westward direction. Eventually, the land dried beneath their feet and the going became less arduous. The ground was primarily flat, interrupted only by a few gently undulating hillocks populated by an increasing number of mature linden, oak, and beech trees. They approached each of these with some trepidation, realizing they could provide concealment to hostiles. Their luck held, however, as the most threatening thing they encountered was a large red deer buck with magnificent antlers, startled from his feed by their approach. After a disgruntled snort, he gave way, allowing them to continue their trek unimpeded.

Christina halted the men for a few minutes of rest. They took the time gladly, gulping down weak ale and wiping sweat from their faces with sleeves already sodden with that activity. Equally soaked, Christina thanked her foresight in deciding against wearing her armor.

Though it assuredly would have afforded greater protection, it would have been of little value had I not the strength to bear its weight over miles of travel. Besides, if everything goes according to plan, I will have no need for it.

She still had her doubts in that regard.

They resumed their march, in a southerly direction now, with the motive of doubling back toward where they believed their objective to be located.

Then, it's only a matter of waiting . . . and keeping from being discovered, she surmised. *Who knows? Everything could be over tomorrow without us having fired an arrow.*

She prayed for that to be true.

Sometime after sunset, Godfrey appeared from the underbrush ahead. He had been scouting the area, his sharp senses alert for any trace of their adversaries. He beckoned Christina forward.

The rest of the group halted as she hurried to his side. Creeping forward, she smelled the villagers' presence before she saw them, the scent of woodsmoke and savory roasted meat

276

wafting on the breeze. She and Godfrey stole forward cautiously, first down on all fours, then crawling on their bellies through the final few feet of withered grass to the crest of a small hillock. Christina swiped at the perspiration stinging her eyes with her sleeve. Spitting the salty dust from her mouth, she focused on what lay before her.

A clear field sloped toward the rivulet approximately four hundred yards distant at its bottom. On the opposite bank a vast plain of reeds stretched into the intensifying gloom. The water before it was about eighty yards across at its widest point and of interminable depth, except through inference from the few small to medium draught vessels that floated at anchor on it.

It was the nearer bank that consumed Christina's interest, however. A small dock, about twenty feet long, extended into the water. There were several small wood houses, all with steep, overhanging roofs thatched with reeds. She imagined the larger buildings at the southern end of the villages were storerooms, holding their ill-gotten gain. A few craftsman's shops were arranged around a small central square; she could identify a smithy, a mill, and a bakery, as a minimum. On the pathways between the structures, men, women, and children made their way to their destinations or merely strolled for the pleasure of it. Though the lively breeze at her back kept Christina from hearing what they were saying, she imagined their conversations to be the same as villagers everywhere.

It's difficult to imagine these are the same people whose livelihood is based upon looting and murdering those weaker than themselves, she mused, experiencing a sudden pang of pity for the men milling below whose lives would likely be snuffed like a candle wick at dawn.

How can humankind be so cruel?

Whether her thought was regarding the freebooters or their soon-to-be attackers, she was undecided.

Then, her heart hardened.

These are the men who murdered Frederick and Father. If they would have taken der Greif, they would have added Ziesolf, Wig and the ship's crewmen to their victims. As for Trudi and me . . .

She gulped, remembering her terror at nearly being raped while a captive at Roxburgh castle

A swift death would have been a mercy we would not have been granted. These fuckers deserve to die!

She did concede to say a silent prayer for the women and children who would be left to fend for themselves, however.

Christina made her way back to where her comrades anxiously awaited. In a low voice, she described the lay of the land and outlined her plan for how their forces would be dispersed. When she finished, Ziesolf accompanied each pair of men, consisting of an archer and a man-at-arms, to their individual station to ensure the entire field before them could be brought under fire. He also instructed them that one man should stand watch while the other slept, ensuring they would not be overwhelmed during the night. Then, there was nothing left to do but chew on the crusts of bread they had brought, drink their weakened ale, and be in position for Geldersen's anticipated attack at morning's first light.

Christina and Alan occupied the center position in the line of two dozen men. His eyes were closed, though whether he truly slept, she did not know. In the last light of the evening, she looked down once more on the tranquil village, populated with contented folk who had no idea of the violence that awaited them at dawn.

How in the hell have I come to this? she thought, nearly laughing aloud at the absurdity of her situation. *It seems I am being carried along*

in life like a twig swept down a rain- swollen river. But is this not of my making? Did I not consent to embark on this wild adventure despite its small possibility of bringing me any gain? Why did I not refuse? Does Katharine Volker's disdain really matter to me?

A few flickers of candlelight were all that could be seen in the village, the moon above just a sliver in the ebony sky.

Is it that Katharine and I are alike in some ways? Christina shuddered, sickened at the thought of likening herself to such a corrupt creature. *But do I revile her solely because of her promiscuous nature? Sybille, the woman who plies her trade at the Nag's Head in Southwark, is a true whore, yet I would have loved her had she only allowed me to. How are the two different? Perhaps Katharine is a rival in my eyes, one who, like me, makes her own way in a man's world? But where I employ subterfuge, living a lie in men's guise, she works her wiles openly, achieving what she will as herself. Does this make her better than me, causing resentment over her freedom and spurring my hatred for her?*

Christina did not fully understand why she felt such loathing against her, but it had filled her from the first minutes they met.

Perhaps one day I will figure it out, she promised herself vaguely.

A sudden hand on her shoulder nearly caused her to cry out. Alan ripped it away, then relaxed when she reached forth and grasped it in a friendly manner. She crawled backwards a few feet until she was completely concealed from the village. Realizing this may be her only opportunity to attend to her body functions unobserved, she retired a short distance away and dropped her braies. After a few minutes, she returned to her position. A few minutes more and she drifted into a fitful sleep, one troubled by visitations from the dead, as well as by some who yet drew breath.

Long before morning, she awakened in a cold sweat, thankful the night was past. She gazed anxiously into the east waiting for the faintest brightening of the horizon. It had not arrived, however, only the dim light of a few stars speckled the blackness. She knew not whether the dawn was an hour hence or four. She had not noticed a church in the small village; even if there was one, the priest was not one so zealous as to toll the earliest hours.

Christina once again slunk toward the hillock's crest. She gestured to Alan, querying him as to whether he had noticed any suspicious activity below. He shook his head, then backed away. Once more, she was alone with her thoughts.

It was less than an hour before the sky went from black to dark gray. She was not the only one to notice as others along the line began to stir, signaling to those behind them the time to wake had come. Some grabbed a few mouthfuls of their meager rations, while others engaged in a morning piss. By the time the first rays of the sun appeared, each was in his assigned place with weapons at the ready.

The sunrise had awakened those in the village as well; a few early risers were already about their everyday tasks. They would not have been so placid had they been gazing through Christina's eyes, placed as they were at a vantage point on the small ridgeline dozens of feet higher.

Far downstream, the upper part of a sail appeared just above the point where the river bent. Within minutes, the vessel beneath it rounded the curve, revealing what she had expected to see; a cog ship progressing slowly towards the village. Soon, another sail appeared not far behind the first.

Christina's attention was diverted by a flurry of activity in the village below. A sturdy pony galloped into the square; soon it was converged upon by a growing crowd of people. The rider dismounted from the beast, whose sides heaved in and out from what surely was unaccustomed exertion. Christina could not hear the rider's words, but saw him frantically gesturing downriver. In minutes, the entire settlement's population was on the move, scurrying to defend against the inevitable forthcoming onslaught.

"It seems as though Geldersen's plan was successful," Ziesolf said solemnly.

"So far," Christina replied grudgingly.

She quieted, observing something curious. Several of the women below were carrying large jugs to two of the schnigges moored to the small dock, then emptying their liquid contents upon the decks. This went on for a few minutes until the decks were thoroughly doused. Then, a few men boarded each, cast off the ropes securing the vessels to the docks, and set the sails to take greatest advantage of the wind. Their intent was obvious, for at least two of the men on each craft carried a lit torch.

"Fireships!" Christina gasped. "They're planning to sail to the oncoming cogs, set their ships afire, then swim to safety, while Geldersen's ships burn."

"A masterful stroke," Ziesolf observed dryly. "It will be interesting to see how he counters this."

Christina watched intently as the pirate crew executed their strategy. The cogs were ponderously approaching now, carried forward by little more than the rising tide as the slight breeze had fallen off another couple of points. The schnigges, on the other hand, gained speed with the change in wind, making the collision of the two in the narrow channel inevitable - and soon.

They will need to decide within a minute or two, Christina thought, transfixed by the terrible spectacle about to occur. *If they turn into the port bank, they will be able to discharge their men, who can then make their way up the trail to attack the village as planned. Should they go to starboard, however, they will become entangled in the reeds and stranded on the wrong side of the river. To turn the entire flotilla to conduct a retreat would be a miracle, so it must be one of the first two alternatives. I can only pray they have spotted the village and realize what must be done.*

As she had hoped, the lead cog threw its rudder over, causing it to veer toward the left riverbank as the crew hastily struck the sail. Christina saw the ship give a slight lurch as its keel apparently struck bottom. Immediately, ropes were cast off over the side toward the shore and men began to disembark into what seemed to be shallow water. Almost simultaneously, the next vessel conducted a similar maneuver. Although she could not see the following ships, she inferred they would soon do the same.

The two schnigges were burning furiously now, orange flames dancing skyward from across most of their hull structures. The sails were also alight, their fabric becoming rent and perforated. This slowed the vessels, but not enough to stop their forward progress entirely. It took minutes for them to travel the final few feet, during which Christina thought they might miss the Lübeckers' ship entirely.

Eventually, however, one of the fireships collided with the first cog, settling in comfortably under the port bow. Sailors from the ship waded into the water, hoping to somehow dislodge it. The small ship had been reduced to a fireball, however, creating a heat that made approaching it impossible. Soon, the clinker-built strakes of the ship's side began to smolder, then burst ablaze. The vessel was doomed. All Christina could hope was the remaining cogs avoided a similar fate.

Now peering intently toward the western end of the village, she began to question whether she should deviate from the existent plan for her men to remain in their current position.

There is nothing we can do to affect the outcome from here. If we moved down into the village, the pirates would be caught between our two forces, she thought, chewing her bottom lip with mounting frustration. *But Geldersen believes we will remain here. Should we venture into the village, how would he know we are friend, not foe? Would we be set upon by both forces, each believing us to be their enemy? Or what if the pirates turn to face us before the arrival of Geldersen's men? We are but a pitiful few, with only Ziesolf, Reiniken, and myself possessing skills clearly the villagers' superior. Our true advantage lies with the archers, whose ranged skill will be negated in the close quarters of the settlement.*

"Damn it!" she muttered. "What should we do, Kurt?"

"It is never a good thing to change a plan involving separate forces unless the tactical situation so requires. In this instance, it does not, at least I believe not yet. Let us hold our water and wait and see, Frederick."

Christina realized her expression betrayed her impatience, knowing she was scowling darkly.

"We can't very well sit here scratching our asses while the battle rages below us, can we?" She spat a glob of dusty saliva on the ground beside her for emphasis.

"Control your impetuousness," Ziesolf ordered. "It seems the battle is joined!"

Christina scanned the area below her, but could see no signs of a struggle. Her ears, however, overhead metal clashing on metal now, counterposed by the din of loud shouts, curses, and the first screams of the injured and dying.

"Shit!" complained Christina, irritated further by the smoke roiling back upon the village as the wind changed.

Here and there, she was able to discern a brief struggle between two combatants before they melted away out of sight once more.

Despite the fact most of the conflict was obscured, the outcome was becoming increasingly apparent. Slowly, Geldersen's forces pushed the line of defenders further into the heart of the settlement. Then, unexpectedly, the will of the villagers began to falter as the battle turned into a rout.

Christina looked on with morbid fascination as the Lübeckers ran down the retreating pirates, dispatching them with blows to the back, rather than fighting them face to face.

"This is a massacre," she muttered grimly, "Why do they not just stand and fight? Better to die with sword in hand than being dispatched like lambs in the slaughterhouse."

It was not long until noises of battle began to diminish and other, more appalling, sounds began. The wind changed once more, allowing Christina to see more clearly what was transpiring in the village. What she saw nauseated and repelled her.

Two of whom she inferred to be Geldersen's men were holding down a naked young woman, deaf to her screams as the naked ass of a third thrust violently between her thighs. Other women were being dragged off, their attackers apparently preferring to conduct their raping more privately. One man had skewered a young child, jigging it like a puppet upon his pike before a group of his fellows, who laughed uproariously.

"How the hell can Geldersen permit this?" Christina shouted with disgust at no one in particular. "Lübeck is a city of civilized people, not a part of the fucking Mongol horde. How can he let them act like animals?"

Without warning, a large group of women and children broke away from where they had been concealed within one of the storerooms. They ran as swiftly as they could manage, up the gentle hill directly in front of Christina's men. After they had made about a hundred yards progress, a couple of the archers nocked an arrow and began to draw their bowstrings.

"Hold!" she screamed at the top of her lungs, "Hold, damn your eyes!"

The bowmen relaxed the pull of their bowstrings, looking toward her quizzically.

"Look at them!" she yelled so that everyone along the line would hear her voice clearly. "They're just women and children, for Christ's sake!"

Reiniken's man Alf ran his thick fingers through his damp mop of red hair and remarked, "A bit of fun with the enemy's whores is a soldier's due. Fuck -em I say!"

A red haze seemed to appear before Christina's eyes, her rage threatening to overcome her.

"What the hell did you say?" she asked in an emotionless, yet menacing voice.

She strode resolutely down the line of men to where Alf stood, then grabbed the front of his sweaty tunic roughly in her left hand, reaching across her body with her right to unsheathe her dagger.

Whether the man was cowed by Christina's violent reaction or merely surprised by her physicality, was indeterminable. He said nothing in response, however.

"Would you feel the same way if it was your mother or sister?" she demanded. "Would you be so happy to let these louts cram their cocks inside them while those you love sobbed and begged for mercy? If so, you are no man yourself!"

She let go of Alf's tunic, but fixed him with an icy stare, challenging him to make the next move.

Alf backed away, muttering, "Sorry," while he dropped his head to break eye contact.

"Let them pass," she ordered, turning both ways to allow each of the men to see the seriousness of her gaze. "If anyone else has a problem with that, say so now so we can settle it!"

No one did. Instead, Reiniken lifted his arm and pointed toward the village.

"Look!"

Although the group of noncombatants had advanced another hundred yards, their presence had finally been noticed by several of Geldersen's men. With profane shouts and laughter, they began their pursuit.

Christina saw the men gaining on the pitiful group of the village's survivors.

"Draw!" she ordered instantly.

The archers recognized the command, but were confused as to what Christina intended as their target. They looked to her, their eyes imploring clarification.

"Draw!" she repeated. "Fire over the villagers, but before Geldersen's men!"

The bowmen complied. In a matter of seconds, nine arrows lay between the retreating women and children and their astonished pursuers. The attackers halted, looking upward to the ridgeline to see Christina's archers had already nocked a second arrow.

"Stop!" Christina bellowed in a voice now hoarse from so much yelling. "These people are harmless and are now under the protection of Sir Frederick Kohl and Herr Kurt Ziesolf. Advance further at your own peril and be damned!"

The men below exchanged baffled looks. They had heard Frederick's name repeated about town as the man who had captured six enemy vessels, overpowering the pirates by employing the English archers who now threatened them. What's more, Kurt

Ziesolf's fighting prowess was a thing of legend among the men of Lübeck. Although they muttered vilely among themselves, none had the pluck to voice a challenge. In mere minutes, the group melted away, returning to the town to search for prey not so fiercely defended.

"There will be a reckoning once we return to Lübeck, I am afraid," Ziesolf, who had now moved beside her, remarked. "Geldersen will not accept his men being used so roughly."

"What would you have me do?" Christina spread her hands before her.

"Exactly what you did do. I would expect nothing else," he replied, his voice tinged with respect. "I speak only to warn and certainly not to condemn you. What you did took courage, but it was a type of bravery not everyone will readily understand."

Christina face flushed red with embarrassment at Ziesolf's sparing praise. The hue of her cheeks did not diminish as anger coursed through her veins at the thought of Geldersen.

Another damned alderman who seeks my ruin! Why can they not just leave me alone?

She watched as the scruffy band of villagers made their way hurriedly up the remainder of the hill, circling wide to avoid Christina and her force of men. The women cast guarded looks their way, some with fear and others in hatred. Several held small children closely guarded within their arms. Other children walked alongside what Christina supposed to be their mothers, reaching out to instinctively clutch their hands or skirts for reassurance from a terror they did not comprehend.

Christina was shocked to see three of the women clasped not the hand of a son or daughter, but instead one end of a stout rope; the other end tied about the necks of three emaciated, raggedly-dressed men. The women pulled them along roughly so that they stumbled and fell, struggling to get back to their feet under the onslaught of the curses and slaps of their captors.

Slaves! These bitches took the time to fetch their slaves before they fled. Undoubtedly, they thought they were the most valuable of their movables they could take with them in such a hurry. Well, they're in for a fucking surprise!

"Halt!" she shouted in a commanding voice that left no room for misinterpretation.

The group hastily obeyed, clustering closer together in their terror. Several of the children were crying now, as many of the women whispered words of comfort or vile threats to bring them to quiet. It was clear they had no idea what to expect, only that they were helpless to prevent whatever it was from happening.

"Bring your slaves out here," Christina ordered, gesturing to indicate the space between the two groups.

"There ain't no slaves," one older woman stepped forward and replied in a surly voice.

"Don't play games with me, damn you!" Christina spat. "Either they come out now or my men go in to take them, and they're not going to be gentle about it either!"

Reluctantly, the three women holding the leads walked into the space. They then pulled in the slack of the ropes and the three prisoners shuffled forward with heads held downward. It was evident they had been sorely mistreated. They were malnourished and filthy, with several unhealed slashes evidencing inhumane whippings. They looked as if they could barely stand. As if as proof, one fell to his knees in exhaustion, turning his head to reveal a massive wound on the side of his head.

Something about this prisoner drew her attention; however, she had no time for to indulge her idle curiosity now.

"Take the nooses from their necks and be on your way!" Christina muttered, her mounting rage threatening to unleash upon the women if they remained in her sight much longer.

"But they belong to us!" one of the women wailed, "You can't just take them! They're worth a lot of money."

Christina ran forward and roughly grabbed the woman by the hair. She led her a few steps back down the hill and shoved her back toward the village.

"You think you're going to get better terms down there, you fucking bitch? Go then, and be damned!"

The simpering woman turned her head back toward Christina and shook it in the negative, mouthing the word, "Apologies." She slowly backed away and still facing Christina, rejoined the group of women and children.

"Any of the rest of you want to negotiate?" Christina asked, looking slowly from face to face. "All right. Be off then before I change my mind and give you back to them."

The villagers skulked away, toward where Christina neither knew nor cared. She had saved their lives, a mercy she was not sure all of them deserved. Perhaps she would be rewarded in heaven for her act, or punished in Lübeck for it. Godfrey stepped forward and offered a skin of ale to two of the freed prisoners, from which they drank greedily. She gave them no further thought for now her attention was focused solely on Ziesolf, and the man before him.

While she had been dealing with the arrogant woman, Ziesolf had stepped forward to examine the formerly enslaved man who lay trembling on the ground. He knelt and gently combed his long, matted hair back from his face, revealing a horrendous partially-healed wound, as if someone had walloped him heavily with a cudgel . . . repeatedly. His jaw had obviously been broken at some point in his beating and his eye was swollen shut. The skin of his cheek was badly abraded and had incompletely healed. Ziesolf leaned closer and whispered gentle words in his ear. The pitiful creature could only make faint mewling sounds in response.

Christina moved forward. Ziesolf turned and gazed up into her face, his remaining eye filled with tears such as she had never before witnessed in the man. She looked at him in confusion, not understanding what was transpiring.

"It . . . it is your . . . cousin," he said softly.

Suddenly, everything became clear. The husk of a man before her was not a cousin. Ziesolf had only been trying to protect her secret from being disclosed. This was her brother, the true Frederick Kohl!

Chapter 13

A Homecoming
Lübeck, July, 1311

Christina paced the passageway betwixt the bedchambers of her family's home nervously. For the tenth time, she wiped her sweaty palms on the lower sides of her tunic, already dampened by her perspiring body.

Why does it have to be so damnably hot? she grumbled, forgetting she had similarly cursed the bone-numbing cold of the winter past.

All such trivial thoughts flew from her head as she saw the door to her brother's room slowly open. She rushed forward, nearly blocking it with her body she was so eager to be told of his chances for recovery. The first to exit was her mother, followed closely behind by Brother Udo.

"How fares he?" Christina blurted out, her anxiety pulling her nearly into hysterics.

"Not very well, I'm afraid," replied the monk, coupling his diagnosis with a gentle sigh. "His injuries are serious, that is true, and he suffers greatly from malnutrition and general neglect. More worrisome, however, is the state of his mind. He has no more cognizance than a small child, incapable of both speech and comprehension. The years he spent in harsh servitude have clouded his mind. Only God in his blessed grace knows whether he will ever regain memory or full function."

The monk crossed himself slowly. He found his own way to the door, leaving Christina and her mother standing alone. As he left the house, Brother Udo turned and crossed himself again, murmuring a prayer for those who dwelt in a house that had experienced such woe and disaster.

The two women progressed to the solar without speaking. There, they sat down facing one another, each silently imploring her counterpart to break the silence between them that seemed to have almost a tangible weight.

Incoherent prayers for her brother's safety filled Christina's thoughts, speeding through her brain as if frenzied horses vying in a wild race.

Finally, she could stand it no longer.

"What can I do for him?"

"Nothing more, for the foreseeable future, at least," replied her mother. "You have brought him home and that is enough."

Christina mulled over her mother's words for a few moments before begrudgingly admitting their truth. Another thought sprang into her mind.

"What am I to do now, Mother?"

"Why, nothing other than what you have been doing."

Her mother's response astounded her.

"Two cups placed upon a table cannot occupy the same space!" Christina's harsh tone reflected her agitation. "One must be moved so the other can take its place. I cannot be Frederick if Frederick is here to resume his life, can I?"

Her mother smiled wearily at Christina and shook her head.

"But Frederick has not returned, my child, not yet at least. He may never do so."

"But what if he does? He is entitled to his life!"

"But so are you to yours, Christina," Mechtild's face was serious. "The life you have made in London is yours and yours alone. Frederick had no part in making it and has no right to live it. If he does regain his senses, we will make him a new life. Here."

Christina sat dumbstruck, amazed by the rationality of her mother's words.

"First, I had one son, who was then taken from me, leaving me with none. Now, I have two. It is true God works in mysterious ways," she said with a benign expression.

Christina left her mother sitting there and walked up the stairs to her room. She opened her window and gazed out upon a brilliant blue sky marred only by a few wispy clouds moving slowly in the high breezes. She looked down toward the cobbled street, where a horse-cart was being loaded with the last of the casks of furs from the storeroom above her head. She recalled a similar scene, nearly two years before, when she had flirted shamelessly with the young laborer Alf, distracting him from his work so completely he had received a cuffing for it.

Now, it was a different Alf involved in the loading, one who dared not look up lest he receive another upbraiding from the intense young warrior who had led them successfully into battle. Unlike his earlier counterpart, he was all too happy when the drover shook his reins and the placid carthorse began its short journey to the wharf-side where *der Greif* was moored.

A knock on her door broke her reminiscence. She turned and invited the caller to enter. Ziesolf strode through the door and sat down in the chair along the side of the room opposite the bed where Christina sat.

"The final schnigge has been sold, I expect the other ewer to go shortly as well. Seems the market is hungry for vessels of any kind now that the pirate threat has been eliminated in the Kattegat," Ziesolf said, avoiding eye contact with her.

Something is bothering him, Christina observed but knew it would be better to let him broach the subject in his own time rather than to press him.

"As you have probably noticed, the loading is nearly finished aboard *der Greif.* What space that remained after Frau Kohl's shares were loaded Matthias has filled with some astute purchases of luxury furs. We will be carrying a king's ransom aboard on our return voyage."

"That is great news indeed." Christina replied. "I have decided to make a short diversion from our course home. I intend to make a Flemish landfall first. With *Seelöwe* already routed to London, it makes little sense to bring another shipload of pelts as well. This is especially true if the political situation remains fraught, as it was when we departed. With good weather, the delay should not be long, a few days, or a week at most. A full cargo will impinge the men's comfort somewhat but, if the weather remains good, a few nights spent sleeping beneath the stars, instead of in a hot and stuffy ship's hold, should not be too great of a hardship."

"A sound plan," Ziesolf remarked dryly. "Although the men long for home, time spent in the baths of Bruges shouldn't be seen by them as too burdensome."

Christina smiled at the old knight's sense of understatement and waited patiently for him to continue.

"The other ships have finally returned," he stated finally.

Christina nodded.

Is this what he was reluctant to mention? Is there some bad news associated with this?

"Four of the five that is. The lead ship was too badly damaged by the fire to salvage. Altogether, thirty-one men were killed in the conflict, nearly the same number again wounded to some degree. It must have been a near thing, down in the village."

Christina was not shocked the casualties had been so high. Vying against an entrenched enemy who fought for the very lives of their families, Geldersen's men must have been greatly surprised by the ferocity of their resistance. She remembered Geldersen's prideful boasts, guaranteeing a glorious victory.

"Their overconfidence certainly worked against them," she replied before changing the subject somewhat. "And what of us? Who will believe we were ordered to hold our position above the village? Certainly, Geldersen will try to shift the blame unto the cowards who stood, doing nothing, while brave men died, at least in his telling of it."

"Geldersen will say nothing, for he lies with the other dead," Ziesolf said. "The accusations of the others would carry little weight and, even then, not a word against us has been voiced so far. Perhaps they do not wish to shake the hornet's nest so that the facts of their un-Christian treatment of the village's women and children come to light. It seems we have nothing to be concerned with from them."

Christina was happy she had not incurred the animosity of yet another resentful alderman. She had no sadness at all for the news Geldersen had perished in the fray.

He was a braggart and a bully and Lübeck is better off without him among its councilors.

She noticed that same, pensive expression had returned to Ziesolf's face.

Growing somewhat peeved by his guardedness, she finally exclaimed, "For the love of sweet Jesus, just tell me man! What is it that troubles you so?"

Ziesolf's singular eye avoided Christina as he began to speak.

"Two years ago, a headstrong young girl appeared on the deck of *der Greif*, hell bent on taking part in the ship's defense. She had little training, only an innate skill, quickness, and an indomitable heart. I expected she would die that day. When she did not, I vowed to train her as I was trained, harshly and with no acceptance of anything less than perfection. Although I felt you hated me at times, I could not ease my efforts, as the foes who you would face would take advantage of any kindness that I showed to you."

Christina remained silent, having no idea where his puzzling words were leading.

"As the months passed your skill with a sword became increasingly formidable. But that was not all. You grew less and less reliant on my advice and knowledge and more and more confident in your own. Now, you are your own master both in right and deed."

A lump began to grow in Christina's throat as she realized what Ziesolf was about to say.

"I will not be departing with you when you leave Lübeck. My place is now here. Your brother needs my support far more than you. I too have been held captive; tortured and treated as an animal. Perhaps he will recover but, if he does not, I will try to ease his pain and fear as he lives out his days. I do this not because I think anything less of you, but because of the mere fact you have outgrown my counsel. I hope you think of me at times while we are apart and judge me not too harshly. I know I will remember you fondly, Christina, as my best student, and as my friend."

Ziesolf offered his hand to her and Christina took it, grasping it tightly. He then drew her into a firm embrace. Tears rolled down her cheeks as she realized the man who had shaped her adulthood would no longer be a part of her daily life. Ziesolf released his hold, then turned and exited the room without further word. Christina stood staring after him, clenching and unclenching her fists unconsciously. She had never before felt so on her own.

A couple of days later, all was in readiness for *der Greif's* departure. Christina stood in her brother's room, staring down at the gaunt body that slept fitfully in his bed. The swelling around his eye had diminished somewhat, but the skin had turned into a mottled mess of diverse hues of purple and yellow. A thick linen bandage had somewhat successfully immobilized his broken jawbone, Ziesolf had hopes he would one day regain at least some function of it. For now, Frederick was able only to gain a small amount of nourishment through spoonfuls of broth dribbled down his throat patiently by their mother.

"Rest easily, my brother. Rest easily and heal. I long for the day when we can again be together, laughing and playing jokes on each other as if we were young children. That day will come once more, I know it!" she said in a choking voice, completely overcome by her love for her brother.

Frederick said nothing.

Christina gave his hand one last squeeze, then bent and kissed him gently on his cheek. She knelt by his bedside and offered a fervent prayer to God for his recovery. She arose and walked to the door, tarrying to take one last look at the shell of a young man she had known so well, but hardly recognized now.

After a final farewell to her mother and Ziesolf, she stepped through the door and into the yard. Seconds later, she was walking down Engelsgrube, back to the life she now knew as her own.

The voyage around the Jutland peninsula was as monotonous as it was uneventful. The water was placid, the sea breezes were mild and balmy, and the sun heated the deck beneath its brilliant rays as if it were a baker's oven and *der Greif* were a pandemain loaf. Their progress was steady, but slow, giving Christina plenty of idle hours to spend in self-doubts.

I should not have left Frederick. How could I have been so callous, so uncaring? What if he should awaken before he dies? Could I have forfeited my last chance to see him alive, or perhaps even speak with him?

Her self-recriminations were only equaled by her anxiety over what might befall her, should her brother regain his senses.

If it became known in Lübeck that Frederick Kohl was alive and residing in his mother's house, it would not be long until some astute merchant traveling to London would question why a doppelgänger of the same name and trade existed in that city. Should that doubt be communicated to one of Christina's adversaries, who knew to what cruel examination she might be required to submit?

Christina shuddered at the thought of her identity being questioned by the likes of Katharine Volker.

Thankfully, they eventually made landfall at the subsidiary port of Sluys, a town she knew well from her previous travels to Bruges. In less than a week's time, she had successfully completed her objective, having sold the entirety of her cargo of pelts to three influential members of the city's skinner's guild. As had become her custom, she walked then to Saint Basil the Great, known colloquially as the Church of the Holy Blood for the vial of Christ's blood it contained, believed to be the most precious of all its relics. Entering the peaceful nave, she knelt before the altar, praying for the souls of those she held most dear; Frederick, Cecily, Ziesolf, her mother, and Trudi. She also asked forgiveness for the souls of those she had dispatched both by her own hand and by those under her command.

Leaving a heavy purse of gold and silver upon the cold, stone floor Christina exited the church, but this time a young priest saw her pass through the doorway. Walking forward to retrieve the purse, he was astonished to discover the degree of the mysterious stranger's largesse. He crossed himself and added his own prayers for those for whom the figure had sought Jesus' blessing.

Christina then headed toward the great square, entering the towered Cloth Hall that dominated its southern side. There, she was fortunate to find Master Pauwels, the mercer with whom she had conducted previous transactions, with an overabundance of fine Flemish cloth in his possession. He was surprised; however, she possessed no fleeces to sell in return.

"So, you see, "Christina continued her explanation as to how her trade had been interrupted by the events in Lübeck, "I will be able to supply the quantity of wool we agreed upon last year, only it will be delayed until I can return to London to fetch it to you."

"I am rather confused." Pauwels stared at Christina intently as he scratched his balding pate. "Your man has already been to see me, promising a cargo of sixty-five sarplars of your fine wool. Did he not speak truly?"

Christina looked at the portly mercer in astonishment.

What man is this?

There could be only one answer.

"Describe this man, please," she was able to choke out, then added, "There are two or three in my service who come to mind."

She hated lying to the fatherly mercer as she had found him to be more than honest in his previous dealings; however, she also did not want him to lose his confidence in her ability to handle her affairs as a merchant.

"A young man, even more so than yourself. Of middling height and a fair face. But I also have his name, which should make it simpler than playing a game of questions."

He said this with a merry look on his face; however, his eyes had narrowed to weigh Christina's response carefully.

"Jost, is it?" Christina managed a mild smile, despite the growing ire rising within her.

"Yes, that was his name."

What in the name of the Blessed Christ was the young whelp playing at? She had left explicit instructions for him to await her return before doing anything more than accepting the wool Master Butiler and she had already agreed upon. Why did he deviate from such a simple instruction? And on what ship did he make this voyage? Surely, there has been no time for *Seelöwe* to arrive in London and complete another voyage. What transpires here?

"No, he did not speak falsely," she remarked. "Please forgive me Master Pauwels, I have been away from London for many months. My business, however, continues on in my absence, as I am sure yours does as well."

Pauwels laughed and shook his head.

"Two years ago, I accompanied a large shipment of fine cloth to set before the French king's chamberlain in Paris. While I was away, my addle-brained son, whom I had stupidly left in charge of my affairs, purchased a cargo of English wool rife with black mold.

When I die, he can and probably will run my business into the ground. But, for now, he does not so much as squeak without my express permission."

Christina's thoughts raced, attempting to make some sense of her apprentice's perplexing overstep of his authority. She considered remaining in Bruges for an additional two weeks, if only to confront him upon his arrival. She decided against it, realizing what was done was done.

I will unravel the strings of this mystery when I am back in London, she decided, *Although I may use these cords to hang my so-called apprentice by his balls if he has erred by too great a measure!*

Christina noticed Pauwels still staring at her keenly, no longer with his customarily pleasant expression. At last, the man spoke in terse, measured tones.

"I have found our past dealings to be fair and profitable, for you as well as I. Despite your youth, I believed you to be a knowledgeable and honest merchant, whose fleeces were exactly as he portrayed them to be. When this Jost appeared, claiming to be your apprentice, I anticipated nothing less than what I had grown to expect from you."

Where is Pauwels going with this?

"As you well know from our past dealings, I personally inspect each cargo of fleeces I intend to purchase, regardless of the amount of trust I have in the seller. When I opened the first sack, I expected to find all in order, requiring no more than a cursory inspection of the remainder. Instead, I found the wool to be so degraded as to be completely worthless."

"What?" Christina managed to reply, stunned to her core.

"Worthless," he repeated with a grim finality in his voice. "And the next, and the next, and the one after that. Finally, after

301

assessing over fifteen sacks, I stopped, sickened by the waste of such a valuable commodity."

"What was it that had ruined the fleeces to such a degree?"

"There were multiple serious mistakes made with this wool. The primary error was it had been packed while quite damp, and too tightly at that. Had this problem been discovered early, the fleeces could have been washed and properly dried. If this would have happened, the value would have been little affected, if at all. Instead, it went unnoticed. After a few days, the wetness of the wool caused the sacks to heat internally. Some were actually steaming when I opened them, emitting a cloyingly sweet smell. Consequently, the wool had become moldy and discolored, with severe brown staining on the tips. Some of the staples were so deteriorated they broke in my fingers."

"I apologize with all my heart, Master Mercer," Christina stated. "Please believe me when I tell you I knew nothing of this. As I told you, I have been in the Baltic region since long before the clip was delivered to my storerooms. I have no desire to cheat you. Even if I did, I know you would certainly catch such a grossly obvious attempt to do so anyway. Rest assured, I will have a reckoning with this apprentice, as well as determine whether my supplier had a hand in this."

"Perhaps I am growing sentimental in my old age," Pauwels replied, the cheerfulness returning to his face. "But I believe you. Let us say nothing more of this for now. Perhaps we will share a drink together later, saluting the sound practice of the regular beating of apprentices."

Christina smiled back, agreeing to Pauwels' suggestion. Her mind, churned, however, as she sought to unravel the calamity that had obviously occurred here.

Sixty-five sarplars, ruined! A trade agreement central to my business endangered. Possible treachery by Butiler, a man I have trusted implicitly. And what was Jost's part in this and what provoked him to do so?

Her anger flared white hot, but she had nowhere to direct it . . . as of yet. She had no doubt, however, the day would come when it would be satisfied. But, for now, she had other business at hand.

Setting thoughts of thrashing Jost senseless aside for the moment, Christina accompanied Pauwels on an easy stroll to a nearby warehouse. There, she focused her attention on selecting the lengths of fabric that would constitute her own cargo for the journey home. With hard coin at her disposal from the sale of her furs, she determined she would purchase only the best of the cloth the mercer had to offer. Christina began with almost thirty ells of a finely woven broadcloth; kermes dyed a brilliant scarlet. Her excitement grew as she discovered two beautiful examples of union cloth; fabric with a warp of one fabric and a weft of another. These combined to form a tiretaine fabric of murrey-died wool and bleached linen of exceptional weave that was wonderfully pleasing to the eye. Next, she began a careful examination of Pauwels' stock of damask and brocades, selecting several lengths of different patterns and colors. She was particularly impressed by twenty ells of damask with a beautifully wrought pattern of golden lovebirds in the warp-faced satin weave against the sateen blue ground. Christina imagined this as a perfect gift for Cecily, whose pale skin and red hair would be accentuated wonderfully against a gown of the exquisite fabric.

In the following days, her fury over Jost's apparently imprudent actions dissipated, as her excitement over their return to England overshadowed all else. By the time of *der Greif's* departure, she could barely contain her impatience for them to be on their way.

Christina stood on the forecastle, looking to the west where the shore of England lay hidden in the distance.

How many times have I trod forward on this deck to join Ziesolf at this very place? she thought nostalgically. *Now, I stand here alone. I hope he is well.*

"Ah misses the miserable old bastard too, Ah does."

The voice beside her startled Christina.

"What?" she managed, shaken from her reverie.

"Old one eye. Ah said it's not the same without -im standin' up here as if it was -im that was drivin' the ship forward and not the fuckin' sail," Reiniken replied.

"Aye, Wig. I do miss him, that's a fact."

"So, what now?" Reiniken asked, a question so broad she had to think for a second as to how to reply.

"Well, after docking in London, I'll try to figure out what the hell possessed my cousin to voyage to Bruges on his own. Then, I'll kill him. Or not. I still haven't decided."

Reiniken laughed, the sound a thunderous boom from his barrel of a chest.

"Ah, boys'll be boys, I guess. Don't go too hard on '-im, Yur Worship. Whup his ass and leave it at that," he advised.

"We'll see," Cristina smiled noncommittally.

"And what of the lady, Cecily?" the large man asked softly, almost shyly.

"What of her?" responded Christina sadly. "She is a married woman and, by now, the mother of her husband's child. There is nothing for me with her, save a treasured friendship."

"A husband, aye, but a bigger chunk of shit," Reiniken said sternly, "and not deserving a woman with such a spirit. If Ah wuz ya, Ah'd hunt the bastard down and split him from cock to gullet. Then, Ah'd sweet talk her like and hope she'd let mi be her man."

Christina grunted.

"You think she'd consent to have me do you, even though I would then be hunted as an outlaw for waging mayhem against the king's peace?"

Reiniken flashed a wry smile, shaking his head from side to side.

"Yur the smartest little fucker Ah know, Yur Worship, but sometimes ya can be as dumb as a stump. Thet woman loves ya, Ah kin see it with mi own eyes. She'd follow ya through hell's hot hinges if only ya asked her."

Reiniken clapped her on the back with his mighty paw, turned, and walked back down on the main deck where he busied himself swigging off a large jug of ale. Fully primed, he turned to the leeward side of the ship, belched mightily, then undid his braies and pissed over the side. He looked back toward where Christina stood and waved. Christina waived back, shaking her head at the irrepressible giant of a man who still held his substantial member guilelessly in the other.

There'll never be another like Wig, and thank God too as I don't think the world could weather a second!

Suddenly, her mirthful appraisal of the man was forgotten and her thoughts turned dark. Despite Reiniken's playful jostling, he had clearly observed there was more than a close friendship between herself and Cecily.

Have others perceived this as well, including members of the court?

She tried to recall.

Have I overstepped myself somehow? I could not bear it if I brought shame or dishonor on the lady. Should I at last bid her adieu, permitting her to carry on with the life she must lead without my constant distraction?

Thoughts of Cecily dominated Christina's mind for the few days it took to cross the waters between Flanders and England. But how their relationship could ever be more than a constant rending of their hearts or only a fond, yet tragic memory, she had no way of knowing.

Chapter 14

Both True and False
London, August, 1311

The sturdy hull of *der Greif* came to a rest against the salt encrusted wooden pilings of their mooring at Queenhithe with a thud. The sky above was a steely gray, with steady raindrops encompassing the space between it and the earth. A cold, swirling wind whipped at the crew as some fought to drop the sail while others secured fore and aft hawsers about the wharf's bollards.

The weather alluded to an inauspicious homecoming. They had had mostly fair weather for the entire voyage, this was the first damnably foul day. She prayed it not to be a portent of evil things to come.

Christina's mood was as dark as the late afternoon sky. She had instructed Matthias to release the crewmen not needed to maintain the watch, leaving the unloading of the cargo to another, hopefully drier, day.

The last thing I need is to have to set about drying hundreds of ells of damp cloth, she thought, imagining her storeroom looking like a massive field of multicolored tentage. *Besides, the lads have definitely earned a bit of respite with their families, or a renewal of old acquaintances at the brothels and taverns, if that is their bent.*

Freed from any immediate responsibilities, Christina began the long trudge back home. The streets were nearly devoid of people, unusual for the time of day and the season. This left her progress unencumbered save for the weight of inquisitive eyes watching her from beneath awnings and inside shadowed doorways. She cared not; her mind was occupied with more vexing matters.

What if I broached my mad plan to escape to the lands of the Mediterranean Sea once more?

She mulled the thought over.

It had seemed almost plausible when she had spoken of it prior to her departure. To ply the warm waters of the southern sea, trading in unusual goods in even more exotic ports, seemed both mysterious and exciting.

This thought does hold allure for me, but what about Cecily? Would she be willing to partake of the nomadic life of a merchant, or would she soon desire more to establish a hearth and home, one to which I returned to at times, then departed from once more? Would living alone amongst strangers be something for her to endure, rather than to enjoy? And what of the child, our child? How could this be a proper upbringing?

With each step, her uncertainty grew.

Would Cecily even consider such an outrageous scheme? If she did, would I have the courage to enact it?

Before she could even begin to decide on any future course, she had arrived at the gate of Bokerel House.

She took a deep breath, imposing calmness as best she could. Her thoughts of Cecily and their futures, either together or apart, were forced into the background as a more immediate concern overtook her attention. She needed to speak with Jost. At once.

She rang the bell sharply and was soon ushered in by a beaming Osbert, the yardman on duty. She thanked him briskly and mounted the steps to enter the great hall. Christina walked quickly to cross the massive chamber, but was soon distracted by swift, light footsteps approaching from behind. Christina turned to see the joyful face of Mary pulling to a stop a few feet in front of her.

Even in her dour mood, Christina smiled in spite of herself as the spritely maid curtsied and words began to tumble from her fetching mouth.

"Oh, Master Frederick! What a wonderful surprise to find you back among us once more! How I . . . I mean, we missed you. Would you like something to eat, or drink? I'll get your chambers freshened immediately. You just give me a few minutes, please."

Christina held her hand up and said laughingly, "Yes, a cup of ale would be most appreciated, Mary. I have missed you as well."

The small girl's smile broadened to its fullest extent, pleased beyond words at her master's notice.

"Now," Christina continued, halting Mary before she could fetch Christina's drink. "Let us please keep my arrival to yourself, shall we? I am greatly weary, but have need to speak to Jost forthwith. Is he about the manor?"

Mary shook her head vigorously, overjoyed to be sharing with her master the secret of his return.

"Nay, Master Frederick, he is away. He is away much these days," she spoke in a low conspiratorial voice.

"Instruct him to find me immediately upon his return, regardless of the hour. Is your mistress in her apartments?"

"Nay, she is in the kitchen, discussing provisioning with Bess."

"Thank you, Mary" Christina replied. Turning to go, she said over her shoulder, "It is indeed good to be back in my own home."

309

Mary expertly balanced as she dipped nearly to the floor, then literally skipped over the flagstones as she sped away to the buttery.

Before Christina could arrive at the passageway door, it swung open and Trudi stepped through. Her mouth gaped open at finding Christina standing before her. Impulsively, she ran forward and clasped Christina in an embrace so robust it threatened to burst her ribs.

Christina emitted a small "Woof" as the air was forced from her lungs.

Trudi released her and stepped back with a look of concern.

"Oh my God!" she exclaimed, "Have you been injured yet again? Did I hurt you?"

Christina laughed heartily, then caught her friend up her own close embrace.

"No on both counts, you silly goose. But thanks to you for asking. My only injury was to my skull and you left that alone, saints be praised!"

"Let me see!" Trudi commanded.

"Later, later. It is well healed and gives me no pain now," Christina replied glibly.

Mary reappeared, balancing a tray laden with a cup of ale, a jug of wine, and several small cakes. Despite her burden, she managed her curtsey well.

"Your ale, Master Frederick," she said merrily, handing Christina the frothy jug. "I though you and my mistress might like to share the bottle while you caught up like."

There was no need to explain the cakes, given Christina's known predilections.

"Thank you once more. It seems you have become even more adept at reading my mind while I have been away."

Mary beamed and, with a farewell curtsey, returned to her duties, leaving the other two women alone.

Within seconds, the two friends had mounted the stairs to the second-floor landing. Instead of retiring to the solar, they continued to Christina's apartments to talk while she dried herself and changed from her sopping garments. Once inside, Trudi closed the door behind them for privacy.

"Oh, Christina! I've missed you so dearly, my sister! You must tell me everything. Did you see your mother? How fares my sister?" Trudi's excitement, like a pot of water over a fierce flame, threatened to boil over at any minute.

Caught in the middle of disrobing, Christina held up her hand to halt Trudi's questioning.

"In time, in time!" she exclaimed. "Firstly, I have important matters to discuss with Jost. Have you any thought as to where I might find him?"

Trudi's eyes narrowed slightly and her expression became slightly brittle.

"No, but that's not unusual for the lad" she replied flatly. "For the past few months, he had become quite secretive as to his whereabouts. Took off for Bruges with hardly a fare thee well, the young scamp. Has he done something wrong then?"

Christina hesitated before answering. Previously, she would have discussed such a matter as this with Ziesolf as Trudi knew little about the dealings of the merchant trade.

Well, he's not here, is he? Although I hate to burden Trudi with woes that have little to do with her duties, she is now my sole confidante. Besides, it seems she is already aware his activities have become suspect.

Trudi's look of amazement grew steadily as Christina related Pauwels's peculiar meeting with Jost, and its woeful outcome.

"You should dismiss the little bastard, Christina!" Trudi interrupted once Christina disclosed that she had not sanctioned his voyage. "You can't have your apprentice conducting business on his own, especially without your knowledge. Better yet, thrash him first, then send him on his way!"

"It may come to that," Christina admitted, "But I feel I must speak with him first before I relent to my ire. If he has no good explanation, however, I will throw his narrow ass from the grounds myself!"

Trudi promised to fetch her at the first sign of the wayward apprentice. That settled, she once more begged Christina to tell her everything that had happened while she was away.

Pausing only to dry her body and finish dressing, Christina began her narrative with the most startling of the events that had occurred, Frederick's return and Ziesolf's decision to remain in Lübeck. Trudi's tears of happiness and sadness intermingled, as did those of Christina, as joy and heartbreak competed to burst their bosoms.

It took several minutes for Christina to provide Trudi with a summary of the remainder of the tale of her voyage. At the end, she relayed Anna's gentle words of love for her younger sister, presenting Trudi with the coverlet Anna had embroidered.

Trudi's ragged sobs threatened to overwhelm her.

"How could I have been such a spiteful little bitch, Christina?" she moaned. "Now, that is how Anna will remember me always!"

"No," Christina rose and stroked her friend's shoulder. "I have told her of your success as the mistress of this house and how you have grown to expertly manage those under your supervision. I also told her you are now a wife and a mother. These words brought her great comfort and pride in you, Trudi."

Trudi smiled radiantly as she thanked Christina for her generous words.

"Now," said Christina with a grin, "where is this strapping boy of yours?"

"Asleep, saints be praised. He's taken to a late afternoon nap to make up for his early morning rise. Takes after his father there, for sure."

"And what have you called him, Trudi?"

"Adam, like in the Bible."

"Truly, a goodly name. Well, please find me when Master Adam decides to rear his head."

"Aye," Trudi replied before asking, "And where will you be? I suppose I should arrange a bath forthwith?"

"I would like nothing better. You know me only too well," Christina laughed. "But I must delay such self-indulgence till a bit later, I'm afraid. Firstly, I have pressing business in the yard requiring my attention."

Christina kissed Trudi lightly on the lips, then departed, expecting the worst to be revealed in the manor's storerooms. Stepping into the yard, she did not notice the rain had ceased as she marched to the wool storeroom. Flinging the doors open, she saw what she had expected and dreaded. The cavernous chamber was completely empty, nary a sack of wool remained. Heartsick, she turned and left, closing the huge doors softly behind her.

Once more outside, she looked about the yard, feeling something was strangely different; yet, not able to place what. Looking left, she realized the source. After such an extended period of heavy downpours, the area to the fore of the right storeroom should have been awash in several inches of water. Strangely, she could see the paving stones clearly, as the rainwater had somehow been magically whisked away. Walking closer, she was amazed to see the large iron grate embedded in the ground in front of the storeroom door, with the sound of running water issuing from beneath.

What the hell is this?

Venturing forward, she slowly pulled open the large doors to the hitherto unusable storeroom. Astonished, she saw the warehouse nearly filled with what must have been hundreds of woolsacks. Fearing the worst, she began to open random sacks, carefully inspecting their contents. To her great surprise, the wool inside each sack was dry and unblemished, with no sign or smell of mold or other decay. Finally, she departed, greatly relieved but also mystified.

Is my mind once more playing me for a fool? she wondered, questioning whether she had somehow experienced a relapse from her head injury. *Did I simply imagine my meeting with Master Pauwels, or was it instead what I just saw?*

With great reluctance, she resisted the urge to once more go inside the storeroom to ensure what she had just seen was real.

There were too many mysteries here! She had thought she had lost an entire season of fleeces, only to discover they were safe and sound. To what wool was Pauwels referring, if not her own? These questions could all likely be answered by one person – Jost! Where in the name of God Almighty had he taken himself?

I care not for this sport, if that is what he believes he is playing!

Christina's taut nerves caused her to jump when she heard the sharp clang of the gate bell sounding.

What now? she thought in irritation. *The only person I would welcome to appear at this moment is Jost. If it is not him, whoever it is can go merrily to hell!*

When she saw the royal livery of the man Osbert let inside the gate, Christina groaned.

Bloody hell!

She gritted her teeth as she walked forward toward the visitor.

Why is it that, as soon as I set foot on London's streets, I am summoned hither and thither, like flotsam and jetsam tossed between the sea and shore? I feel like a cat, belled by a gaggle of crafty mice!

"God's good day to you, Mi 'lord," the liveryman spoke in a surprisingly mild voice. "Would I be having the pleasure to speak with Sir Frederick Kohl?"

What a lovely change, she thought. *Usually, these are the most disagreeable of men, undoubtedly chosen for their surliness and abrupt manner. This fellow, on the other hand, seems almost courtly. I hope his message is similarly pleasant.*

"Aye, and the Lord's blessing upon you as well."

"Excellent!" the messenger remarked, obviously happy he had no need to search any further. "I have been instructed to invite you to Westminster at your earliest convenience."

"Who is it that commands me to do so, and are these your polite phrasings or his?" Christina asked, curious as to the mildness of the summons.

"Alas, I was ordered to deliver this message by my commander. I know not from whose throat the words originally sprang. I am like an obedient hound; someone throws the stick and I fetch it; I have no need to question my master's motive for tossing it."

Despite her anger at being interrupted from her quest to unravel Jost's perplexing activities, Christina grinned at the messenger's dry humor. She told the liveryman to accompany her into the hall, where she had Sarah fetch him a cup of ale. She then went to her chamber and quickly changed into clothing more suitable for a court visit. In a few minutes, she had returned to the hall and the two departed for Westminster Palace.

The rain had ceased, but the atmosphere remained cloudy and cold. Although the sun had not yet set, the skies were already darkening. They had not traveled far when Christina noticed a solitary male figure trudging toward them at a steady pace. He had his head down, perhaps deep in thought or merely protecting his face from the cold wind. Despite this, Christina knew at more than twenty paces distance that it was Jost.

Christina halted and waited for him to draw nearer. Her anger at the apprentice's exasperating actions in Bruges flamed once more and she fought hard against her yearning to throw herself upon him and pummel him with her fists. After a few more steps, Jost raised his head and noticed Christina standing motionless about ten feet before him.

"Good Cousin, welcome back!" he said, his greeting expressed in an overly loud voice.

But his cheer did not extend to his eyes, as they were alight with wariness and fear in equal measure.

When Christina did not respond to his greeting in kind he asked, "Is there something amiss, Master?"

Again, Christina said nothing.

Realizing his master knew some, if not all his transgressions, at least enough to land him in serious trouble, Jost walked forward hesitantly, saying in a weak voice heavy with contrition, "I . . . I can explain."

"Silence!" Christina hissed.

"But . . . but," Jost stammered.

"Another word from your mouth and I'll tear your glib tongue from its very roots, so help me Christ!" she muttered venomously.

Christina was torn between her desires to interrogate the apprentice forthwith and answer her summons to Westminster. She glared into Jost's eyes for nearly a full minute, daring him to speak so her choice would be made easier. She finally shifted her gaze in the direction of the royal liveryman, who watched the unfolding tableau with alarm. She turned her attention once more to Jost, whose face had turned quite pale.

"I have no desire to discuss my affairs in the middle of this misbegotten street for the entertainment of any who care to listen. Go directly to the great hall at Bokerel House and remain there until I return. If not, never cloud my doorstep again. Now, go, go and be damned!"

Jost hurried away, having the sense to say nothing in response.

Christina stood silently for a minute, regaining her composure.

At least I have found him, she thought as she resumed her walk toward Westminster. *He could have already been journeying back to Bruges or creating God knew what mischief here. No, this is a good thing. I will soon have the truth from him and be better for it.*

Her ire ebbed with each passing step. The liveryman said nothing as they made good time through the thinly populated streets, finding themselves before the imposing structure of the palace while a bit of natural light still remained to guide their way. Passing quickly through the gatehouse and through several other sentried guard posts, they penetrated further and further into the cavernous bowels of the palace complex. Christina believed they must be nearing the royal apartments when the messenger abruptly stopped, turned, and directed her into a richly appointed anteroom. He invited her to sit before he excused himself and departed without further word.

Damned mysterious, if you ask me.

Christina settled onto an intricately carved whitish bench of what must have been beechwood, resplendent with friezes of cavorting coneys and other small woodland creatures. There she waited as her mood grew darker, a stark contrast to the whitewashed walls and lightly colored furnishings of the chamber.

Well, who is it who seeks to steal my time from me? Gaveston? No, he seems to favor the Tower for his impromptu assignations. King Edward? Possibly, but I am certain I would have been summoned more forthrightly had it been for his pleasure. Queen Isabella? Hopefully not, as she clearly does not hold me in her favor. An audience with her, especially for a purpose I have no way of knowing, is certain to be uncomfortable.

Lady Cecily then?

Her heart jumped at the thought.

But surely, she would be more straightforward, unless there exists a dark reason for her to assume a clandestine manner. But, if so, is she in danger? Are we both?

Her air of impatience was slowly overshadowed by dread so heavy, it seemed to drain the unlit room of its pleasance as surely as the dipping sun dropped the sky into gloom.

Without warning, the door to the room opened and a maid entered. The woman busied herself going about the room and lighting lamps and candles from a long match she held gingerly in her hand. It was not the servant girl who held Christina's attention, however, but the man following behind her, Sir Giles.

"Frederick!" he cried, bursting forward and catching Christina in a comradely embrace.

"Giles!" she replied, happy to see the man she counted amongst her friends once more.

The two separated and went to sit, Christina on the beechwood bench and Giles upon a short stool he pulled forward to face her.

"I am pleased beyond words to find you safely amongst us," Giles said. "How did the hunt for your pirates go?"

Christina once more related the tale of her journey, naturally omitting the parts related to the recovery of her brother. She did, however, inform him of Ziesolf's decision to remain in Lübeck.

"I know you will miss his counsel sorely, as well as his skilled sword arm," Giles commiserated, "But such a man deserves a respite. Even one of such mighty deeds as he eventually grows old and desires some peace in his life."

"You're right," Christina agreed. "I would not deny him that"

She then finished her telling, with Giles asking a few questions along the way, but far fewer than his want. Clearly, he had something else on his mind.

"Now, friend Giles, I am certain I was asked here for more than my excellent personality and a retelling of the sagas of the North. What is it that worries your mind so?"

Giles breathed a heavy sigh before he began.

"There is trouble within the kingdom that threatens to draw it asunder. The Lords Ordainers had struggled to arrive at a consensus for nearly a year, so evenly were they divided between those foes of the king who sought radical reform and those more moderate in their views. Chief among the latter was the Earl of Lincoln, a firm supporter of the monarchy. When he died in February, the king lost his staunchest ally while his most despised foe, Thomas, Earl of Lancaster, was strengthened through his wife's inheritance of Lincoln's estates. Through Lancaster's influence, the Ordainers have finally come to an accord; one which neither favors the king, nor those around him, I'm afraid."

Christina said nothing, instead listening intently to Giles' worrisome tidings.

Bad tidings for the king and kingdom indeed, and even worse for Gaveston.

"King Edward had hoped a resounding victory over the Scots would raise his popularity among the nobility as well as the ordinary people, allowing him to resist the power of the Ordainers. Alas, that was not to be as, try as he might, the king could not bring the Bruce to battle. This served only to enrage his magnates further. Now, his subjects only see the tremendous expenditure of putting an army in the field and nothing to show for it."

I know their consternation, Christina thought glumly. *I must begrudgingly give thanks to Katherine Volker for advising me to seek surety for my loan to the king. Had I not, I am sure I would now stand small chance of seeing it recouped.*

"Now, with support for the monarchy at its weakest, the Ordainers have chosen to strike, demanding the king summon parliament to hear the ordinances of reform. Left with no alternative, Edward has acquiesced, setting the date for what is now two days' hence, the 8th of August. There are to be forty-one ordinances in all, limiting his royal power severely. But there is one above all others that causes him the greatest dismay."

Giles looked at Christina sharply, as if to appraise her reaction to his next words.

"The twentieth ordinance directly addresses the proposed fate of a great friend to us both, the Earl of Cornwall. It states, 'Piers Gaveston, as a public enemy of the king and of the kingdom, shall be utterly cast out and exiled . . . forever and without return.' The king, of course, protests this greatly, but to no avail. Lancaster has even communicated that, should Edward not consent to Gaveston's banishment, the king could mayhaps be deprived of his throne and his kingdom. Clearly, this is the greatest threat to royal privilege since the rule of King John."

If Giles had been searching for astonishment on Christina's face, he most readily found it.

"But, to depose an anointed king?" Christina gasped, "Why, this is sacrilege! How can the Ordainers threaten such a thing?"

"They have and they will," replied Giles. "Edward has not yet decided what he will do; Earl Piers awaits his decision at Bamburgh Castle. For now, the king has asked me to question those who support him to determine whether they would remain loyal to him, or side with Lancaster and his cronies."

Giles paused, again staring into Christina's face as if to determine the veracity of her words to follow.

"How say you, Sir Frederick?"

Christina was startled, not realizing he was posing the question to her.

Is this man, whom I consider to be a friend, really asking me if I could betray the king?

Recovering her wits, it dawned on her that her response could have substantial repercussions upon not just herself, but also those she loved.

What if the Ordainers seek revenge on those who support the king? Although I am of the Hansa, its rights here, as well as my own, are precarious and may be withdrawn at the king's whim, whomever that monarch may be. Can I risk the life and livelihood of so many of my countrymen?

Giles remained quietly seated, awaiting her response.

On the other hand, it was the king himself who knighted me, a high honor in itself, but also an agreement between us that cannot be honorably broken.

Her way forward became clear.

He is my liege lord. It is as simple as that.

"I stand with King Edward, now and forever, Sir Giles," Christina said in a firm voice.

Giles reached forward and clasped the right hand of Christina.

"I had no doubt, brother knight. I judge well a man's mettle, and I reckon yours to be strong and true. Now, before I depart to attend to less agreeable matters, have you questions of me?"

Christina hesitated. With all the problems of the kingdom weighing heavy upon Giles, did she have the right to trouble him with one that concerned her only?

"Aye, one. How fares the Lady Cecily?"

Giles locked eyes with Christina for a few seconds, an inscrutable expression on his face that gradually softened into a hint of a smile.

"Wait here, my friend," he said. "I have not the right to speak on these matters."

With that cryptic statement, Giles arose and departed the chamber, leaving Christina feeling confused and with a growing fear in her heart sprouting like a slip of henbane in a farmer's kitchen garden.

Why could he not tell Christina of her? Surely, he could say whether she was in good health. Could a fatal malady have overtaken her during her pregnancy or even her delivery? Death was a frequent visitor to many a birthing chamber, royal or not. Could Cecily even now be residing in a cold dark tomb, gone from Christina for eternity?

Dread overwhelmed her.

The door opened and all of Christina's fears evaporated. Giles entered, but Christina had no eyes for him. Instead, she was solely focused on one of the two women who followed him inside. One was clearly a lady of the palace household. The other was Cecily.

She was unexpectedly gaunt, a mere shadow from the last time Christina had beheld her, but her beauty remained undiminished.

Her brilliant red tresses were interwoven with green silk ribbons, braided and affixed to the sides of her head in two ramshorns. Cecily's beautiful face was as perfectly featured as she remembered, with red lips fixing her with such a merry smile it made her knees weak.

"Perhaps, Lady Darel, you would be so kind as to accompany me on a walk through the gardens? I believe the roses are now in bloom and fill the air with a heavenly scent," Giles asked the woman accompanying Cecily.

"I cannot accept your kind offer, Sir Giles," Lady Darel replied, although obviously tempted by the renowned knight's invitation. "The Lady Cecily should not be left alone with an unknown foreign man, be he gentlemanly or no."

"Have no fear, Mi' lady," Giles protested, "Sir Frederick was knighted by his majesty himself. I equally vouch for his honor as strongly as I would mine own. These two have important words to pass between them and the gardens beckon. Come."

Reluctantly, Lady Darel acquiesced. In a matter of seconds, Christina and Cecily were alone in the room, divided by the gulf of uncertainty that existed between them as surely as by the twenty feet that separated them.

"Are you well then, Mi 'Lady?" Christina asked, her voice soft as she fought to keep it from cracking.

"Yes," answered Cecily, her chin beginning to quiver. "And how fare you, Mi 'Lord?"

"I'm well enough, better now perhaps. May I be so bold to ask as to the health of your babe?"

"She is a happy and spritely child, growing stronger with each passing day. I have called her Rosamunde, as her hair and complexion favor those of my own."

"A name well chosen," replied Christina, her mouth forming a slight, hesitant, smile.

"But where are my manners? Please, do be seated, Sir Frederick," Cecily stated before gracefully crossing the room to seat herself on the stool opposite Christina that Giles had so recently favored.

Christina did as she was told, though she scrutinized the face of the other woman, seeking to perceive her rationale for the formality she was imposing upon them.

As if reading Christina's mind, she leaned in close and whispered conspiratorially, "Have caution; this chamber could have many ears."

Christina looked about, as if she could somehow ferret-out a well-hidden eavesdropper. She could not, so her attention became once more fixed upon Cecily.

"So, was your voyage successful, dear knight?" Cecily's lips formed into a wistful smile; the meaning of which Christina was unable to ken.

"Aye, Mi' lady, but not without hardship and loss," Christina refrained from beginning yet another telling of her saga.

"Have ill tidings befell any of those I hold dear?" the other woman asked, a tinge of fear evident in her voice.

"No, none of whom you have known. Ziesolf has chosen to remain in Lübeck, but of his own accord."

"It is bothersome you have lost one of your staunchest supporters, especially in such troublesome times as these. He will be sorely missed."

"Aye," agreed Christina, though her frustration with the stiffness of their conversation was mounting steadily.

Bloody hell! she raged to herself.

She comprehended the need for restraint from their passions within the palace, but she could withstand this no more! This was the woman she loved! The last time she saw her, they had considered a mad escapade, one of running away together to the Mediterranean and living the lives of itinerant traders. What had become of them? Were they the same who now sat within reach of one another, yet would not rush into each other's arms?

"Frederick," Cecily spoke softly, but with urgency.

Christina said the other woman's name almost simultaneously.

"I have something to tell you," Cecily replied.

Christina said nothing, steeling herself for news that she anticipated would tear her heart asunder.

"When King Edward and Queen Isabella returned from Berwick, my aunt, Eleanor de Clare, accompanied them. When we spoke, she informed me the king's army had sallied throughout the Marches and even into Scotland itself, but in vain. The Bruce's forces could not be brought to battle."

"Yes, Giles informed me of as much," Christina remarked, sensing her beloved had more to reveal than Edward's futile military endeavors.

"Eventually, the soldiers were recalled and much of the army was made ready to return to the south. One night, at Berwick Castle, two such men were making a report to their liegelord, Baron de Percy. They told of how they had ventured into the woodlands between Berwick and Roxburgh. There, they came upon a corpse, but one that had been so ravaged by weather and the forest beasts, it was unrecognizable."

Christina gasped.

Could this be the remains of Cecily's husband? The craven coward who deserted her to suffer the pleasure of the Scots while he sought to save his own damnable skin? But, if he was so mutilated, how could anyone be certain as to his identity?

Oh, please, sweet Jesus, let there be more to this!

"Then, one of the men reached into his purse and drew out a cloth. In it were two items. The first was a small silver cross, one which had been hung around a chain from the dead man's neck. Although clever work, there was naught remarkable about it to separate it from many others of the same ilk. Consequently, it provided the baron with no hint as to the man's identity."

Christina mind raged, worrying her lower lip between her teeth as her anxiety mounted.

But it must! How can Fate play such a cruel jest?

"I said the cross gave no clue to the baron as to the body's identity," Cecily continued. "It was proof positive to me, however." She reached into her purse and lifted the cross and chain forth. "This was my father's, given to him by my mother on their wedding day. In turn, I presented it to Sir Edgar on ours."

"So, this does provide the proof Sir Edgar Baldewyne is dead?" Christina asked incredulously.

"No, sorely it does not. As I said, Baron de Percy had no acquaintance with the item and the only one who claimed such familiarity with it was a wife who had already chosen to abandon her family demesne."

Cecily sighed and her lips assumed a tired smile.

"Once again, a woman's word was not to be trusted unless seconded by that of a man."

Christina sat frozen, her mind refusing to register how her hopes had just been dashed.

"Now," said Cecily, a mysterious smile appearing. "Did I mention a second item?"

326

"Speak! You slay me with your hesitation!" cried Christina.

"Oh, yes, I believe I did," replied Cecily, her mouth widening into a merry grin. "Well, the other article in the cloth was a ring, but not just any bauble. It was the signet ring of my husband, one which he used to seal all his correspondence - correspondence that often came to Baron de Percy, where he broke the seal himself. Consequently, there is a baronial attestation as to my husband's death. I am now a free woman."

Christina's eyes welled with tears of happiness. A sudden fear sprang into her mind like one of Satan's merry imps.

But she mentions nothing of us being together. Has she somehow chilled towards me?

Her questions were swiftly answered.

"The two soldiers buried my husband where he lay, in grounds unconsecrated and lonely, save for the grace of God above. I am free to marry once more, as soon as King Edward provides his consent. That is, if the one whose love I hold dearest in my heart will have me, have us, Rosamunde and I?" Cecily asked in a small voice choked with emotion.

Christina's thoughts raced.

She had been involved in the mention of marriage twice before. Once to Albrecht Revel, whom she could not wed as she had assumed the identity of Frederick. The other was Katharine Revel, whom she could not marry while holding such repugnance of her. Now, the one who claimed her heart asked, and she had no words to express her happiness, only her most heartfelt acquiescence.

"With every firmament of my body and soul, I agree to marry you, dearest Cecily, and to raise Rosamunde as if she were my own issue," Christina said, leaping forward and catching Cecily in a tender embrace as she rose from her seat.

All uncertainties concerning Jost, Katharine Volker, even her brother, were forgotten. The universe existed only within the scope of their love.

Their lips met with a gentleness that belied the intense passions racing inside their two young bodies. Regardless of the dangers that loomed in their futures, for this one brief moment, they knew perfect happiness.

Alphabetical Listing of Characters

Adam – infant son of Trudi and Peter
Agnes, Lady – one of Queen Isabella's ladies-in-waiting
Alan – the leader of Christina's longbowmen
Albrecht Revele – brother of Katharine Volker
Aldstan – one of the sailors on Christina's ship *der Greif*
Alf – one of the fighting men recruited by Reiniken
Anna – Mechtild Kohl's servant in Lübeck and Trudi's sister
Avery Robinson – a London cordwainer Christina favors
Beatrix – a servant girl in Christina's household
Bess – chief cook at Christina's London manor, Bokerel House
Black Peter, Christina's smith and husband of Trudi
Brand, Father – priest who marries Trudi and Peter
Brother Udo – healer at Hospital of the Holy Spirit in Lübeck
Butiler, Master – London wool merchant
Cecily, Lady Baldewyne (de Vere) – Christina's love interest
Christina Kohl - knight and merchant in the guise of her brother
Darel, Lady – one of Queen Isabella's ladies-in-waiting
De Percy, Baron – liegelord of Sir Edgar Baldewyne
Edgar Baldewyne (Sir) – Lady Cecily's husband
Edward – one of Christina's longbowmen
Edward II – king of England
Eleanor de Clare, Lady of Glamorgan – Cecily's aunt
Fox - one of the fighting men recruited by Reiniken
Frederick Kohl – Christina's brother presumed killed by pirates
Gilbert – one of Christina's longbowmen
Giles d' Argentan (Sir) – household knight of Edward II
Godfrey – one of Christina's longbowmen
Gotz – assistant helmsman of *der Greif*
Ham - one of the fighting men recruited by Reiniken
Heloise - a servant girl in Christina's household
Henry – a fighting man recruited by Reiniken and father of John
Henry de Lacy, Earl of Lincoln – one of the Lords Ordainers

Henry the Lion, Duke – founder of Lübeck
Hugh – member of the Norwich town weaver's guild
Isabella, Queen of England – wife of Edward II
John – A young beggar boy
John Levestan – a member of London's Weavers Guild
Jost – Christina's cousin and apprentice
Juliana – a servant girl in Christina's household
Katharine Volker – alderman's wife and Christina's enemy
Katrey Wendler – childhood friend of Christina
Kurt Ziesolf (Sir) - Teutonic knight and Christina's mentor
Lizzy – a prostitute
Lords Ordainers – powerful noblemen against King Edward II
Louis IX, King – crusader and King of France
Luit — one of the sailors on Christina's ship *der Greif*
Malcolm – Christina's deceased stableboy killed by the Scots
Manekin le Hauberger – renowned London armorer
Margaret (Margery) – cook at the Golden Fleece inn in Norwich
Margaret de Clare - wife of Piers Gaveston
Margery – a servant girl in Christina's household
Marguerite – Christina's deceased sister
Mary - a servant girl in Christina's household
Matthias – master of Christina's ship *der Greif*
Mechtild Kohl – mother of Christina
Nicholas – one of Christina's longbowmen
Osbert – one of Christina's watchmen at Bokerel House
Pauwels, Master – a Bruges mercer who trades with Christina
Pearl – Christina's horse
Penny – Christina's stablemaster
Piers Gaveston, Earl of Cornwall – Christina's friend
Ranulf – a master smith and friend of Black Peter
Richard – Christina's enemy she maimed in a duel
Robert the Bruce – King of the Scots
Rosamunde – infant daughter of Lady Cecily
Sarah – scullery maid in Christina's household

Siegfried – a deceased mercenary who was Reiniken's friend
Sybille – a Flemish prostitute and Christina's first lover
Thomas – Sir Giles' squire
Thomas Kohl – Christina's deceased father
Thomas, Earl of Lancaster – one of the Lords Ordainers
Thorsten – sailing master of Christina's ship *Seelöwe*
Tiny Tom - one of the fighting men recruited by Reiniken
Trudi – Christina's best friend and the keeper of her household
Tuck – barman at the Golden Fleece in Norwich
Ulbert Geldersen – Lübeck alderman
Volker, Herr – London alderman and husband of Katherine
Walter - member of the Norwich town weaver's guild
Warin - one of Christina's watchmen at Bokerel House
Wig Reiniken – mercenary warrior and Christina's friend
Will – one of Christina's longbowmen
William Bateman – Norwich bailiff

Historical Notes

Although medieval maritime merchants could realize tremendous wealth from their voyages, bad luck was known to just as easily bring them to ruin. Depressed markets, spoilage of goods, and trade privileges withdrawn by capricious monarchs all could adversely affect the profitability of a ship's cargo. There were greater calamities that could be suffered, however. Storms or unseaworthiness could cause ships to founder, often with total loss of the ship, cargo, and lives of those unfortunates aboard. There was little to be done to affect the whims of nature except to build and maintain stout ships, keep a wary eye on the skies, and remain in the good graces of the Lord. Another, less divine, means by which a merchant could be devastated was through a pirate attack upon his investment.

Piracy was a constant threat to early fourteenth century maritime trade and this was particularly true to the ships of the Hansa. The Hanseatic fleet was huge, perhaps numbering as many as six to eight hundred ocean-going ships; thus, potential targets were plentiful. The ubiquitous cog ships were painfully slow, achieving only four to five knots in favorable winds. Hanseatic statutes had not yet prescribed a convoy system, with ships' masters often setting sail in no more than pairs, or even alone. Crews averaged only twelve to fifteen men aboard to repel the attack of determined foes often many times their number.

Geography provided the sea-going brigands with further advantages over the Hanseatic ships. With navigational means still unreliable, merchant craft preferred to sail within sight of land, except for the route from Norway south to England. This custom severely limited their possible routes and greatly simplified the pirates' task of locating potential targets. For ships traveling to and fro between Lübeck and Bruges, London, and other Western European destinations, their danger was intensified by the necessity of travel through the Kattegat, the sea area bounded by the Jutland peninsula to the west and Sweden to the east. This shallow sea area is difficult to navigate as there are numerous sandy and stony reefs, tricky currents, and extensive shallows along the Danish coast. The islands of Samsø, Læsø, and Anholt further constrict the possible sea-lanes of the Kattegat, as well as many, much smaller islets often consisting of no more than a rocky outcropping.

Once a victim has been identified by a sharp-eyed lookout on one of these close shores, he would signal his comrades as to the target's presence. Usually, the pursuit was undertaken by several vessels that were often smaller, faster, and more maneuverable than the cog. Among these types were the kraier and the ewer, which were half the size of their victim, as well as the schnigge, an even smaller boat of ten to twenty lasts (approximately twenty to forty tons) which enjoyed the additional option of being immediately propelled away by oars if necessary. Overtaking or outmaneuvering the merchant ship, the pirates would endeavor to halt the cog with grappling hooks while pelting the other ship with crossbow bolts, javelins, and even stones to reduce the crew's will to fight. Not surprisingly, these encounters were often brief, ending with the embattled crew's surrender once boarded, or after only a brief resistance primarily conducted to demonstrate to the ship's investors that collaboration had not occurred.

Even after surrendering, the wellbeing of the merchantman's crew was not guaranteed. At best, the cogs and their crews were released to travel on unhindered or were at least put ashore when their ship was confiscated. Alternatively, the prisoners could be taken for ransom or kept or sold as slaves. In one instance, captured crewmen were sealed in barrels aboard their ship while awaiting their final fate. At worst, the victims might be murdered in cold blood and committed to a watery grave far from home.

Obviously, one would expect the Hanse to take action to eradicate this menace to the confederation's existence, and they eventually did. By the late fourteenth century, statutes required merchant ships to travel in larger convoys, usually accompanied by a warship financed by members of the convoy, which provided one or two soldiers each. In 1376, a general assembly of representatives from the Hanseatic cities declared war on piracy and levied a tax for a period of two years to pay to equip warships. Their martial and diplomatic efforts were so effective that, by 1400, the threat of piracy had been all but eliminated in the Baltic.

These measures were not taken until much later than the time-period in which the novels of this series are set, however. Organized retaliation against the pirates was still limited by the fact the Germans did not possess a navy. Furthermore, there was as yet no military specialization or particularity of construction in the fourteenth century; all Hanseatic ships were designed as cargo vessels. Artillery was in its infancy in Europe; consequently, there were no cannons carried aboard. What differentiated those intended for war was the large number of fighting men carried aboard a wartime cog, sometimes as many as sixty. If threatened, a city such as Lübeck would put out a call, hiring available ships from private citizens and then man and equip them at its own expense to fight.

In *Her Dangerous Journey Home*, Herr Volker, the London chief alderman, alerts Christina Kohl to such a summons. But it is her desire for revenge against those responsible for the deaths of her father and brother that takes her from her life as a merchant and the love of those she holds dear to finally still the demons who haunt her dreams.

About the Author

Lee Swanson

Lee Swanson has enjoyed a lifelong interest in medieval history. He lived in Germany and England for over twenty-five years, first as a soldier and then as a teacher before returning to the United States.

Graduating summa cum laude from the University of North Florida with a master's degree in European History, Lee's thesis centered on the Hansa, a confederation of merchants from primarily northern German cities. Many of the colorful characters who populate his novels are drawn from the lives of these resolute wayfarers who traveled the waterways of Europe in search of profit and prestige.

Lee, his wife Karine, and their dog Banjo now split their time between coastal Maine and San Miguel de Allende, Mexico.

www.LeeSwansonAuthor.com